HARLEY MERLIN AND THE BROKEN SPELL

Harley Merlin 5

BELLA FORREST

ONE

Harley

I screamed, smothering my face with a pillow to muffle the sound. Tears streamed down my face, and my lungs felt starved of air. Sharp, agonizing jolts tore through my limbs like forks of lightning, setting my blood on fire.

A half-empty mug of cold coffee sat on the edge of my desk, lying just out of reach. It wouldn't fix the problem, but at least it'd take away the metallic tang of blood in my mouth. I'd bitten down on the insides of my cheeks when the attack had started, an hour ago, just after dawn. It was the same torture every morning since my Suppressor had cracked, a little over a week ago.

Squeezing the pillow, I dragged it and my body across the sweat-soaked bed and crawled down to the floor. Each movement made the pain worse, as if every surface were covered in needles. All I wanted to do was curl up in a ball and die... just until the pain went away. I'd have taken a year's worth of the worst cramps imaginable or a thousand bullet-ant bites over this. *Make it stop... Please, make it stop.*

I braced for what always came next—the seeping cold that crept through my veins. I clutched the pillow and gritted my teeth as the shivering took over. The cracked Suppressor leaked more and more of the pent-up Chaos into me every single day, flooding me with uncontrollable energy. The attacks always came around the same time each morning, but further attacks could hit me at any time of day. And the pain was only the half of it. The lack of control was worse. Way worse. My body and mind were no longer my own.

With each new wave of agony, I wondered if the time might've come, if this might be the day the Suppressor fully broke and unleashed hell. I wanted to reach into myself and rip it out of me. I didn't care how, but I wanted—needed—it gone. But there was always a chance the rest of the Suppressor could rupture by itself. The thought was as terrifying as it was welcome. So many things could still go wrong.

At least this can't go on forever, right? I mean, it'd kill me long before then, if I couldn't get it to properly break. And, from Isadora's warnings, I knew I didn't have much time left to break the damn thing. Days. Weeks, if I was lucky.

"COME ON!" I roared into the pillow with everything I had. A few expletives followed, the thick fabric muting the sounds to a faint squeal. I'd become an expert in the art of muffled screaming, desperate not to wake anyone up with my howls of pain. They didn't need that kind of misery to start their days off.

A loud bang went off like a thunderclap, followed by a jolt of searing pain that shot behind my eyes. I shrank around the pillow.

Oh crap, this is it. The bang, the pain...The Suppressor...

"Harley? What the—" A shadowy figure ducked beside me and peeled my clamped fingers away from my arms. I hadn't realized my nails had been digging into my skin, forming tiny crescents.

"Did it break?" I whispered, my throat raw.

"The Suppressor?"

I nodded slowly, the tiny movements sending a blinding sting through my eye sockets.

"I don't think so," he murmured. His emotions hit me in a wave of fear and heartbreak and concern, his adrenaline pumping. I tried to push back against his feelings, not wanting his adrenaline to spike my own, but it was no good; I didn't have the strength to resist. The Suppressor was amplifying his emotions, making them impossible to ignore.

Wade rested his hand on my shoulder, evidently trying to figure out what to do with me. "Didn't you hear me knocking? I've been out there for ten minutes."

"I... didn't... hear," I panted through a fresh onslaught of stabbing blades in the pit of my stomach. His fear had fed into mine, and the coursing chemicals made everything ten times worse. My muscles constricted, battling the agony instead of relaxing against it. All I wanted was total unconsciousness.

I gasped in surprise as strong arms gripped me, pillow and all, scooping me up off the floor. Wade carried me over to the edge of the bed, where he set me down and wrapped the blanket around my shoulders. He rubbed circles across my back, while his worried eyes gazed down into mine. As the pain eased up, I saw him properly for the first time, the blurry haze clearing to reveal his handsome face.

Lookin' good with a little stubble, Crowley.

"You want to tell me what all this is about?" he asked gently.

"The Chaos... attacks. They've been... getting worse." I grimaced as a few aftershocks of pain shot through me.

"For how long?"

I shrugged. "A week."

"Is it like this each time?"

"Pretty much."

"Every day?" I could hear the disbelief in his voice.

"Like clockwork."

He shook his head, running a hand through his dark curls. "Why the hell didn't you say anything if it's been this bad?"

"I did tell you," I said. "I told all of you that I was dealing with… some pain."

"Yeah, you said *some* pain. Not… this." He swept a hand over the bed. A flurry of sadness drifted over me—his sadness. "If I'd known the crack in your Suppressor was causing *this*, then I'd have had you sent to the infirmary. I'm sure Krieger has some potion or spell he could use to make this easier."

"I already asked him for a sleeping potion," I replied. "I took it, and the same thing happened. Worse, actually. Unless I want to be knocked out twenty-four-seven, I just have to push through the pain."

He frowned. "You should've told us. You didn't have to sugarcoat it."

"You're all freaking out enough as it is, and I didn't want to add to that. Santana nearly rallied all of Mexico when I said there was a little bit of pain—imagine what would've happened if I'd told you all the real… extent of it." I gripped the edge of the mattress as more seeping Chaos edged under my skin. My teeth chattered like crazy, and my legs jiggled to try and stop the coldness from getting too deep.

"It's our job to worry, especially when we can't actually do anything to help you right now," Wade said, the subtext glaring like a beacon. The situation must've made him feel pretty helpless. I could feel his despair as it rolled over him like a bank of fog, choking out everything else. But just having him beside me made me feel a bit better.

"Honestly, you're making a mountain out of a molehill." I pulled the covers tighter around me. "It's mostly under control. It just hurts like hell, that's all. Coffee helps a little."

"I've noticed your increased caffeine intake, actually. You were bad enough at three mugs a day, but you're downing at least a gallon these days," he joked. "I'm surprised you're not bouncing off the walls."

"Barely makes a dent. I could drink a truckload and still feel like somebody hit me with a sack of wrenches."

"Well, drink away, then." He got up and crossed over to the desk, where he plucked up the cold cup of coffee and passed it to me. I drank it in one go as he sat back down beside me. I hoped it wouldn't be long before I started to feel more like myself again.

"Nomura's been helping a lot, too. Mostly with meditation and a few herbal teas that he got in Nepal," I added, wiping my mouth on the back of my hand. "I was hoping we could get started right away on the whole Euphoria thing, but he says it's a bad idea with the crack and whatnot."

Wade nodded. "He's worried about your control."

"I guess so. I can't really blame him," I replied. "Anyway, he gave me this herbal mulch stuff that I've got to take every night for ten days. I mix a spoonful in water, drink it down at midnight, whisper a little chant, and bingo!"

"Bingo? What do you mean? What happens?" He looked adorably confused.

"Well, I don't know right now, but it's supposed to put me in a slightly better state, spiritually speaking, to get this Euphoria show on the road. Once my ten days are up, I can start practicing with him." A flicker of excitement pierced my exhaustion and lingering pain. "It'll still be risky, but it's safer than doing it now, when I'm a total mess."

Wade chuckled. "You aren't a *total* mess. You're just more of a mess than you've let on."

"Yeah, although obviously I'm not hiding it as well as I thought," I said. "It's not just these attacks that are causing problems, though. The Suppressor has been playing havoc with my abilities, too. Nomura's already benched me because of it."

"Benched you?"

I nodded. "He's been really helpful and everything, but I think this Suppressor business is stressing him out, too. I guess it's a lot of pressure on him to teach me Euphoria and get me to do it right in such a short span of time. The only time I see him calm is when we meditate. In the training room, he just keeps snapping at me."

"He has a lot on his plate right now, with teaching other students. I wouldn't take it personally," Wade said.

"You're probably right. It just sucks that I can't even practice my abilities until I get the Suppressor out, and my Chaos under control." I sighed, wishing I had more coffee. Hot, this time.

"Wait, he's not letting you practice at all?"

"Nope. He doesn't think it's safe... and he may have a point. I did almost kill him in the training room the other day, when I accidentally engulfed him in a bubble of water and took a few minutes to get him out. So... yeah."

"I didn't realize it was a total ban," Wade said, with sympathy in his eyes. "But like you said, it's for the best. Things have gotten a little crazy since that crack appeared."

I smiled at him as the pain gradually subsided. He was sitting so close, his hand still casually rubbing circles across my back. Looking up into his eyes, I nestled a little closer. His arm moved around my shoulders. *You know what'd make me feel* way *better, Wade? Another one of those sweet, sweet kisses.* I hoped my gaze conveyed what my lips wouldn't. I definitely hadn't forgotten the kiss we'd shared—there'd just been a lot going on. And, anyway, we'd both agreed to wait to talk about "us" until after we'd dealt with the Suppressor, when we had a moment to breathe and think. For now, we were left in this weird limbo between "friends" and "something more."

His Adam's apple bobbed as he swallowed, and his emotions revealed a streak of desire that mirrored my own. He held my gaze, his arm drawing me in ever closer. My heart pounded. *He's going to kiss me again!* Our faces were practically touching.

"I bet it's Alton's resignation that's got Nomura stressed," Wade said, pulling away suddenly. "Everyone's worried about what it might mean for the future of the SDC, and I know the preceptors are especially on edge."

"That's probably true." I sighed, a little disappointed at the lack of a kiss. Although, if I were less of a coward when it came to this lovey-dovey stuff, *I* would've kissed *him* already.

"There's every chance that this temporary director might want a reshuffle, and that, combined with all this Euphoria research, would be enough to put anyone in a bad mood. Even cool-as-a-cucumber Nomura," he added. "Alton leaving has had a domino effect."

No one besides the Rag Team, Jacob, and Isadora knew the real reason why Alton had resigned, with us keeping the secret of his deal with Katherine and his involvement in Quetzi's abduction, escape, and subsequent murder. Still, his stepping down from the role had dealt a huge blow to everyone. The whole coven loved him, and nobody knew who would be taking his place.

"Don't even get me started on this new director," I muttered. "I wish they'd just hurry up and get here so we can move things along. Some of us are dying while they're deciding who gets to sit in the big chair."

"Hey, stop saying that," Wade chided. "You aren't dying. You're just sick. And we've got a way to make you better."

"Yeah, which needs a director's approval."

Right now, I couldn't request approval to travel to New Orleans via the mirrors until a new director was appointed temporarily. And that meant I couldn't break the Suppressor in the interim, even though time was running out.

With each passing day, I grew more and more desperate to get to Marie Laveau's tomb. After all, the Voodoo Queen of New Orleans was my key to breaking this stupid Dempsey Suppressor. With her expertise in Sanguine spells, I figured she could help me perform the spell that'd give me the balance between Light and Darkness that I really freaking needed, once I broke my Suppressor for good. Plus, as the most powerful Dark witch of all time, she could likely point me toward a spell on astral projection. Remington had mentioned it as a viable way of summoning a Child of Chaos, which, right now, was our only way of stopping Katherine in her tracks.

And yet, I was stuck here... endlessly waiting. I even had the damned Sanguine spell that had come from the Reykjavik repository—Alton had given it to me as a parting gift. I had all the pieces, and I couldn't do anything with them. Yep, I was all dressed up with no place to go.

"That's actually why I was banging your door down," Wade said, surprising me. "Which reminds me, you might need a new lock. I, uh, had to melt the old one to break in."

I shot a weary look at the door. Trails of melted silver streaked the spot where the lock used to be. "Are you kidding me? Wade, what the hell?"

"You weren't answering!" He rubbed the back of his neck. "After ten minutes, I had no choice. I could hear you screaming in here, and I had to get inside to make sure you were okay. A lock is replaceable. You're not."

I smiled weakly. "Well, you're paying to fix it."

"Fair deal." His gaze flickered down to my lips.

"You were about to tell me *why* you broke down my door?"

He cleared his throat. "Yes, that's right. I came running because you weren't answering your phone and we're all expected in the Assembly Hall ASAP."

"Why so early?" It wasn't even eight yet.

"They're about to announce the new interim director of the coven."

TWO

Harley

———————

"Seriously, I can make up some excuse for you," Wade whispered as we walked toward the Assembly Hall. A few stragglers wandered beside us like zombies, rubbing sleepy eyes and yawning loudly. He'd been trying to convince me to stay in my room, but I wasn't going to miss out on this. I needed to know what we were up against if I'd have a hope in hell of getting to New Orleans.

"Nah, I'll be okay." On still-shaky legs, I gripped his arm, determined to make it to this meeting. The pain had all but gone now, leaving a pins-and-needles sensation in my hands and feet. That would fade, too. It always did.

The rest of the Rag Team waved to us as we entered the crowded room, the sight of them bringing a smile to my face. They stood to one side, in front of the nearest window, away from the main throng. Astrid normally liked to get a front-row seat to this kind of thing, but she'd been taking a back seat lately, after everything that had happened with her. Being resurrected changed a person, even though she continued to put on a brave face.

"Still no Garrett?" I asked, leaning up against the wall for support. Wade kept close, watching me.

"Nope, he's still cloak-and-daggering it up at the LA Coven," Santana replied, with a roll of her eyes. He'd gone away a couple of days ago, and we had no idea when he'd be back. He hadn't given us any details about it, even though we'd all been desperate for a snippet of information. His announcement about it had come out of the blue, so of course we were curious. Plus, Astrid missed him. Even with the weird void inside her, I could tell she wished he was still around.

"Any idea what he's up to over there?" I asked, eager to take the focus off the fact that I looked like death warmed over. I could sense the confusion and concern radiating off my friends, and I wanted to nip it in the bud before they started asking too many questions. They knew the Suppressor crack was causing me some pain, and that was enough.

Astrid shook her head. "I tried to hack into the LA Coven's system yesterday, to see if I could get the scoop on what work they've got him doing. Call it professional concern." She gave a tight, nervous laugh. "Anyway, it turns out that LA has their own version of me and Smartie fending off cyberattacks."

"Personally, I think every coven should have one of you," I said with a smile. Some of her emotions had drifted back in after the resurrection, but I knew the lack of feeling was still bothering her. With Alton in his own personal turmoil, she hadn't wanted to trouble him with it. I guess she thought it would go away by itself, eventually.

"I agree," Tatyana said. "It's just annoying that we can't find out what Garrett is doing."

Wade frowned. "You think he'll tell us?"

"I wouldn't count on it," I replied, steadying myself on the windowsill.

Jacob and Isadora walked into the room. Jacob still had the guise of Tarver, while Isadora was herself. Nobody knew about her, aside from the Council and the preceptors, so it seemed pointless to disguise her. Besides, the spy had been caught. Alton seemed certain there had only been the one, and the rest of us were eager to believe him.

Louella snuck over from the back of the room and attached herself to our group. *My favorite troublemaker.* With so much upheaval, we were the only people she felt comfortable around. She was kind of a badass, in her own way, and I was glad she had decided to stay at the SDC, instead of moving to LA like Marjorie had. Maybe we weren't doing such a bad job at highlighting the good in this place.

Glancing around at the gathered coven, I was struck by the number of people who lived and worked here. It always hit me, when everyone was together like this. In the vast hallways and labyrinth of corridors and rooms, it was easy to forget that there were hundreds of other magicals inhabiting the same interdimensional pocket.

A sudden, sharp pain throbbed at my temples, making me wince. A stampede of feelings followed. I closed my eyes. I tried, I really tried, but no amount of concentration could get rid of the swirling vortex of other people's emotions. With the crack in the Suppressor, all of my abilities had become more temperamental, Empathy included.

"You okay?" Wade murmured.

"Empathy overload," I whispered back.

"Do you want to leave?"

I shook my head defiantly. "Just give me a minute." I grasped for his wrist almost without thinking, using his solid presence to steady myself. It reminded me of the first time I'd stood here, in the Assembly Hall. He'd been here then, too, with his arm more than willing to take the heat as I sought to control my Empathy. None of who I was, or what I was, had fully made sense back then. Weird, how things could change so drastically in such a relatively short amount of time. Back then, the name Katherine Shipton didn't mean anything to me—I'd have thought she was some new actress, or a news anchor, or a member of *Real Housewives,* or something.

In that moment, all I could feel was a powerful punch of anger and sadness. The coven as a whole had been through a lot, and this was the emotional fallout of Quetzi's escape and ensuing death, Jacintha's death, and Alton's resignation. During his resignation announcement, Alton had told everyone that Quetzi had died during a recapture operation. Even now, his presence was sorely missed in the Bestiary, especially by Tobe. That single glass box stood out like a sore thumb, serving as a stark reminder of his loss.

I looked up at the Beast Master, who was standing with Alton on the mirror platform. His expression seemed sort of lost. He hadn't been told the truth about Alton's underhanded deal with Katherine, but part of me wondered if he knew more than he was letting on. He was a wise, ancient creature, after all—he'd surely seen his fair share of deceptions and betrayals in his long life.

Meanwhile, Alton was trying not to make eye contact with anyone, though he offered a warm and reassuring smile to those who managed to hold his gaze.

"Pretend it's just us in the room," Wade said, taking my hand. He drew it behind him so nobody would see, but the action comforted me more than he knew.

"I'll try." I struggled to relax against the artillery of emotions, hoping it might help if I could loosen up, but they just came on stronger and fiercer than before. Everyone's feelings mingled with mine, emphasizing my own grief and anger and confusion. And I had more reason to feel those emotions than most. Katherine had succeeded in performing the first of the five rituals, and I desperately needed to get ahead of her if we were going to stand any chance of stopping her.

One comfort came in the fact that we didn't know whether, or how, she'd managed to escape the Asphodel Meadows. Santana, Astrid, and Louella were convinced that Nyx had booted her out after she'd overstayed her welcome. That seemed to be the deal with these Children of

Chaos—if you stayed too long in their otherworld, especially after performing a ritual in their domain, you got a one-way ticket out of there. Still, she hadn't raised her ugly head again yet, which gave me hope.

Now, I just need this interim director to let me go to New Orleans. That was the only way we were going to get the jump on Katherine. But the nerves in the room were overwhelming, everyone unsure about this new director. It could either be a smooth, painless transition, or get a million times worse. Given our track record, I couldn't help but feel pessimistic.

"Harley, is something the matter?" Isadora stood in front of me, her brow furrowed in concern. I hadn't even noticed her walk up to me, I'd been so intent on trying to push back the barrage of feelings.

"There's a lot of emotions going on, that's all," I replied. "I'm struggling a bit."

"We should get you out of here," she suggested.

"No, I'm fine. I'll be fine, I swear."

"It's the Suppressor, isn't it?" Her eyes fixed on mine with a knowing look, and I couldn't bend the truth anymore. After all, she'd already seen me collapse in the Aquarium because of this thing, and she was constantly asking if I was doing okay.

Sweat trickled down my face as I nodded. "The pains I told you all about... well, they're getting worse. I keep getting these Chaos attacks every morning, and sometimes during the day. Mostly in the mornings, though."

"So that's why we've been seeing less of you?" Tatyana asked quietly. I turned to find the whole Rag Team staring at me.

"I get so tired because of these morning attacks that sometimes I'm ready to drop by mid-afternoon," I admitted. "I've been trying to sleep it off, but I guess it isn't working so well."

"Can't Krieger prescribe something for you?" Raffe asked.

"I tried that—heck, I tried every painkiller he had available—but they don't do anything. They help me sleep, but then the attacks come back with a vengeance," I replied.

Santana tutted, making me drop Wade's hand as she gathered me to her bosom in a way I imagined Mrs. Catemaco might have done. "Why didn't you tell us it was this bad? You said it was a bit of pain now and again, but not full-blown attacks! Come on, *mi hermosa*, if something is *attacking* you, you tell us about it. *Dios mio*, I thought we'd learned our lesson about not telling the truth, the whole truth, and nothing but the truth?" She stroked my hair, though I caught her eyeing Wade. She'd clearly seen him holding my hand.

"I didn't want to worry anyone, and I was dealing with it just fine until a few days ago. That's when it really kicked up a notch," I said wryly. Wade's gaze didn't leave me for a moment.

"Here, you should try this." Isadora took a small leather pouch from the inside of her jacket. "If Krieger doesn't have anything you can use, this is always a good alternative."

I frowned. "What is it?"

"An herbal remedy."

I pulled the strings apart and lifted it to my nose, inhaling a hideous odor that stabbed at my nostrils without warning. It smelled like moldy banana skins, festering seaweed, cat food, and the back end of a garbage truck, all blended into one. Bile rose in my throat. Clamping my hand across my mouth to keep the puke in, I held the pouch as far from my nose as possible.

Isadora laughed. "It's not for sniffing, although it probably would wake you up if you ever got knocked out. This is ancient stuff—the very best."

"Nomura already gave me an herbal mix for my spiritual healing," I muttered, wrinkling my nose as I closed the pouch. "Don't tell me I have to take this, too?"

"If you want it to stop hurting for a while, then I have to insist," she replied kindly. "Fortunately for you, you don't actually have to 'take' this stuff. You just wear it around your neck, and it does the rest."

"I just wear it?" I glanced down at the nasty-smelling pouch, wondering if that scent would follow me around.

She nodded. "I don't think there'll be any kind of side effects from wearing this and taking Nomura's concoction. It's herbal and neutral, and it's intended to focus on the root of the pain. It's like the witches of old always used to say: one can never have too many herbal concoctions."

I flashed her a weak grin. "They used to say that?"

"No idea, but it sounded convincing, right?" She smiled back.

"How did you get it?" I doubted it was the kind of thing most people just carried around in their pocket.

"Preceptor Bellmore gave me a few bags after she removed Katherine's hex, so I always keep a spare handy," Isadora explained.

"You have to wear one, too?" I knew Bellmore had removed the hex, at great personal cost to herself, but I didn't know about any stinky pouches.

"I have to wear one for the rest of my life, to ease the after-effects of that vicious little spell. In a way, it's similar to what you're going through. If I take the pouch off, I get these bad pains that come and go. I can deal with them, but it takes a lot out of me and makes me want to sleep for days."

"When I get my hands on Katherine Shipton, I'm gonna—" Jacob interjected, only to be cut off by Wade.

"You don't need to get close to Katherine. We'll handle her."

Jacob dropped his chin to his chest. He'd been seeking the Rag Team's forgiveness since his mishap in the Asphodel Meadows—the one that had cost Quetzi his life—and, though we'd all understood his actions, Wade seemed the least forgiving.

"Don't you need this pouch?" I asked, turning back to Isadora.

"No, as I said, Bellmore gave me spares, in case one dries out or gets lost. This one is all yours."

I smiled. "Thank you."

"I'll do anything I can to help ease your pain, Harley—you know that. It's my pleasure. I just hope it works as well for you as it has for me."

I looped the leather strings around my neck and tucked the pouch under my t-shirt. After what my aunt had said, it felt fitting that the pouch now lay beside the pendant that Imogene had given me—a replica of the one I'd seen in my dreams, before I even knew that Isadora was still alive. The Merlin heirloom and a healing herb pouch, both balms for my soul. Both reminding me of the family I still had, and the one I'd lost.

A hush fell over the crowd as the mirrors shimmered like a desert mirage. A moment later, the California Mage Council stepped out onto the platform. Alton crossed the stage to meet them in the center, where a lectern had been set up for the announcement. I watched them intently as all seven members of the Mage Council joined Alton in a hushed conversation. I'd never seen all of them together before. Four I recognized—Leonidas Levi, Imogene Whitehall, Remington Knight-shade, and Nicholas Mephiles—but three were brand new to me.

"Members of the San Diego Coven," Alton announced as he took his place at the lectern. I frowned as six of the Mage Council went to take their seats, leaving only one beside Alton. *No, no, no, no, no... don't you dare, Alton!* "I know you're all eager to discover who will be taking my position as director of the SDC, albeit temporarily, so that we may resume normality. I've said all that I can say, during my last meeting. And so, without further ado, it is my pleasure to inform you that Leonidas Levi will be your interim director, until someone else can be found to take the role permanently."

The crowd gasped, and my stomach dropped like a stone. Levi swaggered forward a few steps, opening out his arms as if he expected rapt applause. He was going to enjoy this, whether we wanted him there or not.

"You've got to be freaking kidding me!" The words slipped out before I knew I'd said them.

Judging by the faces around me, I wasn't the only one with that thought. Raffe looked about ready to blow. Clearly, Daddy Levi hadn't passed this one by his son.

THREE

Harley

"It is with deepest regret that I'm standing down from my position, but, for personal reasons, it's necessary," Alton went on. He looked at the Rag Team—those words were for us. An apology of sorts. "I will continue to remain in the coven during this transitional period, in which I'll help support Leonidas in the daily running of the SDC. I'll do the same for the future, permanent director, whoever they may be. As yet, we don't have anyone in the running, but rest assured, we're looking for the ideal candidate." He glanced back at Leonidas, who wore a smug smile on his face.

Oh, you've been waiting a long time to get your hands on this place, haven't you?

"I assure you that you'll be in the best of hands," Alton continued brightly. "Leonidas Levi has experience running covens, and I know he will do all he can to uphold our tradition of working hard to keep magicals safe and thriving everywhere. It has been the greatest honor of my life to serve as your director, and I thank you for embracing me with warmth and generosity. I'll be sorry to leave you all."

If this was his attempt to butter us up, it'd failed miserably.

Beside me, Raffe stood in stony silence, red pulsing beneath his skin. His eyes flashed, his hands balling into fists. Though sensing emotions from Raffe was always confusing, the fierce rage twisting inside him told me the djinn and Raffe were in agreement on this.

"Calm down, *mi amor*," Santana urged, touching his face and forcing him to look at her. "This isn't the time or place. I need you to ease up on the anger. Otherwise, we'll have people screaming. Don't give your dad the satisfaction—either of you." Having a boyfriend with a djinn inside him came with extra responsibilities, and keeping said djinn from ripping Daddy's throat out seemed to be one of them.

Levi stepped up to the lectern, practically shoving Alton back toward Tobe. He looked like a stuffed peacock, his chest puffed out, his face so smug I wanted to bring down the chandelier again and wipe that smirk off his lips.

"It is my pleasure to take on the role of interim director." His voice boomed across the hall. "The San Diego Coven has been languishing in a lack of discipline and talent for many years, with little sign of improvement, perpetuated by a casual acceptance of Mediocrity. There has never been any sense of ambition or perseverance here, even though you have one of the finest examples of a Mediocre overcoming their label within your ranks—Hiro Nomura. Indeed, it will be the greatest challenge of my life to attempt to turn this coven around and ensure you find your place amongst the upper echelons of national institutions.

"Moreover, the California Mage Council has been bombarded with tales of the SDC's perpetual inability to abide by the rules and coop-erate with higher authorities, especially in these trying times. This coven's recklessness and continual endangerment of others cannot be allowed to continue. We must become a unit, instead of splintered cells who do as they please and fear nothing for the consequences of their actions."

Levi looked directly at us, and a spike of searing resentment jumped through my nerves. *How freaking dare you!* I'd have loved nothing more than to join Raffe and snap Levi's neck.

Imogene stood and closed the gap between herself and Levi, the room falling silent as she moved. "That is not strictly correct, Leonidas," she said. "The SDC has a great many young talents, whose abilities are being well nurtured here. Harley Merlin, Wade Crowley, Santana Catemaco, and the rest of their team, to name but a few. Your son is also amongst the great talents that reside here."

Levi opened his mouth to speak, but Imogene bulldozed on.

"Then there's Hattie Hawthorne, who is one of the most senior magicals here—as a former magical champion in her retirement, you cannot deny her prowess. We have Gregoire and Delphine LaSalle also, who were former Angels. You know the skillset required to become one of those, Leonidas. And, as you have said, the SDC has the likes of Hiro Nomura to teach and guide all those who seek further education. It would be unfair to say that this coven lacks talent *or* discipline, nor is it particularly steeped in Mediocrity. Although, I do loathe that term."

Levi looked about ready to burst. Imogene had well and truly stolen his thunder. I noticed that Nomura was unmoved by the accolades; he sat off to the side in stony silence.

"The leadership is still to blame," Levi declared, narrowing his eyes at the Rag Team. Repentance wasn't in his vocabulary. "The leadership here has poisoned the youth, utilizing their so-called talents in a way that consistently exacerbates the situation. Of course, I have the utmost respect for the likes of Ms. Hawthorne, the LaSalles, and Hiro Nomura, and many other senior members of the coven. The younger generation has yet to earn that, in my opinion."

"Perhaps this is not the time, Leonidas," Imogene murmured, with a hard stare.

"Nonsense, this is the perfect time. It was the SDC's incompetence that resulted in the loss of Quetzalcoatl, and the aftermath of *that* travesty." He didn't need to elaborate. We knew he was talking about the first ritual, and Katherine's completion of it. "Alton was directly responsible for what happened."

My eyes widened. *Does he know about the deal?*

"He was unfit to handle and protect the Bestiary in the first place. It should never have been granted to this coven, not with Alton at the helm. Tobe requires better leadership, and deserves as much," Levi railed on. I breathed a sigh of relief—he didn't know about Alton's part in Quetzi's escape. "Fortunately, I have the answer to all of these shortcomings. There is much work to be done."

Whispers susurrated around the hall, everyone speculating about what that sweeping statement might mean. *Nothing good, that's for damn sure.*

"If you have questions about the upcoming changes, please address them to Alton. I will have much to do in the coming days, and I can't deal with every minor issue. I have a Bestiary to protect and laws to enforce, all of which will ensure that you become better magicals. The SDC has languished too long, and I will change that."

Alton walked toward Levi with a grim expression, his eyes glinting with anger. Evidently seeing that his moment was about to be taken away, Levi turned back to the audience.

"We must not forget that it was this same incompetency that resulted in the death of Preceptor Jacintha Parks. Had this coven's director been more ruthless, her murder would never have been allowed to happen," he said. Alton looked like he might be the one who'd kill Levi, right then and there. I didn't blame him. He couldn't get a word in edgewise, not with Levi hogging the mic like a true dictator.

"To ensure that this temporary era begins the right way, I would like to introduce you to the new preceptor of Alchemy and Magical Chemistry, Rita Bonnello," Levi continued. "She has moved here from the Rome Coven."

He gestured to a woman in the front row, who dutifully rose and lifted her hand in an elegant wave. She was an all-Italian brunette, with olive skin and a killer sense of style that screamed sophistication—sleek lines and expensive-looking black fabrics, all tailored to fit her perfectly.

Levi cleared his throat. "Last, but not least, the Annual Magical Assembly is taking place in Washington, DC, in a few days' time. I will be attending on behalf of the SDC, and I hope to have good news to report. Much can be achieved in a short time if we're all on the same page. The president of the United Covens has heard of the SDC's troubles, and he has asked that I brief him, personally, after his usual address."

I shook my head. Levi was basically positioning himself as the single most valuable link between our bunch of magical misfits and the leader of the free magical world. I'd have bet money on Levi being the one who'd *insisted* on briefing the president personally, not the other way around. He was a lap dog when it came to the bigwigs in authority —anyone could see that.

"Are you done?" Raffe shouted, his outburst drawing the stares of everyone in the hall.

Levi shot his son an icy look. "Yes, for now, that should be all. You are dismissed."

With the speech over, an air of impending doom hung over the inhabitants of the coven. Judging by the wave of disappointment and misery that ebbed and flowed around me, no one was happy about Levi being the new boss. Even Imogene seemed to be on the fence. I wished I could get her to take that bracelet off, so I could really find out what she was thinking, but it was written pretty clearly on her face. Her expressions were nervous and doubtful.

Not like the rest of those cackling hyenas. I glanced at the other members of the Mage Council, who seemed thrilled. They might as well have been slapping each other on the back. In one fell swoop, Levi had given the California Mage Council infinitely more control over the SDC. Something they'd likely wanted for a while now.

"I'm going to go and ask Levi about New Orleans," I said, heaving myself up off the windowsill.

Wade frowned. "Right now?"

"Seems like as good a time as any. He's probably buzzing that he got to roast Alton like that, in front of everyone. It might make him more cooperative."

I took off before anyone could stop me, arriving at the edge of the platform as Levi was descending. He paused to exchange pleasantries with the preceptors, including the new Italian addition. "I'm very much looking forward to working with you all," he said, with that same smug grin.

Nomura was barely paying attention, his foul mood gathering like a storm. I felt a sudden stab of annoyance brimming out of him. He left a moment later with a cursory, "I must attend to something, Leonidas. Please, excuse me."

Weird. Alton's departure was really hitting Nomura hard. Harder than I'd expected.

"Councilor... uh, Director Levi," I said, approaching him. "I was wondering if I could have a quick word? It's pretty urgent, and I think you'll want to hear what I have to say."

He sneered. "Did you not hear what I said about trivial issues? Address your concerns to Alton, not me."

"This isn't a minor issue, Director," I replied. "We'd like your permission to visit New Orleans. We've got reason to believe Marie Laveau has the answers we need about the rituals. I know you want to stop the second ritual as much as the rest of us. Also, we believe she might have something that I need to help with my Suppressor. As you know, it cracked, and the energy that's flowing out will poison me if I don't get help quickly." I didn't mention the Sanguine spell specifically, since nobody knew Alton had gifted it to me. To protect our mission and our investigation, it was best if Levi wasn't told everything. "So, if you would just let me go to—"

A tight laugh barked from Levi's throat. "Absolutely not!"

"But, Director, I really think that—"

"My answer is final!" he snapped. "I planned to speak with you later about this, but since you're here—I'd advise you to stay in your own lane. All of you."

Wade stepped up beside me. "Her request was a simple one, Director. One that could be of benefit to everyone."

"Yeah, maybe you should listen," Raffe added. Santana held on to his arm, attempting to keep the djinn at bay.

"Ms. Merlin is unstable and a danger to you all, though you are much too blind to see it," Levi shot back. "From here on out, she is not allowed off of coven premises. She will receive her surgery, as planned, in several months' time. This talk of poisoning is nonsense; it is merely an excuse to get away from the coven, and I won't allow it."

I stiffened, hardly believing the words I was hearing. "You can't be serious!"

"Oh, I am very serious. If you focused more on obeying the rules, instead of getting into trouble, then you wouldn't be in this mess," Levi said. "Whenever something unfortunate happens, your name pops up— a Merlin through and through."

I scowled at him. He was basically blaming me for Quetzi's death, for Katherine completing the first ritual—everything. I could hear it in his bitter tone. "You can't keep me locked up in here!" I stared at Alton, wanting some kind of backup. He flashed me an apologetic look.

"Levi's word is law now." Alton descended from the platform. He probably hadn't heard what preceded Levi's jibes, but it didn't take a genius to guess.

"Director Levi, this isn't right. She's not lying about the poisoning," Wade said. "And you can't lock her up like a prisoner. She hasn't done anything wrong."

Levi smiled. "Yet."

"She had no more part in this than any of the others." Alton found some semblance of guts, spurred on by Wade. "You shouldn't allow your own prejudices to bleed into your directorship here. That's not how you gain the respect of your peers and your residents."

Levi's lip curled. "I don't need you to tell me how to run a coven, Alton."

"My apologies," Alton replied, his shoulders slumping.

I looked closely at the former director for the first time in a long while. He looked exhausted and broken. As angry as I was with Alton for agreeing to put Levi in the temporary post—although I got the feeling he hadn't had much say in it—I felt sorry for him. He was losing everything because of the deal he'd made to save Astrid's life. None of us would breathe a word of it. If we did, he'd be shipped off to Purgatory. Plus, there was no way any of us were giving Levi another reason to sneer at the SDC.

One thing was certain: if Levi wouldn't let me go to New Orleans with his blessing, I'd have to find another way. The mirrors were out of the question anyway, at least for now.

"And we did manage to rescue Isadora," Jacob, wearing his Tarver mask, chimed in. Levi didn't know his real identity, and we planned to keep it that way.

Levi shot Jacob a withering look. "Meet me in my office in five minutes, all of you. Isadora, you come too."

The others reluctantly headed out of the Assembly Hall. I moved to go with them, dreading another crap-storm from Levi, but he stood in my way. "Not you, Harley. You're not required at this meeting."

"If it concerns the Rag Team, it concerns me," I replied. My knees were still shaky, but I wasn't going to be pushed around by this punk.

"Not this time it doesn't. Tarver, Louella, you aren't needed, either." Levi ushered the rest of the Rag Team out. They cast reluctant glances back at me, but what could they do? If they didn't obey, they'd get a one-way ticket out of here. Levi was on a warpath, and we were obstacles in his way.

I watched them go. I still felt sick to my stomach, and this was only making matters worse. How could he boot me out like that? My focus turned toward Alton, who offered me a small smile. Tobe had joined him at the bottom of the platform steps, with no evident bad blood between them. As wise as the Beast Master was, maybe he didn't know what Alton had done. But I did. Despite his good intentions, this was all his fault. Levi was the director now, and who knew how far those ripples would spread?

"Is this how you hoped things would play out?" I asked, sarcasm dripping from my tongue. I looked at the now-closed doors of the Assembly Hall, my exasperation reaching a fever pitch. The rest of the crowd had dispersed, leaving the room all but empty.

"I'm sure the others will fill you in when they get back. Levi is a showman—he's merely trying to make a point. I'm sure it's nothing to worry yourself over," Alton replied. He had the decency to look embarrassed. If it wasn't for Astrid, and me wanting to protect her feelings, I'd have laid into Alton right about then.

I held his gaze. "That's not the point, Alton. This—all of this—is on you."

Unable to handle another moment in his presence without screaming out the truth, I walked away. Jacob and Louella flanked me, both equally put out at being left behind by Levi. I sensed their disappointment as keenly as my own.

"What was that about?" I heard Tobe ask from behind me.

Alton sighed. "It's nothing... It doesn't matter anymore."

It matters, Alton. Don't you dare forget that.

FOUR

Wade

I swallowed my discomfort at leaving Harley behind. She still looked drained. Seeing her suffering this morning had been a kick to the gut. At least she had Jacob and Louella to look out for her until this meeting was over. She'd be pissed at Levi until the end of time, but we'd catch her up on everything later. It was best to stay on the new director's good side for the time being. Kicking up a stink wasn't the right way to go about things.

Not that I wanted Levi anywhere near this coven; he was a power-hungry autocrat, and he'd bring a whole world of trouble for Harley. The man had had it in for her from day one, and that wasn't about to change. Case in point, he'd barred her from joining us. A petty, juvenile act. Not the behavior of a good leader. If the rest of us could be cooperative citizens, at least it'd steer Levi's wrath away from Harley. That was my plan.

It was easier to think without Harley here, to be frank. My head had cleared the moment I left the Assembly Room. When she was around, my brain was all over the place. I kept looking at her lips, her face, her hair, wanting to put my arms around her all the time, as if I could keep her safe from harm just by keeping her close. It was that cracked Suppressor, leaking her Empathy everywhere, bringing that protective streak out in me.

"This way," Levi said, like we'd never been to Alton's office before. It wasn't Alton's anymore. I'd have to get used to that.

As he pushed open the black double doors, I froze in my tracks. All the sleek mahogany and monochrome décor had gone. In its place stood a room that had been plucked straight out of a Persian palace. The entire office had been renovated overnight, the style dripping in Middle Eastern influence. Mosaics of blue-and-white tiles now made up two of the walls, while silk wallpaper depicting Babylonian motifs covered the other two in complementary tones of silver and cobalt. He'd played around with the illusion of the interdimensional pocket, too, the ceiling now arching toward a central apex. Walnut furniture had replaced the old pieces, the desk included. Glass cases revealed ancient-looking statuettes that transported me into a mysterious tale of great kings and sabered warriors.

Talk about your fixer-upper.

"Well, you made yourself at home," Santana said, with a low whistle. She was always the one to break the ice.

"Did you have the decorators in the moment you heard Alton was resigning, or did you wait a while first?" Raffe added. He was struggling with this. His face said everything I needed to know, not to mention the still-pulsing trails of red under his skin.

Levi waved his hand and settled behind the desk. "It is vital that a director's workspace befits their position. Anyway, you must be wondering why I've brought you here." He let a moment of dramatic tension pass. None of us responded, which clearly irked him, his gaze shifting between us.

"Why did you bring us here?" I asked, finally. We needed to play along to keep him sweet. The visit to New Orleans wasn't just going to land in our laps, and Harley needed that trip.

He smiled triumphantly. "Well, I've brought you here because I wanted you all to be the first to know of my new implementations. The rest of the coven will find out in due course, but you are my primary targets, since you have a history of disobeying the rules and regulations."

"So why leave Harley out?" Dylan asked. I wanted to know the answer, too. Spite was my guess.

Tatyana nodded. "She is as much a part of our group as anyone."

"Whom I choose to include and whom I choose to exclude is none of your concern," Levi replied. "Funnily enough, you bring me to my first order of business: disobedience and backchat. I won't have it while I am director of this coven. You do as you are told, without question. If you can't do that, you will be punished appropriately."

"Alton believed that—" Astrid began, but Levi cut her off with a savage stare. I stood closer to her, trying to shield her from Levi's wrath. After being resurrected over a week ago, she was still dealing with some after-effects. I wasn't going to let Levi make that worse.

"Alton is no longer director here, and his rules—or lack thereof—no longer apply," he muttered. "Imogene was right when she said you were a talented bunch, but you have no discipline. There have been far too many reckless outings and near misses for my liking."

"We secured Finch, and we imprisoned Emily Ryder, in addition to disposing of Emmett Ryder," I said, meeting Levi's eye with a firm stare. I wasn't being contradictory; I was merely stating the facts.

"Yes, that's true. But you also got those magical kids captured and couldn't retrieve Quetzalcoatl when he escaped." Levi gave a crooked smile. "Not to mention putting a lot of lives at risk when you faced Katherine in that otherworld. We might have her in our grasp right now, if you had only waited for the approval of the Council. We could have sent more boots on the ground, but you are all much too willful. You act on impulse, and that must be stopped."

He was completely missing the point. Yeah, we'd messed up, but we'd made advances, too. And the mayhem in the Asphodel Meadows had been mostly down to Jacob. Not the rest of us. I still hadn't quite forgiven him for that. There'd been so much more at stake, but he was young. He wasn't a big-picture thinker yet. But our entire goal was to make amends for the mistakes we'd made as a group. Why couldn't Levi see that? Why was he just fixed on the bad? We were already taking steps to atone.

Astrid frowned. "So, are you moving us elsewhere?"

Levi leaned back in his chair. "It's better to have you here, where I can keep an eye on you, rather than risk an outside enemy exploiting you. I am a fair man, and I believe in second chances. Although, there would be slight satisfaction in knowing you were all at the Juneau Coven, right now, freezing your hind ends off."

I'd like to see you try. I forced down my anger, knowing it wouldn't get me anywhere.

Raffe, on the other hand, wasn't coping so well with his rage. He was shaking with anger, despite Santana's hand on his arm. It took exceptional strength for Raffe to contain his djinn at the best of times, and the two were clearly in the middle of a war of wills. It didn't happen often, but I sensed that Raffe wanted to let the djinn loose. Just this once. Just to wipe that smirk off his father's face. All families were dysfunctional, but the Levis were definitely on the volatile end of the spectrum.

"Calm down," Santana whispered.

"Keep things under control," I urged, giving Raffe a stern gaze. We couldn't lose him, and his father would have no qualms about moving him to another coven. Or a prison.

Levi, ignoring his son's battle, continued. "To ensure that my new rules are adhered to, there will be a penalty system. Breaking a rule once will lead to the deduction of points from the coven, and limited movement for a one-week probationary period. Repeated disobedience will lead to room arrest for forty-eight hours. Multiple offenses will be punished with a week in the basement jail. If, after the third penalty is implemented, the perpetrator insists on further disobedience, they will be written up and shipped off to the Juneau Coven in Alaska. If the transfer is resisted, they'll go straight to Avarice until they've learned their lesson."

"Avarice?" Dylan asked.

"Ah yes, I forget you haven't been here all that long, Mr. Blight," Levi purred. "Avarice is a prison for lesser crimes and criminals, though it is no less severe than Purgatory. It will not be a vacation, you may be assured of that."

That sounded like a gross misuse of magical penal resources. He had to be bluffing.

Isadora stepped forward. "This is precisely the kind of dictatorship hokum that made me stay away from covens in the first place," she snapped. "You don't hold the monopoly on how people should live their lives. This isn't a prison, or a military barracks, nor is this a boarding school where people need to be micromanaged. You don't get to implement rules like this. That's not what covens are supposed to be here for."

Levi smirked. "The SDC must be better, and that means reining in the loose cannons. You're entitled to your own opinion, Isadora, but, as per my new rules, you won't be permitted to leave the premises. You are much too valuable to us, and I would hate for you to fall into Katherine's hands again."

"I can't leave? Says who?" Isadora shot back. Levi flinched, but a scowl remained on his face. She scared him, that much was obvious, and he'd resorted to petty vindictiveness. There was no reason to keep Isadora cooped up here; he was only flexing his bureaucratic muscles.

"The director of this coven," he replied. *You want a crown to go with that?*

Isadora's eyes narrowed to reptilian slits. "You think these rules of yours will stop me from leaving if I want to? If it weren't for Harley, I'd pop off right now, just to prove a point. If you do this, you will lose the respect of every resident in this coven. Fear isn't as potent a motivator as you might think. It only breeds rebellion and resentment."

Levi glared back. "Is that a threat, Isadora?"

"Not a threat, but a warning."

"Speaking of which, we've got a warning of our own for you," Raffe growled. He broke away from Santana and strode up to the desk, slamming his fists on the smooth surface. His skin shifted to crimson, and black smoke billowed from his shoulders. The djinn was loose.

Levi stiffened in his chair; the flash of the djinn's eyes had paralyzed him with fear. Smoky black magic snaked across the desk.

I pulled Raffe back before it could get physical. Terrifying Levi was one thing, but if we let Raffe go over the edge and use his djinn energy, we might never get him back.

"Raffe, you still in there?" I shook him by the shoulders. His face remained stoic and scarlet.

I pulled back, and Santana put her hand on Raffe's face. "I know you're angry, but you can't come out right now, Kadar."

"You named him?" I looked at Santana in surprise.

"*He* is standing right here," Raffe shot back, with a wry smile. "I asked for a name, and they named me. Or, rather, this Mexican beauty gave me the name. Raffe just agreed. Pliable, flexible Raffe, always doing as he's told. See, that's why he needs me, to deal with ingrates like *that*." His red eyes glowered at the still-frozen Levi.

"Right, well, we need Raffe back. He'll end up in Purgatory, and you along with him, if you do anything to Levi right now," I warned.

"You mortals are no fun at all. No idea why Raffe hangs out with the likes of you… with the obvious exception." The djinn winked at Santana, before shrugging off the crimson shade of his skin. He was giving Raffe back to us.

Across the room, Levi sat up straight and cleared his throat. "Have you got him under control?"

"Yes, *he* is under control," Raffe retorted. "Kadar just wanted to give you a little warning, that's all."

"If he rears his ugly head again, you may consider that one rule broken." Levi's voice was firm, but he looked shaken, his cheeks nearly purple. "As for the rest of you, I trust you accept my new legislature? If you do not, I may have to make arrangements right away. It's getting colder up in Juneau already, and I hear the winter darkness can turn some people quite mad."

I looked to each member, and they looked back. A mumble of assent ran around the group. Yet again, what choice did we have?

"From now on, the National Council will be the only ones to continue their work against Katherine," Levi added. "You will stand down, although you may be required at a later date, if the Council needs more boots on the ground for their missions. Until you are called up, you are not to go prancing around and looking for ways to disable Katherine yourselves. You've done enough harm with that, already."

I nodded on behalf of the group. "Understood, Director Levi."

"Does everyone understand?" Levi asked.

The others agreed, albeit reluctantly.

"Will we be assigned new duties, now that we're off the investigation?" I asked.

"I will find plenty to keep you occupied. There's a huge backlog of paperwork to be done, and we wouldn't want the devil making work of your idle hands now, would we?"

I nodded again. "Understood." He'd likely find the most boring stuff for us to do, to keep us busy.

"Our first meeting has been a success, then. You may leave," he said in a bright tone that annoyed the heck out of me. I might've sounded obedient on the outside, but I wanted to punch him as hard as anyone. If not more so, for the way he'd treated Harley. She deserved his respect. She'd earned it. *I'd like to see you face off against Katherine Shipton and live.*

Not that my pretense of obedience mattered. We were going to break the rules as soon as we walked out the door. There was no way we could leave something as important as Katherine's investigation to Levi and the other members of the Council. They were in over their heads, even if they wouldn't admit it, whereas we'd faced Katherine twice. We knew what we were up against.

Santana led the way with Raffe, while Dylan and I tried to put some distance between him and his father. Tatyana and Astrid provided added support, flanking Raffe on our way to the exit. I'd almost stepped out into the hallway when Levi called me back.

"Wade, would you mind staying for a moment?" He looked at me expectantly. "I have something I need to speak with you about."

I glanced at the others, who offered sympathetic looks. They needed to get Raffe away from the office before Kadar showed himself again. I understood that, but I really didn't want to spend another minute alone with Levi.

"Of course, Director," I replied, wary and frustrated. Harley was my main concern. She'd be on edge about New Orleans, and we had to figure out a way to get her there. Her life depended on it.

Taking my time to turn back around, I struggled to keep my eyes from rolling hard. I wasn't supposed to be in here with Levi. I was supposed to be out there, staying close to Harley. I couldn't protect her from here.

I got the feeling that was the point.

FIVE

Harley

"At least Alton isn't leaving completely," Louella said, as she sat on the low wall beside the dragon fountain. All three of us rejects —Louella, Jacob, and I—had come out here to find some peace away from prying eyes and curious ears. A gloomy mood hung over the garden as we sat there, discussing how peeved we were at Levi. Still, it was a nice place to recover after the events of the morning, and my pouch of rancid herbs seemed to be doing the trick in keeping the pain at bay.

"Not that he'll be able to do much," I replied. "He can't stop Levi from being an ass, and you'd better believe he's going to be. That dude laps up power like it's going to run out at any moment. He'll rule over this place like a freaking emperor. I wouldn't be surprised if he has us on our knees, scrubbing the floor with toothbrushes by this time tomorrow."

Jacob stretched out with a loud yawn. "Alton might still be able to help us move around without catching Levi's attention. He knows this place better than anyone—nooks and crannies included."

"Why did it have to be him, of all people? Seriously!" I muttered.

"Ugh, he's probably been waiting for a moment like this. I bet he did a little dance of glee when he heard Alton wanted to resign."

Louella smiled. "I can't picture Leonidas dancing."

"I bet it went something like this." Jacob scooted backward around the dragon fountain, half moonwalk, half running man. Louella giggled, her face lighting up. I had to admit, it was pretty funny, and it was even nicer to see the two new recruits laughing. They hadn't had much chance for normal teenage silliness recently.

"Well, one thing's for sure: we're not telling Levi about you," I said to Jacob, as he came to a halt in his dancing. "We can't have any slip-ups, not even if the mask gets too hot. It's the only thing keeping you safe right now, and Alton hasn't told Levi about your true identity. We already covered your portal-making ass by telling them we followed Katherine through to the Asphodel Meadows, but you're not exactly off the hook."

Levi probably already had Isadora in his crosshairs, which was why he'd called her into his selective meeting. Portal Openers were exceptionally rare and of huge strategic value. There was no way Levi would let her slip through his fingers. If Levi found out he had two at his disposal, he'd wet himself out of sheer happiness.

I walked over to the wall and leaned on the stone, staring out at the familiar sight of Balboa Park. Sadness hit me in an unexpected wave, emphasized by my cracked Suppressor. I wished Quetzi were still alive, and that we'd managed to stop Katherine. I wished we'd rescued Isadora without compromising Quetzi's life. I wished Alton hadn't made his deal, and he was still director of this coven. Either that, or he'd just covered it up and stayed the director here anyway. Now, I was slowly dying of Chaos poisoning and had been denied permission to go to New Orleans to fix it. Not only that, but I wasn't allowed to leave the coven, and Katherine was still out there, cooking up her next plan of action with even more power at her disposal. I would have given anything for an easier way out of this mess.

This is the Suppressor talking, giving me stupid mood swings. Right now, it was taking all the bad stuff and making it ten times worse. I couldn't afford to wallow in self-pity, not with so much at stake. *Get it together, Harley.* If I was going to break my Suppressor and get the jump on Katherine, I needed to focus on what I *could* do, not what was out of my control.

First and foremost, I had to find another way to get to New Orleans without Levi knowing I'd even left the coven.

Simple, right?

The rest of the Rag Team found us in the garden twenty minutes later, and I was no closer to coming up with a solution to my travel problem. A mixture of emotions hit me as they walked out into the courtyard—anger, disappointment, exasperation, and a hint of pure hatred. The only person I couldn't quite feel was Astrid, but I'd sort of gotten used to the weird, cold void inside her. It wasn't right—I knew that—and I didn't want that to be her reality, but neither of us knew what to do about it. We'd talked about it a lot since her resurrection, and she couldn't find anything in her books that could reverse it.

"So, what did our new leader have to say?" I asked as I approached the group. Looking around, I realized Wade wasn't with them.

"Nothing good," Santana replied, before launching into a brief rundown of everything Levi had told them. The new rules and regulations, and the threat of Alaska and Avarice if we didn't comply. She also mentioned the spat that Isadora and Levi had had, and the near miss with Raffe and the djinn. That outburst had worried her the most, I could sense it.

"He said what to you, Isadora?" I gasped in disbelief.

"He's essentially holding me prisoner, though I'd like to see him try and keep me here," she muttered. "I will stay as long as I need to, and not a moment longer. He can shove it where the sun doesn't shine if he thinks he can stand in my way." A startled laugh rippled from my throat. I'd never heard her speak like that before. If Levi thought he could trap my aunt, he had another thing coming. She was a force to be reckoned with.

"And Avarice? Is that some kind of prison?" I asked.

"Yeah, for misdemeanors," Dylan replied. "I didn't know about it either."

"And you're okay now, Raffe?" I asked.

He nodded. "Just about. Kadar seems to have retreated for now." He paused, a subtle flash of red sparking in his eyes for a millisecond. "Although, I kind of wanted him to beat the crap out of my dad this time."

"I'd have paid to see that," I replied, bitterness twisting up my words. "Who does he think he is? I know he was on the Mage Council, but that man has one major ego."

My anger spiked, spurred on by the knowledge that Levi was keeping Wade in his office for a "private chat." *Arrogant little creep.* Part of me kind of wished the djinn *had* stayed out a while longer, just to bring Levi down a peg or two. Then again, the djinn was temperamental, and we might well have ended up with a bunch of mulch on the wall and no director at all.

"That's my father for you." Raffe gave a harsh sigh.

Astrid nodded. "It's going to be so strange without Alton at the helm. I thought it would be okay, since he's still going to be around, but now I'm not so sure. All of these rules and regulations… They can only spell bad news."

"I've seen this happen time and time again," Isadora replied. "A director gets these big ideas and lets the power go to their head, and the covens end up in total disarray. Or worse."

"Well, Levi isn't stopping me from breaking this Suppressor," I said, determined. "If he's happy to sign my death warrant because he thinks

I'm a liar, then that's his business, but I'm not giving up until my time has run out. I just need to find another way to get to New Orleans without him catching me, especially now with this new penalty system. I mean, I don't really feel like dying in this Avarice place. Or Alaska."

Santana's eyes brightened. "I could always get my Orishas to build a duplicate of you, like they did back at the New York Coven. It fooled Salinger, and as long as Levi only sees it for short bursts at a time, we might get away with it again."

"I'm sorry, what?" Isadora asked, confused.

"Oh… uh, Santana and I went to the New York Coven and kind of broke into the Special Collections room by fooling one of the preceptors with a pair of duplicates." I smiled sheepishly. "The guy was also a bit drunk, after Santana had plied him with about a million whiskey sours and tequila chasers. What did you say to him—it would be an insult to you if he didn't?"

"I said it would be an affront to my entire culture if he refused a drink from me, as the daughter of the coven leaders of Catemaco," Santana replied, with a grin.

The memory still made me nervous. "I wanted to see my mom and dad's Grimoire, and that was the only way to do it without jumping through a bunch of hoops. I saw it again afterward, after going through all the red tape, but the first time was on impulse."

"And you saw it?" Isadora looked sad, her hand pressed to her heart.

"Twice now, yeah."

"Such a shame they never got to finish it. I would've loved to have seen the spells they created together, brought to life." She sighed, dropping her chin to her chest.

Yeah… about that. Between my aunt getting her hex removed and my Chaos attacks, I hadn't had the chance to tell her about my ability to read from unfinished Grimoires. Nor had she seen me perform the summoning spell in the Asphodel Meadows, without me even having my parents' Grimoire near, but I knew she'd be fascinated to hear about it. Now wasn't the time, but I planned to tell her as soon as we had a moment alone.

"I wonder how Salinger was, after all that?" Santana said. "He was so serious until we got him drunk. Man, he was like a different person!"

I laughed. "He really was."

"I must say, I'm impressed with your ingenuity." Isadora recovered her smile and put her hand on my shoulder. "It's not every day that two young magicals can fool a well-respected, senior preceptor."

"Do you think it could work? The duplicates?" I looked to Santana and Isadora, though I wanted the rest of the Rag Team's approval, as well.

Santana nodded. "We could definitely do that, and just have your duplicate spend most of its time in your room or lost in one of the training halls. With you being sick a lot lately, nobody's going to question it. I'll even convince Krieger to back us up, if we need to use someone more convincing." She tapped her chin in thought. "I'll have to stay here to keep the duplicate going, and I'll need some help to keep up the charade. It'll be the only way to keep you safe from Levi's eagle eyes."

Raffe raised his hand. "I'll stay and run interference."

"Me too." Astrid folded her arms across her chest. "I can alter cameras and track Levi's movements, to warn Santana if he gets too close. That way, we can stay one step ahead of him."

"I can stay, too," Louella said. "Levi doesn't know that I'm fully on your side, so he's more likely to trust me if you need an instant distraction. Plus, I can listen out for him coming with my Audial senses. I might try to use my Telepathy on him, to see if he suspects anything, but it's still not very good."

"I can portal you to New Orleans, since he'll be keeping Isadora under close watch," Jacob offered. "I'll zap myself right back before anyone knows I'm gone. You'll just need an alarm or something, when you need me to pick you up."

"I can do that," Astrid replied, looking at me. "I'll hook you up with upgraded earpieces, with a unique channel just for you and Jacob, and whoever else is going with you. The two of you aren't going there alone, I presume?" She narrowed her eyes at me, but no feeling of concern drifted away from her. It was an unsettling thing, to see an emotion on someone's face and not feel it.

"I'm coming with you," Tatyana interjected. "You'll need me if you want to reach out to Marie Laveau effectively. I'm also excellent with finding gifts for the dead, and we'll have to shop around for a fitting offering for Marie, if the legend is true about her tomb and the curse."

"Thank you," I whispered, my voice catching in my throat. Tears filled my eyes, and my heart swelled with gratitude. *Cheers, Suppressor— being overly emotional is just what I need right now.*

Tatyana smiled. "My pleasure. I could never let you visit the great Marie Laveau alone. It is as much an opportunity for me as it is for you."

"Dylan?" I turned to him, realizing he'd yet to say anything.

"I'd like to come along," he replied.

Tatyana put her hand in his. "It might raise suspicion if so many of us are missing. Better that you sit this one out and help the others here, love."

I tried not to raise my eyebrows at the term of endearment. It seemed like Tatyana and Dylan's romance was still very much alive.

He looped his arm around Tatyana's waist. "You're right. If we all disappear, Levi will smell a rat." He nodded, as if coming to terms with the idea. "I'll keep the duplicate safe so you can do your thing and get back to us without worrying you'll end up in Alaska or something."

"Perfect," Tatyana said, kissing him on the cheek.

Jacob stared at the happy couple, then scuffed his shoe on the ground. He was sulking. I smiled at him sympathetically, but he just dropped his gaze. *Poor guy. That first crush is always a killer.*

Dylan grinned. "Plus, Harley's in the best hands with you and your abilities. How would she speak to Marie without you? I'd just be there as a bit of brute force. I guess Wade can handle that… and Harley, to be honest."

"Couldn't agree more," I said.

Isadora squeezed my shoulder gently. "I'll help distract Levi. He's interested in my abilities, which is useful. Even if I have to talk his ear off for an hour, that's what I'll do. You're in good hands, Harley. We're all looking out for you."

"Thank you, Isadora. I already feel better, knowing you'll be here."

As I glanced at the Rag Team, a spark of hope burst in my chest. It was small and fragile, but it was there. We had a plan, and if we could do this, then I'd have the means to break the Suppressor safely, with my Light and Dark in balance. We still had a lot of hurdles to leap over, but at least we were getting somewhere. We were going to New Orleans.

I only had one lingering concern—what did Levi want from Wade?

SIX

Wade

I sat opposite Levi and waited for him to speak. Five minutes had passed and... nothing. Was this some sort of game? Who would break the silence first? It seemed pretty pointless. He'd been the one to call me back, not the other way around. Fed up with his nonsense, I spoke first. Harley was waiting.

"You wanted to talk to me about something?"

He nodded.

"Does it have to do with Alton?" He clearly needed a prompt.

"I'm trying to find the right words to say this, without causing offense," he replied, with a casual air. I knew what came next. *I don't mean to offend you, but...* followed by something undeniably offensive. That was always the way. I'd heard it enough with my Irish roots. That's why I'd softened my accent in the first place.

"I'm all ears." I smiled tightly, wanting him to get this over with.

"I've thought long and hard about it, despite only recently being inaugurated as temporary director, and I've decided—I'm ready to transfer you to the LA Coven."

My stomach dropped. "The LA Coven...?"

"Imogene was the one who brought your talents to my attention," Levi rambled on. "Your abilities and professionalism are wasted here, especially as you seem to be the only one who understands the role obedience and discipline have to play in a coven. Imogene would like to see you with the LA Coven, and I happen to agree with her."

"Did she not tell you that I decided to stay here?" I couldn't have been clearer when we spoke about it a couple of days ago. With Alton stepping down and Garrett gone, I wasn't abandoning ship.

"She did, and she was very disappointed. Naturally, I understand your emotional attachment to this place. A coven becomes like a home and a team, all wrapped up into one. It can be hard to move on. However, I find it rather childish that you would ignore such a valuable opportunity for the sake of that comfort. One can only grow when one steps out of one's comfort zone."

And one is generally an ass when one refers to oneself in such a way.

"Still, I'd like to stay. My abilities and professionalism are better served here," I said.

"I'm sure you would, but that's not the plan," Levi replied bluntly. "Arrangements are being made as we speak, and I'm preparing the documents for your transfer to the LA Coven."

I shook my head. "You can't do that, not without my agreement."

"Ah, well, legislation is a somewhat flexible thing at times. A loophole in coven law states that if one coven is in dire need of assistance and a magical from another coven has a certain set of skills at their disposal, then provisions can be made for a temporary transfer of said magical... without their approval."

"In other words, you can transfer me without me being able to oppose your ruling?" I bit out through gritted teeth. *Dictatorship 101. Do what you damn well please, and screw everyone else.*

"Excellent, I'm glad you understand."

"No, Director Levi, this won't fly." I bristled with irritation. "Who's in dire need? The LA Coven? They've got better resources than we have, and clearly you think they're more talented than the members of the SDC. I couldn't possibly add anything."

He smiled. "Think of it as magical martial law, implemented in times of war. The threat of Katherine Shipton is close enough to war, and it's a good enough cause to stir up some old laws and put them back into motion. We're in a fight for our lives, Mr. Crowley, and we need you."

Why not get a big poster with a finger pointing right at me? LEONIDAS LEVI NEEDS YOU! This was bull at its finest. He was bending the rules for his own purposes.

"No." The word echoed across the silent room. I tried to keep cool, but it was proving difficult. He had no right to do this, martial law or no martial law. We weren't at war yet.

"Excuse me?" Ice dripped from his tongue.

"With all due respect, Director, I said no." My eyes narrowed, and my heart pounded. I wasn't leaving Harley. For all I knew, she could be dead when I got back from this "temporary transfer." He'd banned her from going to New Orleans, which didn't leave many options.

"The choice has been taken out of your hands," Levi said simply.

"You can't do this, Director." I didn't want to leave the SDC. He was right, it was my home—but it was also so much more than that. Someday, I hoped to be the new director. Ideally, it would have been when Alton retired, but my trajectory hadn't changed; I'd take over when the next permanent director retired instead. It had been my hope all along. It was why I'd joined in the first place. Alton and I shared a vision of the SDC, and I would see that come to fruition. The only trouble was, I couldn't do that if I was somewhere else.

"It has been done."

I balled my hands into fists. "You don't understand my attachment to this place at all. It's a professional attachment as much as it's a personal one. The SDC needs me more than LA does. How are you going to spin that one? The Council will see that the SDC is in greater need."

"I still sit on the Council. Don't worry about their approval—it's already been received," he replied. So, there was an endgame here. He didn't care about my professional prospects, not with the SDC. *Then what have you got up your sleeve?* It didn't make sense.

I clenched my jaw to keep a calm head. "What do you want from me? You've clearly got some other idea in mind, if you feel the need to threaten me with a provisional transfer to the LA Coven. So, what is it?"

Levi smirked. "You've always been sharp, Wade. That's one of your most admirable qualities." He paused for dramatic effect. He really liked doing that. "I think you will make a tremendous director one day, and I imagine it's already your destiny to be a great magical. You wouldn't have chosen a coven like this if you didn't have a bigger picture for your future. Is that fair to say?"

"It is."

"And, maybe, you'll even find yourself with a seat on the California Mage Council one day. If you play the game, that is. We've all jumped through the same hoops. Now, it's your turn. Until you achieve that greatness you desire, you must pick your battles carefully. You could defy me, and try to challenge this motion, but what would that achieve in the long run? Let me tell you: nothing. This isn't a fight you can win."

Anger bubbled up inside me. "Are you going to tell me what you want or not?"

"I want every snippet of information you can provide on Harley Merlin," he said, the words hanging in the air between us. "I want to know of her whereabouts, her thoughts, her actions, and even her damned bathroom breaks, at all times—from now until I tell you we're done."

My throat constricted. "You want me to *spy* on her?"

"If you want to put it so crassly, yes. I want you to spy on her. Do that, and we can postpone your transfer." He sat back in his big wicker chair and grinned like the cat who'd gotten the cream. He might as well have been stroking one, with the villainous vibes he was giving off.

No matter what, he wouldn't see me break. He might've been playing games with his new authority, but I had a few tricks up my sleeve, too.

My brain sparked into motion, the cogs whirring overtime. I'd play him like a fiddle, and he wouldn't know until it was too late. *You think you're smart, but I'm smarter.* He didn't know half the things I'd learned since joining the SDC. This coven had a scrappy fighting spirit that no other coven had. This was where great magical warriors were made, ones who fought tooth and nail to endure and persevere. Two former Angels had chosen to stay here—that spoke volumes. No matter what the coven's reputation gave off, I knew better. I was proud to be one of the warriors who bled and battled and sweated here.

"If you agree to postpone my transfer, like you said, I'll play my part," I said, doing just that. I could be very convincing when I wanted to be. And, right now, I needed to be. "If I want the SDC to progress, then I need to set a good example. Obedience and discipline, right?"

Levi grinned. "I'm glad we could come to an agreement."

"And you'll definitely postpone my transfer?" I pressed.

"I'm a man of my word, Mr. Crowley. If you scratch my back, I'll scratch yours."

Stab me in the back, more like. I'd play along. If it meant buying time, then I had to.

"Then I'll do as you've asked. You should understand that it won't be easy, but I won't defy you on this," I said, to really seal the deal. He had to know I was earnest and sincere. Judging by the smug look on his face, he believed me. I was a Crowley after all, and our recent legacy was built on following orders. He knew I'd never risk my reputation by making a fuss. Moreover, he knew I'd never try to oppose the wishes of the Mage Council. I'd proven my obedience in the past, and he was using it against me. I realized that's why he'd picked me. Of everyone, I was the least likely to go against him. To be honest, I wasn't sure whether to be insulted or complimented.

Well, we Crowleys could bend the rules too. We hadn't always been pillars of the community. One of my ancestors had been an occultist who'd started a religion all his own and had once been referred to as "the wickedest man in the world." I wasn't anywhere near that bad, nor did I want to be, but I wasn't the type of man to roll over and play dead, either. Levi had no idea what I was capable of.

"I should warn you, if I hear of any deceit or find that you have lied to me, there will be no second chances," Levi said, leaning forward over the desk. "I am putting my trust in you, for our mutual benefit. Do not disappoint me."

"I won't, Director."

"Then you are free to go... and begin your endeavors."

I stood from my chair. "I won't disappoint you, Director."

Feeling his eyes burning into my back, I left the office with my head held high. I had to make this spying lark look genuine, to please Levi and keep him from handing me over to LA.

As I walked out of the room, I couldn't help thinking of the office's former resident. Alton could have stopped this from happening. He could have made this easier. Instead, he'd put us all in an awkward position to appease his guilt. It might've looked like the right thing to do, at the time, but hindsight was twenty-twenty. He should've known it would end in trouble, and I wasn't letting him off the hook for this. It'd be a long time before we could trust him again, if ever.

I turned my mind away from Alton. That would only make me angrier, and I couldn't afford to have my judgment clouded. Right now, a bigger obstacle loomed large, the biggest one: Harley. I could only imagine what she would make of me turning spy for Levi.

SEVEN

Wade

_____

Halfway down the hallway, my phone pinged. Harley's name flashed up on the screen with a message underneath: *In the infirmary with J/T and Krieger. Need to talk. X*

The kiss surprised me. She never usually put a kiss on the end of her messages. I figured it was the Suppressor toying with her emotions again. Her moods had been swinging hard ever since she'd cracked the thing. One moment, she'd be all smiles. The next, tears filled her eyes for no reason at all. I didn't mind, but it was tricky to keep track of.

Be there in five, W, I texted back. My fingertip lingered over the *X*, but I decided not to press it. We'd agreed not to get too romantic, and I didn't want to make her swinging emotions any worse. It seemed we both had something we needed to say to each other, which was good. At least I could let her tell me her news first, before bringing my bad news down on her. Unless her news was just as bad. I guessed I'd find out soon enough.

I walked quickly to the infirmary and found them in Krieger's private office. Harley sat off to one side while Jacob and Krieger fiddled with a bulky machine. It looked like something out of a steampunk novel, all brass and cogs and dials. A golden orb sat in the middle of the machine, emitting a purple pulse of light.

"I didn't realize I'd walked into Frankenstein's laboratory," I said, drawing their attention toward me. Krieger was sweating, his glasses practically falling off the end of his nose. Jacob, who'd taken his mask off, looked flustered too. His cheeks were like tomatoes.

"They're trying to get the magical-searching device to work," Harley explained.

Krieger swiped his forearm across his brow. "I don't understand the problem! I have calibrated it over and over again, but it won't connect to Jacob's sliver of Chaos. It keeps sputtering and flashing purple, as you see." He gestured to the orb in the middle of the machine, which continued to glow. It was slightly menacing. From what I knew of Chaos, purple light tended to lean toward death-related magic. Not the sort of magic anyone ought to be around for too long.

"Basically, it's making all the right noises, but it's not doing any readings," Jacob added. He twisted one of the dials, but it only changed the light to a faint blue pulse instead.

"Are you any closer to fixing the issue?" I sat down on one of the stools near them.

Krieger shook his head. "We keep adjusting the Chaos values inside the device, but we are a long way from completing this. The vibrations are so subtle. It's like finding a very specific fish in the entire expanse of an ocean." He gave an exasperated sigh and flung a wrench onto the table.

"I'm sure you'll crack it." I could only offer encouragement. They'd been working away at this for a while now, and I didn't want them getting disheartened. If they figured this out, it would be one of the greatest magical advancements of the twenty-first century.

Harley smiled. "That's what I keep telling them. I mean, we can't rely on chance meetings for every single lone magical out there, can we?" Her eyes glinted with random tears again, and she was staring right at me. My throat constricted as I realized what she was getting at. She meant our chance meeting, outside the casino that night. I often wondered where the two of us would be if I hadn't gone out Purge-beast hunting that day. I didn't believe in anything as trite as destiny or fate, but it'd been a stroke of luck to stumble across a magical as powerful as her.

"No, it's not a very efficient method," I replied plainly. I didn't want those tears falling.

She looked a little crestfallen.

"Anyway, what did you want to talk to me about?" I changed the subject quickly. Krieger and Jacob were on one side of the room, tinkering away with the scanning device. It gave us the perfect opportunity to speak one-on-one.

Her expression brightened, and I breathed a silent sigh of relief. "I'm going to New Orleans," she said. "Santana is going to stay here and create a duplicate to fool Levi. The rest of the Rag Team is staying, too, to run interference, apart from Tatyana. She's coming with me, so she can give me her Kolduny assistance when we get to Marie Laveau's tomb. Jacob is going to portal us there."

She sounded so hopeful and determined. I liked her best when she was like this, even though I felt a bit left out. She seemed to be heading into this dangerous mission solo, with only Tatyana to back her up. She was tough as nails, for sure, but she was in no state to do something like this alone. She might not be able to hold it together, with all these Chaos attacks and mood swings. *How do I say that without pissing her off?*

"That sounds… interesting." I was building up to my concerns.

"Anyway, I was wondering if you'd come with us, too?" A flush of pink hit her cheeks. "I've been thinking about it, and the Suppressor's leaks are a frigging nightmare. They're making things difficult already, and I can't risk things going to hell when we get to New Orleans. So I'll need some emotional support to get through this, especially while

Tatyana is busy doing her Kolduny thing. I figured you could keep me on the straight and narrow."

I'd been ready to give her my reasons for not going alone, but now my chest puffed up. She needed me. She'd actually said it. Right then, I felt like I should have had a sword and a shield and been trotting around on a big white warhorse. *Get me my shining armor. Harley needs me.*

I'd never expected her to admit that to me. I had to say, it was welcome. I still didn't know if a relationship between us was a good idea, but I couldn't deny the spark between us. I'd been pushing it to one side, but why hide from it? It was already there. We'd kissed. If I closed my eyes, I could still feel her lips on mine. I wasn't one for sappiness, yet it was one of those kisses that was unforgettable.

But that was Harley in a nutshell... unforgettable. Even the night I met her, she'd stayed on my mind. *Man, that black dress.* It had clung to every curve. Funny that I preferred her in her jeans and leather jacket, but she'd made one knockout impression that night. *And that ruby-red hair.* Up, down, ponytail, braid, it always looked good. *Those inquisitive sky-blue eyes.* They were looking at me right now, and I couldn't look away. I didn't want to.

I remembered the way she'd reacted to the gargoyle, and the sass she'd given me. She'd really hated me then. But I knew she was something else, from that first moment. Anyone else would have screamed and freaked out. She'd been weirded out, yeah, but she'd been brave regardless. For so long, she'd been wandering around in the human world by herself—lost and confused, in a way. Always toughing things out on her own. And I'd brought her into the fold. Now, she was asking not to be alone. It was an unexpected turn of events, but I liked it.

"You okay there, Wade?" Her brow was furrowed in concern.

"Just thinking," I replied, my mind still wandering.

On the one hand, I was glad I'd brought her here. Her potential was unbelievable. She could blow us all out of the water with her capabilities once this Suppressor was gone. It was hard not to feel jealous of that, to be honest. All I had was Fire, some Telekinesis, and a ton of knowledge. She had more Chaos in her little finger than I'd ever have. On the other hand, I wished I'd left her to her quiet life at the casino. She'd have been alone, but Katherine would never have gotten wind of her. She wouldn't be in grave danger now, if I'd just left her be. I might have felt like her protector, but I'd also put her in a position where she needed protecting, and that didn't feel so good. Not that I'd tell Harley that. She didn't need to know how responsible I felt.

"So, are you coming or not?" Harley's tone was impatient.

"I'll come with you," I replied. *She's going to hate me for this.* "I kind of have to."

She smiled. "That's weirdly sweet of you to say."

"Not exactly." I took a breath. "Levi has asked me to spy on you."

She froze. "What did you just say?"

"Levi wants me to track your every move. He threatened me with a transfer to the LA Coven if I didn't comply, but I'm telling you so we're on the same page. We can engineer this so everyone wins." My heart raced. She had to understand.

"Where does he get off, asking you to do that?" she spat. A moment later, she grinned like the devil. "No, wait! This is perfect! I couldn't have planned it better if I'd tried."

I frowned. "I don't follow."

"Levi trusts you enough to have you spy on me. Yeah, he's threatening you with some transfer, but he must feel confident enough in you doing what he's asked. He thinks you're a lapdog. He doesn't doubt you the way he doubts the rest of us."

"Thanks?"

She laughed. "See, the thing is, I know something he doesn't. I know where your loyalty lies. You'll cover my back in what we're doing, no matter what he's asked you to do. Your support will be the final piece in the interference work we're running, because you can lie about where you are, and where I am, and he'll believe you. It's freaking perfect!"

I fought a grin; her enthusiasm was contagious. "You could be on to something there."

"The Rag Team is made up of geniuses… or is it genii? Either way, this is going to work. I know it is. I've got a good feeling."

Truthfully, I did too. I wouldn't say it out loud, but I felt it. She was right. With me by her side, we could cover our tracks with Levi. He trusted me. *Mistake number one.* What lay ahead wasn't going to be easy, by any stretch of the imagination, but it was only a matter of time before Katherine exploded into the world again. Nyx would have kicked her out of her otherworld by now, and Katherine would be focusing on the next ritual. As soon as Harley had the means to break the Suppressor, that was our next point of business: find out what the remaining four rituals were. I could almost taste success. I wouldn't enjoy it until the job was done, but I could feel good things afoot.

"So we're doing this?" I smiled at her. "We're going to New Orleans?"

"If you think you can put up with me a while longer," she teased.

"I think I can manage."

I was heading for another whirlwind of crazy with her. And, right now, I wouldn't have had my life any other way.

EIGHT

Harley

Bright and early the next morning, after successfully evading a sea of potential eavesdroppers, the Rag Team gathered in the Luis Paoletti Room. Louella had used her Audial senses to get us there without detection. Her Telepathy would have been pretty great right now, but she'd said it herself—it was still far from perfect, and glitched in and out beyond her control.

Levi's authoritarian rules were already coming into immediate effect, and they were bugging not just the Rag Team, but the rest of the coven as well. The senior members were particularly bitter about it. I'd heard a group of them gossiping about the different strikes, with one muttering, "If I wanted to be treated like a kid, I'd have stayed at my mom's house and never left." The others had agreed, wearing gloomy expressions. It made me wonder how our most famous members were dealing with the rules, but I hadn't seen them since they'd been mentioned at Levi's inauguration. I hadn't even known we'd had legends like that in our midst, and I kind of wanted the chance to speak to them. I didn't know what I'd say, but their lives must have been fascinating, the retired Angels in particular.

"You sure nobody followed us?" Wade looked at Louella.

She nodded anxiously. "Nobody. The corridors are clear."

"Anyone else think this is ridiculous?" Santana murmured. She'd already been yelled at by security for swiping a cup of coffee from the kitchens after breakfast hours had ended. "I'd like to knock him off his friggin' pedestal. What kind of *pendejo* puts breakfast between five and six-thirty in the morning? It's sadistic." Santana without her coffee was not something anyone should have to witness.

"Totally ridiculous, but that's my father for you," Raffe replied, his arm draped around her shoulders.

"At least with Alton there was a bit of leeway," Dylan added.

Astrid nodded. "He liked to abide by the rules, but there was always wiggle room."

"I saw one of the security staff screaming at a child for being late to his first class. He was literally screaming in this poor boy's face," Tatyana said. "I don't usually disagree with discipline as a principle, but that was too much."

I grimaced. "We've got to hope this coven doesn't turn into the Stanford prison experiment."

It seemed that, with Levi, nobody was allowed a scrap of freedom, if it violated the tiniest of his new coven regulations. There'd been a clampdown on clothing, as well, with a set of guidelines delivered to every coven member: *Casual clothes may be worn in downtime, but only within the confines of the living quarters or during permitted outside excursions, if a pass has been acquired. Coven members are expected to wear coven uniforms during weekdays, and beyond the living quarters. Uniforms are expected to be ironed and crisp when worn. Smart shoes are also required. No sneakers.*

The SDC was starting to sound more like Gilead from *The Handmaid's Tale* and less like a free coven of magicals. *No way he's turning me into Oflevi.* I could understand why the senior inhabitants were particularly peeved. This wasn't a military facility or a school in its truest form, but he was treating everyone like lesser beings, morphing us all into one entity. Levi was turning it from a sanctuary into an institution.

"Well, hopefully his term will be short. We can't think about his leadership now, not when someone could walk through that door at any moment," Wade said, bringing us all back into the right mindset. We had a job to do. Levi and his rules could wait.

"Still clear, just so you know," Louella chimed in.

He smiled at her, and her cheeks reddened. *Right there with you, sister.* "Thank you, Louella. Now, let's get this show on the road, shall we?"

"I'm ready when you are." I opened my leather jacket and showed him the taser in my inside pocket. Dicky had delivered it in his cab to the front of the Fleet Science Center, after Astrid had put in an order with Cabot's. It meant I wasn't technically leaving the premises. *Can't get mad, Levi.* She'd also ordered a knife for me, which was inside my boot. With my Chaos glitching all over the place, traditional weapons seemed like good backup. I just hoped I wouldn't have to use them.

"You'll need these first." Astrid handed out four earpieces, one each for me, Wade, Tatyana, and Jacob. We fitted them into our ears, my nerves building. I'd soon step past the point of no return, with no idea what we'd come back to. We had our job to do, and the rest was in the hands of the others. Santana and Isadora were in charge of managing the duplicate illusion and its movements through the coven, while Dylan, Astrid, Jacob, Louella, and Raffe were going to provide the necessary distractions and tech work to make this a success.

"Is it tuned to the right channel?" Wade asked.

Astrid nodded. "It can be switched between two channels. The first is the main channel, through which we'll all communicate. The second is an emergency channel, in case anything happens while you're in New Orleans."

"In case anything happens here, you mean?" I said.

"Either here or there. If you need to get out of New Orleans, use it and we'll send Jacob to get you. If anything happens here, we'll use it to let you know what to do. Rest assured, we'll have contingencies in place. Isadora and I have been drawing up some exit strategies."

"Comforting," I murmured.

Louella's eyes widened in alarm. "Someone's coming!"

"What?" I hissed, as all of us whirled around to face the door of the Luis Paoletti Room. *Not now!*

A minute passed, and nobody came through. Nevertheless, we all kept our gaze fixed on the door. If we were caught here, we'd be through the next mirror to Juneau… or worse. Levi was just begging for an excuse to lock me up in Avarice.

"Over here," a voice announced from behind us. We spun around in unison. Alton stood at the back of the Luis Paoletti Room.

"How the—?" Wade gasped.

Alton winked. "The coven is full of secret passageways, if you know where to look. This bookshelf, for example." He gestured to a nearby bookcase, which looked totally legit.

"I knew I could hear someone," Louella said with satisfaction.

"Very good, Louella," Alton replied. "Unfortunately, I've been forced to use some of the lesser-known routes around the coven to continue my investigative work. It's not only the regular inhabitants who are being watched."

"He's on you too, huh?" Santana surmised.

He nodded. "If not more so than most. It's lucky that I took the coven blueprints before he could get his hands on them. They're safely stowed away and have been replaced with a different set of blueprints that don't show the secret passageways." A small, sad smile crept onto his lips. "I used my last days wisely."

"No offense, Alton, but what are you doing here?" Wade's tone held an undercurrent of annoyance, shared by the rest of the Rag Team. I could feel it emanating off them. Alton's good intentions had put us in this situation, but he was standing in front of us regardless, with a renewed sense of determination flowing through his veins. Was this his way of trying to make amends?

"Levi might be watching me, but I haven't given up on capturing Katherine or rescuing the Librarian. I will help you however I can, in a way I never could have as director. I have my ways of getting around him, and I can be useful to you in this," he said.

Panic ricocheted through me. "What do you mean 'this'? What do you know?"

He smiled. "You're going to New Orleans. I heard Levi block your request, and I know you all well enough by now to know that you'd never have accepted that, not with so much at stake. I don't accept it, either. I understand that you have to do this. Your *life* is on the line here, Harley."

"We've got a pretty watertight plan in place, Alton. I don't know if —" I started to object, but he interrupted.

"I'll liaise with Isadora and make sure nobody catches on to what you're doing. I still have access to parts of the coven's security system that nobody else does and can use that to your benefit." He sounded so earnest. "All I need to know is, how long do you plan to be gone?"

"If everything goes smoothly, the three of us will be back by night-fall. Tomorrow morning, at the latest," Wade replied. This was going to be a tight turnaround.

Alton nodded. "Good luck."

"Thanks," I said with a smile. We were going to need it.

"You ready to go?" Jacob asked.

I exhaled a shaky breath. "I think so."

"Everybody stand back." Jacob moved to the far side of the room and lifted his hands, closing his eyes. Streams of Chaos twisted around his fingers. His body glistened with gold specks, the energy flowing out of him and into the cracks in space and time. He tore the seam of reality and opened the gaping mouth of a portal.

"See you soon," I said over my shoulder, looking at those we were leaving behind.

Santana grinned. "You'd better, *mi hermana.*"

Without another glance back, the three of us stepped through.

The portal spat us out on Decatur Street, on the southern edge of the French Quarter, with us almost careening into the long line that spilled out from Café du Monde. I recognized the café instantly by its green-and-white striped awning, which matched the pictures I'd seen. The portal had gone, but panic hit me in a wave. What if someone had seen us arrive? I looked around, checking the expressions of those around us. To my relief, nobody seemed to be paying attention to three people suddenly appearing out of nowhere. With the way we were staggering, they probably thought we'd had one too many cocktails at some local bar.

An unexpected figure stood next to me.

"Jacob? What are you doing here?" I whispered. "You were supposed to stay behind."

"I thought I'd check that you got to the right place. I'm still learning a thing or two about controlling my abilities when it comes to new destinations, and I wanted to be sure. I'll need to feel this place out again to get you out, so I figured I should come along," he explained. "I'll find a more discreet place to zap out again."

I nodded breathlessly. "Good thinking."

"Everyone okay?" He looked to Wade and Tatyana.

"All good," Wade replied.

"I'm in one piece," Tatyana agreed.

"I'm *very* glad." Jacob gazed at her adoringly, but she didn't seem to notice.

I cleared my throat. "Be careful on the way back, Jake."

"I'll duck behind that place there and portal back to the coven." He gestured to the wide path behind Café du Monde.

"We'll come with you," I insisted, all of us heading around the back of the building. A few employees had just gone back inside the building, leaving it empty.

With nobody around, he opened another portal with ease. I thought he'd go straight through, but instead he gave me a quick hug. "I hope everything goes well, Harley."

I hugged him back, surprised by the gesture. Pulling away, he looked like he was about to try to hug Tatyana but thought better of it. With a shy smile, he disappeared through the portal, and it snapped shut behind him. The three of us were left in the side alley, with the chatter of New Orleans babbling away beyond the café.

"I suggest we select our gifts first," Tatyana said.

Wade nodded. "We'll also need to find Marie's tomb."

"Wait, what?" I asked. "I thought it was a famous landmark. I've seen it in pictures. It's in the St. Louis Cemetery, on the other side of the French Quarter. I looked it up before we came here."

"You mean that Greek-style mausoleum?"

"Yeah, that one. People mark three crosses on it and leave gifts. Although, I think they might have stopped that now."

He smiled. "You can't always trust Google with these things. That's the supposed location of her tomb, but the real site was hidden from public knowledge a long time ago."

Tatyana made a noise of agreement. "A magical as famous as her would not have a tomb that people could easily find. The one in the cemetery is a spot for tourists, nothing more. Humans like to think they can have their wishes granted by the supernatural."

"Then who do we ask? I thought we knew where we were going?" This was news to me. I'd expected to land in New Orleans and take a quick trip to the St. Louis Cemetery, and be back by dinnertime.

"When I mentioned it to Nomura, he said we should seek out Dominic Etye, a magical who serves Papa Legba," Wade replied.

I arched an eyebrow at him. "Papa who-said-what-now? Nomura didn't tell me any of this."

Wade shrugged. "Maybe you caught him at a bad time. Like you said, he's been down lately. Alton resigning has hit him pretty hard. It'd be like one of the original Rag Team jumping ship."

"I hadn't thought of it like that." I paused for a moment, feeling sad for Nomura. "So, who is he—this Papa guy?" I looked at Tatyana.

"Papa Legba is an extremely rare instance of a magical's spirit who persists within the earthly world and continues to attain followers long after his death. Given his transitory state, he can speak with humans and spirits alike. Think of him as a bridge between both worlds," Tatyana said.

"He's allowed to do that?"

She smiled. "Forcefully sending a magical's spirit into the next plane of existence is, as yet, impossible. Nobody has achieved it. So, New Orleans is somewhat stuck with Papa Legba and his antics."

"And Dominic is one of his followers?" I pressed, wanting to get up to speed.

"That's the theory. He fashions himself as a soothsayer," Wade replied. "He takes on a lot of human clients who require spiritual help. He charges magicals, too. We don't get a freebie, unfortunately."

"Right then," I said firmly. "Gifts can wait. He's the one we need to talk to first."

NINE

Harley

I t didn't take us long to track down Dominic Etye. He'd made quite the name for himself, advertising his services to humans as a clairvoyant—with a lower-case "c." He definitely wasn't a Clairvoyant. *A Charlatan, more like—big capital C.* The kind of guy who said what a person wanted to hear and took their money without a hint of guilt. He likely had a talent in cold-reading people, with no actual ability for the skill he hawked. Plus, Nomura had given Wade a note that simply said, *Tourist Info—Ursulines Station* and told him the address moved every few years, so he'd need to double check.

After walking along the banks of the mighty Mississippi, heading east away from Café du Monde, we found a tourist information stall to the side of Ursulines Station. The red-and-yellow streetcars trundled by, their bells ringing as they passed and stopped. Locals boarded and alighted, getting on with their days. There wasn't a tourist information stand, but I spotted a noticeboard with the familiar "i" above it. Dominic Etye's leaflets were plastered all over it, alongside advertisements for nighttime Voodoo tours and Mardi Gras experiences. All the usual touristy stuff that no doubt made the New Orleans natives cringe.

Fed up with your present? Let me look into your future! the leaflet read, screaming "scam" with every word. I figured that was just for the humans. *Visions and fortunes at a low price. Can you afford not to see what lies ahead?*

Wade peered over my shoulder as I read the leaflet. "Seems like he's one of these people who blurs the line between fiction and reality for humans."

There was an address on the bottom: No. 361, Pirate Alley. That didn't exactly fill me with confidence. What kind of crook were we going to meet?

Tatyana spoke from behind us. "I know a little about Papa Legba. From the basic Voodoo teachings we Kolduny have to learn, we were told his previous servants have continued the same legacy of 'soothsaying.' They provide a gateway between what is natural and what is supernatural, at least to a human mind. These wishes he grants humans can appear as miracles when, in reality, they may be simple magic. Many of these soothsayers are impostors, but at least we know that Dominic is a true follower of Papa Legba."

"Yeah, cheers to Nomura for that nugget of intel. Otherwise, we'd be screwed." I smiled, though I still doubted the legitimacy of this Etye guy. What did it even mean to be a follower of Papa Legba? Was that a good thing or a bad thing? It was difficult to tell, and neither Wade nor Tatyana seemed to have the answer.

After looking up the address on Google Maps, we wandered back along the riverbank, retracing our steps. As it happened, Pirate Alley was a short walk from where we'd arrived. My gaze turned out toward the vast, murky waters of the Mississippi, with Algiers opposite. I couldn't help but remember the violent destruction this river had caused in the wake of Hurricane Katrina, not so long ago. It looked calm enough now, but water held a deadly power. As someone who could wield it, I knew that better than anyone.

The devastation remained throughout much of New Orleans, in the water-stained walls that had been hastily painted over, and the sagging structures of several buildings. Some were still boarded up, where the windows had shattered inward. It was hard to comprehend that these streets had been under feet of water, with countless lives ruined in the aftermath.

But some beauty remained. Nothing could take away from the elaborate balconies that ran around the upper floors of the buildings. They were awe-inspiring, giving off a Spanish flavor, with hanging baskets full of ferns and flowers. And the colors were striking, each building painted a different shade of the rainbow, both bold and pastel. Neon lights flashed in windows. Meanwhile—and it almost sounded too cliché to be true—jazz rolled out from the bars and restaurants, the smooth saxophones making me smile. Grief and grit filled these streets, the hurricane having failed to break the spirits of the city's people.

We decided to walk through Jackson Square instead of skirting around it. With it being a warm day, there were a few other people out on the grass, enjoying the sunshine. One was playing guitar, strumming the vaguely familiar notes of "Hallelujah." All down the central path leading toward the statue of Andrew Jackson, caricaturists called out to draw our likenesses, while painters and sketchers sat off in peace, concentrating on their works.

The white-and-gray majesty of St. Louis Cathedral loomed ahead, with its trio of Gothic spires. The statue was almost framed against the white exterior, as if President Jackson were reaching up to touch the clock in the middle. Two streets led to either side of the cathedral, with Pirate Alley on the left and Pere Antoine Alley on the right.

"It's down the side of St. Anthony's Garden, which is around the back of the cathedral." Wade glanced down at his phone, the arrow icon leading us in the right direction.

Tatyana frowned. "Did you say St. Anthony?"

Wade nodded.

"Very odd," she mused.

"How so?" I looked at her expectantly.

"Well, from what I can remember of Papa Legba—and they didn't teach us all that much—he is often associated with St. Anthony. The two are interchangeable in many religious stories. Christianity merely uses St. Anthony instead."

A wry smile turned up the corners of Wade's lips. "Good thing I don't believe in coincidences."

Walking along Pirate Alley, we stopped outside a coral-colored building with a green door. Number 361. A single balcony jutted out, but the windows and French doors were shuttered closed. If it hadn't been for the stretch of neon signs above the door flashing "FOR-TUNES, FORTUNES, FORTUNES," we wouldn't have known it was open for business. It reminded me of one of those ten-cent crystal ball ladies with weird moles on their faces who pitched tents at county fairs. I hoped he'd be more useful than that.

"I guess this is it." Wade walked up to the door and knocked.

A dark-haired woman with jet-black eyes poked her head out. "Yes?"

"Is this Dominic Etye's place?"

"It is."

I stepped up beside Wade. "Can we see him?"

"Yes." She didn't say another word. She simply opened the door and ushered us up a narrow set of stairs to the first floor. The layout was incredible, with exposed brick walls and low beams. Flickering faux candlelight set the mood, glowing from mounted brass lamps. It was nothing like the gimmicky neon lights had suggested. This was pure Southern class.

We froze as a figure dressed in a green kaftan that trailed across the wooden floor burst out from behind a beaded curtain. He wore so many bracelets on his wrists that he jangled as he walked. An elegant silk wrap covered his head, the end flowing down like a ponytail. Dangling from his ears were two enormous emerald teardrops, while his neck was covered in glinting jewels and colored beads. He was impressive—almost beautiful. Startling, gray-brown eyes stood out against smoky eye makeup, and his lips were plump with red lipstick. His skin was tan and velvety, his every movement elegant. And yet, somehow, he gave off a masculine energy that compelled me to flash a shy smile.

"And what rare jewels be gracing my doorstep this day?" he asked, in an accent spiced with Creole origins.

"Keep your wits about you," Wade whispered, distracting me from Dominic's beauty.

"We're here to ask you about Marie Laveau." I snapped out of it and focused my energies on getting the answers we needed. This Suppressor was likely to blame, anyway. It heightened everything, including the hotness of interesting men.

"Ah, no path is decided. There are forks and diversions along every road. Who's to say that be your end goal, when all's said and done?" He flashed a megawatt smile.

"We need to find out where her tomb is," I pressed. *What are you, a sphinx?*

"Follow the trawler, and go where all the gulls go," he replied, with a rattle of pearls.

I frowned. "What?"

"Where the most fish are gathered is where the good eating is."

I glanced at Wade and Tatyana, but they both looked as confused as I felt.

"Do you mean the tourist spot?" Tatyana asked. "We don't want that one. We want the real one."

"There's some mighty power in you, daughter of the Kolduny. The ghosts around you be vibrating through the roof!" Dominic gave a low whistle, that grin never leaving his face. He'd gotten uglier real fast. "The spirits don't stay too quiet here in New Orleans. Listen a little and see what they say."

Wade interrupted. "Will they guide us to Marie Laveau's tomb?"

"Who can say what these here spirits will do and not do? I live amongst them, but I'm not one of them. No man, nor woman, can know a ghost's heart." His turns of phrase made everything he said sound poetic, but his riddles were starting to annoy me.

"Look, will you just tell us where her tomb is?" I snapped. *This is what I was afraid of.* I kept telling myself to calm down, but my mind and body were separating, and the reins were slipping from my grasp.

"Tic hen gen fos devan kay met li," he purred, in a language I couldn't understand. It had hints of French, mixed with something else —something more ancient.

I glared at him. "What?"

"A little dog is very brave in front of its master's house," he replied. "But you are not in front of your master's house. Are you brave still?"

Tatyana's eyes widened. "Kreyol pale, kreyol komprann."

"Am I going mad here?" I muttered, my rage bubbling over.

Dominic laughed. "I didn't know they taught the Kolduny the proverbs of my mother tongue."

"What did you say?" I turned to Tatyana.

"I said, 'Speak plainly, don't try to deceive.' It's the only one I know."

"You might speak a sliver of my mother tongue, but you don't speak it well. The meaning is of no meaning to you." Dominic's grin widened, making him look borderline manic.

"Will you just tell us where we can find Marie's tomb?" I shot back at him. "It's really freaking urgent, and it won't just be us who suffer if you don't spill the beans. Katherine Shipton will come for you, too. She'll come for every magical and wannabe magical in this whole country, and then she'll start on the rest of the world."

"The trials of roaches do not stir the dreams of lions," he replied.

"You're not listening. If you don't help us, you'll have more than lions and roaches to deal with!" A pulse of white-hot energy surged through me before I could hold it back, spreading outward in a violent ripple. Everything went black, with the others lingering like ghosts in my peripheral vision. I heard pots smash and lamps crack, the wooden floor splintering under my feet. Wade and Tatyana dove to the ground, while Dominic hurtled back against a wall I could barely see anymore. To me, there were only shadows.

That cold, syrupy feeling followed a gut-wrenching twist of pain that made it hard to stand. I recognized the sensation. This wasn't an ordinary Chaos attack—the crack in my Suppressor had widened. I was sure of it.

My vision cleared, and my breath came in sharp gasps. Dominic scrambled to his feet as Wade helped Tatyana back up. For the first time, Dominic looked genuinely frightened. I could sense fear pouring out of him.

"No more riddles." His hands trembled. "I can see that there is no use in toying with a power like yours. I will help all I can."

"Thank you," I said quietly. *I'm sorry...* I hadn't wanted to scare him into helping us, but this was bigger than his games.

"In order to give you what you seek, I must summon the might of Papa Legba himself, for only he knows the true site of Marie Laveau's final resting place. A secret most treasured, given only to those who dance the line of life and death."

Yeah? Well, I'm doing that right now.

"A husband's final vow," Dominic whispered.

I frowned. "Husband?"

"Marie Laveau and Papa Legba were married through the binds wrought by life and death. Their love traverses all," he replied. "Side by side they lie, in secret peace for none to disturb. Their bodies be more precious than all the world's riches. Many would seek to feast upon their belongings and their tomes of majesty."

A lightbulb flickered in my head. "Their Grimoires?"

"If that be the word you care to use."

"Did Marie serve Papa Legba, the same way you serve him?" Tatyana asked, dusting herself off. It seemed like Remington's information had gaps that needed filling.

"Not exactly the same, no. She served him long before me. They were bound in blood and fire, in a way none can hope for in this mortal realm. He served her as much as she served him. Not even death could halt their love, for it was stronger than she who takes life. He never loved her as man loves woman, but as only a spirit can—he fed upon her body and she upon his soul. None would dare try part them." His eyes had gotten so wide it creeped me out. There was definitely something wrong with this all-consuming love, considering Papa Legba had been dead at the time. And still was.

I guess it's a little romantic. I couldn't even imagine that kind of legendary love. Although, it begged a couple of questions. Like, how did they… I didn't want to think about it too hard, in case my brain fell out. Not much of a relationship if they couldn't even touch. Then again, maybe they could now that they were both dead, but that was another creepy can of worms I didn't want to open. If Papa Legba had waited until she was dead to have a physical relationship, that seemed like a *lot* of time and effort. *Marie Laveau must be some woman.*

"Will you summon him for us?" Wade asked, while my mind was off in a strange place.

"I will, for I sense he'll be wanting to see this power for himself." Dominic sat down on the now-cracked floor and closed his eyes. White light pulsated beneath his skin, highlighting his veins. I frowned at him and wondered why this seemed familiar. He arched backward at a sickening angle, and his face turned up to the ceiling. His eyes sparked with white light, the striking gray-brown turning milky.

"He's a Kolduny!" Tatyana gasped. Now I understood how he'd been able to figure out what she was—because he was one too.

"Is that possible?" I asked. "I thought you were all Russian."

"Ordinarily, we are. I suppose it makes sense that our practices found their way into Creole culture, as there are a lot of similarities between Voodoo and Kolduny magic."

Wade grasped my wrist and pulled me behind him sharply. "Something's happening."

"You didn't sense it in him, daughter of the Kolduny?" a weird, echoey voice bellowed out of Dominic's mouth. "The blood has weakened, through pride and purity. We soldiers of Voodoo recognize the glory in fresh blood. We treasure it, and know it brings new life. But your vain leaders lost the knowledge with many moons passed. My humble servant had a grandmama of noble heart who wielded the vibrant spirit of the Kolduny in her palms—a daughter of St. Petersburg. Cast out for loving one of my own, she came to me and made true sacrifice. Two generations later, a promise was fulfilled. The son of her daughter came back to serve me. All roads lead to Papa Legba in New Orleans. All roads."

Dominic's milky white eyes fixed on me. Only, they weren't milky white or gray-brown anymore. They'd turned a vivid violet that sparked with an inner fire. He inhaled like a predator taking its first sniff of prey.

"That scent... such power." He shivered with eerie glee, his mouth twisting up in a leer. "Do not cower behind weaker blood. You can't hide from me. I have scented you, *tifi*... and I want you."

TEN

Wade

I stood firmly in front of Harley. She was breathing hard. Through her wrist, I felt her pulse racing. This guy might've been some line-dancing spirit who wouldn't cross over, but I'd fight with everything I had if this guy got too weird.

"I want you, *tifi*," Papa Legba repeated.

What do you mean, you "want" her, you dead creep? This spirit needed to keep his phantom schlong in his pants. Or Dominic's pants. I didn't know how the possession aspect worked. Either way, I'd have killed him all over again if he'd tried anything with Harley. I gripped her hand tighter, to let her know I was there for her.

"What do you mean?" Harley's voice shook.

"I want you to serve me," he purred. "I see the barrier inside you, resisting all that sweet glory that might flood your veins, if only it could break free. You fear what it may do to you, *wi?*"

She nodded slowly.

"I can rid you of it. I can take it out and balance the rivers of Light and Dark that flow through you, creating one fluid tide that will make you a true force of nature. There are none like you and will not be again. The blood is weakening. I have seen the ebb."

"You can do that?" she gasped.

"If it sounds too good to be true, it probably is," I whispered to her. Meanwhile, Tatyana was transfixed by Dominic-slash-Papa-Legba.

"An honest proverb." Papa Legba laughed. "But beggars also cannot be choosers. I believe you are familiar with that one?"

Harley peered out from behind my shoulder. "What's the catch?"

"Ah, *tifi*, what do you take me for? A simple exchange is all I ask."

"What's the catch?" she pressed.

"I'll rid you of your limitations if you sign your life over to me. Your *nanm* in my hands, for a world of power." I didn't know what a *nanm* was, but I'd heard this one before. It hadn't turned out too well for Faust.

I fixed my gaze on Papa Legba, certain that Harley would give him a sharp "hell no." When it didn't come right away, I turned to look at her in disbelief. Who would be foolish enough to serve and hand their life over to a dead and way-too-powerful magical? I glanced back at Dominic. *Ah, yes. Him.*

"I don't think so," Harley said, after what felt like forever. I almost turned and shouted "finally," but I kept my cool. Of course, Harley wouldn't be that stupid.

"You don't want the true extent of your talents, *tifi?*"

She smiled and stepped out from behind me. "What I really want is the location of Marie Laveau's tomb."

"Ah, *renmen anpil*. And what are you seeking my love for? Do you want to join in our eternal *renmen*? Are you willing to part with your heart instead of your life?" He smiled at her creepily. I wanted to knock him straight into the afterlife. One punch and he'd be ringing the bell at the pearly gates.

"There's something I want to speak with her about, woman-to-woman, magical-to-magical," Harley replied.

"A secret?" His eyes widened. "Tell me more."

"Then it wouldn't be a secret, now would it?"

I had to say, she was holding her own better than I could've done. She was playing him to perfection. I just didn't like the tone in his voice. He sounded like he wanted to eat her alive.

"Nothing in life is free, secrets least of all," Papa Legba said. "If there is something you want, something must be paid. If you want to know where my love lies, my sweetest *renmen*, then an offer must be made in return. That's the balance of life and death, the sides of every coin, the flutter of a butterfly's wings causing a hurricane."

"Kind of in poor taste, don't you think?" Harley folded her arms across her chest.

"That is the way of the world, *tifi*. Decay and beauty are bedfellows. Destruction and resurrection. Death and life. Dark and Light. All in harmony. The balance cannot be tipped—it is universal law."

She frowned. "You keep calling me *tifi*. What does it mean?"

"Girl."

"Should I be insulted?" Harley muttered.

At least it wasn't a nickname, but I was affronted on her behalf.

"It is affectionately meant," he replied. "I see you wish to diverge from the subject. All roads lead back to me, remember?"

Harley nodded. "So, where is Marie's tomb?"

"Where is my reward?" he shot back.

"Why won't you tell me where she is, if this concerns your wife and not you? Surely, she should be the one who decides what price I have to pay for speaking to her?" Even Tatyana was staring at Harley now. She had him on the ropes.

"My love and I are one. I protect her, as your love protects you." He looked straight at me. My heart stopped for a second, not only because those purple eyes were terrifying but because of what he'd said. Could he feel what I felt for her? I had a hard enough time with *her* being able to feel my every emotion. I didn't need every creepy magical pointing it out. I cast a subtle glance at Harley. She was looking at me, a shy look on her face. *Then again, maybe if every magical points it out, it could work in my favor.*

"You're worried we might hurt her?" Harley asked in disbelief, turning back to Papa Legba. "You're worried that *we* might try and threaten the greatest Dark witch of all time?"

He sighed. "No one discovers my love without my permission. The stakes are much too high. The secrets that lie with her mortal form must stay buried… unless you can offer me your life, your *nanm*, in return. That price would be high enough to match the peril in my heart."

"What does *nanm* mean?" I asked, disrupting their verbal sparring.

Papa Legba smiled through Dominic's lips. "Soul."

"You'd take her soul?" Anger spiked inside me.

"What else did you think I meant, when I asked for her life?"

"I don't know."

He laughed coldly. "How could she fall for one so weak of mind and magic? Love is truly blind, when found in the wrong places. I would advise you to find another, *tifi*, but the youth do not listen and the aged cannot turn back the clocks."

Now, he was really pissing me off. "Listen, she can fall for whomever she damn well pleases. Not all relationships have to be crazy, death-defying feats of love. They can be simple, too, and that's just as good. At least I can touch—"

"It's okay, Wade," Harley interrupted. She placed her hand on my shoulder and flashed me a bright smile. I was aware of Tatyana gaping at me. I'd never seen her shocked. *That was Harley's Suppressor leaking into me again, right?* It had to be.

"Allow me to show you the painless nature of what I ask," Papa Legba suggested. "This does not have to get so heated, although I must say, I'm now convinced there is at least passion in your love affair." My throat constricted and left me speechless. I couldn't look at Harley.

His vessel, Dominic, walked over to a safe in the corner of the room. Once he twisted the dial, the door popped open with a click. Inside were rows upon rows of tiny jars, with white lights twinkling inside. Harley, Tatyana, and I followed him over to take a closer look.

"Are they souls?" Harley whispered in awe.

"They are," he replied. "Some, I keep for an hour or two. Others, for days. And some for eternity, depending on the cost of what they seek. For that is the price that mortals, both human and magical, must pay, if they desire favors from Papa Legba. I say again… nothing is free."

I just knew he'd be the kind of man who spoke about himself in the third person. Then again, he was already speaking through another person. I held my tongue regardless. Snark wouldn't help convince this guy to help us.

"And you want to add me to this collection?" Harley eyed the jars dubiously.

"For a short time, as reflects the price of your favor," he replied. "I will return your soul to you as soon as you have returned from my immortal beloved's tomb and I know she is without harm."

I glanced at Harley, who'd gone white as a sheet. Even Tatyana looked paler than normal, which was no mean feat. I imagined I looked the same. Papa Legba was asking a lot. I already knew my thoughts on it, but Harley wouldn't necessarily share them. At the end of the day, this was her decision. When had she ever listened before? Still, I couldn't let her do something stupid and reckless.

I jumped right in. "This is a bad idea, Harley."

"What else can I do?" She turned to me with wide eyes. It wasn't really a question.

"You can't make a deal like this."

Tatyana nodded. "I wouldn't advise it. Making deals with spirits rarely ends well, and I say that from personal experience." She looked at Papa Legba. "I mean no offense to you."

"I do not take any," he replied.

"But what else can I do?" Her voice was more urgent this time. "We're running out of time, and we don't have the magical methods we'd need to find the tomb ourselves. If Papa Legba is the only one who knows where the real site is, then he's our only choice."

Papa Legba laughed. "You would never discover it on your own. Ancient measures have been taken to protect my beloved. Everyone who has ever desired to see her tomb, and meet her directly, has had to pay the price of their soul. Just as the ancient Greeks paid Charon to reach Hades."

Nice image there. As long as we weren't sailing toward death, too.

"Why the difference in times?" Harley returned her focus to Papa Legba. "Why do some souls stay with you for a short time, and others stay with you for eternity? I know you've said it has to do with the price of what someone is asking, but *why* do you collect them? What's the benefit to you?"

He smiled. "An excellent question, *tifi*. It is related to my bread and butter—my business, my existence, my purpose. My unique connection, as a magical spirit dancing the line between this earthly realm and the next, allows me insight beyond your imagining. Even a Kolduny cannot see what I can see." He flashed a grin at Tatyana. "Sometimes, I even have the opportunity to intervene where I see due cause. Humans or magicals, it doesn't matter. But it takes energy to perform these tasks."

Grim realization dawned on me. "The souls fuel you?"

"Your tongue is crass, but yes," he answered. "The harder and more consuming a deed may be, or the more precious the information within me, the longer the soul remains in my grasp. I like to think of them as ethereal investments and occasional spell invigoration. There is no power like soul power. It breathes of ancient sinew. The more I possess, the stronger my magic becomes. There is a reason in everything I do."

"What, so short-term souls are like batteries and long-term souls are like investments?" Harley pressed.

"Precisely."

"An investment in what?" Tatyana asked. She knew more about this kind of thing than anyone. If she was worried, so was I.

"In my future, as all investments are," he said simply.

Harley edged away from the safe full of souls. "And I'd be a short-term soul? A few hours?"

"You would. I would hold your soul in my embrace for as long as it takes you to return from my beloved. That is all."

This was a bad idea. There was nothing this spirit could say to convince me his intentions were good. I needed to stay calm and pragmatic, but terror jolted through my nerves. It was proving hard to mask from Harley. This was way too much for her to shoulder alone. Only, this time, I couldn't carry any weight for her. I'd have given my soul if I'd thought it would make a difference. But he didn't want me. He wanted his *tifi*.

Harley cleared her throat. "Why should I trust you? Who's to say you won't twist this around and cheat me out of my *nanm*?"

Papa Legba's violet eyes burned with sudden rage. Around us, the walls vibrated violently, and the few pots and lamps that remained shattered completely. "I am a spirit of my word. My word is sacred. I am no devil sent to pilfer lost souls. I would never cheat those who enter into an agreement with me, as long as they do not harbor ill intentions toward me. Everything in balance." Dominic's body strained, a vein bulging out of his neck.

"How can you tell if someone harbors ill intentions?" I asked.

He cast me a withering look. "I am a dead man. I see what others do not."

"I didn't mean any offense," Harley said quickly. "I just wanted to be clear."

Papa Legba calmed. "It is a grave decision ahead of you."

Poor choice of words, pal.

Harley nodded. "Can I have a minute to talk it over?"

"Time is irrelevant to me." He flicked his wrist at us, Dominic's bracelets jangling. Papa Legba stared at the jewelry. "Ah, why must he wear so many?" Leaving us to talk, he moved over to the opposite side of the room and sat down on one of the sleek leather sofas.

"What are you thinking?" I stared at Harley. This was down to her.

"I think I have to accept."

Tatyana pulled a doubtful face. "It isn't wise. He's very strong."

"Like I said, what choice do we have? If we don't get to Marie Laveau's tomb, I die anyway. If I accept, then I might not die. Which seems like the better option, if I put it like that?"

She had a point. "Just… be careful, okay?"

A smile spread across her lips. "Don't worry, I've got this."

Her smile always warmed me up on the inside, but it didn't change my doubts. She was putting on a brave face in typical Harley style. I admired her for it as much as I feared for her. She was about to step into a world of danger. And I couldn't stop her or protect her.

I had to hope that, even in death, Papa Legba was a man of his word.

ELEVEN

Harley

"Have you made your decision, *tifi?*" Papa Legba asked. He was draped across the leather sofa in Dominic's body, the emerald kaftan pooling over the edge. *This guy is giving off way too many Elizabeth Taylor vibes.* I needed to take my mind off what was about to happen, and humor tended to work.

I nodded. "I'll accept your deal."

He jumped up. "Glad to hear it. Shall we begin? With your little problem, I am guessing you don't want to waste any time. Death knocks for us all, and she is not far from your front door."

I tried not to shudder. Feeling the ice-cold, syrupy spread of the Suppressor leak was bad enough in reminding me of my own mortality. He didn't need to lay the doom and gloom on so thick.

He crossed the room and took a small jar out of the safe. I hadn't noticed before, but there were tiny symbols etched in the glass. *This must be how the Purge beasts feel.* The memory of Quetzi popped into my head, but I quickly pushed it down.

"Come here, *tifi,*" he instructed. With Wade and Tatyana watching me, their expressions filled with dread, I went to Papa Legba. He removed the lid and took my hand, bringing me closer. Being face-to-face with those scary violet eyes wasn't exactly comfortable, and my heartbeat was going haywire. It was all I could do not to run from the place screaming.

"Will it hurt?" I found myself asking.

"It will hurt a bit, and you may feel strange afterward." His free hand shot out and slammed into my chest. Wade lurched forward, but a sharp look from Papa Legba kept him back. His palm was bitterly cold, and strands of purple magic slithered out like tendrils. I winced as they sank beneath my skin, though the tendrils themselves were oddly warm. It felt like coming in out of the cold to a blazing fire and feeling the sensation come back into your fingers and toes.

Then everything changed. The comforting warmth turned to stabbing pain, the tendrils spiking like barbed wire through my body. I grasped Papa Legba's arms to steady myself, my nails digging into Dominic's flesh. A sickening pull in the core of my chest let me know that my soul was coming away. It was like having the air knocked out of me, only way more painful.

With one excruciating tear, my soul came loose and filtered out of my body and into his palm. White light mingled with the purple strands, forming a perfect orb in the center of his hand as he drew it away from my chest. *I take it back—give me the Chaos attacks any day of the week.* With a smile, he dropped the orb into the jar and screwed the lid on tight. The glass lit up white, the etched charms glowing.

"All done," he said. Leaving me to shake on the spot and draw in ragged breaths, he went over to the safe and took out a red tag. With a deft hand, he wrote my name on it and tied it around the neck of the jar. Had he not been a powerful spirit, I'd have thought it weird that he even knew my name. I couldn't remember telling him who I was.

It took a moment for me to realize that Wade had his arms around me, his strength propping me up. Tatyana was there too, and my hand was somehow in hers. *I don't like this.* But it was too late to change my mind.

"Harley?" I realized Wade had been calling my name.

I blinked at him in a daze. "Yeah?"

"Are you okay?"

"A bit shaky, but I think so." That wasn't completely true. I felt weird and almost hollow. With a sinking realization, I started to understand the odd void inside Astrid. Right now, my body felt the way she felt, whenever I reached my Empathy toward her. Did that mean part of her soul was gone for good? I couldn't bring myself to think about it. It was too sad, if that were the case. There was no jar with her name on it.

"You don't look too good," Tatyana said.

I forced a smile onto my face. "Thanks."

"Is everything working?" Wade gazed into my eyes, worry written across his face.

"I… I don't know." I felt oddly light. Focusing on him, I tried to feel for his emotions… but nothing drifted back. I knew I should have panicked, but I felt nothing. Still, it came as a surprise. "My Empathy —it's gone!"

Papa Legba laughed. "That is to be expected, *tifi.* There is nothing to fear. Your abilities will return along with your soul. The two are intrinsically connected, though these modern magical teachers don't care to delve too deeply into the symbiosis of it. A shame, to not know the depth of the roots that twist beneath the soil of your being."

"Do you mean *all* my abilities?" *Why don't I feel more panicked?* It was a weird state to be in, knowing I should be feeling something but being unable to do so.

"Of course. That is the price."

"You didn't think that was something you should've told me?" I glared at him. Papa Legba had creeped me out enough for one day,

though I did feel sort of excited. There was no pain and no syrupy feeling, and no buzz of Chaos in my veins. For all intents and purposes, I
was normal. In a way, he'd fixed me, albeit temporarily.

"Your abilities will be returned," he repeated, bordering on blasé.
Well, I couldn't change it now.

"Now can we have the directions to Marie Laveau's tomb?" I
pressed, eager to get on with it. The sooner we got there, the sooner I
could come back and get my soul. And then, I'd break this bastard
Suppressor once and for all.

He nodded with a rattle of beads. "My immortal *renmen's* tomb is
hidden in the garden behind St. Mary's Chapel, on Jackson Avenue in
the Garden District. It is better to greet her as the sun fades, but time is
of the essence. You will find her there, regardless. Give her my love
when you look upon her." A sad smile turned up the corners of
Dominic's mouth, and the violet of his eyes dimmed for a moment.

"How will we know we've got the right one?"

"You ask the right questions, *tifi*. Her resting place is marked with
the veve of Erzulie."

I frowned. "I don't know what that means."

Tatyana smiled. "A veve is a Haitian symbol. I believe Erzulie was
the Voodoo goddess of love."

"Perhaps the Russians have not been completely remiss in their
teachings of us," Papa Legba remarked. He pulled a pendant out of the
lapels of Dominic's kaftan. It was shaped like a winged heart, with
curled fronds and a scepter running through the middle. "Take this and
it will lead you to her. Bring it back when you return."

I took the pendant and hung it around my neck, letting it rest
beside the herb pouch and the pendant that Imogene had given me. I
was only missing the St. Christopher necklace from the Smiths, which I
could've done with right now. Safe passage and all that.

"Thank you." I gave an awkward bow and hurried out of the townhouse, with the other two in tow.

Stepping out into the real world felt strange after our time in the townhouse. My instincts hit me all at once, heightening the void inside me. There was no pain, no emotion, no nothing. I didn't feel a thing, not even for Wade. I looked at him, just to be sure, but a dead calm had taken over. I tried Tatyana too, but didn't even feel a flicker of warmth. It was like I was dead inside. *Weird... so weird.*

"I've got the location on my phone." Wade brandished his device at me.

"We don't need it," I replied.

"What do you mean?"

"The pendant knows where we need to go." Somehow, it was already guiding me, to the point where I knew every step we had to take. I set off down the narrow flagstones of Pirate Alley and turned right onto Chartres Street. I'd barely walked half a yard down this new path when I pulled to a halt. A prickle crept up the back of my neck. As subtly as I could, I turned over my shoulder and squinted at the corner we'd just come from.

"Is something wrong?" Tatyana whispered.

"We've got company," I said.

"What do you mean?" Wade murmured beside me.

"What do you think I mean? We're being followed. Now come on, hurry up." I pressed on without another word. I would've suggested trying to lose our shadows, but that meant defying the pendant. I didn't know if it would set us on the right path again if we diverged, and there was no way I was risking it.

He frowned. "Are you sure you're okay? You don't seem right to me."

"I was about to say the same thing," Tatyana added.

"I'm fine. Never better." It was actually a relief to be free from all the pain and emotional bombardments. My head felt clearer than it had in a long time. In fact, it had never felt this clear before.

"Well, shouldn't we try and lose whoever's following us?" Wade suggested.

I shook my head. "There's no time. We have to keep going." If they didn't want to carry on, I'd leave them behind. That might've sounded blunt and uncaring, but the loss of my soul had granted me a freedom I'd never had before. The freedom to focus solely on one task. No emotional distractions getting in the way.

We walked on through the streets of New Orleans, following the guiding pull of the pendant. All the while, I kept a close eye on the shadows on our tail. The prickle up the back of my neck didn't stop, which let me know they were still watching. Every time we turned, and I cast a glance behind us, I couldn't see anyone. But I knew they were there.

After ten minutes of walking, I was suitably convinced they were part of the Cult of Eris. I'd run the possibilities through my super-clear head. If they were from a coven, they'd have announced themselves or tried to stop us. The fact that they were watching from a distance gave the impression that they didn't want *us* to see *them*. They were merely observing, not intervening. The people most likely to practice that kind of furtive behavior were Katherine's cronies.

"Let's capture one, once we reach the church," I whispered. We'd just crossed over the famous Canal Street to where Chartres Street connected with Camp Street. The elegant palm trees fluttered in the breeze coming off the river and heading inland. It smelled pungently of the sea, reminding me of teenage evenings down by the San Diego waterfront. Still, no emotion came with those memories, only an endless blankness.

"You think they're from the Cult of Eris?" Wade whispered back.

I nodded. "Who else would be following us? If Levi sent them, they'd have dragged us back to the SDC by now."

"I have a bad feeling about them," Tatyana muttered, keeping her gaze fixed forward. "They're staying back, which makes me think they'll strike when we find the tomb. We're doing the dirty work for them."

I smiled. "Then let's lead them to it and get this over with. We can beat them at their own game and take a prisoner while we're at it." It was a dangerous play, but it was crazy enough to work. Right now, they thought they were the hunters. *Let them think that a while longer.*

Thirty minutes later, we turned right onto Jackson Avenue. A huge building of gray and white sat ahead of us, with a gated driveway and a high wall topped with hedges. It gave off colonial and Gothic vibes and looked like it cost more than I'd make in my lifetime. The tree-lined street was pretty, the rest of the buildings a mixture of modern concrete and that unique, New-Orleans blend of Spanish and colonial.

"Is this it?" Wade pointed to a quaint little chapel that sat right next to the huge house. With a whitewashed, wooden-slatted exterior and double doors that took up most of the front, it wasn't what I'd expected. From what I knew of Marie Laveau and her legacy, I'd expected something more like the St. Louis Cathedral that we'd just come from—something big and elegant and Gothic that matched her status. This chapel had a single steeple with a bell and a white cross on the slanted porch roof. It was too simple and too small, as pretty as it was.

"I guess so." I walked up to the gate and let myself in. There were small gardens to the front and side of the chapel, all neatly kept and blooming with pale pink flowers. "We need to start searching." The pendant had stopped giving me directions. Clearly, finding the tomb was going to be up to us.

Trying not to draw attention to ourselves, we wandered through the gardens and peered behind every bush in the hopes of discovering this veve of Erzulie marker. All the landscaping looked way too new to be hiding Marie Laveau's resting place, but there were no other gardens around. A wooden fence blocked the side path, but after peering through the gaps in the slats, I couldn't see a secret garden beyond it.

"The pendant isn't saying anything else?" Wade wiped his brow with the back of his hand. It was hot and sticky, and the shade of the over-hanging trees was doing nothing to help.

"I'm starting to think we've been lied to," I said bitterly.

Wade pinched his brows together. "Well, if he's conned us, then that would render the deal null and void. He'll have to give you your soul back straightaway." I could tell he preferred the more emotional version of me, but he'd have to wait for her to come back. I wasn't giving up yet.

Tatyana shook her head. "I don't think he was lying to us. He abides by Chaos rules, and he made an agreement bound in the Chaos of your soul. Those rules are absolute. He wouldn't risk lying to us."

"Maybe there's another garden around the back," I suggested, looking up at the double doors at the top of the steps. "We might have to go through the chapel to get to it; those fences look pretty high, and I don't see a gate. Maybe that's why the pendant stopped working—because we're looking in the wrong place."

Wade shrugged. "Can't hurt to try."

The three of us headed up the steps and slipped into the chapel. The inside was even simpler than the outside, with rows of neat, empty pews and a single balcony over our heads for the organ. The walls were painted a plain shade of cream, and plain adornments hung there: wooden shield-like things with a cross on each.

With the silence echoing through the empty chapel, we took a look around. I approached one of the wooden shield adornments, peering more closely. To my surprise, there was a small, heart-shaped design at the bottom of the first one, with flourishing symbols that matched the veve of Erzulie. Each engraving had been turned on its side, so the top of the scepter pointed toward the back of the chapel, behind the altar. I moved to the next one and found the same thing.

"Over here!" I whispered to the others. They came running, and we followed the veves all the way down to a narrow white door in the wall. It looked plain enough, aside from the brass doorknob. The veve of Erzulie had been embossed around the keyhole. This had to be it.

"It's charmed," Wade said. Putting his hands on the doorknob, he whispered the *Aperi Portam* spell. It clicked and opened, swinging wide onto the most beautiful lily garden I'd ever seen. I wished I could've had my emotions, to properly appreciate it.

A patchwork path of flagstones led down between two ponds, where dragonflies flitted, and lily-pads rested on the water. Purple flowers opened to the sun, while the walkway itself was bordered with vibrantly colored, star-shaped lilies. We stepped out onto the path and looked at the garden in a daze. Everything fell silent, aside from the gentle trickle of running water coming from a small waterfall at the far end of each pond.

"It's an interdimensional pocket," I gasped, as we moved along the central path toward a small island in the near distance. A marble mausoleum stood on the island, surrounded by more lilies and sculpted shrubs that bore tiny white blooms.

I froze. Someone was already standing in front of the mausoleum. The tall, familiar figure turned over his shoulder.

Wade broke the silence. "Garrett? What the hell are you doing here?"

A pendant hung around Garrett's neck, identical to the one Papa Legba had given me. He must've left his soul with Papa Legba, too—a glimmer of life was missing from his eyes.

He opened his mouth to speak, but no sound came out. Instead, his eyes widened at something behind us. I whirled around in time to see six cloaked figures sprinting up the path toward us. I shot a cold look back at Garrett. Had he switched sides? Was that why these cultists were here? There was no time to ask him outright. The figures were almost on us.

My throat closed as I saw a familiar face amongst them. Naima, Katherine's lieutenant. Her lips parted to show glinting fangs as she led the pack in our direction.

This garden was the most beautiful thing I'd ever seen, but it was about to get *very* ugly.

TWELVE

Harley

I lifted my hands to create a fireball, but nothing happened. No sparks, nothing. *Crap, no abilities.* I'd forgotten.

Thinking fast, I ducked and whipped the knife out of my boot. With my powers tucked up in a jar in Dominic's townhouse, I'd have to rely on brute force. The cultists leapt onto the island with fireballs blazing and water hurtling in all directions. I flung my knife at the first cloaked figure. Her hood flew back as it grazed her shoulder, and her eyes burned with anger.

"Harley, get down!" Wade shouted. A fireball skimmed over my head and hit another cultist full in the chest. She was down for a moment before she sprang up again. Within seconds, she was on me, pushing me to the ground.

"I've been waiting for this!" she spat in my face. "Eris will honor me!"

So, she's got you calling her that now, has she? That was the image Katherine wanted to create for herself, and the metamorphosis was already in full swing.

I stared up into the cultist's dark brown eyes as she pressed her hands to my chest and fed a sparking burst of frosty energy into me, muttering a spell. *Not today.* I punched her hard in the side of the face. Using her confusion, I slipped out from under her and ran to the others.

"Let me guess, no abilities?" Garrett said. He joined us in a line, facing the onslaught. Tatyana flung out a barrage of Telekinesis that swiped at the ankles of the six women. Two went down and got straight back up. *Man, they're like Weebles.*

"You trying to fool us into thinking you're on our side?" I shouted at Garrett. He'd pulled out a knife of his own, the two of us looking like something out of a crime thriller.

"I am on your side!" he shot back, as he sent one of the cultists flying with a kick to the stomach.

"Didn't look like it." I ducked Wade's fireball, which was headed toward Naima.

"This is my mission," he replied. He shoved me to the side, knocking me clear of an oncoming twister of water.

I caught my breath and stared at him. "What do you mean?"

"The LA Coven sent me here, to get to Marie Laveau and find out what the rituals are. I had to go to Papa Legba first." He dodged a barrage of strange, crackling attacks from a fierce, dark-skinned woman. "You weren't supposed to be here!"

"No sh—" A fireball hit me in the shoulder and sent me sprawling backward. Wade stood over me a second later, his hand hauling me back to my feet.

"You're not supposed to be here, either," Wade snapped at Garrett.

Garrett shook his head. "If Levi finds out about this, he'll throw your asses straight into Purgatory."

"Bigger things to worry about right now!" I said. These cultists were agile and powerful, and I was getting major Ryder twins flashbacks. One slammed her fists down onto the ground and sent a shockwave at us. I stumbled and fell, twisting out of the way of Naima's bared fangs.

"You won't escape," she snarled.

"Oh yeah?" I lashed out with a fist, wishing I had brass knuckles to make the blow harder, and caught Katherine's lieutenant square in the jaw. It didn't stop her for long. She'd have torn out my throat with those fangs if Wade hadn't swooped in with a flurry of burning orbs. Tatyana did the honors and swiped Naima out of the way, launching her into one of the ponds. *Cats hate water, right?*

The other five had no intention of stopping. Even the one who'd been on the ground was back on her feet and heading right at us, magic oozing from her hands. Having my soul removed had been a brief respite. Now, I understood what price I'd really paid.

Sprinting across the mound, weaving in and out of the assailants, I snatched up my knife and hurled it straight at one of the cultists. It hit her in back of the knee, downing her. Aware of Naima lunging out of the pond and back onto the path, I raced back toward the others and pulled the blade out of the cultist's leg. Blood pooled, but without my soul, the sight made me feel nothing. Instead, I wiped the knife clean and held it out, ready to protect myself.

Tatyana leapt over us like a kung-fu artist and sent a pulse of Telekinesis at the relentless cultists. It sent them scattering, even Naima.

"Harley!" Tatyana's scream pierced the air. I turned to see a woman practically flying through the air toward me, the same one who'd pinned me down before. She hit me like a wrecking ball, pushing the air out of my lungs. Then, to my surprise, her face twisted in confusion. Something warm trickled over my hand, and I knew what had happened. She'd landed on the blade. Staring into her eyes, I watched the life leave her.

With an almighty push, I rolled her away from me. The blade was still stuck in her side, and the grass below her was turning red. I tried to feel some kind of guilt or sorrow, but it didn't come. That hollow calm remained. *It'll hit me when I get my soul back.* That wasn't a particularly comforting prospect.

"You okay?" Wade helped me up and held me by the shoulders.

"I'm fine." I shook him off. "We've got more incoming."

Naima and her four remaining cultists attacked us at once. There might have only been five of them now, but it felt like fifty. They hit us from all sides in a blur of Elements and good old-fashioned brawling. Naima bit down into Garrett's arm, and he gave a guttural cry. Wade whirled around and shot a fireball right at her. She withdrew, but the bite was nasty. And she'd be back in a couple of seconds with another attack.

I blinked rapidly, not believing my eyes. Two Wades and two Tatyanas were in the fray, and I couldn't tell the difference. Apparently, some of these cultists were also Shapeshifters, and without my Empathy, I was fighting blind.

Cultist number three grabbed me around the waist and tackled me to the ground. Thrashing to get away from her, I managed to grip the handle of the taser in my inside pocket. As I pressed down hard on the button, her body went into spasms. I shoved her back and ran for the front of the mausoleum. I needed a better view of the battlefield, especially as I'd lost sight of cultist number four as the Shapeshifters took center stage.

Wade and Tatyana were facing off… and Wade and Tatyana were facing off.

"Just hit her, Wade!" the real Tatyana yelled.

In that moment, I knew which one was the real Wade. While Garrett didn't seem to have a problem round-housing a woman in the stomach, Wade hesitated. I mean, this wasn't just any woman—this was a Shapeshifter pretending to be Tatyana.

The fake Tatyana had no issue kicking seven shades of crap out of someone else, though. She spun around like a dervish and smacked him in the head with her boot. Wade shook it off and grabbed her arm. He paused again, a grimace twisting up his face as he punched her hard in the sternum. She bent backward. He hit her with a ball of fire, sending her to her knees.

Meanwhile, Tatyana whirled in front of the fake Wade and sent out a blast of Telekinesis so fierce it took him way up into the sky. The Shapeshifter dropped down a moment later, hitting the ground with a sickening thud. Wade's crumpled body shivered and sparked for a few seconds, before morphing back into the cultist. She didn't get up.

"Well, now I know what you really think of me," Wade said. He was evidently trying to distract her from what she'd done. She looked horrified, after watching the fake Wade die. Even though the cultist was a Shapeshifter, I imagined it was still hard to watch the likeness of a friend get killed.

Garrett staggered toward me with his arm bleeding. The elegant pillars provided some cover, but we still had three cultists, plus Naima, to fight. And they were coming right for us—picking off the weak, magicless links. Wade sprinted after the dark-skinned woman and pulled her back, taking her down in one swift move. Next to him, Tatyana had snapped out of her shock and lassoed the second and third cultists, sending them flying into the pond.

I grasped the handle of my taser and raced toward Wade, who was now in the middle of a brawl with his opponent. *Not on my watch!* I jabbed the taser into her side, but it barely affected her.

She flashed me a sour grin. "Nice try." She gripped me by the neck. Her palms crackled with electricity that shot violent bolts through my body. I sank to the ground, flailing uncontrollably. *What the heck are you? Electro-girl?* Whatever she was, her powers seemed to be in keeping with Katherine's line of special collections.

I struggled to get back up, helpless to do anything for Wade. Electro-girl had him by the throat, and her palms were crackling again. He'd be a mess on the floor in a few seconds if I couldn't reach him. Tatyana was busy keeping the last two cultists at bay, and Garrett was binding up the wound on his shoulder with the ripped-off edge of his t-shirt. I crawled across the grass toward Wade. I might not have had any emotions, but that didn't mean I was going to let this psycho kill him. My true feelings hadn't changed—they were just in a glass jar right now.

Garrett sprinted forward to help Wade, knocking Electro-girl to the side. It gave Wade the moment he needed to catch his breath and stagger to his feet. However, before he could dust himself off and join the fight again, a whoosh of air passed close to my face. A flash of black fabric pounced on Garrett, sharp claws throwing him back, before she turned her attention to Wade. He lifted his hands to defend himself, but she moved too quickly. In one leap, she was on him, slamming him down into the ground. Wade landed with a thud, Naima leaning over him in a menacing pose.

"Don't you know what happens to heroes?" Naima growled. Her voice was oddly musical, like Tobe's. Only *way* more menacing. Her clawed hands shot out and gripped Wade's throat. His eyes bulged as she squeezed.

I fought to reach him, heaving my body along the grass. Behind me, Garrett struggled to get to his feet, his movements unsteady. Electro-girl had risen, too, and she shot a crackle of electricity through the air that sent Garrett flying. He hit the deck, wincing as he landed on his bad shoulder.

"You aren't necessary, Crowley," Naima hissed. "I'm going to enjoy this."

I couldn't look away as she bared her fangs and moved toward his neck. My muscles weren't functioning properly. There was no way I could get to him before she killed him. *WADE IS GOING TO DIE.*

"Sweet dreams," she purred, as her mouth clamped around his throat.

"Ah, but what if it turns in te a nightmare?" a voice spoke, in a rich, mystical accent that had the same flavor as Dominic's, only more prominent. Naima and the cultist froze. We all did. I glanced over my shoulder to see a striking figure sauntering down the mound from the crypt. Draped in red silk, she moved like water. She had ebony skin and jet-black eyes that glinted with a center of violet, and her powerful features spoke of Haitian ancestry. Marie Laveau in the flesh… sort of.

And just like that, in a snap of red mist, Marie was gone.

Ahead of me, a gasp of pain brought my attention back. Tatyana convulsed, and her eyes lit up violet. Naima pulled away from Wade and stared at my friend. Clearly, she hadn't seen this coming. Her wide, feline eyes said everything.

Marie Laveau showing up wasn't part of the plan.

THIRTEEN

Harley

Tatyana turned slowly and pointed to Naima. "Ye may leave us, unless ye want te become someone's gumbo dinner? And take ye little pets." That definitely wasn't Tatyana anymore.

Naima staggered away from Wade.

"Oh, and I've got a message for ya mighty leader. If Kassrine Shipton wants te talk to me, woman-te-woman, she better be coming down here te do it herself. I despise them witches that don't have the guts te face me." She said "guts"—or more like "gots" in her amazing accent—with such vehemence that I could feel it shaking through the ground. I was mesmerized. It was hard to see Tatyana at all, and not the vision in red that had swept down from the crypt.

A rush of air barreled across the garden and swiped Naima, Electro-girl, and the two drowned rats into the air. They vanished in a snap of energy, all of them kicked out of the interdimensional pocket. We were on Marie's turf, and she didn't want them here.

"Weren't we supposed to summon you, to… uh, appease your spirit?" My voice came out as a squeak. This was… unexpected, to say the least. And it could get us all killed. If we couldn't appease Marie properly, then a curse or death would follow. That's what we'd been told.

"See, this is why you should've stayed away," Garret said. He dragged himself to his feet and clutched his shoulder. "If you'd left this to the National Council and the LA Coven, the way you were supposed to, none of this would be happening."

I shot him a cold look. "You're seriously trying to blame me? How about telling us what you were up to, huh, instead of sneaking around all cloak and dagger?"

"You just can't follow orders, can you?"

"Says you! Let's not forget how you behaved with those bodycams. You wouldn't even answer a bunch of simple questions. You're the one who can't follow orders."

"That was a matter of principle; this is just your stubbornness," he sniped back.

"I'm *dying*, Garrett! Did you expect me to sit back and let you fix this for me? Levi banned me from coming here, for crying out loud. He doesn't believe me! Either that, or he knows exactly what's going on with me and freaking wants me dead. That doesn't exactly give me much reason to trust him, now, does it? Or any of you LA-ites for that matter!"

"Enough!" Marie's voice shivered through the air, silencing us both. That single word made every muscle in my body seize up. I couldn't have disobeyed if I'd tried. It felt like a kind of Telekinesis, but so much stronger than anything I'd ever seen before. She hadn't even lifted her hands—she was doing all of this with her voice alone.

Wade forced his head to turn. "You don't have to restrain us, Ms. Laveau. We're not here to cause harm."

"I'll be the judge of that. Tell me, boy, do you know what it feels like te be cursed?" She fixed her gaze on Wade. My eyes widened in alarm as his skin morphed from his healthy tone to a sick, decaying gray. His face collapsed in on itself, his cheeks hollowed, his eye sockets sunken like a skull, his flesh drooping. I wanted to scream or run to him, but I got the feeling that would only lead to something worse. Even without my emotions, this was horrifying.

"What did you do?" I snapped.

"A curse. Only temporary," Marie said with a wild chuckle. I'd never seen Tatyana's face wear such an evil expression.

I tried to control the tone of my voice. "Change him back. Please, change him back. We meant to do this the proper way, we really did, but things got out of hand."

She smiled, eying me up and down. "*Wi*, it doesn't seem right to see a handsome face in that mess, anyway. I thought I'd let ye know I meant business, in case ye thought to deceive me." She glanced at Wade and the decay receded, his face puffing back up to its normal shape and his body doing the same. I breathed a sigh of relief.

Wade wheezed out a terrified breath. "Remind me never to get on your bad side," he muttered, his whole body shaking. "The whole world went dark there for a moment."

Marie stretched out Tatyana's arms like a cat unfurling after a long nap. "Comin' te ye in spirit form ain't no easy task, ye should know," she said. "That curse be me last drop of juju for now, but I've got more where it came from. Good that ye brought a Kolduny to me door, though, so I can speak more freely. It be a nice body at that. It been a long time since I had a body." She reveled in Tatyana's form, smoothing her fingertips down her forearms and smiling. Tatyana had clearly left the building—she had no say in this whatsoever.

With us frozen, and Wade catching his breath, she walked toward us. Reaching Garrett, she brushed her finger across his wounded shoulder and touched the blood to her lips with a chuckle. He looked deeply uncomfortable, but he apparently thought it wisest not to speak. *Don't blame you there, buddy.* She leaned closer and kissed the injury. As she pulled away, I gasped. The wound had gone, leaving a few streaks of blood and nothing else.

"I don't like te leave a man bleedin'," she purred. "But what to do with all of ye, hm? Nobody disturbs me slumber, and yet ye stumble in like newborn lambs, makin' a racket te raise the dead. Not only that, but ye brought the scourge of Eris wit ye. See me lilies—see how they're droopin' now? Ye soiled the precious earth beneath them. Ye brought ya mortal poison to their door. And ye know what price got to be paid for their death?"

More death? I knew I should have felt fear, but I didn't have the means anymore. In front of a woman like Marie Laveau, I guessed that was a good thing.

"Trouble is, *ptit mwen*, how te gain me price? Do I take it slow and painful, or savor the taste? Curse ye to perpetual decay, like ya man there was, or give ye the eternal pain of the tortured souls of the other-world? Ye might wish for death then. Might that be price enough te satisfy?"

I realized I had less to lose than the others. If she killed me on the spot, she'd only be speeding up that eventuality. If she didn't help us—and she didn't seem to be in a particularly helpful mood—then death was coming for me anyway. Papa Legba had said Death was almost at my door.

"Marie Laveau, you say there's a price for the death of your lilies, but doesn't everything in this world have two sides? If we've brought death to your flowers, I'm sorry for that, but surely the price for death is life? The other side of the coin, right?" My voice was weirdly steady. "Please accept our humble apologies for waking you so rudely. We were desperate. *I* was desperate. I needed your help, but I see now that I should've thought of you first. We had no right to barge in here. This wasn't meant to happen."

"Oh? And how did ye mean to make this happen, huh?" She eyed me curiously.

"We planned to summon you the proper way, as I said—in a way that gave you the respect you deserve. I left my soul with Papa Legba to come here."

She smiled. "Ah, me immortal beloved. I've not seen me man since last All Hallow's. Chaos rules being what they are, it's forbid te spend our days side by side. Once a year, and that be all. It's what allows our spirits te stay on in this world, long after we ought to have left it. This is me place of rest and thought and meditation, in this here chapel garden. This be where the wandrin' spirits come te gossip before thems pass. Ye hear all if ye only listen, and I hear *all* them whispers."

"Spirits come here?" I glanced around, as if there might be one behind me.

She chuckled. "This place be a mighty power for receivin' thoughts and secrets from the dead, *brav nanm.*"

"Sorry?"

"Brave soul." Her violet eyes flickered.

"And you only see your husband once a year? That must suck."

A vibrant laugh poured out of Tatyana's mouth. "*Wi*, that it does. Once a year is all we have to ourselves. I go to him, the *renmen* of me life. He chose his afterlife on Earth long before me, and I chose the same when me end of days loomed. I see he's still at his work, gatherin' his souls."

"He said he's only allowed to stay on Earth if he does his spiritual duty... or something like that."

She clapped her hands together. "Is that what he be tellin' ye?"

"Is that *not* what the souls are for?"

"He be collectin' them for us, *brav nanm*. One day, he goin' te break the rules of Chaos with all them souls, and join me again, eternal. In this world, not the one what follows. Our hearts will be one again, when that mighty day dawns."

I frowned. "Why didn't you just move on together, after you died?" This seemed like a *lot* of hassle just to be together, when there was a simpler solution.

"I don't expect ye te understand, for ya be mortal still. When life in the flesh is done, nobody knows what comes after, not even Papa Legba," she replied, her tone soft. "There be no guarantee that we'd be together there, wherever and whatever 'there' may be. A love like ours —we didn't care te risk the loss of it."

So, you loop-holed the crap out of the system and got stuck like this? Their bodies together in the crypt, but their souls apart, only able to unite once a year, for a few hours, on All Hallow's Eve. To me, the risk seemed worth it, instead of the alternative of being forever separated. Not that I dared say so out loud.

"That's rough," I said.

"It ain't every day that I come te a mortal's aid," she replied, the soft edge gone. "On any other day, I'd have let ye battle that fanged *tigrès* critter and let ye do me summonin' ritual. I like te watch people go through the effort just te speak te me. Makes me feel alive. But you... mmm, you are different. Not right now, with ya soul in a jar, but I know there's power in ya bones, *ma brav nanm*. My love knew what he was takin' when ye came to his door. Power I've not seen in decades, if not centuries. I could scent it from the other side of my city. The spirits be whisperin' about ya more than any."

"That's why you intervened?"

She shrugged. "I chose te show up and get the ritual part out of the way. It be a waste of time, in circumstances like these. Those cloaked intruders gave the game away. Kassrine is still after you, *wi*?" I liked the way she said Katherine's name. It almost made it palatable.

"Uh... oui, madam."

She laughed. "There is a sayin' in Haiti: *li pale franse*. It means, 'he speaks French, so is likely to be deceiving you,' but I respect the effort."

"Sorry." I dropped my gaze. "So, you've been keeping tabs on the magical world, then?" I wasn't all that surprised.

"I admit, the powerful ones have always fascinated me. When the barrier inside ye cracked, I could feel it in me own spirit. It vibrated like nothing else."

I gaped at her. "You *felt* that? So you know I have a Suppressor inside me?"

"Dancin' the line between life and death, there've got te be some perks. I listen, remember? I hear all and feel all." She smiled and made me feel like an idiot. "Still, me intervenin' doesn't mean all parts of me ritual should be left aside. I have traditions to be upholdin'. Did ye bring me a gift?"

My heart sank. We'd totally forgotten about that part. I needed to buy some time so I could figure this out.

She squinted at us. "Now... did ye bring old Marie a gift?"

Garrett stepped forward and spared me a torrent of excuses. "I've brought you a gold coin from the Tomb of Midas."

She waved him away. "Ten a penny. Ye dishonor me, *ti gason*." From the withering way she was looking at him, I guessed that meant "boy."

Wade fumbled in his pockets for a moment. His eyes brightened as he pulled a small object out and walked toward her. "I've got a sprig of heather from the Wallace Monument in Stirling, blessed by his spirit. I picked it up when I was in Scotland a few years ago, to bring me luck. I bought it from a magical who was descended from Wallace himself." The dried-out flower had been pressed between two squares of laminate. I stared at him. I'd never have had him down as the sentimental type, but then I didn't know much about his family.

Marie snorted. "There'll be a thousand of those driftin' about. No good, *ti gason*."

Panicked, I checked my own pockets. I only had one thing to give. I thought about parting with the pendant Imogene had given me, but it didn't seem right to regift a gift. *She won't accept it. It's not good enough.* Still, it was all I had.

"I have this. It's pretty much the most precious thing I've ever owned, but you can have it if it means you'll help us." I handed her a crinkled, folded-up note. The words inside were etched into my mind: *Harley, I am so sorry for doing this to you, but there is no other way. Stay safe. Stay smart. I love you. Dad.* I'd slipped it into my jeans for the same reason that Wade had kept the sprig on him—to bring me luck and keep me safe. Right now, I felt no pull of guilt or reluctance in handing it over, but I knew I would once I had my soul back.

Marie smiled. "Now there's a gift worth takin'. The grief still lingers… mmm, so potent I could lick it clean." She plucked the note from my hand and pressed it between her own. Her eyes closed, and she inhaled deeply, as if drawing something from the paper. "I would've asked for ya soul, Harley, but it seems like me husband beat me te that one." A cackle split the air, sending a chill down my spine. Wade and Garrett shuddered, too.

"Does that mean you'll help?"

"I'll help." She didn't bother to ask what I wanted, exactly. "Kassrine is ambitious, and there's admiration te be found in that, but I'd rather cross over or end up in someone else's soul jar than let that bitch become a Child of Chaos. She'd never have faced me in the old days, when I had me body as well as me power. I was wise enough to know never to bite the hand that feeds ye, and she be chewin' off hands."

Way to go, Katherine—pissing off the greatest Dark witch of all time. Nice one.

Marie shook her, or rather Tatyana's, head. "Who do she think she is, huh? It's disrespect in the highest form, to think yourself as mighty as the very beings what made us magicals possible. Well, pride do come before a fall, and I'm only too happy to help ye build them gallows high."

Wade, Garrett, and I stood in baffled silence for a minute. I hadn't expected Marie Laveau to be so accommodating, but it was a welcome break. After Quetzi's death and Katherine completing the first ritual, I'd been desperate for a bit of luck. *And this could very well be it.*

FOURTEEN

Wade

Harley looked relieved. I was, too. Getting Marie Laveau on our side was one major thing ticked off our list. I knew firsthand what it meant to *not* have her on our side. Her curse still lingered in my head. It had felt like a living death, which I guessed was the point, my body hollow and weak and decaying. I shuddered at the memory. I'd been able to hear and see what was going on, but it had been muffled and blurry. My eyes had misted over as if I had cataracts. And my heart... ugh, that had been the worst. I'd been able to feel it slowing, like the last seconds of my life were ticking down and I could sense every single one.

I'd been shocked by Harley's gift, though. I'd wanted to stop her from giving it to Marie, but the loss of her soul had done something odd to her. It was like she didn't feel anything at all. She'd handed over her father's note as if it were a dime she didn't need. *This is temporary.* I kept reminding myself of that.

"First of all, we need your help with a Sanguine spell." Harley was all business right now.

Marie-as-Tatyana smiled. "Me specialty. Though ye know that, else ye wouldn't be here." It sucked that Tatyana was being used against her will. She didn't deserve it. I wondered if she could even hear us in there. Being a conduit to the spirits came with a lot of downsides.

"We had some info on your skillset before we came. As the Voodoo Queen of New Orleans, we figured blood-related spells would be your field of expertise," Harley replied. "We heard you might be able to tell us about astral projection, too."

"Ye got me." Marie chuckled, which wasn't a comforting sound. It could flit from a throaty laugh to an eerie cackle in two seconds flat. At least Remington had been right; Marie was our woman.

"This is the Sanguine spell I need help with." Harley whipped a slim brass tube out of her leather jacket and handed it over. Alton had given it to her as a parting gift to save her life, after the mess he'd made. I hadn't considered the risks he must've taken to obtain it. My residual anger toward him softened a bit. He was still looking out for us.

Marie gave a low whistle as she took a threadbare scroll out of the tube. "Powerful stuff, *brav nanm*. Mighty powerful. I'd ask ye where ye got ya hands on it, but it don't suit me to pry so deep. I listen, I don't go lookin' for secrets." She looked over the faded words on the page. A smile curved up the corners of Tatyana's lips. "Ye realize ya brought me one of me own?"

"I did?" Harley looked surprised.

"Me own fair hand. I remember the dawn light, rosy with the sun's blood, as I wrote them words." Her violet eyes took on a faraway expression. "So, it ain't just the barrier ya seekin' to break? Ye seek balance, too? Understandable in a *sòseyè* of your kind. Wit so much energy built up in ya bones, ye'd put Kassrine to shame when the barrier broke. Dark or Light, no tellin' where ye'd turn. Dark be my guess. I sensed the creep of it in ya veins, pulsing deep and deadly, when that barrier cracked."

My chest gripped in a vice. I didn't want that for Harley. Not because being a Dark magical was inherently bad, but if it overwhelmed her... well, it wouldn't be good. She'd lose all sense of who she was. And if it made her more like this—emotionless—it wasn't happening. Plain and simple.

Harley nodded. "That's why I need to balance the Light and Dark in me. My heritage isn't exactly comforting. I know I might turn to the Dark side if I can't fix this."

"Wise *fanm*." She flashed a mischievous grin. "That means 'woman,' in case ye think I be cursin' ye."

"Can it be done?" Harley pressed.

"It's all in the quantities," Marie explained. "For this, ye need thirteen drops of Light and thirteen of Dark, not a drop more or less. Although, this won't do you no good. It's provident that ye came to me first, else ye'd have had a nasty surprise in store. Well, not nasty... maybe disappointin' might be a better word." She waved the scroll. "My love distracted me that *maten*, when I had ink to paper. The dawn bein' so pretty, we walked in the sun's light and lay together in her embrace."

TMI, Marie. TMI.

She glanced at me as if she could read my thoughts. "Ye've not been livin' if ye've not lain together in the first light of *maten*." A wink followed. I dropped my gaze and tried not to flush with heat. She stared at me with a worrying hunger. Her kissing Garrett's shoulder had been uncomfortable enough. Speaking of which, he looked just as embarrassed as I felt. He shuffled in silence, kicking the grass with his foot.

"So it *can't* be done?" Harley ignored our discomfort and kept on track.

"Rest here awhile." Marie turned, in Tatyana's body, and walked up to the crypt. She still held the scroll in her hand. She disappeared inside, leaving us to watch the crypt door like meerkats. *What if she doesn't come back out again?*

Garrett found his voice now that Marie had gone. "At least you didn't try the spell before you came here. I suppose you get props for not being *that* reckless."

Harley glared at him. "Dying, remember? Do I have to keep reminding you? You weren't here to fix this mess inside me, so how about you shut it?"

"I'm glad she's helping you." He stumbled over his words. "It was just a shock, seeing you all here. And it kind of threw a wrench into what I was here for."

"Yeah, well, I suggest you get over it," she shot back. "Marie healed you, so you can't moan about getting injured because of us, either."

He fidgeted. "If you could not mention that to anyone, I'd appreciate it."

"You embarrassed, Garrett? Not like you to blush over a woman taking a fancy to you," I teased.

"You jealous, Crowley?"

I chuckled. "Not in the slightest. You should've seen your face, though."

"Not another word," he warned.

A second later, Marie emerged with a book in her hands. It looked ancient, the leather cover cracked and veined with years of love and effort. Gold-and-red vines twisted across the exterior. And, in the center, the veve of Erzulie took pride of place. A Voodoo Queen's Grimoire. I could feel the power of it, even from a distance. There were magicals all over the world who would've killed their own mothers to get their hands on this.

"For the *brav nanm.*" Marie opened it to a certain page and handed the Grimoire to Harley. "Feast ya eyes upon me complete words. I finished them when my love and I parted, and me time was me own once more. Be warned, love is bad for productivity."

Harley took it graciously. I was stunned. This was an incredible honor, and I didn't think she realized the significance of the act. This was a book that the whole magical world wanted, and she was being given a glimpse. Nerves jangled through me, too. I knew what Harley could do with Grimoires and how they affected her. Even with her soul in lockup, there was no telling what might happen.

"It's different," Harley said with a smile. "The chant is different."

Marie nodded. "Couldn't have people usin' it for they own devices. Thieves took that scroll you gave me. Had they stolen the true words, I'd have brought me wrath down on them. Instead, I only cursed them *yon ti kras*—a little. A lifelong ague and a few lost minds. Served them right." That eerie cackle slipped from her throat.

"I think I've got it," Harley said, looking back up at Marie. "But what about the blood needed? We think we might know how to get the Light part of it. Giverny Le Fay is the most powerful Light magical, so we were kind of gunning for her."

Marie spat violently. "I know the vile *tifi* all too well. Another disrespectful poison on this earth. Ye be right, though—her blood would be perfect. Only, she won't give it away so easy."

I frowned. "Well, she's in Purgatory and clapped in Atomic Cuffs whenever she leaves her cell. It's not like she can do much about it, if we try and take it from her."

"A danger, to rest on ye laurels and think so simple. Ya parents taught ye better than that, son of Crowley." She shot me a piercing glare that wrenched at my soul. I didn't want to be reduced to a skeleton again. "Oh *wi*, I know ya parents as if they were me own followers. They came to old Marie when they were young. Stood where you're standin'."

My mouth fell open. I'd never have expected my uppity parents to come and seek information from Marie Laveau. They already looked down their noses at less-mainstream magic, and Voodoo seemed like a stretch.

"Why would they come to you?" I asked.

She laughed. "Te be gifted with a child."

"Me?" I gasped.

"Well, I don't see no other Crowley child standin' before me."

"They came to you to have *me?*"

Marie nodded. "Ya *manman* couldn't conceive. Years they tried, and the fertility gods didn't grace them with a child. They came to me, as all do when they need true power. I gave them a spell from me Grimoire to perform, and gift ya *manman* with the fertility she craved. Ya standin' here today because of me."

I gaped at her. That didn't sound like my parents. They were never desperate. They were strong and proud, and never let anything get to them. It was as much their flaw as it was their greatest attribute. To think of my mother, here, begging to have a child... it didn't seem possible. But here I was. Living proof that she had. They'd always been loving parents, but they came from the kind of people who kept children at a distance. They'd raised me the way they'd been raised. I'd never seen a glimpse of that desperation or obsession in my mother.

"That's very interesting, but where do we get the Dark blood from?" Harley asked. *Geez, Harley, can't I get a moment?* The spell was important, but so was this. At least to me. Then again, the sooner she got her soul back, the sooner she'd stop being... well, soulless.

"It won't be easy, *brav nanm.*" Marie's voice held a note of warning.

"Please don't say Katherine Shipton," Harley muttered. "If I have to go right into the belly of the beast and get it from her, I won't survive. I might as well stay here and let my time tick out."

Marie grinned. "Like I say, it won't be easy. Nothing in this life is. For the ultimate prize, we must pay the ultimate price. And you seek an ingredient that is not easy te come by. If you get it, it'll show the strength of ya resolve."

"It's her, isn't it?" Harley's face fell. I wanted to comfort her, but I stayed back.

"Funny ye should say you'll have te go to the belly of the beast. That's exactly where ye must go, te fulfill ya wish of bein' a balanced child of Dark and Light."

Harley shook her head. "Well then, this is a wasted trip. I should have known!" She glanced at Marie. "Sorry for disturbing your slumber. We won't take up any more of your time."

Gloomy silence settled across us humans. Even Garrett looked sad about it. He might have been an ass at times, but he didn't want Harley to die. If Katherine held the Dark blood we needed, then Harley was out of options. It broke my heart. Worse, I didn't know what to say or do to make it better for her.

Raucous laughter spilled out of Marie, startling us all. "The looks on ye faces! So gullible. Ah, ye can't blame an old spirit for findin' amusement where she may. As if Kassrine is the most powerful source of Darkness. She wishes!"

"Is it you?" Harley asked, a hint of irritation in her voice.

"Once upon a time, but me body be dust and me blood with it," Marie replied sadly.

"Then who?"

Marie's eyes brightened. "No magical alive will ever have more Darkness streamin' through they veins than the Mother of Monsters."

"Mother of Monsters?" I chimed in.

"Echidna." The word hung in the air, vaguely familiar.

"Those cute, spiky things from Australia?" Garrett sounded confused.

Marie howled with laughter. "The stupid ones are always the nicest to look at."

Garrett flushed with mortification, and I stifled a laugh. The name rang a bell, but I knew it wouldn't be cute, spiky creatures. I wracked my brain, trying to think where I'd heard the name before.

The Bestiary. That's where.

"Echidna be the oldest and most powerful of the Purge beasts. Her blood, in her physical form, is rich in the highest concentration of Darkness anywhere on this earth. It be her gift. The thing that allows her te give birth to other Purge beasts of fearsome might—Leviathan,

Medusa, Chimera, to name a few. No other creature has the power." Marie sounded almost awestruck. Which was saying something, considering *her* power.

Memory came rushing back. I knew about Echidna. Tobe had told me about her once, but I hadn't been paying much attention. Now, I could hear his voice. Ages ago, I'd asked why one of the boxes was frosted over. Tobe had explained it. Her box was literally frozen under a powerful barrier spell. She couldn't be granted any of the freedoms of other Purge beasts, not even the ability to move around her box. Echidna made Quetzi look like a kitten.

"I know about her. She's in the Bestiary," I said excitedly. "Some of her children, too." Leviathan was in his own room of the Bestiary, in a box filled with charmed oil. A stasis less potent than his mother's, but no less powerful. Their energy alone could sustain half the magical planet. That's why they were kept so deep in the Bestiary.

"There be danger lurkin' in those glass boxes. More than anythin' ye might've faced up to now," Marie said in a low voice. "If ye be wantin' her blood, *brav nanm*, ye'll need to approach the Mother of Monsters with due caution. But, first, ye'll have te survive the encounter. She could fill half an underworld with the spirits she's created in her time, for she births Death as well as Purge beasts."

The mental image made me shudder. I'd known this wasn't going to be easy, but Echidna? Harley seemed to attract danger like a magnet. She jumped from one flaming hoop of terror to another.

"We'll have to thaw her out," I said. "And she'll be pissed after being restrained like that for so long. She's literally been frozen for decades. But I guess it has to be done." Getting blood from Giverny Le Fay was going to seem like child's play compared to this.

Harley looked at me. "Why did they freeze her?"

"Something about birthing monsters faster than the Bestiary could keep up."

She nodded slowly. "So... a monster has the blood I need. Better than Katherine Shipton, I guess."

Marie chuckled. "I like ya spirit, *brav nanm*. If ye manage te get through to Echidna without her swipin' ya head off ya shoulders, that's when ye'll be able to ask for the blood. It won't come cheap. High gain, high price. The Mother is goin' te want somethin' in return."

Harley rolled her eyes. "I suppose I should've expected that. Why does everyone want something in return? What happened to charitable giving, huh?"

"A note torn from the deepest part of ya heart won't cut it, neither," Marie replied. "She's more discernin' than me. When ye get her in a bargainin' sort of mood, ye'll have te be ready te do whatever she asks of ye. And I mean *whatever* she asks of ye. She don't barter, and ye won't be able te appeal te her charitable spirit." Marie flashed a wink, but Harley didn't smile.

With each step forward we took, we seemed to be taking two backward.

FIFTEEN

Harley

"You should have this back," I said, handing the Grimoire to Marie.

Marie smiled. "You give it back to me so easily?"

"It belongs to you."

"Others would be on they knees, beggin' to have this in their possession for the rest of time. Those what touch it and try to snatch get sent away with a bad case of shingles if I'm feelin' generous, and razorblades when they pass water for when I'm less kind in me heart. Pesterin' gets nobody nowhere."

I flashed a wry smile. "I'd never try and take something of yours. Grimoires are deeply personal. It'd almost be like me trying to take your soul from you."

"Ye wisecrack too?" Marie chuckled. "*Brav nanm*, you're a rare one."

I wasn't going to deny that trying to take the Grimoire, or begging for more time with it, was a tempting idea. The way it felt in my hands, it was like it wanted me to take it. Even without my soul, the whispers coming off it were deafening. The pull was intoxicating, as if my body was responding to the sheer power inside it. But I had a leaky

Suppressor to deal with. My absent soul had made me forget for a while, but the truth remained. If I tried any kind of big-ass spell in this state... I didn't even want to think about what might happen. My last show of power in front of Papa Legba had almost brought the house down, literally, and widened the crack to boot.

"You've already been generous. I'm not going to push my luck," I replied.

"Ye'll be eager to get away, if me thinkin' is correct." A grin twisted up her mouth. "Tick tock, Harley Merlin. Your clock is ticking, and I'm afraid there ain't long left."

It still didn't seem real that if I didn't make this happen, I'd end up dead. Marie's words made it tangible, the stark reality hitting me in the pit of my stomach. *Will I find my way back here if I don't make it?* There were a lot of obstacles still in our way, and my survival wasn't guaranteed. It reminded me that we had more information to gain from Marie Laveau.

"Before we go, there's one more thing."

She seemed surprised. "Oh? And what might that be? I thought ye weren't one for pushin' ya luck?"

"Once I've broken this Suppressor, we're going after Katherine," I explained. "You already know what she's trying to do, and we want to stop her. To do that, we need to know what these rituals are and what they're about. Can you help us?"

Marie bristled with sudden anger. "Those kinds of secrets I'd kill for, just so I could destroy them—so no magical on this fair earth would ever dare te challenge a Child of Chaos and think so high of themselves again. I'd cross over just so I could take them to me true grave."

"You don't know anything about them?" Wade asked. Garrett, on the other hand, had been uncharacteristically silent in front of Marie. I guessed her kiss was still lingering in his mind. *Must be weird to have a powerful spirit flirt with you.*

"Sadly not, though I wish with all me heart that I did. I listen, and I hear all, but those secrets are whispered so quiet that not even I can grasp them. I've tried, ye may rest assured of that." Her violet eyes sparked.

It was a disappointing outcome. With her being the greatest Dark witch of all time, I'd hoped for more. Still, it wouldn't stop me trying to figure these rituals out. I'd dig as deep as I had to until I found out what Katherine was up to. Plus, we weren't completely out of options. Katherine had the Librarian—that woman was our key to getting ahead. Maybe Marie knew something about her instead?

"We have another way," I said. "Do you know anything about a woman called Odette... uh, I don't know her surname, but you might know her better as the Librarian?"

"Odette de Salignac?" Marie's full focus was on me, her eyes wide.

I shrugged. "That sounds French enough to be her, but I'm not sure."

"The Clairvoyant?"

"Bingo."

Marie shivered. "Serendipity shines on us, *brav nanm*."

"Then you know about her?"

"Are ye not listenin' te me? I hear a lot of things in this place. And I hear many a whisperin' about her," Marie replied. "She was a captive of Kassrine not so long ago, if my spirits be talkin' right."

I nodded, feeling a flicker of dread. "She still is, as far as we know. Don't tell me she's passed through here as a spirit, or I might just drown myself in that pond." I was only half joking.

She chuckled. "Fear not, she ain't passed through here in no spirit form. I heard a rumblin' last night that Odette freed herself from Kassrine's grasp while the ungrateful bitch was busy dealin' with the first ritual. A smart *fanm*, Miss Odette—the smartest. Wily, too."

I looked at Wade and Garrett, my shock reflected on their faces. Odette had escaped Katherine! We'd been so busy worrying about how we were going to rescue her that we hadn't even considered that she'd free herself. That was my kind of woman!

"Have you heard anyone say where she might be?" I pressed.

"Afraid not. These whisperings can only reveal so much," she confessed. "But all's not lost. There's one man who *does* know where she's hidin' herself. I feel the vibration of they love, even now. Ooh, how it swells through the veve of Erzulie and into my soul. Delicious. She's recently seen the man who holds her heart. That lover of hers, Remington Knightshade."

"Whoa, *lover?*" Garrett spluttered.

"A classic story of romance, where tutor and student fall helplessly under love's spell." Marie sighed wistfully. "He didn't just *study* under her, if ye catch me drift." A cackle ricocheted through the air, turning my cheeks pink. I didn't have my emotions, but that kind of blue talk from her had the power to shock anyone.

I cleared my throat. "Are they still… um, lovers?"

"A love like that don't go away so easy. It clings on, long after the decision to part," she replied with a wink. "There was more to them nights in each other's company. Much, much more. I feel the echoes of it, even now. One of the greatest romantic tragedies in recent history, maybe sadder than me own. To love and not be loved in return… nothing hurts like it."

"Who doesn't love whom?" Wade asked unexpectedly.

"Remington loves her still, and always will. Someday, it will ruin the boy's soul and break him into fragments, to be scattered in starlight. Ye can't love the Librarian, whoever they may be. She is Odette now, but when she dies, another will take her place."

I frowned. "I don't understand. There have been others before her?"

"And will be more after. When a person becomes a Librarian, they got to forsake all that's mortal and ordinary in their lives and devote themselves te the task of preservin' all the magical knowledge this world has te offer." Marie smiled sadly. "They endure an ancient ritual

—as ancient as Earth's first magical—to gain the power and the knowledge. It's a sacred bond that not even Kassrine can break or take for her own means."

All of these women had given up so much in the pursuit of power. Odette, Katherine, even Marie to some extent. I wondered if I'd do the same, if I was ever faced with that choice. What would I be willing to give up in exchange? *High price, high gain, as everyone keeps telling me.* I glanced at Wade, but I still felt nothing. Would he be on the list of things I'd give up? Would my friends? Would my family? Maybe that was what separated me from the likes of Katherine. Maybe I didn't have it in me.

"Thank you, Marie." I turned back to her. "We'll find Remington and, hopefully, Odette."

She bowed her head. "I wish ye luck, *brav nanm.* May the loa watch over ye in ya trials to come. And here's ya spell for that astral projection ye seek. It ain't me forte, but I'm sure ye'll make good sense of it. Ye didn't think I'd forget now, did ye?" She handed over a small slip of paper that had materialized from nowhere and pressed it into my palm.

I pushed the yellowed slip of paper into my pocket to look at later and returned the bow. "You've been too kind, Marie. I can't thank you enough. Sleep well, and I hope All Hallows' Eve comes around quickly."

"So lies a good heart." A strange smile flitted across Tatyana's lips. "I wish ye greater luck in gettin' ya soul back from my love."

"But I thought the deal was made? I give my soul, I see you, I get it back." I was grateful not to have my soul at that very moment; otherwise, I'd have been freaking out. But I sure as hell wanted it back.

"*Orevwa, brav nanm.*"

Before any of us could say another word, the interdimensional pocket disappeared in the blink of an eye. Air rushed around me and a weird, weightless feeling carried me upward. A moment later, I crashed down on the parquet floor in front of the chapel's altar. Three more thuds told me that Wade, Garrett, and Tatyana had landed next to me.

Aching, I got to my feet. The others did the same. It was good to see Tatyana again, her eyes no longer violet. She seemed even more confused than the rest of us, looking around as if she didn't quite remember where she was. I would have felt sympathy for her if I'd been able to.

"Feeling okay?" I took her by the hand.

She blinked rapidly. "That was… unusual. Even for me."

"All good?"

"I think so." She shook her head like a dog after a bath. "It feels like she shoved me into the back of my own skull. Very, very strange. It's never been like that before."

I smiled. "I guess that's Marie Laveau for you."

"Ugh, never again. I've had enough of spirits using me as their personal conduit. To have to sit there and hear everything and not be able to do anything. It's fine when I'm the one in control, but that… I wasn't even near the driver's seat."

"We should go," Wade urged. He was even more anxious to get my soul back than I was.

I nodded. "Lead the way."

We hurried down the central aisle and back out into the balmy afternoon. Pausing to catch our breath on the steps, we glanced at one another. Garrett's eyes were oddly wary, and Wade was staring at him intently. The Sanguine spell was safely tucked up in my head, and we knew we had to speak to Remington in order to get to the Librarian, but there was one other thing to deal with first. Garrett was supposed to be on a mission for the LA Coven. Technically speaking, he was our competition.

Wade broke the tense silence first. "Don't you dare think you can go back to Levi with this so you can get ahead of us." He'd said exactly what I wanted to. I suspected Garrett might kick us to the curb and sell us out to Levi so he could use Marie's info to improve his standing with the LA Coven and, by proxy, the National Council. They didn't want us anywhere near their investigation. What they didn't seem to understand was that we were in this way deeper than they were. For us, it was personal.

"You don't have a leg to stand on, Wade. You shouldn't have been here," Garrett shot back. "You don't get control over this."

I raised my hands to quiet them before they could get into a slinging match. "We don't need to be on opposite sides here. Let's collaborate instead and pool our resources." I leveled my gaze at Garrett. "If you want to gain any kind of brownie points with Astrid, you'll work with us instead of against us. She's dealing with enough without finding out that you screwed us over. Don't think she'll forgive that, so I suggest you choose wisely."

After a minute of tense silence, he sighed. "What are you suggesting?"

"You go to Remington and get the Librarian's new location, while the rest of us hit Purgatory to get the Sanguine spell going," I replied. "We can look into astral projection when the time comes, after everything else is done."

Wade shook his head. "No way. He'll just go to the Librarian himself. He won't share a damn thing."

"Wade." Tatyana shot him a stern look. "He's still part of the Rag Team."

"*He* is standing right here," Garrett muttered.

I smiled. "Garrett won't betray the only people who actually care about him. The LA Coven is just using him, the way all covens use people. All you need to do, Garrett, is make sure you take us with you when you find out where Odette is. That's all. You're not technically breaking any rules, and you're still on mission, as far as the LA Coven will be concerned."

He shrugged. "I guess I haven't had any problems with your investigation so far, not with the Katherine-capturing stuff. LA has, like, an encyclopedia of rules and regulations that I have to stick to. To be honest, I kind of prefer the maverick approach." A small smile turned up the corners of his mouth. "And hell, if anyone's got the motivation to take crazy old Shipton down, it's Harley."

Then there's Astrid... He didn't need to say it—I could see it on his face. Even with the void inside her, she'd been confused by his departure. She'd told me as much. And, honestly, she missed him. The sooner we could get this madness over and done with, the sooner everyone could go back to figuring out the ordinary stuff. Including me.

"Is that a yes?" I prompted.

Garrett nodded. "It makes sense to me. Two heads are better than one, and all that."

"All right, time to send a message to our one-woman dynamo." I pressed down on the earpiece in my ear, which had been silent ever since we'd arrived. It crackled to life and hissed with white noise. "Astrid, do you read?"

For a moment, nobody replied.

"Hello! Yes, I'm here. Sorry, I had to rush into the ladies' room. Louella has been scoping out safe spots, and this is one of them." Astrid's voice echoed through my ear with a screech of feedback. Tatyana and Wade recoiled, while Garrett stared at us, baffled. "How did it go?"

"We saw Marie and got the details for the Sanguine spell. We had an... unexpected visitor while we were there," I replied.

Garrett paled. "Are you speaking to her right now?" he whispered.

I smirked at him. "Garrett was already there. The LA Coven sent him."

"Garrett?" Astrid replied, after a brief pause.

"He's decided to help us out instead of turning us in to Levi." I filled her in on the rest of the events at Marie's crypt, from the cultists to the Grimoire. She listened in silence while I rambled on, the cogs in her head no doubt whirring. "Anyway, we're headed to Purgatory while

Garrett goes to Remington. We're going to reconvene and find the Librarian together."

She took a raspy breath. "Am I reading between the lines here?"

"I think you understand." I kept my response vague, aware that Garrett was listening in.

"You want me to make sure Garrett doesn't screw us over?"

"Perfect."

Another pause stretched. "Leave it to me."

SIXTEEN

Wade

After telling Astrid to put Jacob on standby for an extraction—or more like a change of location—we headed back to the townhouse. I walked beside Harley, but she wasn't very talkative. Soulless Harley excited and scared me in equal measure. She'd never been so fierce, but the lack of emotion was killing me. When she looked at me, it was like she was looking through me. And that dead expression in her eyes was eerie. Garrett, too—I just didn't care about him in the same way.

"I can't wait to get my soul back," Garrett announced. "It's been weird without it."

Harley shrugged. "I don't know, I'm getting used to it." *Getting scarier by the second, Merlin.*

"Very funny, Harley." Garrett smiled but Harley didn't laugh. She clearly meant it.

Forty-odd minutes later, we turned the corner onto Pirate Alley. The coral-colored townhouse sat in the middle of the row, exactly where we'd left it. With magicals, there was always the fear that a building might just up and disappear. Harley froze a few steps from the front door. The rest of us halted behind her.

Something was wrong.

The neon lights had stopped flashing, and the door dangled on its hinges. Someone had kicked it in. Harley sprinted through the broken doorway and pounded up the stairs, with the rest of us in hot pursuit. Reaching the first floor, my worst nightmare turned to reality. The house had been ransacked completely. Tables had been flipped, drawers yanked out, everything swiped off the tables, the stuffing spilling out of the sofas. The windows were smashed, the lamps destroyed, every door broken. The wooden beams had caved in across the far side of the open-plan room, and the exposed brick walls had huge holes in them.

There was a fight here.

Papers were scattered across the damaged floor, a giant fissure running through it. Harley had caused some damage earlier, but she definitely hadn't broken the floor that much.

In the distance, sirens blared. Whatever had happened here, it had happened recently. Cops and firemen would swarm this place soon. We needed more time. I lifted my palms and poured my Chaos energy into making a time-lapse bubble. It'd been a while since I'd made one, but it was like riding a bike. My ten rings lit up, the magic flowing out and encompassing the townhouse in a glinting dome.

"We need to be quick," I said. "The bubble will slow things down, but we should get out of here ASAP."

"The safe," Garrett breathed. "Where is it?"

As I looked to Harley, her expression remained blank, and I figured I'd have to be horrified on her behalf. She needed her soul back whether she liked it or not. It was what made her who she was; it was what made me fall in love with her. Not that I'd say that out loud. Ours might not have been a legendary love like Marie and Papa Legba's, or Remington and Odette's, but it *was* ours. Awkward and amazing and unexplored.

"Garrett, help me with this." I raced over to the pile of rubble and started hauling beams away. Garrett sprinted to join me, the two of us working in unison to clear a path to the safe. Halfway through, I stopped. A flood of nausea rose up my throat. There was a body under here.

"Is that...?" Garrett murmured, turning away.

I nodded. "Yeah, it's Dominic." The wooden floor beneath him had turned a rusty red, and his blood pooled out. His eyes were wide open, staring blankly at the ceiling.

"Did you say 'Dominic'?" Harley walked over, with Tatyana at her side. Neither of them looked away. One of them feared nothing right now, while the other didn't fear death.

"Tatyana, can you search for Dominic's spirit while we clear the rest of this?" I asked. We'd have to move him to get to the safe, since his back was blocking the door. "Harley, look around, see if there's anything that might indicate what happened here."

Harley nodded and retreated to the opposite end of the room. Meanwhile, Tatyana lit up with white light. *At least there's no purple this time.*

As she searched for Dominic's spirit, Garrett and I finished clearing away the rubble. We looked at each other grimly. Dominic still blocked the way. Silently, Garret took Dominic's legs and I took his arms, the two of us carrying him off to the side. Laying him carefully down, we returned to the safe. It stood before us, covered in dust and splintered wood, but the door was firmly locked. An expletive lingered on my tongue. This was becoming way more than a joke.

"Is Dominic still here?" I turned to Tatyana. Dominic's spirit might have a way to open the door.

She shook her head. "He's moved on. I can't feel his energy here any —" She choked on the last word. Her eyes bulged for a moment and her body convulsed. Where her eyes had been white, they now turned that familiar shade of violet. *Guess I spoke too soon.* Papa Legba had taken over, against her will. She'd been working hard on her Kolduny powers since the mess-up with Oberon, but they were clearly still weak against the likes of Papa Legba and Marie Laveau.

"You see what you've done!" Papa Legba's voice roared out of Tatyana's mouth. "You brought nothing but danger to my door, after the favor I gave to you. I showed you the way to my dearest love, and you do this! Well, if you and your Shapeshifter traitor came for your souls, you can forget about it. My generosity is at its end. Chaos rules or no Chaos rules."

"Papa Legba, this wasn't us," Harley insisted as she ran back over.

"I scented the rich wealth of power within you, Merlin. I ought to have known that your arrival would spell nothing but trouble. Decades of your kind, your ancestry, and I still did not think to refuse you. I sought the strength of your soul, and this is my reward for that greed," Papa Legba raged on. His violet eyes were practically burning. Purple tendrils snaked across Tatyana's skin, following the lines of her veins.

I stepped between Harley and Papa Legba's fury. "We didn't do this."

"Your henchmen killed Dominic. You severed the spiritual connection that bound us. I was supposed to hold on to his spirit forever, and you have stolen that from me. That beast of yours knew some old Voodoo, it seems. Very clever, to send your most knowledgeable to steal from me and seek to ruin everything I have built all these years. Do you know how hard it is to discover a follower of his caliber? Very clever indeed, *tifi!*" He spat the word.

Beast? Realization dawned. After Marie kicked Naima out of the garden, she must have come here with more cultists and killed Dominic. They must have tried to get into the safe and found it locked. Either that, or they didn't know the value of what was in it.

"Papa Legba, we had nothing to do with this," Harley insisted. "Look into my eyes. You'll see that we're innocent!"

"The people who did this are the ones we're trying to fight against," I added.

Garrett nodded. "If you saw a feathered tigress, then you saw Katherine Shipton's lieutenant. And we're not on her side."

"You would say anything to have your souls returned to you," Papa Legba hissed. "I can never believe the word of mere mortals. You lie as easily as you breathe. I have known mortals long enough to know their treachery."

"How can we prove it to you?" Harley was impossibly calm.

"A blood oath judged on the scales of Erzulie herself. That is the only way now," Papa Legba bellowed. "If you lie, you will find yourselves forever cursed. Eternal misery and disease the likes of which the magical world has never seen. I will fuel the oath with my deadliest hex —one I vowed never to use upon mortal beings."

I hoped this wasn't like a polygraph test. We were innocent, but fear might play a part in skewing the results. My heart was already hammering. If we didn't take it, though, I guessed we'd end up hexed regardless.

"We'll do it," Harley answered without any discussion.

"Give those pendants back to me," Papa Legba demanded. Harley took hers off and placed it in Tatyana's hand. Garrett did the same. "I have no blade—your henchmen destroyed everything. Do you have one?"

"They weren't our henchmen," Harley replied.

"Nevertheless, I need a blade!" he snapped.

Harley pulled the small knife out of her boot and gave it to him. Walking to the safe in Tatyana's body, he paused beside Dominic and pulled a third necklace from around his throat. *How many of these does he have?* Then he lay the pendants flat on top of the safe and took the blade, setting it beside the pendants. "One by one, you must approach and drop blood upon the veve of Erzulie. A red glow excuses you from any wrongdoing. A blue glow means you are guilty and will receive the full fury of my curse."

No pressure...

Harley stepped up first. She took the knife in her hand and drew the sharp edge across her palm, then squeezed her fist. Two drops of blood trickled out and landed on the surface of the pendant. I waited with bated breath. A moment later, the heart motif lit up. I'd never been so uncertain of the color red in all my life. But there it was… red. She was clear.

Garrett went next, wiping the blade clean before he swiped it across his palm. He lifted his hand over the second pendant. Once again, it lit up red. And then it was my turn. Cleaning the knife on the edge of my shirt, I cut a small groove along my index finger and brushed it over the third pendant. For a long time, nothing happened. At least, it felt like a long time.

Thank God. The pendant glowed red. I was off the hook. Not that I'd done anything to get *on* the hook.

"Very well, do as you please," Papa Legba muttered. He almost sounded disappointed. Leaning down, he pressed a glimmering dial on the front of the safe. It shimmered purple and opened with a click. To my relief, the rows of soul jars were intact and undisturbed. Naima hadn't gotten to them.

Papa Legba moved away and crouched beside Dominic. With Tatyana's hands, he fixed his former follower's beads back into place and adjusted the front of his silk headscarf. It was an oddly sweet gesture. The guy had clearly meant a lot to Papa Legba, beyond being a soul he could use.

Garrett ducked down once Papa Legba had moved away and took out his labeled jar. Almost tearing off the lid, he swallowed the firefly of light down in one gulp, like it was a glowing, white pill. An instant later he smiled, and his shoulders relaxed. The life had come back into his eyes.

"Better?" I asked.

"Hell yes. It was pretty cool without a soul, but it'd make me suicidal in the long run," he remarked. "There was no flavor to life without it.

No sense in living, really. Nothing felt real. Plus, there's the no-abilities thing to deal with."

"Harley, you're up," I prompted.

"I'm getting to it," she replied. She seemed oddly reluctant.

I went to the safe myself and plucked her jar out. As I approached, she took a step back. She glanced at the staircase. Everything about her body language screamed deer-in-headlights. Her fight-or-flight was kicking in, and I had no idea which way it would go. I couldn't begin to understand what being without a soul felt like. Somehow, it seemed as if she enjoyed it. Like it was easier that way. *Emotions are what make us human, Harley.*

"I know you don't want to feel the pain again," I said softly. "But your soul is the one thing that sets you apart from Katherine. You're as powerful as her—or you will be—and you have as much potential as she does. But it's the differences that make you better than she'll ever be. Your soul is good, and sweet, and pure. She might as well have lost hers, because she doesn't feel anything. Whatever she has left is dark, and twisted, and brutal. She killed children, Harley. She has the kind of soul that lets her do that without remorse."

She dipped her head and refused to look at me.

"It's your kindness and your valiant spirit that make you greater than she could ever be," I continued. "If you want to defeat her and show her what you're made of, then you need this spark back inside you. This spark *is* you."

Garrett nodded. "I get not wanting to, Harley. I can understand better than anyone, but it'll start to feel more hollow soon. The emptiness is kind of freeing, but it'll turn cold inside you if you don't take your soul back. You need it. Wade's right—Katherine's the soulless one."

She lifted her head, and there were tears in her eyes. "But it hurts so much."

"It'll hurt more to lose yourself," I replied.

"Can't I just get my other abilities back and lose the Empathy?" She turned to Papa Legba.

He shrugged. "I can accommodate that if you choose."

"Harley, that Empathy is what makes you… you. It's a gift, not a curse. I know it doesn't feel like that right now, but you need all your abilities. I've made digs at you for your Empathy a million times, but you wouldn't be you without it. I'll deal with you reading my emotions for the rest of my life—just take it back." I offered the jar to her.

Slowly, she took it from me and unscrewed the lid. Her hands were shaking. Keeping her eyes fixed on me, she lifted it to her lips and swallowed the white firefly of her soul. A second later, she dropped to her knees. Her arms wrapped around her stomach, and her face contorted in pain as a bloodcurdling scream burst out of her.

"No, no, no, no, no…" she gasped. Sweat glistened on her forehead. The Suppressor was making its presence known. Everything she'd felt before was back with a vengeance. Watching her suffer felt like breaking down her bedroom door and seeing her on the ground all over again. I could be with her, but I couldn't take the pain away.

Closing the gap between us, I sank down and pulled her into my lap. I held her tight and rocked her gently. I held on with everything I had, like I could send my strength into her. She clung to me with desperate hands, her fists grasping my shirt. As she buried her face in my neck, I could feel the hot tears streaming down her face.

"You're okay," I murmured. "I'm here. You're okay. You're going to break that thing and get through this. I promise."

"It… hurts… so much." She pounded her fist into my chest, and I let her. Whatever eased her pain.

"I've got you, Harley. I've got you."

I held her like that until the pain subsided. Garrett stared at us, but I didn't pay any attention. I guessed it was giving him flashbacks. He'd held Astrid like this after she'd cracked her skull on the altar in the Asphodel

Meadows. I couldn't imagine what that had felt like, and Garrett wouldn't talk about it. If Harley were dead in my arms, I'd have broken there and then. It was a possibility I'd refused to think about. The Suppressor could still kill her, but my Harley was tougher than that. She'd beat this.

"I feel better now," she murmured, pulling away from me. My shirt was stained with tears, but I didn't mind.

Instinctively, I held her face in my hands. "Are you sure?"

"Pretty sure." She forced a weak smile onto her face.

Man, I want to kiss you right now. I didn't, but I wanted to. We'd decided not to revisit that kind of thing until after the Suppressor break, and I wanted to honor that. Then again, did we really want to be like Remington and Odette? An unresolved, painful love?

"We should go," I said.

She nodded, and I helped her to stand. Keeping an arm around her, I glanced at Papa Legba. He was still taking pains over Dominic's body, shifting the silk of his kaftan this way and that. But his time playing with Tatyana was over.

"Papa Legba, we need our friend back." I kept my gaze on him.

He shook his head. "You may not have caused this, but this destruction has everything to do with you. They came because you sought to irk them, and I require suitable recompense. Unlike my love, I lack patience. Dominic was more to my liking, but this body will do just as well. They are both of Kolduny blood, after all."

"You don't have the right," Harley rasped. "Give her back!"

He smirked. "No, I don't think I will."

Suddenly, his expression turned to one of surprise. A bolt of white light pierced the violet in his eyes, and the snaking purple tendrils retreated. Tatyana was fighting him, and it looked like she was winning. *Yes!*

Tatyana's body convulsed, and her eyes rolled back into her head. Wisps of silvery violet energy smoked from her skin as the very floor vibrated. Her eyes sparked white, then violet, then white again. She was really putting up a battle, and I wished we could've helped her.

"STOP!" Papa Legba's voice roared, but another voice shouted over it a second later.

"Go find a disciple who's willing!" Tatyana was coming through.

"STOP!" Papa Legba cried again. Tatyana's body bent double, and her limbs flew out at awkward, painful angles. *This is an exorcism.*

"I'm sick of you spirits thinking you can take what doesn't belong to you!" Tatyana cried as she emerged victorious. She staggered forward with a scowl on her face. "No means no!"

"All that training paid off, huh?" I grinned at her.

"You bet your sweet ass it did!" She punched the air in a very un-Tatyana manner. The rest of us laughed, happy to have her back in full fighting form.

Our joy didn't last. The walls started to shake, and the shards of glass on the floor jumped. A howling wind tore through the room and knocked us back toward the staircase. Papa Legba's spirit was tethered to the townhouse, and he wasn't happy at all.

"GET OUT!" he bellowed, his voice echoing all around us.

The fallen chairs and upended tables hurtled toward us. I pulled Harley out of the way as a plant pot whizzed by her head and hit the wall beyond. Garrett, meanwhile, was dodging a hailstorm of glass, and Tatyana was using her Telekinesis to fling a chest of drawers back across the room.

"We need to leave before this whole place falls down." I scooped Harley up into my arms and sprinted down the staircase and out of the townhouse. Garrett and Tatyana followed, the two of them running out onto the street just as the house collapsed in on itself. The time-lapse bubble broke and revealed the debris. The cops would be all over this like a bad rash.

Standing outside, we stared up at the chaos.

"How's he going to get another disciple if he's got no place of business?" Garrett asked.

Harley leaned against me for support. "Marie might send someone his way. She'll hear about this soon enough, I imagine, if Dominic hasn't already told her. She won't leave him to suffer on his own." She turned to Tatyana. "But when he comes back, you'd better stay away from this place. Even if he doesn't try and take over your body, he'll probably whip you with a hex or something."

She smiled. "I gave him a bit of a shock back there."

"He's lived for decades, if not centuries," I said. "This townhouse will be rebuilt, and he'll continue to collect the souls of the willing. He's got the greatest motivation in the world—his immortal beloved. He'll keep going until he finds a way to be with Marie, in both spirit and body, forever."

"My Suppressor is definitely back in full force," Harley teased. "You've gone all sappy."

"Hey, I can admire a love like that, as long as it's not trying to kill us." I kissed her forehead, grateful that she had her soul back. I couldn't help myself.

"Should we get going?" she suggested with a shy look.

I nodded. "I think it's safe to say we've overstayed our welcome, and we've got a lot to do."

Purgatory and Remington beckoned. Still, I took a second to hold Harley that little bit tighter. I was glad to have her back. Properly back. As I glanced down, I noticed how pale and down she seemed. Her eyes weren't as dead as they'd been without her soul, but they weren't far off.

"We won't stop until you're okay and fully ready to tackle Katherine. We're already way ahead of where we were this morning. So come on, Merlin, chin up. You've got this." I sounded less like a concerned lover and more like an enthusiastic coach, but that's what she needed right now.

She smiled. "Thanks, Wade."

"Ready?"

"Ready." She pressed down on her earpiece. "Jacob, do you read?"

"Harley! It's so good to hear your voice!" Jacob's voice crackled through. "I heard your conversation with Astrid earlier, but I didn't want to interrupt. I was in the hallway, and you don't know who might be listening."

"Good thinking, Jake. Anyway, we're ready to be extracted."

"Give me two minutes. Just need to get up to the Luis Paoletti Room. Hang tight." He sounded breathless, like he was running.

"Will do. Over and out."

"Over and out."

Less than five minutes later, a portal tore open in the street beside us. Fortunately, it was quiet and there were no tourists about. Those sirens were almost here, though.

Jacob lurched out of the fissure. He had a big grin on his face, which I took as a good sign.

"How's the SDC? Are there wanted posters yet?" Harley asked.

He shook his head. "Nah, Isadora and Santana have got this thing running like clockwork. Nobody's noticed you've gone."

Not yet. We couldn't afford to get cocky.

Harley

Isadora's voice crackled through the earpieces. "You can't portal into Purgatory. If you try it, you'll set off every single alarm. Sorry for the delay—I had to find a safe place to speak to you. Levi's on the prowl, ordering this and that to be changed. Feels like he's settling into his new palace or something, making sure everything's 'just so.'" She sounded irritated.

"Is everything all right?" A flicker of worry pushed through me. If Levi caught on to what we were doing, we'd be toast.

"Nothing we can't handle. We've still got everything under control with the duplicates, so nothing to worry about there. I've lost Raffe and Santana for the time being, though, so we're running a bit of a skeleton crew. Raffe's gone to calm down, and Santana is with him. At just the sight of Levi, Raffe starts to lose it, and we didn't want to give Levi a reason to cart him off to Alaska."

"That's great, but what did you say about the portal?" Wade asked, pressing his ear like a bodyguard.

"If you portal into Purgatory, you'll trigger their alarms. And that's only if they don't notice the great big tear in time and space first."

I'd been worried about that. "Well, we can't come back and use the mirrors at the SDC. Levi will know," I said.

"You'll have to find different mirrors. I've got to go, someone's coming. Keep in touch." The earpiece crackled, and she was gone.

"Great, because we've got mirrors coming out of our asses," I muttered. The Suppressor was back in action, heightening my every emotion. Which, at the moment, seemed to be grumpiness.

Tatyana's eyes brightened. "We can use the ones in San Francisco. Garrett is heading there anyway, and I'm sure we could persuade Remington to let us use them."

"The same Remington who's on the same Council as Levi?" I replied.

She smiled. "No, the Remington who's hiding the most valuable woman in the world from that Council and doesn't like Levi a whole lot either. He'll help us." She had a point. Although Remington didn't show his dislike in public, it was common knowledge that the two men didn't exactly see eye-to-eye. They were from different schools of authority and often clashed over Council issues, while Imogene acted as mediator.

"Then we'd better get going." I looked to Jacob. "Can you portal us into the San Francisco Coven?"

He nodded. "I'm getting the hang of this destination stuff. It shouldn't be too hard."

"Wait, you're coming with me now?" Garrett frowned. "But you'll all be going on to Purgatory from there, right?"

I flashed him an irritated look. "We'll decide what's best when we get there."

"You good to go?" Jacob glanced anxiously between us.

"Yes, we're good to go."

He raised his hands and let his energy swirl around his fingertips. As he released it in one powerful pulse, the fabric of time and space tore in front of us with a rush of air. The portal gaped like a crooked mouth, the edges sparking and crackling. Jacob had to be tired by now, but he didn't show it. That boy had come so far and was only continuing to improve. Yeah, he'd made mistakes—one pretty freaking big one—but I was proud of him for pushing forward.

We stepped through the portal, with it snapping shut behind us, while Jacob went on to the SDC. A moment later, we stumbled out into the familiar surroundings of the San Francisco Coven. It really was beautiful here, like a fairy grotto deep beneath the earth, a stark contrast to the grim ex-prison above. To my relief, the same lazy receptionist was on duty, his back turned to us. He whirled around in surprise, but the portal had already gone; it'd be easy enough to lie our way through this.

"You again," he said as our eyes met. He pocketed his phone and leaned over the desk.

I flashed him a grin. "Our new director is annoyed about some paperwork that Remington left at the SDC and wants us to pass the message on. Is he in?"

The receptionist shrugged. "Sure, you know where his office is. Saves me the job of calling him up here. He hates that. We don't call him the troglodyte for nothing."

I stifled a laugh. "Thanks."

"The troglodyte?" Wade whispered as we set off through the carved rock tunnel. I remembered the way, even though these corridors all looked the same.

I smirked. "I guess he keeps to himself."

We arrived outside the right door ten minutes later. I knocked, and the four of us waited patiently for a reply. None came. Instead, I heard someone shuffling around inside before the door creaked open and Remington's face peered out. He reeled back in shock when he saw us standing there. I guessed Levi had already filled the other Council members in on his new rules, especially where we—or rather, I—was concerned.

"Harley? What are you doing here?" Remington hissed. "Does Levi know about this?"

"What do you think?" I replied.

"You can't be here." His eyes were wide and scared.

"Levi isn't listening to me, Remington. He wouldn't let me take the right steps to break my Suppressor and stop the leaking energy from poisoning me. He thinks I'm lying through my teeth, so I had to take matters into my own hands."

He paused. "He really wouldn't let you?"

"Again, what do you think?"

"Well, come in before someone sees you." He opened the door wide to let us in, but I shook my head.

"This is just a pit stop. We need to use the mirrors here to get to Purgatory so I can beat this," I explained. "Garrett's going to stay behind, but the rest of us need to go. *Right now.*" The ice-cold syrup of the Suppressor was edging deeper and deeper into my bones. I didn't know how much longer I had before the expanded crack wreaked havoc.

Tatyana raised her hand. "Actually, I'll be staying behind as well."

I glanced at her. "You will?"

"Call it insurance," she replied, giving Garrett a warning look. This wasn't negotiable.

"Okay then, Tatyana and Garrett will be staying behind to speak to you, but Wade and I need to get through those mirrors."

Wade nodded. "We figured you could cover us the way we'll cover for you."

"Cover for *me?* I haven't done anything that needs covering up," Remington protested.

"We went to see Marie." I arched a knowing eyebrow. "She told us your secret."

Remington paled. "I imagine that's what Garrett and Tatyana wish to talk to me about?" He looked crestfallen. But we already knew he couldn't risk us exposing the truth about his former lover, not for the sake of ratting us out to Levi. Love wasn't just a potent motivator—it provided a foolproof way of extorting someone, too. Not that I felt particularly good about that.

I smiled. "Got it in one."

"Very well, then come with me and I'll see you safely through the mirrors. I can make an excuse for you if anyone asks why the mirrors were used. I'm currently writing an article on the 'psychopath gene,' so I can just say you were assisting me in gathering interview material. The mirrors here don't keep a record of *who* has passed through, just *when*. It should work." He nodded, as if trying to convince himself. "You two stay in my office. I'll be back as soon as I've dealt with Wade and Harley."

Garrett looked sullen as he stepped into the office with Tatyana, but he didn't have much of a choice, not if he wanted to stay in Astrid's favor. Wade and I followed Remington back through the labyrinth of corridors to the main foyer. The receptionist was engrossed in some game as Remington led us right up to the mirror on the far right. Dust lay thick on the frame, as if it hadn't been used in a long time.

"Hurry," he whispered.

"Thank you," I said, before whispering, "*Volat in Purgatoris*" and stepping through. Only when my body was immersed in the mirror did I have a sudden flash of doubt. What if Remington was double-crossing us? What if he was sending us somewhere else entirely?

However, as I strode out into the familiar, sterile entrance hall of Purgatory, my fears fell away. Remington, it seemed, was on our side, even if he'd been forced into helping us. Wade came through a second later, with a similar look of concern on his face. The expression relaxed as he looked around, taking in the glass-and-steel cells, and the walkways that crisscrossed overhead like the threads of a spider's web.

"To be honest, I wasn't sure where we'd end up," he confessed.

I smiled. "Me neither."

A familiar figure dressed in thick black Kevlar, a baton on each hip, stood at the officer's station nearby. *Crap, what was his name again? Mellencamp? Melanin? Merryweather?* It definitely started with an *M*.

He crossed over to us with a smile. "You here to see Finch Shipton again?"

"Not today, Officer Mallenberg," I replied brightly, noting his name badge. *That's the one.* While I had his full attention, I ramped up my Empathy in an attempt to get him to trust me. "We've been sent by Remington Knightshade to collect some interview material for his research. The 'psychopath gene'—interesting stuff. It's part of an inter-coven program to get gifted and talented magicals involved in criminal rehabilitation." The words spilled out with ease. *Oh Remington, you beauty!* He'd given us the perfect excuse.

My heightened, unruly Empathy seemed to be taking effect on poor Officer Mallenberg. It was already going mad after the restoration of my soul, with all of the things that had happened hitting me like a ton of bricks. The note weighed heaviest on my mind, and my remorse about giving it away was nearly impossible to suppress, seeping into Mallenberg alongside the rest of my turbulent emotions. He'd started to sway as if he'd had one too many beers at lunch, his expression disoriented.

"Sure, sure, sounds fascinating," he murmured. "Man, it's hot in here. Reminds me of my last vacation to Jamaica. Nothing like Jamaica to get this place out of your system, am I right?"

"Uh... yeah, sure."

Beside me, Wade looked equally alarmed and amused. "We're here to see Giverny Le Fay, as part of this interview program." He cast me a look that said, *This had better work.*

He nodded, bobbing his head to some unknown rhythm. "Sure thing. Follow me and I'll take you to her. Nasty woman, though. Not the kind you young folks should be seeing. Then again, kids do all sorts of things these days, don't they? At least you're doing something productive instead of loitering on street corners with beers in hand."

How old does he think we are? I chuckled internally. Maybe he meant underage drinking.

We followed him across the entrance hall and up one of the elevators to the very top floor. I'd thought Finch was being kept in maximum security, but I'd been way wrong. *This* was maximum security. They'd done away with the glass floors, replacing them with solid steel walkways and a perilous drop to either side. If anyone fell from there, they'd be mush when they landed on the entrance hall floor, stories below. The cell walls were entirely glass here, but superpowerful charms thrummed from every single one, far stronger than the ones on Finch's cell. Not only that, but there only seemed to be five cells on this entire floor. Furious eyes watched us as we walked along. A few of the prisoners looked like they were shouting at us, but we couldn't hear a word through the reinforced walls.

Mallenberg took us to the cell at the end of the steel walkway, where two officers stood to either side of the glass door. They both wore leather-peaked military hats and long black coats that reminded me of every World War II film I'd ever seen. On their feet, they wore boots that seemed to be reinforced with metal. As I glanced up the walkway, I realized the other guards wore the same kind. Maybe the metal kept them from falling over the edge if anyone broke loose—magnetic boots to keep them on solid ground.

The two officers in front of us had their heads down, with smoky glasses covering their eyes and a springy cord running down from their ears. Sunglasses indoors were for bodyguards and Bono, but these looked like they might serve a purpose.

"These two are here to speak to Ms. Le Fay," Mallenberg instructed, his voice wobbly. I prayed it wouldn't give us away. "They're doing research for Remington Knightshade."

The officers nodded in unison. It was almost comical.

"You'll need these." Mallenberg took two sets of the same smoky glasses from a box on the floor and handed them to us.

I frowned as I took mine and put them on. "Why? To make us look cool?"

He howled with laughter. "Good one! To make you look cool!" It took him a good minute to recover. "No, no, these are to stop Ms. Le Fay from hypnotizing you."

"She's got Atomic Cuffs on, right?" Wade sounded concerned.

"Oh yeah, for sure, but for some reason they don't work on her Hypno abilities. I guess it's because it's such a rare ability. It wasn't included in the Cuffs when they were designed, I suppose. Who really knows." He shrugged woozily. "All I know is, thirty guards killed themselves in her first week here, and nobody could figure out why. Turns out they looked into her eyes, and she worked her magic on them. Hypno wasn't on her list of abilities from her Reading, so we didn't know to look out for it. She tricked the system somehow, sneaky witch. Weird woman, very weird." He waggled his finger as if he was telling off a naughty schoolkid.

So she's not just evil—she's rare and weird, too? After our recent run of bad luck, that felt just great to know.

Mallenberg suddenly stopped and doubled over. We watched him, not sure what to do. The other officers didn't seem too bothered, but I guess they had shock sticks and magnetic boots to defend themselves if anything went south. We didn't. One false step and we'd stumble over the edge. Mallenberg, too. When he stood back up, he looked green around the gills and was sweating profusely.

"You'll have to excuse me for a minute. I'm not feeling too good. I'll check back with you in a bit, once I... Oh God, I have to go," he muttered. Guilt twisted in my stomach. My temperamental, leaky Empathy had made him sick. With a hand clamped over his mouth, he turned around and hurried for the exit.

"Do you think he'll be okay?" I murmured, watching him go.

"He'll be fine." Wade put his hand on my arm. Reading between the lines, I knew he was trying to tell me that it wasn't my fault. I was glitchy as heck, but I'd gotten the job done. We were here because he'd trusted us, all thanks to my faulty Empathy.

EIGHTEEN

Harley

"Keep a distance between yourselves and the prisoner," the officer on the right warned, as he opened the door to Giverny's cell and let us in. "And keep your glasses on at all times. No exceptions. You have ten minutes, starting now."

It felt like I'd walked into some weird gameshow, and the clock was ticking. With Wade at my side, I stepped into the glass box and approached the figure in the center. She was sitting at a table, her hands Atomic Cuffed to the middle, with long, glowing chains tightly pulled to four corners of the walls.

The first thing I noticed was how beautiful she was. It wasn't a normal kind of beauty, but the kind you saw once in a lifetime on a Paris runway or by chance in the street. Tumbling dark curls flowed past her slender shoulders, and huge, piercing, pale gray eyes stared at us. Her skin was unbelievably smooth, with rosy cheeks that gave some softness to the impressive cut of her cheekbones. Her mouth was a perfect heart shape, and a sweet smile rested across it. She looked like an angel, but I had a feeling her heart leaned more toward the devil.

"*Bonjour, mes amis.* How delightful it is to have visitors. *Mais,* you are *étrangers.* I do not know you, I do not sink?" she said in a strong French accent. Every word rolled musically off her tongue. I could have listened to her all day. *She doesn't even need to look at anyone to hypnotize them!* I had to remind myself that she was a total psychopath.

"No, you don't know us." I took a step closer. "But we know you, and you've got something we need."

She gasped in mock delight. "I do? What is it? Zis is very exciting."

"I need thirteen drops of your blood." I still had the little jar from Papa Legba's townhouse, now empty. Plus, I had the knife in my boot to get the job done, since I'd swiped it back after the blood oath.

She covered her mouth and laughed raucously, the sound both sweet and cold at once. "Zis is a joke, *non*? You are comedians, sent to amuse *moi* in my endless days here? Zat must be it, ozerwise I would sink you idiots wiz a dess-wish."

"We're asking nicely, Giverny, not taking it by force. You should appreciate that," Wade said. "Remember where you are."

"Oh, so I should be grateful for zis? Is zat what you sink?" She laughed louder. "You come to take my blood and I should be *grateful*? Do not make me laugh harder than I already am. You are *des imbéciles.*"

That translated perfectly into English. She was mocking us. "We need your blood. It's very important for the safety of the magical world." I softened my tone and tried a different tactic, but she just shot me a withering look.

"Aww, ze heart breaks."

"Don't make us take it from you," Wade warned.

"I would like to see you attempt zis. I am in need of comedy." She shrugged and tossed her hair over her shoulder. "You would almost certainly slice an artery wiz your *incompétence* and see me bleed out all over zese lovely, clean floors. Alzough, it would be amusing to see ze faces of ze guards when zey discover what you have done. Torture and blackmail me all you please; zere is nothing worse zan being cooped up in zis *très minuscule* cell."

"Giverny, we aren't leaving here without your blood." I glowered at her, though I realized she probably couldn't see because of my glasses.

She giggled. "Let me guess. We can do zis ze easy way or ze hard way, *non*? Well, I have always preferred ze hard way. How do you Americans say... come at me, bro? No pain, no gain?" Her eyes sparkled with amusement. "Les Américains. You really are so very coarse."

I glanced at Wade, who was already staring at me. We'd have to take it from her, whether she liked it or not. But her casual attitude worried me. She didn't seem fazed in the slightest, which meant she probably had something up her sleeve. After all, she was the most powerful Light magical in current existence. We had to bear that in mind at all times. I mean, she'd already killed thirty guards just by looking at them. What else could she do? What other hidden things was she keeping for a rainy day like this?

"But wait a moment. What is that scent?" She was toying with us. "It has been a long time since I have smelled zose particular lilies. And ze smell of New Orleans is on your skin, even now. It cannot have been long since you were zere, *oui*? You have seen *ma douce*, Marie. I would know her scent anywhere. Sweeter zan any *parfum*."

"How do you know that?" I blurted out, caught off guard.

"She was *mon prof*, once upon a time," she replied wistfully. "All I know, I learned from her. I spent my youth as a nun in training, if you can believe zat? I met her when I went on a pilgrimage to New Orleans and found myself drawn to zat chapel of hers. Her sweet voice drew me into zat place, and into zat garden beyond ze door. She was ze one who discovered what I was. She gave me all zat I have, and all zat I am capable of."

"And you squandered it." Wade's voice was blunt and cold. "You had the best start in life that any magical could hope for, with all that power and Marie Laveau guiding you, and yet you ended up here? Seems like a tragic waste to me."

Giverny's cheeks flushed a deeper shade of pink. "She sought to hold me back. She feared my power. I could have been so much more zan zis, so much more zan any *magique* before me," she replied bitterly. "I could have had ze world in my hands if I had gotten away wiz Marie's Grimoire. I would have achieved it, had it not been for zat man." Her face twisted in a mask of fury.

"Which man?" I pressed, curious.

"*Alton Waterhouse.*" She spat his name like a curse. "He came to me to recruit me for some foolish American sing, and he discovered my plan to take Marie's Grimoire. He fooled me. We were drinking good wine, and I whispered it to him while he fell asleep in my arms. He had stolen *ma cœur*—ze first man to ever do so—and I had sought him hypnotized, but he was only pretending. He is ze only *magique* I have ever happened upon zat was immune to my special abilities," she muttered. "I planned to take the Grimoire once I had overcome ze European Council, and had ze force of ze Angels bent to my will, so I could cast my spell upon ze rest of ze world. He acted his part to perfection, I must give him zat—quite the *acteur*. He even came to Europe wiz me, keeping up ze act every moment he was wiz me. And when I left him sleeping in our hotel room so I could make ze arrangements, he went to ze Angels and told zem of my plan to take over. Zey caught me and srew me in here."

You and Katherine should talk. They seemed to share a desire for all-powerful leadership. To be honest, I didn't quite know what to make of her story. The idea of Giverny and Alton together was weird, but then again, she was stunning. And he'd had to stop her somehow. Even with his forewarning to the Angels, she'd managed to kill a bunch of high-up European leaders.

I wondered if Alton's immunity to her hypnosis had something to do with his Necromancy. It was the only thing I could think of that set him apart from the others, in terms of Chaos. Alton's Necromancy shared the same violet energy that had glinted in Marie's eyes. Maybe the Queen of Voodoo had seen what might happen if Giverny was let loose on the world and had taken steps to prevent it. After all, Marie had essentially made her what she was.

An idea sparked in my head. "What if I gave you something juicy on Alton in return for the blood? You'll like what I've got to say. It might make you feel better about being here because of him."

"You know him?" She eyed me suspiciously.

I nodded. "He was our director."

She spat. "So he achieved *his* dream and shattered my own. *Salaud!*"

"If you give us the blood, I'll tell you," I urged.

"Tell me and zen I will give you ze blood."

"It doesn't work like that."

She frowned. "Take zose glasses off, and I will believe you. Zat way, you will have to keep your end of ze bargain."

"Harley…" Wade reached out for me, but I'd already moved toward her and sat down opposite. My glasses were off, but I refused to look at her. It was a risky move, but Wade was here to snap me out of any hypnosis. I took out the jar and set it on the table before removing the knife from my boot.

She smiled. "You came prepared."

"We had to," I replied. "Now, hold out your wrist."

"Will it hurt?" She flashed me a grin and lay her arm across the table.

"Not if you behave," I replied.

I'd just made the incision, the blood starting to spill out, when the door burst open and one of the guards sprinted across the room. The second guard lay sprawled across the door, a pool of scarlet stretching across the first yard of the cell, while the rest had disappeared from their posts. I didn't even want to think about where they'd gone, imagining them tumbling to their deaths.

The guard took Wade by surprise, tackling him to the floor and whispering something dark and familiar in his ear. Wade's body twisted up in pain, his arms wrapped around his stomach. The guard looked up at me, a twisted grin on his face. For the first time, I got a proper look at his face. My stomach sank.

Kenneth Willow. He was disguised as a guard, wearing the same peaked cap and long coat. *How did you get in here?* More to the point, how were we going to get out?

"Did you miss me?" he growled as he tore me from the seat and sent me flying against the wall. Giverny stared in disbelief, frozen in place by the chains on her wrists. Blood trickled out of her wrist, but it was no good to me now. Kenneth would kill me before I could collect it.

I struggled to get up, but he was already on me. He gripped my throat and squeezed. "*Ardenti Pellis,*" he whispered. Immediately, my skin felt as if it had been set alight. I howled in pain as I fought against it, but I couldn't escape the searing agony. Blinking through hot tears, I saw Wade barrel into Kenneth and knock him to the side. The two men brawled, each trying to get the upper hand.

"*Oculi caecorum!*" Kenneth screamed at Wade and slammed his hands across his eyes. For a moment, I thought he was going to gouge them out. Instead, golden light slipped out of his palms and into Wade's eyes. I tried to get to him, but the pain was too intense. A milky white sheen had covered Wade's eyes, and he fumbled blindly to grasp at Kenneth again. The evil son of a bitch managed to slip away from under Wade and made a beeline for Giverny.

"I've got work for you. Eris wants a word," Kenneth said. As I writhed in pain, I watched him remove the Atomic Cuffs and set Giverny free.

Desperation flooded my senses. I couldn't let Giverny leave. I needed her blood, but I also couldn't let *that* loose. Not after I'd heard what she wanted from the world. Despite the agony, I gathered my Chaos and pushed it through my hands, attempting to send a lasso of Telekinesis at Giverny and Kenneth.

A scream tore out of my throat. Something was wrong. Something deep inside me snapped. Everything went white.

NINETEEN

Harley

As the roar from my lungs faded, I stood tall with my hands balled into fists, my chest heaving with the exertion. My abilities were on steroids, cracks slithering up the sides of the glass walls on every side thanks to my blast of superpowered Telekinesis. Kenneth was on the floor, the table overturned. Giverny was in a heap beside him, one wrist still cuffed to the table, while the wave of energy seemed to have skirted over Wade completely, as if I'd somehow protected him as I'd shot the blast outward.

The burning skin spell had gone, though it left a slight tingle across my body. I couldn't explain it, but it looked like I'd broken Kenneth's curse by sheer magical strength alone. However, Wade's eyes were still shrouded in that white sheen, his head whipping around in confusion. I hadn't managed to break his curse.

"Wade!" I ran to him and grabbed his arm, helping him to his feet. His eyes scrunched up suddenly, and he dragged me back down to the ground.

"Watch out!" he shouted, covering me as a puff of colored smoke whizzed over our heads.

"How did you do that?"

"I heard it coming."

My gaze snapped to the direction it had come from, my reflexes pulsing with tiny electric shocks that shivered through every nerve in the most intoxicating way. In that moment, I felt like I could take on the whole damn world and still have room for the rest of the universe. That sharpened focus homed in on Kenneth. He was back on his feet, hurling a flurry of hexes toward us in the form of small clouds of colored smoke. He looked like he'd rolled an ankle, because he was hobbling as he made for the door. Evidently, he'd decided to cut his losses and make a run for it, leaving Giverny to fend for herself.

Coward.

I pulled against Wade as if to sprint after Kenneth, but he held on to my hand. "Watch out for those hexes," he warned. "They're incredibly dangerous, and you can never tell what might be lurking inside the smoke. It might be a blinding hex, a paralyzing hex, or something way worse."

"I've got this," I shot back, leaping to my feet. Kenneth wasn't getting away, not with me all supercharged like this. It was scary and exciting at once—almost like handing over my soul but much, much better.

In mid-run toward Kenneth, I skidded across the floor on my knees and swiped my knife from where it had fallen on the floor after the table had overturned. I realized I must have dropped it when Kenneth flung me from my chair, the blade still streaked with Giverny's blood. Without missing a beat, I was back on my feet and hurtling toward Kenneth, who was struggling to put weight on his right foot. Still, if he made it through the door, all he'd have to do was close the door behind him, and we'd all be stuck in here.

"Get back here!" I yelled.

With an arm that would have put the Padres' pitcher to shame, I hurled the knife at the back of Kenneth's leg, aiming for the Achilles tendon. Instead, it thudded into the back of his knee, giving me flash-backs of Marie's lily garden and the cultist I'd taken down in the same way. I didn't want this becoming my MO—*Harley Merlin, knee-slicer extraordinaire.* He stumbled and fell to the ground with a crunch of kneecaps, letting out a pained roar as blood sprayed out. It mingled with the slippery pool that had already been spilled by Kenneth's hand, from the downed guard. Kenneth thrashed about in the slick blood, slipping and sliding as he tried to get back up.

"Eris will come for you! Her eyes are everywhere!" Kenneth declared as he crashed into the ground once more, sending up a spray of scarlet.

My stomach turned as he used the blood to pull himself along, like a penguin sliding on its belly across the ice. The kid was desperate to get out of here, even though Katherine would likely eat him alive for coming back empty-handed. He shot one last glance over his shoulder at me, before slithering right over the edge of the steel walkway. I ran to the spot where he'd disappeared in time to see him land effortlessly on one of the walkways below in a puff of green smoke. *Slimy snake!*

"Wade, we need to—" I turned back around to get him, only to find myself face-to-face with Giverny Le Fay. With one arm free of the Atomic Cuffs, she'd managed to get right up close to me without me realizing... and I was standing there without my glasses on. I hadn't looked her in the eyes while we were making the exchange, but now I was gazing right into those striking gray pools. I couldn't have looked away if I'd wanted to. Which, oddly enough, I didn't.

"So beautiful," Giverny purred. "Look at zis face. Much prettier wizout all zat worrying, *non?*"

"I—" I'd forgotten everything I'd wanted to say.

"Harley, don't look into her eyes!" Wade shouted, but Giverny's voice was the only thing I wanted to listen to, and her face was the only thing I wanted to look at.

"Do not listen to him, *ma belle.* What does he know, hmm? Zese foolish men, zey know nothing. All zey do is hurt us and torment us and break our hearts in ze end anyway. You might say I am doing you a favor, Harley. And zere will be no pain for you, because I will make sure you do not remember it. Zat will be my gift to you, one woman to anozer—ze way Marie taught me."

I nodded slowly, my body moving against my will, as if someone else were forcibly bending my limbs. It felt like the daze after waking from a dream, where nothing quite seemed real. My head knew that something was wrong and that I should run, but my body had checked out. I watched my palms lift and a fireball form in my palm. Giverny stepped out of the way as I aimed the sparking orb at Wade.

He was on the ground, a trickle of blood running down the side of his face. He was trying his best to find his way across the floor, his white eyes shot through with thready veins of red. I didn't know how I'd missed it, but Giverny must have hit him while I was dealing with Kenneth. The blood definitely hadn't been there before. Still, it would take more than a blow to the head to keep Wade down—the blindness was more of a problem right now.

Harley! You'll kill him! my brain screamed, and I listened, but my body was still on someone else's time. *You broke Kenneth's curse with your powers; you can break hypnosis, too. COME ON!*

I grimaced as pain twisted my stomach, releasing a flood of icy Chaos syrup through my veins. The Suppressor crack was getting even bigger, and I was losing control. One moment, I was full of sparking jolts of electricity so invigorating I could have flipped a car. The next, I couldn't even feel my hands and feet anymore. Using every scrap of strength I had left, I tried to bring Telekinesis into my palms instead.

Come on, come on, come on...

A silent scream ravaged my throat. Overwhelming pain and pressure surged through my body, the leaking Chaos energy pressing down on me like a concrete block. My bones felt like they were all breaking at once. It was creeping deeper into my cells, expanding them and poisoning them, leaving no room for anything else.

But, however terrifying it might have been, it seemed to be helping. The agony and the pressure were diverting my mind away from Giverny's magnetic pull, severing the link that she'd made between us. Seizing the opportunity while I had it, I ignored the burning fireball in my hands and fixed my gaze on Wade's white eyes.

"Damnum factum est, ut dissolvat," I whispered, remembering one of the spells Bellmore had taught us. It didn't always work, but with Kenneth now miles away, I figured the hex he'd hurled would already be in a weakened state.

"What did you say?" Giverny's eyes narrowed. Behind her, the white fog across Wade's vision cleared, returning them to the deep green shade that I loved so much. Playing up the part of the hypnotized victim, I stared blankly into her eyes until she seemed satisfied that I was still completely under her spell. Her magnetic grip took hold of me again, the fireball lifting higher and burning brighter. Giverny steered me toward Wade, but he was already one step ahead. As the fireball flew from my hands, he darted out of the way and launched himself at Giverny.

She whirled around, but he drove a savage backhand against her rosy cheek, smacking her silly. Her hold on me broke. I raced across the room and snatched up the smoky glasses. I put them back on as quickly as I could, knowing Giverny would be looking for any way to get control back.

"I thought you had a rule against hitting girls," I teased as I walked back over to Wade.

He frowned, catching his breath. "What do you mean?"

"You wouldn't hit the Tatyana lookalike back in Marie's tomb. Seems like you got over that fast enough."

"I'll do anything when it's your life on the line," he replied. My Suppressor heightened the swell of sudden happiness inside me. *Not the time!* Giverny had been knocked back, but she was straining at her restraints, trying to find a way to get the last one off.

"Quick, get the jar." I pointed at Giverny and the blood dripping from her wrist. We had one shot at this before security came running.

Wade hurried over to the upended table. He ducked behind it and shot back up with the jar in his hand, brandishing it like he'd just caught a twenty-pound catfish. We met in the middle, with me gripping Giverny's arm as hard as I could. She thrashed against me, trying to tear her hand away, but I held on fast. I thought about using some more of my Telekinesis to hold her in place, but that seemed like a *really* stupid idea right now. The glass walls were already splintering; one more blast of badly timed Telekinesis and this whole place would shatter, sending us on a one-way trip down to the ground floor.

"Here, you take this." Wade pushed the jar into my hand and took over for me. He held her tight and squeezed, the veins in his forearms popping out as the blood oozed from the cut I'd made earlier in her skin. I was done being delicate about this blood-gathering procedure. She'd had her chance to do things the easy way, and if she didn't like it —well, she could blame Kenneth Willow and Katherine Shipton.

"You made me *un promettre*," Giverny hissed as the blood dropped into the jar.

I glanced at her, a curious twist of guilt turning my stomach. She'd been willing in the end. "Alton resigned as director of the San Diego Coven. He didn't get his dream. It shattered too, just like yours," I said, ignoring Wade's stare. "Let's just say he's not in a good place. There, I kept my side of the bargain. We're even."

A cold smile turned up the corners of Giverny's heart-shaped mouth. "Everything in balance. I am glad to hear zat zere is some justice in zis world."

"Well, now you can't say I didn't give you anything in return for this." I nodded to the third-full jar, which was already more than we needed. Still, it wouldn't hurt to have reserves, just in case.

My eyes flitted toward the door, where the sound of heavy boots clanged along the walkway beyond. The cavalry had arrived. *Better late than never, I guess.*

"I will be very interested to see how you talk your way out of zis one." Giverny chuckled as Wade pocketed the jar and tore a strip of fabric from his shirt. He bound it around the oozing wound, tying it tight to stem the bleeding.

"You!" one of the guards barked as they stormed into the cell. "What the hell happened here?"

I put on my most terrified face. "We were speaking with the prisoner about Remington's research when this officer just burst in and started attacking us. Only, he wasn't an officer. He was in disguise. He tried to free Giverny, but we managed to stop him," I explained rapidly. "He got away before we could capture him, but he could still be loose in Purgatory. His name is Kenneth Willow, and he works for Katherine Shipton. He's very dangerous—he needs to be caught before he can escape and get back to her. You can't let him get out."

The guards exchanged worried looks. "Hewitt, pull the lever," the leader instructed.

"Yes, sir." The guard, presumably Hewitt, stepped toward a silver box on the wall and placed his palm against a security panel. A green light flashed, checking his biometrics, before the door popped open. Inside, there was a single black lever. Hewitt yanked down hard on the lever, triggering a blaring siren that echoed through the entire building like a banshee scream. Red lights flashed down the walkway, illuminating everything in a grisly crimson glow.

"What's that?" I yelled over the din.

"The intruder alert," the leader replied.

I nodded. "I guessed as much."

The whole group turned as another set of boots pounded on the steel walkway, and Mallenberg appeared a moment later. He stared at the mess in the cell, stunned into silence. His eyes darted between Wade, Giverny, and me as he tried to put the pieces together.

"What happened?" he gasped.

"Kenneth Willow, an associate of Katherine Shipton, attacked us while we were speaking to the prisoner. He tried to free her, and now he's on the loose," I replied.

"And the guards stationed along here?" He gestured back at the walkway.

I hesitated. "I think they might be dead. I'm sorry, Officer."

He swore loudly and punched the wall. "I should never have left you. I'm sorry for this. Killingworth, take two men and carry this guard's body down to the infirmary." He pointed to the figure on the floor, who blocked the doorway. "We need to get Ms. Le Fay locked up again. You two, wait outside until I've got everything handled."

Wade and I didn't need to be told twice. As Mallenberg clapped the Atomic Cuff back onto Giverny's wrist, we watched from the outside ledge.

"We'll have to take her to a different cell once the alarms stop. I'll put this floor on lockdown until we can find one," Mallenberg said, his voice drifting through from the cell. As he worked at double-cuffing Giverny, the dead guard was carried away between three of the additional officers, all of them disappearing into the elevator at the far side of the cavernous hallway. I watched them take him away, feeling the heavy weight of his death.

Meanwhile, the other four maximum-security prisoners were going ape in their cells, slamming their fists into the walls and howling wildly. We couldn't hear them, but we could see the expressions of glee on their twisted faces.

I felt terrible for the way things had gone. I'd caused Mallenberg's sudden sickness with my Empathy, but if he'd been here, would he have survived Kenneth? The other guards hadn't been that lucky. Even so, I'd been the one to loosen him up too much, and now he was riddled with regret and self-loathing. I had a feeling some of it was mine, feeding into him and emphasizing his own guilt. Back in New Orleans, I'd killed a person, and I'd handed over my dad's note as if it were nothing. With my soul restored, those thoughts had pounced into my head, filling me with remorse and a gut-wrenching hatred for what I'd given up so easily. Mallenberg had been on the receiving end of it. After all, the Suppressor was going haywire. I could still feel the sluggish ooze of its poisonous Chaos moving through my veins, pushing me toward the brink of death.

TWENTY

Harley

With Giverny safely secured in a new cell, Mallenberg returned to us. The other guards had gone to investigate how Kenneth had managed to get into Purgatory undetected, leaving us alone on the ledge. I tried not to look down, but it was impossible not to.

"I just got word that Kenneth Willow escaped," Mallenberg said bitterly, wiping blood onto his uniform.

"How do you know that?" Wade asked.

"We saw him on the security footage, running outside the compound. The guards couldn't apprehend him," he replied. "On his way out, though, he made an attempt on Finch Shipton's life."

I stared at him with wide eyes. "Kenneth tried to kill Finch?"

Mallenberg nodded. "Yeah, not too long ago."

"Is he okay?"

"He's in a bad state, but a couple of guards took him down to the infirmary."

The news hit me harder than I'd ever have expected. Panic flooded my senses, mixed with a deep-rooted sadness. We may not have had the best relationship, but still, he was my brother, and I'd had hopes of getting him back on the right side of things. The thought of him almost dying at Kenneth's hands made my blood boil and my heart ache, all of it intensified tenfold by the leaking Suppressor. I knew I was running out of time to break this thing, and the pain in my body was only getting worse, but I *had* to go and see Finch. I had to see what Kenneth had done, with my own eyes, and make sure Finch was okay.

"Can you take us to him?"

Wade frowned. "Harley, we have to get going."

"No, we have to do this first. I need to see him." The desperation in my voice silenced Wade.

"Then follow me," Mallenberg said.

We took the elevator all the way below ground, riding it down as far as it would go, to "Level -10." I didn't know what was on the other subterranean floors, but I guessed it'd be boring day-to-day stuff. Five minutes later, the doors pinged and opened out onto an enormous hospital, a world away from the small facility at the SDC. Doctors and nurses rushed around full rows of beds, seeing to all kinds of nasties— wounds, hexes, curses, missing limbs.

Mallenberg led us through two massive wards with most of their beds occupied and down a sterile hallway toward a smaller unit. There were officers absolutely everywhere, covering every possible means of escape. *Yet nobody noticed a complete stranger snooping about?* Then again, his disguise had fooled us, too.

"He's over there." Mallenberg pointed to a bed at the far end of the quieter ward, where eight of the ten beds had people sleeping in them.

I smiled. "Thank you, and I… uh, I'm sorry that all of this mess has happened on your watch. For what it's worth, I don't think any of it was your fault. Kenneth came in here knowing what he wanted. You wouldn't have been able to stop him."

Mallenberg nodded. "Nevertheless, it's my job to try. I left my post. I am solely responsible, whether I could have prevented it or not."

I didn't know what else to say to that, so I walked toward Finch's bedside without saying anything at all. Mallenberg joined us, his hand resting on the hilt of one of his shock sticks. Finch lay curled up beneath the covers, looking oddly small and vulnerable. He had a pair of Atomic Cuffs on his wrists, the same as everyone else in the infirmary, even though he was out cold. A physician was working away on some deep wounds in his shoulder, dangerously close to his heart, using charms and potions to try to heal them back up.

"We must stay on alert," Mallenberg warned. "A team has been sent to look beyond the prison for Kenneth Willow, but that doesn't mean you're safe."

"Someone overlooked him somewhere. That has to be how he got in," I mused. "Either that, or there's someone in this place who's working for Katherine or is at least on her freaking payroll."

Mallenberg's frown deepened. "That may be so, but that's not your concern, Miss Merlin. Allow us to do the investigating. The sooner you're done here, the sooner I may safely see you back out."

I looked down at Finch again, rage boiling my blood. Katherine had sent one of her cronies to get the job done—the job she couldn't bring herself to do. But why had Katherine chosen now to kill Finch? He was out of her way here, no threat to anyone. What was she so afraid of?

"You remember I asked if you were here to see Finch again, Miss Merlin?" Mallenberg's tone softened.

I nodded.

"Well, there was a reason for that. I know you've been to see him a couple of times since he came here, but the thing is, *he* has been the one asking for you lately. He's entitled to one visit a week, and he was demanding to get in touch with you over the last three or so days."

"Me? But he hates me." I glanced at his sleeping figure and wondered what was going on in his unconscious mind.

Mallenberg shrugged. "Maybe he had a change of heart. The isolation gets to a lot of our inmates, and they end up begging to see just about anyone."

I turned to Wade. "Do you think it might have something to do with Adley's death? Astrid said that Garrett had visited Finch and told him what had happened to her, and that Katherine was responsible. Maybe he wants to cooperate now."

"I was wondering the same thing," he replied. "It'd definitely explain why Kenneth was sent to kill him on Katherine's behalf, and it makes sense why she wants Le Fay. That Hypno ability would probably be useful. Just think, she could persuade world leaders to do what she wants."

I shuddered. "I don't even want to think about that. Still, killing Finch? That seems like too much, even for Katherine. He's her son! She loves him, somewhere in that hollow shell she calls a soul—she risked the success of a hugely powerful spell just to spare him. Plus, she would've killed him sooner if she'd wanted to. Why now?"

Wade smiled sadly. "It's about love."

"I don't follow."

"Finch's love for Adley. Katherine hadn't counted on it being real, especially as Finch made it look like she was just a way in to all the right places," he explained. "But it was real. Garrett confirmed as much to me, from the way Finch talked about her. I guess Katherine didn't care what it would do to Finch if she got Adley killed, or didn't think it would matter, anyway. She probably just offed Adley as a diversion to get Quetzi out of there, which would make her collateral damage. Katherine didn't see the bigger picture."

I frowned. "I'm still not seeing it."

"The loss of the one you love can change you forever, Harley," he continued. "To that person, it's so much more than collateral damage. It's their heart breaking irreparably."

I couldn't help but sense a hidden meaning in his words... one addressed to me, personally. We hadn't really had much time to talk about what had happened today, and we'd quickly swept our kiss under the rug. Had I somehow hurt him when I'd lost my soul? Did he think he'd lost me? I wanted to tell him that wasn't true, that he hadn't and would never lose me, but now wasn't the time. Especially considering I couldn't actually promise that he wouldn't lose me. There was so much we needed to do before I could break the Suppressor properly, and if I didn't get the spell right or get it done in time… game over.

"You think hearing about Adley's death made him change his mind about Katherine?" I asked, skipping over the hidden message.

"She probably decided he was a liability now. He knows a lot about her and likely knows some things she doesn't want us finding out about," he replied. "If he's been asking for you, then, clearly, he may want to cooperate with us. Katherine could never allow that. Killing him was, and still is, a necessity for her, even if she doesn't necessarily want to do it."

I gingerly touched Finch's hand. He stirred and mumbled something incoherent. His face contorted as if he was having a nightmare, his fingertips curling around my palm like he was grasping for a lifejacket. *I guess your whole life has been a nightmare, huh?* I couldn't escape the similarities between us, no matter how hard I tried. Only, he'd had a mother who'd abandoned him to someone else, while my mother had been killed by his. Still, that kind of thing could destroy a child's mental stability. Finch was living proof of that, and, though I hated to admit it, I sort of felt sorry for him.

"If that's true, and his life is still in danger, then I need to be the first one to know when he wakes up." I looked at the physician and then at Mallenberg. "This is personal to me, but it also involves the wellbeing of the entire magical world. Sounds dramatic, I know, but it's the truth. I need to be the first one to know."

Mallenberg crossed his arms. "We can let you know when he wakes up, but other authorities might want to speak with him first if he has information regarding Katherine."

"I'm the only one he'll talk to when he wakes up," I said. "If you want to get anything out of him, then you have to call me. So much rests on this. Please, make sure it happens."

Mallenberg sighed. "All right. We'll mark you as top priority when he wakes up. Dr. Ganglion, can you ensure that Miss Merlin is called the instant he's alert?"

The physician nodded. "Certainly, Officer. I'll place her name and number on the top of the list."

After exchanging details and saying a quiet goodbye to Finch, we followed Mallenberg back out of the infirmary and down to the main entrance hall. The sirens were still blaring, and Kenneth was still on the loose somewhere beyond the prison, but we had a Suppressor to break. I could feel the seconds of my life ticking away. We had the blood of Giverny Le Fay, which would give us the thirteen drops of Light for the Sanguine spell. Now we needed the Dark, and that was going to be a whole new challenge. *And don't even get me started on the Librarian.* I really couldn't see the light at the end of this mission's tunnel. Not yet, anyway.

"Back to San Francisco?" Wade prompted as I made a beeline for the mirror that usually led back to the SDC.

I paused and backtracked quickly, realizing that Mallenberg was still close by. "Yes, of course. We've got to get this research to Remington." I didn't want him to start suspecting us of being involved in this. Plus, I didn't want Levi catching us if we came through the SDC mirrors.

"After you, then." He directed me toward the San Francisco mirror and urged me through.

I stepped into the welcoming foyer of the San Francisco Coven, with its twinkling lights and rock walls. The receptionist just rolled his eyes and gestured for us to head through to Remington's office. We walked through the corridors until we came to his office, only to find it empty of people.

"Garrett and Tatyana must have the information by now." Wade's tone was worried. I was worried, too.

"Let's head back to the SDC and see if they've gone back there first," I suggested.

"Good idea."

I pressed my earpiece and waited for the telltale crackle. "Jacob, do you read?"

"Loud and clear," he replied a second or two later.

"We need you to come and get us from San Francisco."

"Okie doke, I'll be with you in a couple of minutes." He didn't sound too perturbed, which calmed me slightly.

"Oh, and Jacob?"

"Yeah."

"Is Tatyana with you?"

There was a brief silence, in which my heart was firmly in my throat. "Yeah, she's here. Garrett, too. They came back about half an hour ago—looks like Tatyana dragged him back with her."

I breathed a sigh of relief. "That's good. We'll see you in a couple of minutes, then. We need you to get us from outside Remington's office, so if you can ask one of them to give you directions, that'd be great. We don't want you ending up in someone else's office."

"Will do. Hang tight." With that, he was gone. All we could do now was wait.

TWENTY-ONE

Harley

After portaling back to the SDC, we'd all gathered in the dining hall, where dinner was being served. I needed to make a show of being around to appease "Lord Levi," who sat at the top table with the rest of the preceptors. Wade and I had already brought everyone up to speed on what had happened in Purgatory, while Tatyana and Garrett had told them about New Orleans—everything they hadn't heard over the earpieces, anyway. A tense atmosphere had settled around us; we were eager to move forward with the tasks at hand, but we had to make sure Levi saw us around in case he started to smell a rat.

Only Raffe was absent from the party. "He's not good at being in a room with Levi, not even one this big," Santana explained, packing up some food for him. "We don't want a djinn loose at dinnertime. Blood and guts spilling everywhere is the quickest way to ruin everyone's appetite."

I noticed that Garrett was pretty quiet too. "What happened in San Francisco?" I asked. The dinner bell had rung before we could get to that part, and everyone was required to attend these "family" meals. Another stupid rule of Levi's creation.

"Remington didn't tell us where she was, if that's what you're getting at," Garrett replied sullenly. "He's mega paranoid about people finding out where she is and wouldn't give the location to us straight. He mentioned something about bugs and microphones, but I think he's being a bit melodramatic. Anyway, he said he'd text a message through but we'd have to decipher the location. We're still waiting. I sent word to LA that I'd be here for a bit, for 'research,' so they won't be on my case for a while."

Tatyana nodded. "He was extremely on edge. I think he's more terrified of Levi than we are."

I glanced up at the top table, where the big kahuna himself was chatting with the rest of the preceptors. Nobody seemed comfortable around him, which was both sad and funny at the same time. The most uncomfortable one was Nomura, who sat as far from Levi as possible. Even so, the angst, grief, and fear oozed off him in a palpable wave, slamming into my Suppressor to the point where I was starting to feel queasy. Then again, with this thing inside me, queasiness had become my constant state.

What's going on in that head of yours, huh, Nomura? What had Levi done to make him feel like this? Maybe they'd clashed over Alton, or these new rules—it was hard to tell from a bunch of random, intense emotions.

"Do you think there's a chance he might not text?" I wondered aloud.

Garrett shrugged. "It's up to him, but he seemed pretty worried we might spill the beans if he didn't."

"Maybe he's trying to think of the right cryptic message," Jacob, still wearing his Tarver mask, suggested.

Astrid nodded. "That makes sense. He'd need something vague enough to confuse any potential snoopers, but clear enough that we'll understand what he's trying to say." I felt much closer to Astrid after my lost soul incident, now that I could understand the void inside her much better. She seemed to know that, too, from the way she kept glancing at me with curious eyes.

It worried me that Garrett and Tatyana had left San Francisco without an answer, but at least we were one step closer to breaking the Suppressor. After dinner, we were heading to the Bestiary to speak with Tobe, which would hopefully lead to the Dark blood from Echidna. Once we had that, I could get this thing out of me for good.

"How is Raffe?" I turned to Santana, who hadn't eaten much of her own food. That wasn't like her at all.

She tilted her head from side to side. "We're working on some self-control techniques, but I've never seen him like this. He's struggling, to be honest—really struggling. Levi is the only person I know who can boil his oysters like this. And if he can't get his anger under control, he'll have to stay put, which isn't exactly an option. He can't just hide until Levi leaves."

"So how do we get rid of Leonidas Levi?" Louella whispered.

Santana grinned. "Box him up with a big red ribbon and send him as a peace offering to Katherine?"

"Or 'accidentally' shove him into the Ibong Adarna's cage?" Dylan added.

"Slip something into his dinner?" Jacob replied with a smirk.

Tatyana chuckled. "Maybe let Harley's Suppressor loose on him?"

"We need to focus on the task at hand," Isadora cut in. "I'll come up with something for Levi, even if it's just to get him off our backs."

"How very mysterious of you." I smiled at her, knowing the problem would be in good hands. She was still seething at him after being told she couldn't leave, and that anger was a great motivator. Plus, she had experience with this kind of thing that we didn't. After what she'd told me in her letter, about being held captive by other covens, I figured she'd know a thing or two about getting people to do what she wanted to get them off her case.

"Everyone done?" Wade asked impatiently. A rumble of assent murmured around the group. "Right, then we should get going." He'd been jittery ever since we'd come back from Purgatory, though I couldn't blame him. He'd witnessed my Suppressor cracking even more, and now that Kenneth was on the loose, we were facing a lot of potential trouble.

We waited until a few more people got up to leave before heading out of the dining hall and toward the Bestiary. Levi watched us go with suspicious eyes. I was starting to wonder whether that was just what his eyes looked like—he'd stared suspiciously for so long that they'd stuck that way. Mrs. Smith had always warned me it could happen. Still, it was creepy and annoying to be constantly under observation. *George Orwell, eat your heart out.*

Just before he exited, I noticed Wade throw a subtle nod in Levi's direction, with the boss man giving a small nod back. An instant expression of smug satisfaction spread across Levi's face.

"What was that about?" I whispered to Wade.

"Just letting him know I'm still 'spying' on his behalf." An amused smile twitched at his lips.

"What have you been telling him about me? All the gory details?"

Wade chuckled. "I told him you've been holing yourself up in the Forbidden Zone's library and spending a lot of time going through all the medicines in Dr. Krieger's pharmacy. I also told him you'd taken a new interest in observing the creatures in the Bestiary. I figured Tobe and Krieger would cover for us if Levi decided to follow up."

"Is he buying it?"

Wade nodded. "You should have seen how smug he was when I fed him all that info. He thinks he's got us on the end of a tight leash, and he's got no idea that the collar is actually around *his* neck."

I chuckled. "Man, that feels good."

"Doesn't it?" Wade flashed me a pleased grin as we continued on through the corridors.

Garrett's phone was glued to his hand as we walked to the Bestiary and pushed through the huge double doors, citing a meeting with Tobe to get past the hordes of security personnel that crowded the place. A few scorch marks and cracked cages were all that remained of Quetzi's escape, aside from a new steel tube that had been fitted around the Bestiary's central conductor to protect it from any external blasts. Charms thrummed all the way along it, the engraved symbols glowing in the dim light.

"Looks like you haven't escaped Levi's new rules," I said as we approached Tobe. He was wiping a cloth across the glass of a small red imp's cage, a look of irritation fixed on his feline features. Annoyance swelled from him, directed at the security personnel who stood at intervals all the way down the main hall.

"I have no privacy anymore. It is quite ridiculous," he muttered, stowing his cloth away beneath his wing. "They don't seem to realize that it is making the Purge beasts anxious, and it is hardly doing wonders for my own nerves. At any moment, I fear they may clap me in irons and carry me away, for no reason other than breathing too hard. Bull-headed imbeciles, the lot of them, smearing their greasy fingertips on every surface they can find."

I'd never really seen Tobe annoyed. He was normally the one person I could count on to be level-headed, but normalcy seemed to have gone right out the window.

"If it makes you feel any better, he's pissing all of us off," Santana chimed in.

Tobe smiled. "It doesn't, but I thank you for your humor. Now, what brings you to my proverbial door on this irksome evening?"

"We've got a favor to ask," I replied. This was going to be a tough one to explain without Tobe immediately kicking us out for being reckless. "We need to visit Echidna, and it's literally a matter of life and death. My Suppressor is slowly killing me, and I need some blood from her in order to break it. You know us, Tobe—we wouldn't be here asking you this if it wasn't serious."

He furrowed his furry brow. "You know who you're dealing with, yes? Echidna is not called the Mother of Monsters for no reason. She is extraordinarily dangerous, Harley. It really wouldn't be safe for you to visit her in any capacity."

"Even if it means me dying?"

A sad glint flickered in his amber eyes. "It has really become so dire?"

I nodded. "Afraid so. I've cracked it, and it's leaking like crazy. That much pent-up Chaos is apparently poisonous to a magical. Who knew, right? The very thing that makes us magicals strong is also the thing that's going to end me."

"And there is no other way you can break this Suppressor?" He tapped his claws together nervously.

"This is the only way to get the right spell to work."

After a moment's pause, he nodded. "Then there is no other choice but to allow you this, for I will not be held responsible for your death. I will do what I can for you, Harley. I will bring Echidna out of the freezing curse that binds her to her box, but it will take some time to thaw her out in the proper manner."

"How long?"

"That, I cannot say. I will have to contact you when the process is complete. Are your time constraints really so pressing?" He sounded like a concerned mother worried about her brood.

I smiled wryly. "Kind of, yeah."

"I will make it as swift as I'm able," he promised. He was about to open his mouth and say something else when Garrett's and Astrid's phones pinged loudly. Astrid didn't bother to check hers, but we all turned toward Garrett, no doubt thinking the same thing: had

Remington finally gotten in touch with the message that would lead us to the Librarian?

Garrett frowned. "'Where the Elysian Fields meet great Triumph, that is where you will find the Sacred Heart. It is in the hands of Our Lady.' What the heck does that mean?"

Astrid grinned. "Paris. She's in Paris."

"Eh?" Garrett looked up, bemused.

"Elysian Fields equals Champs-Elysées. At the top of the Champs-Elysées is the Arc de Triomphe, which means Arch of Triumph. Sacré-Cœur is another Parisian landmark, which means Sacred Heart. And the last one translates to Notre Dame in French. That must be where she is." We all stared at her in awe and admiration. I definitely wouldn't have figured it out so quickly, if at all.

Garrett smiled. "See, this is why you're the best. I have a hard enough time with English."

"What on earth are you up to?" Tobe interjected, looking surprised and confused by the random outburst of French. I realized we probably shouldn't have said so much in front of him. He wasn't exactly on Levi's side, but he had to toe the line. That was part of his job description. Still, with so much at stake, I hoped we could persuade him not to say anything.

"You can't tell a soul what you've heard," I whispered. "This has to do with stopping Katherine."

"Harley, I really don't think you should be—"

I cut him off. "If Levi gets his hands on the woman we're looking for, he'll just lock her in a box somewhere and throw away the key for 'safety reasons' or some other bullcrap. He doesn't care about any of us." I took a deep breath. "I know this sounds crazy, but I feel powerful enough to take on Katherine. I just need this woman's help to do that. I can't do anything if Levi finds out what we're up to. He'll probably lock me up, too, and let the Suppressor kill me."

Tobe was silent for a full minute after I'd finished, which kept us all on edge. Everyone's anxiety hit me at once, again and again, like I was on the ropes getting pummeled by a heavyweight. This Suppressor was already taking way too much out of me; I didn't know how much longer I could deal with it without crumbling under the weight of the stress. That would probably get me long before the poison could.

"I'm sorry for these trials that you are facing," he said at last. "I sympathize with your plight, I truly do. And it is no secret that I am not particularly fond of our new director, even though I have little choice but to cooperate with him. Nevertheless, the Bestiary will always be my domain, quite apart from the everyday running of the coven. What goes on within these walls stays within these walls. To the best of my ability, anyway." His eyes turned sad, the subtext clear—he missed Quetzi. We all did.

"Does that mean you'll help us?" Wade pressed.

He nodded. "I will work with all of you and ensure that Echidna is suitably defrosted upon your return from… wherever it is you're going. I have no idea what it is you are up to, and I don't wish to know." He flashed a comical wink. "Isadora may assist me in the defrosting procedure, as I require a powerful magical to achieve it."

"I would be happy to help," Isadora replied. Being called on by Tobe was a noble thing; he didn't do that for just anyone, and I knew Isadora had to feel proud of the fact that he'd asked her.

I looked at Santana. "You might have to do that thing again." I arched a conspiratorial eyebrow.

"No problem. I'll get on it right away."

"And we're going to need you." I smiled at Jacob, who was already nodding.

To my surprise, Wade stepped in. "We can head off at first light. You've had the longest day in living history, and you'll be no good to anyone if you haven't slept, Harley. *Tarver* here has had a pretty exhausting day, too. This is non-negotiable. You at least need a few hours' rest before we leave."

I pulled a sour face, but I knew he was right. I was tired to the very center of my bones, my entire body aching from the lack of soul, the running, the fighting, and the fear that had taken hold of me over the last twelve or so hours. Paris wasn't going to go anywhere—I just hoped Odette wouldn't either.

Tatyana chuckled and slipped her arms around Dylan's waist, hugging him from behind. "Isn't it sweet when these boys look out for us?" Jacob turned beet red and stared into the nearest box, catching the eye of a Redcap goblin. It made me smile, even though I knew he was struggling with his teenage emotions. *Poor kid.* He'd have been better off staring at a Victoria's Secret catalogue, for all the good his crush would do him.

"That goes for the rest of you, too, since you'll be the ones running diversions again," Wade said.

"I'm pretty beat," Louella admitted. She'd spent the day listening out for every single noise in the coven to make sure the coast was constantly clear. She needed to be properly focused if she was going to do it again tomorrow.

Isadora smiled. "I think it's a very sensible suggestion. We should reconvene in the usual place just before dawn."

Déjà vu... Realizing this was an argument I probably wasn't going to win, I made a grunt of agreement.

Leaving Isadora to discuss Echidna proceedings with Tobe, the rest of us headed out of the Bestiary and back to the living quarters. I found myself walking alongside Tatyana, Santana, and Astrid, while Louella and the boys went on ahead. Wade had lagged behind for a moment before Dylan had dragged him away to give us women the chance to talk.

"So that ping that went off at the same time as Garrett's? I'm guessing that wasn't a coincidence," I said as we wandered along.

Astrid smiled shyly. "That was my insurance. I cloned his phone after he got back from San Francisco so that every message would be directed to me." A sudden expression of alarm rippled across her face. "I've deleted the clone now, though. I just wanted to make sure he couldn't hide anything that Remington might send through."

She and I looked at one another, two matching grins spreading over our faces. "You did good, Hepler."

"Not too stalkerish?"

"Not now that you've deleted it," I replied with a wink.

Tatyana smiled at us. "Dylan was asking how we'd managed to get Remington on our side like that. He wouldn't stop asking, the moment we got back. I figured it was just the threat of us exposing his lover, but Dylan seemed to think there was something more."

Astrid and I exchanged another look.

"Maybe he felt like he owed us another favor," I said cryptically. We'd promised to keep Remington's relation to Dylan private, since it wasn't really our business. But, deep down, I hoped that Remington would tell Dylan the truth soon. He deserved to know he still had family out there, even if what had happened to his parents was heartbreaking. I was just grateful that the secrecy, alongside the Odette thing, had worked to our advantage. And that Astrid had been bold enough to do what she'd done with Garrett's phone. We cared about Garrett, as a group, but we knew he could be quite the sociopath when he wanted to get something done. We couldn't have risked him keeping the text from us.

Anyway, at least now we knew where to find the Librarian. One thought remained as we headed for our rooms: with Marie Laveau, Giverny Le Fay, and now Odette, I was really going to have to start learning French.

TWENTY-TWO

Harley

I n a twist of time-zone wizardry, we technically arrived in what turned out to be the Paris Coven earlier than we'd left San Diego. It was five in the morning for us but eight o'clock the previous evening for them as Jacob opened a portal right below the beautiful architecture of Notre Dame Cathedral. I was sort of sad we wouldn't actually get to see any of it, but at least we were on our way to finding the Librarian.

Back at the SDC, half an hour before we'd been due to leave, we'd received news that Garrett had been called back to LA and wouldn't be coming. With no time to waste, we'd had to go on without him. If he didn't like that, then it was his tough luck; he should've been there with us instead of running errands for LA.

I fumbled around in the darkness of the room that Jacob had brought us to, searching for a light switch. My Fire abilities were way too temperamental to use to light our way, and we didn't want to draw attention with Wade doing the honors. A crash of metal made me freeze. I'd knocked something over, but I wasn't sure what. A moment later, my hand closed over a string dangling from the ceiling. I pulled it, and an anemic bulb shed its sickly yellow glow on what appeared to be a broom closet.

"Really, Jacob?" I teased.

He shrugged shyly. "My destinations are still glitchy sometimes. I'm getting the hang of it, though. Just be grateful we didn't end up in the Vatican instead."

"What makes you think we haven't?" Wade smiled and nudged Jacob in the arm. It looked like the relationship between them was thawing after the Quetzi incident, and I was glad to see it. Wade had been harder on Jacob than anyone since then, but I guessed all this portal stuff was bringing him around. Plus, he was staying with us this time in case we needed to make a quick getaway, and there was no room for grudges. Heck, there was no room at all in this tiny broom closet.

"Why am I thinking about sardines?" I grinned, moving toward the door. I opened it and peered out into the single most beautiful corridor I'd ever freaking seen. Gabled archways curved across the ceiling, an explosion of gilded craftsmanship embellishing every single surface, my eyes blinded by mirrors and gold. I wondered if we'd somehow ended up in Versailles, rather than Notre Dame. All it was missing was Marie Antoinette appearing in a fluffy wig and a dress as wide as a house, shouting, "Let them eat cake!"

With the coast clear, we tumbled out of the broom closet and dusted ourselves off. In the distance, people were walking the halls, dressed in head-to-toe couture. Givenchy, Dior, Louis Vuitton, Chanel—they had all the labels, apparently fresh from the runway. One woman was wearing a dress so outlandish—made from a patchwork of brightly colored brocade fabrics, with a near six-foot train flowing behind her—that I thought my eyes might pop out of my head. Most of the magicals were more understated, in ascots, neutral-toned garments that were perfectly tailored, and sharp three-piece suits, but each one screamed elegance and style… and huge expense.

Welcome to Paris. Wade looked like he belonged, in a smart white shirt and a dark gray waistcoat, complete with matching suit pants, but I… well, I looked like I'd been dragged in off the street, with my biker boots and leather jacket and a scruffy band t-shirt underneath. Jacob wasn't exactly high fashion, either, in jeans and an old sports sweater.

"We're going to get the whole 'coarse Americans' thing again, aren't we?" I mumbled.

Wade smiled. "I told you, you should've dressed up."

"This *is* me dressing up."

"Come on, we need to be stealthy here. Just zip your jacket up and try to look presentable."

I scowled at him. *Easy for you to say.* Jacob, on the other hand, was staring up at the architecture, his mouth hanging open. We definitely looked like tourists, but maybe that was a better excuse than the real reason we were here. I mean, the magical world had to have magical tourists, right? Why else would the Paris Coven have gone to all this effort?

"Follow my lead, and duck behind something whenever we see other people," Wade said as he set off down the hallway. Jacob and I had no choice but to follow, since he seemed to know what he was doing. Each coven had a different layout, and this place was even more labyrinthine than the other ones I'd visited.

Obeying Wade's instructions, Jacob and I darted behind walls, doorways, cabinets, and somewhat raunchy statues whenever magicals appeared in the corridors. Wade didn't look so out of place, and since he was the only one who could speak French, he needed to do all the talking. A second text had come from Remington, stating that we needed to "find the Sacred Heart of healing within," which we'd guessed meant the infirmary. I frowned as Wade caught the attention of a stunning French magical dressed in a sleek blush-colored dress that hugged her figure perfectly.

Don't get jealous, or you might end up blowing these mirrors to smithereens. I struggled with my emotions, trying everything to force them down. I pictured Levi in his boxers, hoping it might make me feel sick enough to distract my attention away from Wade and the French *belle*.

"*Bonjour Mademoiselle, excusez moi. Pouvez-vous m'aider avec un petit problème?*" Wade's smooth French accent, and the way he was rolling those Rs, made it *very* hard to concentrate on anything else.

The woman smiled. "*Oui monsieur, j'ai un moment pour toi. Quel-est le problème?*"

"*Ma tante est malade, et je ne sais pas où se trouve l'infirmerie. Ou l'hôpital? Pardon, je suis Irlandais et mon français n'est pas très bon. En plus, je ne sais pas comment décrire les choses.*" It sounded like fluid poetry coming from his lips.

Focus, Harley. Remember the mirrors!

"*Tu te trompes, Monsieur. Ton français est excellent!*" She giggled, prompting a spike of jealousy to jolt through me. "*Comme pour l'infirmerie, c'est là. Suivez les indications pour la Sacre Cœur, et tu trouveras ta tante.*"

There's a mouthful. Not that I had a clue what they were saying. I guessed he was asking for directions and making up some kind of cover for why we needed to go to the infirmary here.

"*Merci, Mademoiselle. Tu es trop gentil.*" Wade flashed her a polite smile, and I wanted to punch them both in the face. Either that, or I wanted to walk over and pull him away in my usual elephant-in-a-china-shop fashion. My Suppressor was doing the talking, but I didn't mind giving it the reins for this. I guessed it was sort of how Raffe felt with his djinn, now that Levi was around all the time.

"*De rien, Monsieur,*" she replied coyly. "*J'espère que ta tante va bien.*"

"*Merci, Mademoiselle. Moi, aussi.*"

We came out of our hiding place as the slinky woman left, to find a very smug Wade watching her go. Heck, even I was watching her leave —it was impossible to take my eyes off her. It was like she wasn't even made of flesh and bone but some kind of liquid substance instead.

"Did you enjoy that?" I asked coldly.

"It's been ages since I've used my French. I thought I'd be rusty. Turns out I'm okay."

I frowned. "When it counts, right?"

"What did she say?" Jacob cut in, clearly worried I was going to start shooting sparks out of my eyes or something.

"She said to follow the signs that read 'Sacred Heart' and it'll lead us to the infirmary." He pointed up at one of the gilded signposts, which were covered in French words I couldn't understand. Still, as long as he understood, we'd be okay. It looked like the sexy French girl had jogged his memory enough to get us there, as well as a few other things. Not that I was jealous. *Yeah, right.*

"You know, that French girl was pretty hot," Jacob said suddenly as we followed the signs for the hospital. "They're just going about their ordinary days, and they look like supermodels. Don't you think that's funny? It'd be so weird if Harley suddenly started wandering about in some expensive dress."

I shot him a look. "That's hilarious, Jake."

He blushed. "I didn't mean... I just meant you wouldn't look like you if you were dressed like them."

"Word of warning to you, Jacob, *never* get involved with a high-maintenance girl. I prefer the more natural kind of girl, though I suppose it's personal taste." Wade glanced at me with a sweet smile that made my jealousy melt away. *Smooth, Crowley.* I practically buzzed with happiness as we walked the rest of the way to the infirmary, even when another cluster of daring, sexy-as-heck French girls giggled and swooned over him.

Every hallway was like something out of a museum or a stately home, with random chairs of cream and gold that looked too fancy to even sit on. Huge paintings hung from the walls, showing Renaissance scenes of biblical tales alongside ballet dancers in sharp brushstrokes. There even seemed to be an original of Delacroix's "Liberty Leading the People," presumably to remind the Paris coven what they were always fighting for—Liberté, Egalité, Fraternité. I remembered the painting from art class in school, with the powerful image of Liberté as a bare-breasted woman waving a French flag atop a pile of dead bodies. "Haunting and beautiful" didn't even begin to describe it close up, and I paused for a moment to properly admire it.

"I prefer these ones." Wade pointed to a painting nearby showing three beautiful, red-headed women, their skin like peaches and cream. The one in the middle was playing a harp, while the two above her were staring away with a sad wistfulness. "Rossetti, I think. This one reminds me of you." He pointed to the girl with big blue eyes and tumbling red hair in the top-left corner.

"She looks so sad."

He smiled. "So do you, sometimes."

"I hate art." Jacob broke the tension with his blunt commentary. "We used to get dragged around galleries at school. Didn't like it then, don't like it now. I don't get how you can read so many things in a picture, you know? I always thought people were just making it up, saying whatever to make themselves sound smart."

A laugh burst out of my throat, and a broad grin spread across Wade's face. *Way to kill my vibe, Jake.* Then again, it was probably for the best—now wasn't the time for flirting and games. We had the Librarian to track down, preferably before anyone else got to her.

Fifteen minutes of awestruck admiration later, we found ourselves at the door to the infirmary. It was just as impressive as everything else, with carved wooden vines climbing up the frame and branching out across the ivory doors. The winged specter of the medical symbol—the caduceus—had been embossed into each panel, with the customary snakes twisting around the central staff. There was no denying we were in the right place; we just had to hope Odette was here. I'd be having a stern word with Remington if she wasn't.

Wade pushed open the door and ushered us inside. A strange hush blanketed the cavernous room beyond, which looked more like a five-star hotel than a hospital. Most of the beds were empty, the same as at the SDC, but this put our poky little infirmary to shame. A doctor was doing her rounds at the far side of the room, but she turned as we entered. She looked just as elegant as the rest of the coven's inhabitants, wearing a cream silk suit that buttoned all the way to her neck. *No Crocs here.* Instead, she wore cream loafers, with the interlinking Cs of Chanel on the tongue. I wondered how she'd react if anyone dared to bleed all over her designer gear.

"*Bonjour, Madam. Tu parles en Anglais?*" Wade asked as she walked toward us.

She frowned. "*Oui, pourquoi?*" I guessed that kind of defeated the point of being asked if she spoke English. I was starting to admire the spunk of these French folk.

"We're looking for a friend of ours, and we have confirmation that she's here. Odette de Salignac?" Wade replied. "I'm Wade, and these are my… uh, associates. Harley and Jacob."

She dipped her head. "*Bonjour. Je suis Dr. Fenélon.*"

Are you sure you speak English?

"Is Odette here?" I jumped in. Now that we were here, I was all too eager to get Odette and get out again.

"How do you know of her?" Dr. Fenélon asked stiffly. "You should not know zat she is here."

"We're friends, like my associate here said," I lied. A movement in the adjoining room, which could be seen through a gilded archway, caught my eye. Garrett was creeping across the gap, heading for a door in the passageway between the two rooms. He hadn't spotted us, or at least I didn't think he had. And that wasn't the worst of it—it was definitely Garrett, but dressed in a nurse's outfit, sleek pencil skirt and all. I'd caught him mid-Shift, his clothes having switched, but his body still catching up.

What the…

He was up to something. He said he'd been paged to go back to the LA Coven, but here he was.

"Where have you come from?" Dr. Fenélon asked, drawing my attention away from Nurse Garrett.

Wade cleared his throat. "We're from the Houston Coven. My full name is Wade Crowley. You can call the director there to confirm; just ask for Director Crowley—she'll confirm." He was lying so blatantly that I knew he'd never be able to forgive himself. Name-dropping his parents didn't come easily to him, but I figured he was taking the lead so I didn't end up putting Dr. Fenélon in some kind of Empathy coma. We didn't want a repeat of what had happened to Mallenberg.

Dr. Fenélon took out her phone as Wade handed her a business card from the top pocket of his waistcoat. I caught a glimpse of his parents' names—Cormac and Felicity Crowley—with their direct lines written underneath. *Felicity?* It had the elite flavor I'd expected, but it still came as a surprise. I guessed Wade got his Irish side from his dad, judging by the name.

"I know ze Crowleys well," Dr. Fenélon said, and she seemed impressed. Beside me, Wade paled. I guessed he hadn't anticipated his parents knowing the physician here.

She dialed the number and put the phone to her ear. Aside from the intro, where she told Wade's mom what was going on and who she was dealing with, we couldn't hear what was being said. There were just a couple of nods and several *Oui, Madam*'s. Eventually, she hung up and returned her attention to us.

"I am sorry for ze inconvenience, Monsieur Crowley. You must understand, I have to check zese things to avoid impostors."

I realized that Wade's mom had just lied for us, without a heads-up. I had to admit, I was a little jealous; I would've given anything to have a family like that, who'd get my ass out of trouble without hesitation. He'd probably get a phone call later asking what he thought he was playing at, but for now, Felicity Crowley had saved us from a whole heap of trouble.

"I completely understand," Wade replied. "You're just doing your job. I wouldn't expect anything less."

"Odette is through the door over there, in one of our private suites." She pointed to the gold door in the middle of the adjoining passageway. The same door that Garrett had just gone through a few minutes ago.

He smiled politely. "*Merci, Docteur Fenélon.*"

Leaving her behind, we headed for the door she'd pointed to.

"Your mom is going to kill you," I murmured on the way.

He grimaced. "My phone just buzzed. It's a text, but she's going to want a *very* detailed call once we're out of here. That little stunt is going to cost me."

"By the way, Garrett's already in there."

He frowned at me. "In where?"

"In Odette's room. I caught him creeping in. He's… uh, well, I'll let you find out for yourself." I couldn't ruin the delicious surprise Wade was about to get.

We pushed through the door to find Odette sitting on the windowsill, her face turned up to the sunlight. She was mumbling quietly and tracing her fingertips across the glass in a strange pattern. Her body was bruised and battered, and it seemed like she was out of it. A nurse stood close to her, trying to get her to look in their direction.

"I don't see him," Wade whispered.

I grinned despite the trouble we were in. "Well, well, well, that's one hot pair of legs you've got on ya, Nurse Kyteler."

TWENTY-THREE

Wade

"What?" I stared at the nurse. "Garrett… is that you?!"

He toyed with his blond hair and put on a girlish giggle. "What a surprise. I was not expecting visitors. You really should not be here, *madames* et *monsieurs*. Visiting hours are over, and my patient must get her rest. Please, if you would leave, zat would be *très bon*." He really thought he could get away with this.

"Garrett, we know it's you. I saw you come in here." Harley was trying, and failing, to hold in a laugh. "Drop the act."

"Act? Zere is no act. You must go, you really must." He put on another giggle that made me want to collapse on the floor. He was delusional. He couldn't trick us.

"Garrett, just stop. You're embarrassing yourself." I grinned. He wasn't going to live this down anytime soon.

With a furious expression, he lost the face he was copying, but he was too angry to remember to Shift out of the outfit, too. "Yeah, well, you should've known I'd be here. You guys said six, and then I find out you're all going at five. Good thing I thought ahead and arrived before you did. This is my mission, too, in case you've forgotten. I was supposed to come with you, not get left behind!"

"We should work on this together, now that we're all here," Harley said. "And we didn't leave you behind. You were there when we said when we were meeting—same time as the other morning."

He puffed out his cheeks. "Well, how was I to know you meant five? You weren't exactly specific."

"Garrett, I think you're forgetting something." I gestured to the nurse's outfit.

His gaze darkened. "See, you all think I'm some kind of joke. At least the LA Coven gives me some freaking responsibility." He shook his body violently, and the outfit faded away to reveal jeans and a t-shirt.

"We don't think you're a joke." I cast him a sincere look. I could take him seriously now that he was in normal clothes. "You just reminded me of that day you dressed up as my old crush, that's all. I guess I dodged a bullet there."

Garrett looked about ready to burst. "Look, you all shouldn't even be here, and you definitely shouldn't have brought the boy wonder. Levi would literally kill you if he found out you'd brought a Portal Opener out here."

"Well, Levi doesn't know about me," Jacob shot back.

"Garrett, come on. We've got to work together on this, the way we agreed," Harley said.

"The way *you* agreed, you mean?" He scowled at her. "You didn't give me much of a choice, dangling Astrid in front of me like a friggin' carrot. I only said I'd work with you to get you off my back, but I've changed my mind. I'm not putting my career at risk for this. You're not even supposed to know where the Librarian is!"

I flashed him a warning look. "We've all got the same goal, the difference being we're actually in a position where we can do some-thing about Katherine. The Council are dragging their feet; you know they are. They haven't faced her one-on-one. We have. We know what we're up against. Now, either help us or get out of our way." I held his gaze. "You're still a part of the SDC, even if the LAC has got you doing their dirty work. Remember where your loyalties lie, and remember who your true friends are. Don't get sucked up in that Council machine, because it'll just spit you out when it's done with you."

Garrett scoffed. "Like you wouldn't be doing the same in my position."

"I didn't do the same, Garrett. Imogene offered me a position and I turned it down," I said. "I'm not saying you were wrong to take them up on their offer. You're a braver man than me for doing it. You've always pushed people out of their comfort zones. Remember that water thing at school, where we got ducked in a pipe and had to come out the other side? I'd never have done it if you hadn't been the one pulling me back up for air and shouting me on. I admired you then, and I admire you now, but don't be an ass. Because you're not one, no matter what you want people to think."

He frowned. "Did you forget me pushing your head into the mud?"

"No, but you gave me the anger I needed to get through that netting. I wouldn't have done it if I hadn't seen that shit-eating grin on your face and wanted to smack it off." I smirked at him, and he smirked back. We'd shared some good times back then, when our camaraderie had been at its strongest. It got bad after we arrived at the SDC together. For a while, it had felt as if the previous stuff had never happened. Especially when he got in with Finch. Garrett blamed me for ratting him out to Santana; I blamed him for hurting her in the first place. We'd probably have figured it out if Finch hadn't been whispering in his ear. We'd always been at loggerheads, even when we were close. But we'd always made up again. That was how our friendship worked. Even now, I hated him as much as I loved him.

Garrett laughed. "You ever wish we were back at school? Man, those days were simple. If I'd known things would turn out like this, I'd never have graduated."

"They were good times, but we're better now than we ever were then."

Harley and Jacob were staring at us like they were watching an episode of *Oprah*. I didn't care. Garrett needed to remember why he was in this with us, and a bit of nostalgia never hurt. Those school days had felt like we were in the Army sometimes. You didn't get through that and forget who was beside you when you did. I had dirt on him that I'd take to my grave, and he had the same on me. He really was an ass at times, but that didn't change anything. He'd always be my brother, even if we weren't bound by blood.

Garrett's expression softened. "Fine, then we might as well work together."

Harley rolled her eyes. "Thank goodness for that."

"Although, we probably won't get anything out of this one." He nodded to Odette. She was tapping the glass in steady rhythms. Judging by the look on her face, the lights were on, but nobody was home.

"What's wrong with her?" Harley approached tentatively.

Odette was slim but not in a healthy way. Her collarbones protruded, and I could see the indents of her ribcage through her gown. Her cheeks were sunken in, and dark hollows surrounded her jet-black eyes. They couldn't have always been that color; no doubt it had something to do with the ritual to become a Librarian. Her fair hair had been scraped into a bun, dry and straw-like.

"Katherine must have done something terrible to her," Jacob murmured.

Harley nodded. "I've seen trauma like this before, just never quite this bad. A couple of the kids at the foster center used to do this, tapping on the wall and muttering to themselves."

I couldn't think of Harley in a place like that. It hurt to imagine her as a lost kid, abandoned and alone. Jacob, too. They'd been through stuff I couldn't even picture. It was never nice to be reminded of my privilege, but this stung deep.

Meanwhile, Odette continued to mumble to herself. She wasn't making any sense, just babbling incoherently. Harley got closer with slow movements, her eyes narrowed as she listened. I followed her lead and got nearer. Odette's words still didn't make sense, but Harley seemed to be on to something.

"Unleash the dragon's kiss and feel the heat of burning flame," Odette whispered. "Two drops of a witch's blood, five drops of silver…"

Harley's eyes widened. "They're spells. She's mumbling spells and ingredients, listing them one after the other. Listen."

"Five dried toadstool caps, one sprig of holly…" Odette tapped the glass in time to her words. Five taps for the toadstools. One for the holly. Harley was right.

"You think she's going through the whole repository?" I kept listening. The words were tumbling out of her like water from a broken faucet. She must have had thousands of spells in her head—new, old, complete, incomplete. And she was set on saying every single one. She never repeated anything.

Harley nodded. "It sounds like it."

"What the hell did Katherine do to her?" Garrett wondered in a low voice. He looked mad. At least he'd forgotten to be angry at us. This was a surefire way to get him to stay on our side.

"Odette?" Harley murmured. She reached for Odette's hand, but the woman tugged it away and kept tapping. "Odette, can you hear us? We're here to help you."

Nothing.

"Odette, I know you've been through a lot. We're sorry for that. We know you escaped while Katherine was completing the first ritual, but we need to know about the rest." Harley stared at her in earnest.

Odette blinked. "My mind… it's broken."

"Keep talking, Harley," I urged.

"Your mind is broken?" Harley went on. "Did Katherine break it?"

Odette tapped her finger against her forehead. "It's all in pieces…

coming back in pieces. Vital spells in the dark. All in the dark, still. Can't reach them. Can't get them. Can't find them." She tapped harder and broke the skin. Harley's hand shot out and grasped Odette's.

"Are you trying to get to them?" she asked. "Are the doctors here helping you remember?"

"Can't remember. Can't think. Can't get them," Odette whispered. She clung to Harley's hands. "Spells and charms. Medicine and potions. Nothing helps. It's all dark. All gone. All hidden. They don't want to be found. My spells. They run. They hide. Can't unlock. Can't get in."

"Do you know you're saying all your spells out loud?" Harley urged. The three of us—Garrett, Jacob, and I—were holding our breaths. She seemed to be getting through to Odette. Somehow, she was doing it. As far as Odette was concerned, us guys weren't even in the room.

"Must find. Must search. Must speak. Must get in." Odette rocked unsteadily and gripped Harley harder. And then the clarity faded away and left a rambling husk on the windowsill. Harley looked at me desperately. I wracked my brain to find a solution. I could only think of one.

"Keep going," I said. "Keep talking about Katherine."

A glint of pain flashed in Harley's eyes. She didn't want to cause Odette any more suffering. But we had no choice, not if we wanted to beat Katherine. I put my hand on her shoulder and gave it a firm squeeze. *I'm right here. I'm with you in this.* I hoped she understood.

"Odette, I'm sorry to ask this, but we need to know about the second ritual. We need to know so we can stop Katherine before she hurts others, the way she's hurt you," she whispered.

Odette blinked again. "Must kill. Must stop."

"Exactly, we've got to stop her, and you're the only one who can help us."

"Kill... a... Father of Magicals... in the Land... of Gaia. Can't think of three. Four is gone. Five is dark. All gone. All hiding." The strain of remembering showed on Odette's face. Veins bulged at her temples, and her pale cheeks were scarlet with exertion.

"What did you say?" Harley turned to us. "What did she say?"

"Kill a Father of Magicals in the Land of Gaia," Garrett replied.

Jacob nodded. "I don't think she can remember three, four, or five."

"Wade, can you try any of your memory tricks on her?" Harley glanced at me.

"You don't think the doctors here have tried every single one in the book?"

She shrugged. "I don't care, I want you to try. They might have missed one. We have to see if we can make it work."

I stepped forward and placed my hands on either side of Odette's head. She wouldn't let go of Harley's hands, which made things awkward. Ignoring the brush of Harley's forearm against my stomach, I focused on Odette. Wisps of magic slithered across my fingertips and into her skull. I didn't like doing memory spells this way; it intensified the sensations.

"*Claustra deobstruere,*" I chanted. "*Quod depelle nebula. Excommunicare auferat Daemones.*"

A scream howled from her throat, and I stepped back sharply. Her body convulsed, white foam spilling from the corner of her mouth. Her eyes rolled back into her head, and veins bulged like fat worms under her skin. Before she could topple from the windowsill, I caught her in my arms. She weighed almost nothing at all and looked like a child in my grasp. I carried her across to her bed and lay her down.

"I'm sorry," I whispered. Behind me, Garrett hurried over and administered a painkiller, pulling it out of his pocket. He shot it right into her vein, having somehow gotten his hands on a syringe. He'd really gone all out with the nurse thing. She relaxed instantly, but it wouldn't fix her mind. She was definitely suffering from a bad case of retrograde amnesia, and an even worse case of PTSD.

Harley came to sit at her side, holding on to her hand as she tossed and turned. "Odette?"

It was no good. The poor woman was babbling again.

"It doesn't look like she's going to talk again." Jacob sounded nervous.

"She gave us the second ritual, whatever it means. Maybe we should leave her for a while," Garrett interjected.

Harley shook her head. "She told us what the second ritual entails, but we need to know more about astral projection. Remington mentioned it when I spoke to him. It's going to be important if we want to stop Katherine from performing ritual two." She fixed her gaze on Odette. "Odette, there's one more thing, and then I swear I'll let you rest. There are two ways of reaching out to a Child of Chaos, right? One way is through a portal, which takes us straight to the other-worlds. And the other way is through astral projection. I know nobody has tried it for a very long time, and I don't really understand what it means. That's why I need you to help me. Please, Odette."

Odette stirred and stared up at Harley. "Astral... projection. Yes. Will get a Child's attention. Yes. But how? Must think. Must focus. Must remember." She strained, and her back arched. "Need spell. Must get spell. Must think. Must remember."

"That's it, Odette. You've got this." Harley gripped her hand.

"Euphoria," she whispered. "Euphoria. Can talk. Can reach. Can seek. Happened once. Yes. A witch. She sought. She sank. She spoke. Lux. Long ago. Yes. Euphoria."

"Euphoria is a way of doing this astral projection thing? A witch did it, a long time ago? She spoke to Lux when she did it? Is that what you're saying?" I heard the desperation in Harley's voice. The rest of us were watching her in awe. Marie Laveau had given us a small square of paper that gave us some indication of how to perform astral projection, but we hadn't been able to make much sense of it. This was good progress.

Odette nodded very slowly. But it was a definite nod.

"Must rest. Must think. Must remember," she murmured. "Very dark. Very tired. Very scared."

"We'll let you rest now, Odette. But if you can, will you try and remember the other rituals?" Harley pressed.

Odette nodded again. "I find. I tell. I try. Much harder. I try."

"I'll leave my number here in case they come to you. You can call me any time, and I'll be there to answer. If you want us to visit you again, we'll come running, okay?" Harley's voice was soft and sweet. Tears glinted in her eyes. Angry ones. Katherine had pushed this woman to her breaking point, and Harley wouldn't forget or forgive that. None of us would.

Odette smiled. "Very kind. Very sweet. Good soul."

A tear fell down Harley's cheek. It took everything I had not to wipe it away. "I'm sorry Katherine did this to you," she murmured.

"Much pain."

"I know, I can't even imagine what you've been through," she replied. "How did you escape her in the end?"

"Broke rules. Used spell. Powerful spell."

"You broke the rules? What rules?"

"Librarian rules."

Harley shook her head sadly. "I'm so sorry, Odette."

"Human Morph. Woman dead. My hands. Only way."

"You used a Morph spell to take over someone's body?" Harley sounded surprisingly understanding. Anyone who sided with Katherine was our enemy. And Odette had been pushed to her limits by Katherine. Of course she'd snapped eventually. I only wondered what it had cost her. Was this because of Katherine, or was this because she'd broken Librarian rules? There had to be boundaries to being a Librarian. If they could use their knowledge themselves, they'd be the most powerful magical on the planet. It made sense now that she'd said it.

Katherine had forced her to break those rules. Either way, she was the one responsible for this.

Odette smiled. "Yes."

"And that woman is dead now?"

"Only way. No trail. Two spells. Broke rules."

Harley nodded. "You killed her to cover your tracks, which meant you had to use two of the spells you'd learned? Two very powerful ones?"

"Human Morph. Medusa's Gaze."

"Those are the spells you used to escape. One that gave you the ability to use Morph powers on a human, and one called Medusa's Gaze?"

"Yes."

Garrett gave a low whistle. "Man, Katherine must be fuming right now."

"Garrett," I hissed.

"What? She must be!"

Harley's focus never left Odette. "I promise I'll make sure that Katherine doesn't hurt you ever again. She won't touch you, do you hear me?" The woman's eyes closed, and a look of quiet calm settled over her face. "I promise you, I'll stop her."

"We should go," Jacob said. There were tears in his eyes, too.

I nodded. "Just let me set some charms under her bed, and we can head out." Katherine had been dabbing her fingers in the SDC with annoying ease. She wasn't going to do the same here.

"Good idea." Harley placed Odette's hands on her chest and got up. "We need to do what we can to boost this coven's protection. If a Shapeshifter can sneak in without detection, we need to boost the security ourselves. No offense, Garrett."

He shrugged. "None taken. I'll help."

After laying the charms under Odette's bed and around the room, we were ready to portal back to the SDC. Dr. Fenélon would no doubt wonder where we'd gone, but that was the beauty of a Portal Opener. They were so rare that nobody expected them.

"Everyone ready?" I looked at the group.

Garrett shook his head. "I'm going to stay here awhile and do some research. Plus, I can cover for you so Dr. Fenélon doesn't start freaking out about a bunch of missing visitors."

I frowned and opened my mouth to speak. He cut me off before I could.

"Relax, it's all above board. You were right before. We're all in this together. There are just some things I need to look into. If Odette came here, then people know who she is here—I might be able to find out more. Plus, I kind of want to keep an eye on her, just for a bit."

"You're not going to LA about us, are you?"

He grinned. "Wouldn't dream of it. I'll have to tell them about the second ritual, though."

Man, you better not screw us over.

"Fair enough. Let's get going." I turned to Jacob. "Whenever you're ready."

We reappeared in the dragon garden a few minutes later. Fortunately, nobody was there. It was so out of the way that hardly anyone came to this part of the coven. Jacob had chosen well. At some point, I'd have to properly forgive him for the Quetzi incident. Slowly but surely, he was winning me over.

Together, we headed out into the main hallway. A second later, I skidded to a halt and pulled the other two back. Levi had turned the corner into the corridor, and he didn't look happy. He stormed toward us, ready to tear us a new one. I didn't need Empathy to know he was pissed. I could see it on his face—he knew we'd been out.

"Crap, crap, crap!" Harley hissed. *My thoughts exactly.*

Hell was about to rain down on us. I just hoped the rest of the Rag Team wouldn't get soaked along with us. Whatever happened, we had to defend the lie. We had to make sure they weren't embroiled in this. Otherwise, everyone would be screwed.

"You!" Levi roared. "A word. NOW!"

Jacob was frozen stiff. He still wore his Tarver mask, but I could sense his fear at being found out.

"Not you. You can go. This will not be suitable for younger ears." He flicked his wrist at Jacob, who didn't need to be told twice. He scurried away and flashed us an apologetic look. I didn't blame him. I wanted to do the same thing. "I'm *very* interested to hear where the two of you have been." Levi's eyes burned almost as brightly as Raffe's. He might not have had a djinn, but Levi sure had a devil inside him. Right now, we were facing the pointy end of his pitchfork.

"We were taking a walk," I replied. We had to play it cool.

"You don't fool me, you little worms." Levi's chest heaved with the exertion of his anger. "I know about the duplicates, so don't even try to use them to save your asses. I popped them like balloons. I haven't figured out who made them, but I will. You can count on that. And when I find out, there will be hell to pay for that magical!"

Harley cleared her throat. "We wanted some privacy, that's all."

"Yes, some privacy," I added.

"I trusted you, Wade, and you have let me down. I should have known you were too close to the situation to be given any responsibility." He shot me a dark look to let me know my cover was blown. No more spying for me. "You underestimate me, both of you, and you undermine me. And it *will* stop. You two have no idea what I'm capable of, but I'm only too happy to make sure you find out," he growled. "As if I wouldn't spot a duplicate a mile off? I'm no fool."

If you have to say it...

"So, I'll ask again, where have you been?"

A very familiar voice echoed in the hallway behind us. "They were out to dinner. With me."

I whirled around and stared into the eyes of the one person who could possibly be angrier at me than Levi.

My mom.

TWENTY-FOUR

Wade

She held Levi's gaze and barely looked at me and Harley. I didn't know whether to be mortified or relieved. Having my mom suddenly appear was weird enough. The circumstances made it worse. I hadn't called her back after she'd saved our asses in Paris, and she'd be waiting for an answer.

"Felicity?" Levi said, embarrassed. "What an unexpected surprise."

"Wade was giving me a tour after I brought them back from dinner, and I wandered off down one of the hallways. My fault." She gestured down the corridor. Man, she was a good actress. I couldn't see any hint of anger on her face, but I knew it was coming. "I suppose congratulations are in order." She said it with such disinterest that I could see Levi wither in front of my eyes.

"Uh, yes."

"Being a director isn't as easy as it might look, you know. It takes more than authority."

Levi nodded. "I hear the Houston Coven is doing very well."

"That's what I mean. It takes more than brute force and a bit of council experience to make a coven flourish. I trust you have a vision in mind, to lead this one forward?" A Texan twang had found its way into her accent. Levi seemed to bring some Southern clout out of her, not that she needed it. My mom wasn't the kind of woman anyone messed with. She feared nothing and no one.

"I do, Felicity. I have already implemented several new rules which I believe will turn the discipline in this place around." He beamed proudly. It faded a moment later as my mom stepped closer to him.

"I've heard about your rules, Levi. Indeed, it's lucky that we've ended up meeting like this, as I've wanted the opportunity to remind you that nobody likes a bully." Her voice cut like a knife. Even I dropped my gaze, in case she turned her words on me. "You seem to be hounding these two. I don't know why, but it's going to stop. Nobody liked your bullying tactics twenty years ago, and they won't fly now, either."

"If you would allow me, Fliss, I—"

"Felicity, please. Formality between directors is essential. We're not kids anymore, which you must be grateful for. Do you recall that afternoon when Cormac delivered a swift ass-kicking during training for the annual tourneys? I'll never forget that sound you made when you hit the lake." My mom smiled at the memory, covering her mouth as she chuckled. Old habits died hard, and my family rarely showed humor. Following suit, I stifled a laugh in case she smacked me over the back of the head. Watching my mom force Levi to withdraw his fangs was hilarious. Even if she yelled at me for days after this, I'd never forget the sight of Levi shrinking away into an embarrassed little boy.

Levi's cheeks burned. "I was not bullying, Felicity. I thought these two had broken the new rules, and I simply wanted to get to the bottom of it."

"That isn't what it looked like to me, Levi. You were *very* accusatory, as if you'd already decided they were guilty." She eyed him closely. "You should've learned by now that it is a terrible idea to corner a Crowley. It rarely ends well for you. Although, I should warn you that it is a terrible idea to corner anyone. The last thing you need is a public investigation while you're trying to find your feet as a director. You must remember what happened at the Phoenix Coven—I would've thought that served as a cautionary tale to us all, a lesson not to let the power of being director go to our heads."

Levi's mouth hung open. "I am nothing like Emmerich Grisham!"

There'd been an investigation some years ago after Phoenix suddenly cut communications with the rest of the US. When the authorities went in to see what was going on, they discovered that Director Grisham had turned the Phoenix Coven into a cult-like institution. Apparently, he'd convinced everyone that the world had ended, and they were the sole survivors. It had resembled a prison more than a place of magical refuge. My mom clearly knew just how to push Levi's buttons.

"Aren't you? I see some worrying similarities with all these new rules and regulations. It seems rather archaic to have your residents walking about in their uniforms. For a moment there, I wondered if I'd stepped back to the 1930s." She nodded toward a frightened cluster of young students, who were trying to pass by without attracting Levi's attention. They wore the gold-and-blue suits that were meant for special occasions.

"I am doing what's best for this coven," Levi protested.

"Funny, that's exactly what Grisham said when they led him away. Although, you always did have trouble with delusions of grandeur. Remember when you tried to rally the rest of the training program to join you in banning Esprits from the grounds? Sad, really, to see that so little has changed."

Levi looked ready to explode. I hadn't realized that the Crowleys and the Levis knew each other well. My parents had brought them up in conversation now and again, but I'd never had this kind of insight. Their youth was never mentioned much. As forward thinkers, they preferred the future to the past. Me, too, I supposed. I'd never been one to dwell. They were probably the reason why.

"Anyway, you can leave my son and his girlfriend alone now, as they were at an early dinner with me. I haven't had much time to give to this blossoming relationship, and I thought it high time I visited so I could get to know Ms. Merlin better." She flashed Harley a kind gaze, but Harley was fixed firmly in panic mode. Her eyes were close to popping out of her head, and she didn't seem to know where to look. I didn't, either. My mom had just called her my girlfriend. My cheeks felt hot, my throat tight, and Harley seemed to be suffering the same level of mortification.

Levi raised an eyebrow. "Your son is an exceptional magical. You must be very proud." I noticed he didn't say a word about Harley. His feelings about her were clear.

"Don't attempt to suck up now, Levi. Yes, we're very proud." A hard edge lingered in her tone. Right now, she wasn't especially proud of me. "But that is by the by. You ought to go back to your work and have a long, hard think about how you might *actually* improve the state of this coven. If you really want to make your mark, that is. My husband and I have poured enough money into this place, and it is high time we saw some improvement. Now, if you don't mind, I would like to speak with my son and his girlfriend alone before I depart again for Houston."

Levi nodded awkwardly. "Yes, Felicity. Of course." He scurried away with his tail between his legs. I wished I could've enjoyed the satisfaction a bit longer, but that exchange with my mom would come and bite us in the ass later. Levi didn't handle humiliation well, especially at the hands of a woman. And my mom had just slammed him into the ground.

A heavy silence followed. My mom looked at me intently. Harley seemed to be off the hook. My mom wasn't even paying her an ounce of attention. *Am I supposed to speak first? No chance.* If I could get away with never saying another word to my mom, to stave off the imminent tongue-lashing, I would.

"I'm Harley Merlin. It's nice to meet you." Harley stepped forward and held out her hand.

My mom stared at Harley's hand like it was an alien object. "Wade, we need to talk."

Alone. The unspoken word hovered between us.

I sighed. "Harley, I'll meet you later in the Luis Paoletti Room. I'll text you when I'm done, okay?"

She glanced at my mom before nodding. "Sure. Uh… great to meet you, Mrs. Crowley." With that, she headed off down the corridor. I wanted her to look back. I wanted her to stay, but this was between my mom and me.

"We should talk in my office," I said. "It'll be more private."

I didn't wait for her to reply. She'd follow me.

Five minutes later, we arrived outside my study. I held open the door and ushered her inside. Promptly, she swiped her fingertips across every surface and examined the bare room. It was small, but it was mine.

"'Office' seems a little like overkill, wouldn't you say? It's more like a box with a desk inside." This was the first time my mom had set foot in here. She came to the coven when there were important events, but other than that, my parents kept their distance. A form of subtle punishment for choosing the SDC over every other option. The last time I'd even spoken to my mom was at the Family Gathering. None of us were big on phone calls.

"It serves its purpose," I replied. I gestured for her to sit on one of the small chairs that I'd crammed inside.

She shook her head. "I'd prefer to stand. Now, how about we stop beating around the bush? You know I hate to come here, but when that call came in from Paris, I knew you needed help and may, in fact, need someone to cover for you here, too. I've been hearing bad things about

Levi, not that I'd expect anything less from him. Although, I *am* disappointed to find you at the center of some unruly gang."

I shot her a cold look. "It's not an 'unruly gang,' Mam. They're my colleagues, and we're undertaking some very important work." Having her here brought out my Irish twang.

"Work to do with Katherine Shipton?"

I froze. "Partially."

"This is not the way you've been brought up. We didn't raise you to become anti-establishment. We raised you to respect rules and authority, and yet here you are, sneaking around, using my position for your own benefit."

"Like you said, I needed help. I wouldn't have had the physician call you if I'd had any other way."

She sighed. "The company you keep reflects on your character, Wade. You are only as honorable as the people beside you, and you choosing to hang around with that Merlin girl—well, people are beginning to talk. Your father and I are very worried."

"She's not defined by her past, Mam." Anger spiked through me. Her elite prejudices were showing. "If you got to know her, you'd like her."

"I have no desire to get to know the girl," my mom shot back. "Your reputation is the only one that concerns me, as it also affects our own—your father's and mine. We can't afford to have our positions questioned because of your actions."

"I can't see what Harley has to do with any of this."

"She seems to draw Levi's attention, and I have reason to believe that she is a bad influence on you. This behavior would never have happened a few months ago. Suddenly, this girl appears, and you turn into a maverick. Besides, you can't have that bloodhound sniffing you out every hour of every day. It's embarrassing, frankly." She turned up her nose and started to organize the folders on my desk.

I tried very hard to keep my cool. "You don't need to worry about me. Or your precious reputation."

"Your father and I have thought long and hard about it, and we'd prefer it if you came back to Houston with me. You'll be better off there, with all of this Katherine Shipton mess going on. My coven can protect you in a way that the SDC can't—it just doesn't have the facilities or the strength. The rest of the US doesn't call it Mediocre Central for nothing."

I glanced at her in disbelief. Why did everyone seem intent on running from the problems in this magical world, instead of improving things? Why was everyone so scared to go after Katherine directly? What had happened to sticking around and fighting for a change? Levi wanted Raffe gone. Tatyana had gotten the same spiel from her parents. Santana had, too. There was so much skirting around that it was starting to annoy me.

Plus, my mom's words about Harley weren't exactly putting me in a good mood. She didn't even know Harley. She didn't know what her family had been through. She read the magical papers, made her judgments, and fixed them in her head. "Stubborn" didn't even cover it.

"No." The word echoed through the room. Simple and straight to the point, just as I'd told Levi.

"I beg your pardon?" Her eyes narrowed. She had the same deep green eyes and dark hair as me, but we couldn't have been more different. My father, on the other hand, was fair and hazel eyed. He often joked that I wasn't his, and my mom usually smacked him on the back of the head for that.

"I said no. I've got plans here, you know that. One day, I'll be the director, and I'll bring this place up to the same level as New York, Washington, Los Angeles, and Houston. But that takes time. You should know that better than anyone. I can't weasel out at the first sign of trouble. You might have raised me to follow rules, but you also raised me not to be a coward. I won't leave."

My mom snorted. "I doubt even I could bring this place up to snuff."

"That's because you don't know it and its people the way I do." I held my ground. She didn't have the monopoly anymore. "When I first came here, I didn't know if it was the right choice. I'll admit it. But then, as soon as I set foot through the door and saw the potential this place had, I knew I was where I was supposed to be. When people are willing to put the work in, the SDC can be extraordinary. *Better* than those other places. Alton, for all his faults, already made several steps in the right direction."

"You're living in a fantasy land." She shook her head. She hated me contradicting her.

"No, Mam, I'm very much living in reality. The trouble is, I'm the only one in the upper echelons of this magical community who seems to have any faith that this coven can be so much more than a shelter for misfits and inner-city magicals." I didn't mention that one of the best things about being here was the fact that it was out of my parents' circles of influence. But that was definitely a perk. "I'm making a name for myself here, and I'm helping this place and its magicals. So, no. I'm not going anywhere."

My mom sighed. "You always did love a charity case. I'm guessing that's why you're so fond of the Merlin girl." Her expression softened. She knew when to stop, before I blew my lid. "I'm just worried about you. I love you. You're my only son, and if anything were to happen to you... Is it so bad that I want what's best for my boy?" Her voice choked up. I didn't want her to get upset, but she had to understand. This was my home. Not Houston, or anywhere else.

"I can't leave. I'm... attached to the people here." I exhaled sharply. *Cat's out of the bag. Might as well be honest.* If she wouldn't understand the rest of it, maybe she'd understand me falling for someone.

She stared at me in shock. "Wait... you actually *like* that Merlin girl? I only said you were an item to throw Levi off. I never, for a second, thought you might actually be... oh my goodness." She fluffed some more papers in an attempt to distract herself. "Well, I'm not sure how I feel about *that*, to be perfectly honest."

I smiled. "Neither am I."

"There is a great deal at stake here, Wade."

"Danger, risks, reputation? Yeah, I know." I paused. I'd never said this out loud before. "The thing is, I care about her. She's strong, stubborn, powerful. Kind, too. And so funny it would make your eyes water. She has her moments, when all I want to do is shake her by the shoulders for being stupid, and she can be determined to a fault, but I wouldn't have her any other way. There's so much potential in her, and I feel like she might unravel if I leave her side."

My mom turned to look at me. "See, what did I say? You and your fixer-uppers. First the SDC, now this girl."

I tried not to laugh. Harley would have hated being called a fixer-upper. "She needs me for balance and protection, at least until she can get her Chaos under control. After that... who knows. I know what I'd like, but it's in her court as much as it's in mine."

Man, that felt good to say out loud. I could trust my mom not to blab. She'd probably be too mortified by my choice of partner to say anything. Not that I cared what she thought. I wasn't about to start now.

"Yes, I've heard about her Suppressor problem," my mom said after a moment. "It's part of the reason I want you back in Houston. You forget, Wade, that I knew the Merlins. I knew them in a way that neither you nor this girl did. I know what happened, and I witnessed the aftermath. I was one of the magicals who was there to pick up the pieces, to comfort a grieving community. That family is jinxed. They were born under every unlucky star you can think of. And, while I'm glad that Harley survived, I'm wary of what she can do... and what she may become. The good in her family tends to be wiped out."

"Not her. She's good. She's powerful, but she's good." I stood firm. "I just want her to have a chance at happiness. Nobody asks to be born into the family they're born into. I want her to be safe and free, able to live the way she wants to. If I can help her do that, then everything will be okay."

My mom frowned. "With Katherine around? You think that's possible?"

"Trust me, Mam, if we all work together and help Harley get her Chaos under control, we'll have a fighting chance against Katherine. Right now, we're royally screwed. We don't have the power to match her. Harley *is* that power."

She walked over to where I stood and brushed a curl away from my forehead. It was weirdly tender for her, and I didn't know whether to bolt or smile. "You're in love, honey. I could argue with you until I was blue in the face, and it wouldn't change your mind. Love can be stronger than Chaos itself when it wants to be. More stubborn, too."

"So you won't keep hassling me to leave? You'll let me get on with this, my way?" I looked into her eyes—a reflection of my own.

She chuckled. "On one condition."

"Which is?" I struggled to keep my eyes from rolling.

"When all of this is over—provided we all survive—I want to have dinner with both of you. The Merlin girl and you. If she isn't going anywhere, then I probably *should* get to know her better."

I arched a suspicious eyebrow. "Dinner?"

She gave a curt nod. "For real, this time."

TWENTY-FIVE

Harley

The Rag Team had gathered in the Luis Paoletti Room, though Wade was still somewhere in the coven, chatting with his mom. He'd texted us an hour ago to tell us to go ahead without him, but it felt wrong. I'd texted back, asking how it was going, but he hadn't replied. I didn't know if that was a good sign or a bad one.

Felicity Crowley had been on my mind ever since leaving Wade. She hadn't exactly taken to me, which sucked, but she also hadn't been what I was expecting. Honestly, I'd imagined a stuffy, stiff upper-lip sort, but she'd been way more terrifying and way more awesome than that. How she'd taken Levi down would stick in my mind for a long time. Even if we couldn't get rid of him, I'd always have that memory of him running off like a naughty boy who'd been caught with his hand in the cookie jar.

The only members who weren't present were Garrett and the rest of our honorary colleagues: Jacob was busy working on the scanning device with Krieger, and Louella was catching up on magical studies. Being a teenager, she had mandatory classes to attend, as well as the selective ones. *I do* not *miss being in school.* Isadora, meanwhile, was toiling away at keeping Levi busy. I hated that she had to put up with that devil, but it was proving to be the best way to get him away from the Rag Team. Still, it begged the question of *how* she was keeping him busy. I hoped it involved hurling him through multiple portals on a seemingly endless loop, but it was probably more like endless paperwork and discussions about rare abilities.

As for Garrett, he seemed to still be "researching" at the Paris Coven. If it hadn't been for Astrid, I'd have been more worried about his absence. As it was, I knew he'd never risk ruining things with Astrid, not even for the benefit of the LA Coven.

"Merlin, you okay? You're paler than Tatyana, which is a sentence I never thought I'd say." Santana glanced at me from across the table. She didn't exactly look in top form, either, after her djinn-babysitting duties, but she definitely looked better than I felt. I was glad that Raffe had finally joined us again—we'd all been missing him.

I dragged in a shaky breath. "The Suppressor is kicking my ass today." My head was all over the place, and my body was constantly flitting between ice cold and red hot. I'd already gone through two t-shirts, thanks to the endless sweating. I thought I'd been covering my sickness well, but apparently my ghoulish face had given the game away.

"Let us know if you need a break, and we can fetch anything you want from the kitchens." A mischievous glint sparked in Santana's eyes.

Raffe cast her an amused look. "Are you just trying to break the rules now?"

"He'll never catch me. I've already got a stockpile in my room, so I don't have to deal with his ungodly breakfast hours ever again."

Their banter calmed my palpitating heart. It was nice to feel normal, even if it was just for a moment or two. Not that there was anything normal about what we were doing, since we'd gathered to get down to business regarding the second ritual and what we'd learned from Odette. The rest of the team had already been briefed about our sad visit to the Librarian, and they'd all shared our sympathy. However, Odette's face still haunted me. *I promise I'll stop her, Odette. I swear it.*

I forced a smile onto my lips. "I'm fine. No breaks necessary. Although, I might raid your stockpile later."

"It's all yours, *mi preciosa*." Santana grinned, but I could see the worry lurking beneath. It was the same concern that was written on everyone's faces, reinforced by the rush of emotions that flowed away from them. I guessed everyone was half expecting me to drop dead at any minute. Right now, I felt like that might even be a possibility—the Suppressor leak was getting much worse, and even concentrating on the smallest task was proving to be a slog.

"So how about we get going with what comes next before I end up passed out on the floor?" I decided to make a joke of it and was rewarded with an anxious chuckle from the group. "How are things going with Echidna?" I looked to Tatyana, who'd taken over for Isadora with the thawing process.

"Tobe is still waiting for her to defrost," Tatyana replied. "He's keeping his promise to us, though. Nobody knows she's been taken out of the freezing spell, and he's doing an incredible job of keeping the security personnel from sniffing it out."

Astrid smirked. "Alton is helping cover that up, too. I think he's trying to make it up to me. I've never seen him so enthusiastic. Plus, if anyone can keep a secret in this place, it's him... right?" A bittersweet note ran through her words. Alton had proven himself to be the master of deception with his secret deal with Katherine, but it served as a stark reminder of the price he'd paid for that. All of this would've been so much easier if he were still the director.

"So we've got our turkey on defrost," Dylan chimed in. "What do we do about this second ritual while we're waiting?"

Raffe nodded. "What does 'Kill the Father of Magicals' even mean? Are you sure Odette didn't say anything else about it?"

I shook my head. "She wasn't exactly in any state to say more."

"Maybe it has to do with Chaos itself?" Santana suggested. "If Gaia is the mother of magicals, then maybe Chaos is the daddy—so to speak."

"So we're supposed to find a way to *kill* Chaos itself?" Raffe replied.

Santana frowned. "Yeah, maybe not."

"It could be the most powerful male magical?" Dylan said. "Like, a Giverny/Katherine type thing?"

"Could be." I leaned over the table to steady my shaky arms. "But then, why would they be called the 'Father' of magicals? It's the 'Father' bit that doesn't make sense."

"Well, we've got books coming out of our asses here, so why don't we take a look-see?" Santana nodded at the bookcases and shelves that surrounded us. "Stands to reason that the stuff we're looking for might be in the Forbidden Section."

"Louella already spent some time in the Forbidden Section's library, but she couldn't find anything." I huffed out an exasperated breath. "If there'd been a mention of this Father, she'd have found it."

Santana covered my hand with hers. "Did she look in here?"

"I don't think so."

"Then this is where we should start." Santana planted a little kiss on the back of my hand before getting up and starting her search. Raffe joined her, the two of them pulling books down and spreading them out on the table. Nausea rose up my throat as they laid out a couple of Grimoires, the books' whispers overwhelming. On wobbly legs, I crossed to the farthest side of the room, where I perched up on the edge of a desk.

Tatyana came over. "Is it getting that bad?"

"Like you wouldn't believe."

"Can I try something?"

I frowned. "A safe something?"

"Of course."

"Why not? It can't make anything worse, right?"

She smiled and pressed her hands to either side of my head. Silvery-white tendrils snaked out from underneath her palms. I felt their cold bite as they slithered inside my skull and took hold. My mind swirled with a soothing calm, which flowed through my body and slicked over the aches and pains. *A bandage for the soul.*

"How do you feel?" she asked a few minutes later. I hadn't even realized she'd taken her hands away.

I blinked my eyes open. "Better."

"*Much* better?"

"Not really," I admitted. The leak was ever-present, but at least my legs weren't shaking anymore. It was like someone had put a bit of tape over a massive crack in a dam, giving me a short respite from the Suppressor's influence. "Thanks for trying, though."

"Don't mention it."

Half an hour later, we'd exhausted all of our avenues. There was no mention of a Father of Magicals in any of the books in the Luis Paoletti Room, and Louella hadn't been able to find any earlier. Either he'd deliberately been taken out of the history books, or he was so obscure that nobody even knew who he was. I wasn't sure which was more frustrating.

I looked out of the window to find that the sun was setting. An idea leapt into my foggy head. I grasped at it, terrified that it might trickle away like the rest of my thoughts—retention was getting more and more difficult the worse the Suppressor leak got.

"What if this Father of Magicals has something to do with the Primus Anglicus—the first magicals in existence? Maybe it refers to a male descendant, or the spirit of the first male magical." The others turned to me as I spoke.

"They're your family, aren't they?" Santana replied with an excited smile.

I nodded. "The Merlins and the Shiptons were part of the Primus Anglicus. That's why my Chaos energy is so high."

Raffe puffed out a sigh. "Either that, or these rituals are open to a lot more interpretation than we thought. Let's face it, the Father of Magicals could be anyone or anything. Echidna is the Mother of Monsters. What if it's a Purge beast like her, instead? What if it's something older than the Primus Anglicus? Sure, they were the first magicals, but there was magic in the world before them."

Way to burst my bubble, Raffe.

"Man, I thought we were on to something there," Dylan muttered.

"This is hopeless." Tatyana sat down on one of the stools and held her head in her hands. It was unsettling to see her like that, since she almost never broke down. "There are endless interpretations."

Santana groaned. "Why couldn't Odette have just said, 'Kill José Domínguez, aged 54, lives on 42 Calle del Escobar, Medellín, Colombia.' That'd be so much simpler."

"Why Colombia?" I chuckled at her.

"*Narcos* is the only thing keeping me sane right now." She smiled, giving Raffe a nudge.

He blushed. "It's relentless. I keep suggesting a movie, but she won't have it."

"He keeps pretending it'll trigger his djinn."

Although the levity between the two lovebirds had broken the tension in the room, frustration remained. It spiked off everyone, making mine ten times worse. Knowing the name of the second ritual but not having a clue who, or what, the target might be was completely draining. Tatyana was right, it really did feel hopeless. Then again, there was *one* small silver lining: if we were having trouble deciphering the meaning behind it, maybe Katherine was, too. After all, she didn't have Odette to elaborate anymore.

The door burst open and Wade walked in. Anger and exasperation drifted off him in foggy waves, which made me wonder what he and his mom had talked about. That had to be why he was like this, all grim-faced and stern.

"Everything okay?" I asked, keeping it vague so as not to put him on the spot in front of everyone.

He shook his head and slammed a small folder onto the workbench. "Nope."

Astrid opened the folder, a series of papers and photographs spilling out. She picked up the first piece of paper and began to read. "Reports of violent deaths in different covens across the US. Denver has been hit, and so have Baltimore, Montpellier, Atlanta, Des Moines, and a group of smaller institutions. Some attackers have been apprehended, all of them branded with the same golden symbol. They're all from the Cult of Eris."

Wade sank down on one of the stools. "Alton handed this to me a few minutes ago. The magical intelligence services are having a hard time breaking anyone. Looks like Katherine has trained them all in interrogation tactics, and now the bastards won't talk. She's ramping up her presence, which can't be good." He heaved out a sigh. "Important people are dying—preceptors, students, residents, physicians, mostly, but the director of Montpellier is dead, too."

"How many dead?" Dylan asked.

"Ten in the past week, all of them connected to Katherine in some way," Wade replied. "All of them were people with weight and respect in the community. She's targeting them on purpose. She's sending a message."

Tatyana shook her head. "How are they linked?"

"The director was in New York with Katherine. One of the physicians had helped Hester during her pregnancy, and the other one was a former Angel who'd helped to put Giverny out of business in Europe. The rest... intelligence is still working on that."

I was starting to learn one very valuable lesson from being here at the SDC: things could always get worse.

"How's it going here? Any news on the second ritual?" Wade looked up at us.

See?

"Nada," Santana replied.

Dylan nodded. "Dead end."

"Great, just what I wanted to hear." Wade stretched out his arms and yawned loudly. It'd been a long and trying day for all of us, and we were only just recovering from the events of yesterday.

"I say we sleep on it and come back together in the morning." Raffe looked edgy, as if the news had somehow agitated the djinn inside him. It wasn't just Levi who could have this effect on him.

Santana glanced at him, her brow furrowed. "I agree. No use flogging a dead horse. Anyway, you never know, something might come to us in a dream." She laughed, but it didn't reach her eyes.

"Yeah, we could all do with some rest." Dylan was the first to get up as he spoke, with Tatyana following him. She held on to his arm, and the two of them wished us a good night before heading out into the coven. Santana and Raffe were the next to leave, Santana practically dragging him out of the room. The djinn was evidently being especially temperamental right now, and none of us could risk an outburst.

"'Night, guys." Astrid got up and walked to the door. I couldn't feel much emotion coming from her, but it was clear she missed Garrett. And with all these other couples wandering about, I couldn't blame her.

Wade looked at me. "We should probably get going, too."

I grabbed his hand, pulling him back down onto his seat. "In a minute."

We obviously needed to talk, but I felt suddenly nervous. Now we were alone.

TWENTY-SIX

Harley

"We should get some rest," Wade repeated, but I wasn't having any of it. He'd spent ages with his mother, and I wanted to know what had happened. After she'd saved us from having our cover blown, I doubted they'd talked about cupcakes and kittens.

"Not yet." I pulled my chair closer. "How did it go with your mom? I texted you, but you didn't reply."

"Alton cornered me on the way back from my office, so I didn't get to check my messages. He's stressed out about this, as we all are." He nodded to the folder that still lay out on the table. "We poked the bear, I guess. What else did we expect?"

I nodded. "Nice diversion tactics, Crowley. What did your mom have to say?"

"She was pissed about the call, but I knew she would be." He sighed and rested his elbows on the table. "My parents and I... we don't exactly have a close relationship. It's complicated. I know most families are, but us—well, we're more complicated than most."

"How so?"

He shrugged. "I guess it's the world they come from. Kids are supposed to be seen and not heard, that kind of thing. They love me, and they care what happens to me, but there's always been a... I don't know, a wall of some kind between us. That's why it was so weird when she just turned up. Usually, she'd have let me muddle through on my own, doing a bit of character-building. It made me realize that things are really serious. She's worried about Levi as director, mostly, but there's all the Katherine stuff, too."

"I don't think I'll ever get over the way she schooled Levi like that."

"Me, neither. It's going to cost us, though."

I smiled wryly. "I've been thinking the same thing. Isadora's doing her best to keep Levi at bay, but now that we've embarrassed him, there's no way he's going to let it slide. Still, your mom was awesome back there."

"She has her moments." He smiled back, but he looked exhausted.

"Did she say anything else?" I wasn't fishing, but I was interested to know whether she'd mentioned me at all. After the whole "my son's girlfriend" thing, my curiosity was piqued.

"I got a lecture on reputation and upholding the family name. The usual 'weight of responsibility' nonsense that she always lays on thick. Apparently, my actions affect their standing, and I should pay more attention to my behavior. She doesn't like the fact I'm sneaking around, doing things that are against the rules. Oh, and she called the Rag Team 'that unruly gang,' which naturally set me off." He leaned on his hand. "She doesn't get why I'm here. I think she's starting to, but she's always questioned my move here. If she had her way, I'd be safely tucked away in the Houston Coven, constantly under her watch."

"What does your dad think about it?" I kind of liked being part of an unruly gang.

He shrugged. "My dad gets involved as little as possible. He lets my mother do the worrying and the disciplining, and he gets on with his work at the Texas Mage Council. They're pretty hands off, aside from when I'm jeopardizing their positions—they always have been. I haven't even spoken to my parents since the Family Gathering, and I probably wouldn't have spoken to them again until the next big event if that phone call hadn't come up."

"How come?" It seemed sad that he didn't have a close relationship with his parents. As a foster kid, I had always pictured the ideal of a close-knit family who could confide anything in each other and spoke to each other at least once a day. It had never really occurred to me that a happy, united family on the outside could be so distant on the inside. I'd seen my share of broken homes, but I'd always thought they were the exceptions.

"Like I said, it's the way I was brought up. It was the way they were brought up." He smiled to himself. "You should see my mother at Christmas, when my grandma is coming around for dinner. She gets into this panic that nothing is good enough, and my grandma always complains about this and that, just to annoy her, and all I want to say is, 'Doesn't this look familiar to you?' But I never do."

"I'm sorry."

He looked up at me. "Listen to me harping on about how dysfunctional my parents are. You can tell me to shut up. Compared to what you've been through, I should be grateful I have them."

"Hey, family is family. You can hate on them and love on them as much as you want in front of me. Just because I've lost my parents doesn't mean you can't share stories about yours. If I lived by that rule, nobody would even speak to me." I chuckled, a wave of sweet emotion rolling through my veins, temporarily smoothing over the aches of the Suppressor.

"She mentioned you, by the way." A grin split his face. "If we survive this, she wants to take us both out to dinner to get to know you better. I may or may not have insisted on staying here because I wanted to make sure you were okay."

He wanted to make sure I was okay... My heart brimmed with happiness, even though the thought of dinner with his mom was uncomfortable to say the least.

I sensed there was more to it, but I didn't have the energy to press him for every gory detail. Plus, I wasn't sure I'd like what I might hear. Parents didn't tend to like me much, mostly because I said things at the wrong time and could be pretty crass. The Crowleys would have a field day if they took me to some fancy restaurant; I could already envision myself panicking over knives and forks. *Work from the outside in. Or is it inside out? Ah, crap.*

I frowned. "So it'd be dinner with just us and the two of them?"

"Yep."

"Maybe it'll be better for everyone if Katherine kills us all then."

He laughed. "I told her you were funny."

"Who said I was joking?"

"She's got some concerns about your potential power, but I put those to bed. Seems like you're getting pretty famous around the covens because of that Suppressor of yours."

It was my turn to laugh. "I think you mean 'infamous.'"

"That, too."

"You really told her you were sticking around for me?"

He nodded. "It's the truth. I promised I'd get you through this, and I'm not breaking that promise."

He stared at me with such intensity I thought my cheeks might burst from blushing so hard. Those green eyes would be the death of me one of these days. More to the point, I couldn't believe he'd stood up to his mom on my behalf. I'd seen what Felicity Crowley could do, and it took a man with balls of steel to say no to a woman like that. Even Levi didn't have the stones for it, but Wade... well, Wade was something else.

I lunged across the table at him, wrapping my arms around his neck. I couldn't contain myself anymore. Sure, we'd agreed to get through the whole Suppressor fiasco before we decided on what was going on between us, but I didn't care. I couldn't sit on that stool a moment longer and not kiss him, not with his lips looking so delicious and inviting.

"Whoa, what the—" I interrupted him with a kiss, my lips grazing his. His eyes widened for a moment before closing in silent satisfaction. Mine did, too. I wanted to sink into the moment and never leave the bubble surrounding us. His lips pressed to mine, firm and passionate, moving in a slow rhythm that set my pulse racing. *Damn, he's a good kisser.* I slid my fingertips into the tousled mane of his dark curls and kissed him all the harder, his hands cupping my face as he skillfully let his tongue dance with mine.

He reached around my waist and lifted me up onto the edge of the table. The folder went skittering away, sending a flurry of papers and photographs drifting to the floor. I didn't care, because all I could see and feel was him. Katherine didn't exist, as far as I was concerned, and all the bad stuff happening in the magical world belonged to some other person in some other time.

His kisses moved away from my lips, his fingertips running along the length of my bare spine, beneath my t-shirt. I arched my neck as he traced a delicate, passionate trail of kisses along the curve of my throat, before fluttering all the way along my collarbone and back up to my parted lips. He caught my mouth in his and explored with his tongue, his breath catching in his throat as he kissed me deeply. My own lungs were straining for air, coming in short, sharp gasps as I surrendered to his every kiss and touch.

My hands were doing some exploring of their own, running up the firm contours of his stomach and hastily unbuttoning the awkward fastenings of his waistcoat. *Seriously, why so many clothes? This isn't the time for a three-piece Tom Ford.* Undoing the buttons of his shirt beneath, I gulped at the sight of his taut body, his pecs flexing as he leaned over me and lay me down against the table. A pen was digging into my ass cheek, but I didn't give a damn. He smelled of something deep and spicy, the scent completely intoxicating.

In fact, all of this was intoxicating. A little too intoxicating. Sudden dizziness brought black spots into my eyes, my skin creeping hot and cold at the same time.

I pushed my palms against his chest, panic shooting through me. He stood back and helped me to sit, his eyes wide with worry.

"Is something wrong? Did I hurt you?" He was breathless, his bare chest rising and falling rapidly.

I shook my head, catching my breath. "No, no, it's nothing like that. I just... I feel a bit dizzy."

"Can I get you some water?" He glanced around in a fluster.

I shook my head. "I just need a minute."

"Are you sure I didn't hurt you? You look about ready to pass out."

"Might just be the effect you have on me." I forced a smile, but I was still struggling to stay conscious.

"Maybe we should slow things down a bit," he said, still breathing heavily.

"Did I do something wrong?" My heart lurched.

"No, not at all. I'm just worried about sending your Suppressor into overdrive."

I frowned. "You think this is the Suppressor messing with us like this? I guess my abilities are going crazy, and my Empathy is off the charts. Plus, those Grimoires almost made me hurl before."

"I doubt it's the Empathy, Harley." A smile curved up the corners of his kissable lips. But I knew it was too late... the moment was ruined, and sense had returned. Still, his words made me flush. He didn't think the Empathy was exaggerating things, which meant he really did want to kiss me like that. And I did, too. His abs were still very distracting, even as he tried to fasten a couple of buttons on his shirt.

"Sorry..."

He tilted my chin up. "You've got nothing to be sorry for. I meant what I said: we're getting this Suppressor out of you, and I'm not leaving your side until it's gone. Until then, we just need to be careful about putting too much strain on it."

"What is it with this room, huh?"

He laughed. "I blame the forbidden things."

"Me, too." I shuffled off the edge of the table and hastily picked up the papers and photographs that had fallen off. Shoving them back into the folder, I handed it back to Wade. "You should take this, keep it safe."

"We should get to the living quarters before Levi starts his evening prowl." He held out his hand, and I took it without hesitation. Tucking the folder under his arm, he led me out of the room, and together we made our way back to the living quarters. Halfway there, I let go of his hand, standing on my own as we walked the rest of the way.

I felt like a lot had been said between us and yet nothing at all. I was no clearer about our relationship, but that was probably for the best right now. We still had to get the Dark blood from Echidna and figure out the meaning behind the second ritual. Plus, there was the whole Sanguine spell to do, which rested heavily on my mind. Romance didn't really have room to feature, not until the rest of this was over. And if I could get the Suppressor broken... well, at least he wouldn't have to hold his girlfriend in his arms as she died. A friend, yes, but not a lover. I didn't know whether that would make it any easier, but I was trying to convince myself that it would.

Even if we did make it out of this mess alive, there was dinner with Mrs. Crowley to think about. I was dreading it already, although it was still a long way off. I took comfort in that; at least I didn't have to add "impress the parents" to my list of difficult tasks.

Let's survive Katherine first.

TWENTY-SEVEN

Harley

Darkness shrouded me, cold sweat dripping down my back. No matter where I looked, I couldn't see a glimmer of light anywhere in the distance. Panic gripped my heart in a vise, and every time I opened my mouth to speak, something unseen stole the words away. Trying to calm my nerves, I reached inside myself and drew on the familiar hot-cold touch of Chaos. A sparking orb appeared in my palms, crackling and warm. I lifted it higher to cast its light.

Out of the shadows beyond, a faceless beast leapt toward me. I staggered back as the orb fell from my hands and landed with a burst on the ground. It lit up the world for a split second, revealing a crowd of yellow eyes. Shadowed jaws drooled, globules of black oil dripping from their mouths. My screams wouldn't come, though I felt them threatening to explode from my chest.

I lit up another orb, my hands shaking as I swept it around me, trying to scare away the faceless creatures that snapped and snarled. They weren't afraid of a little fire, their muscles straining as they pounced toward me. Dropping the orb, I turned and ran, with no idea where I was going. Claws slashed at my legs, tearing at my clothes and my skin. I ran and ran and ran.

Suddenly, I stopped. Somewhere in the distance, a familiar mechanical beep called to me. I tried to reach out for it, but the beasts descended on me, dragging me to the ground in a frenzy of teeth and claws. I smelled blood in the air and knew it was mine.

I sat up sharply, blinking my eyes awake. I was in my coven bedroom. My body was drenched in sweat, my treasured Springsteen t-shirt and checked flannel pajama bottoms soaked right through to the mattress beneath. A wrenching pain tore through my abdomen, spreading out across my chest. I blinked again, realizing something was wrong. Everything felt... unstable.

Looking around the room, I saw my lamp and side table floating in the air. A chair knocked against the ceiling. The very bed I was lying in hovered above the floor.

My Telekinesis must have gone wild while I was trapped in that dark nightmare with the faceless beasts. As my heart stopped racing and my mind started to clear, everything came down with a thud, the lamp swiveling on the bedside table before I righted it.

You need to get a grip on this, Harley. It was all well and good when I was alone in my room, but what if my Telekinesis stretched out to the rest of the coven? Levi would have me locked up until the Suppressor killed me. I didn't mean to be, but I was becoming a real threat to the people around me.

Smoothing the damp strands of hair away from my face, I glanced down at my phone, which lay beside my pillow. A green light flashed at the top, meaning I'd received a message. I realized that must have been the beep that drew me out of the nightmare. Reminding myself to set a couple of alarms, in case that kind of dream happened again, I picked up the phone and swiped the screen, checking the message. To my surprise, Nomura was the sender. Getting a text from a preceptor was always weird, like getting a message from a teacher after school hours.

I have prepared my office for your requirements, and it is high time we began learning about Euphoria. I will expect you shortly after 7:00 AM. Sincerely, Hiro Nomura. I smiled at the way he'd signed it—very old school, and very Nomura. Not even Mrs. Smith signed her texts with a "Sincerely," and she still typed with one finger.

My entire body felt like I'd run about twenty marathons, and my mind was still lagging behind the rest of me, but I figured I might as well get going with the Euphoria stuff. I couldn't let tiredness get in my way, even if I felt on the edge of a breakdown. The Suppressor wasn't going to hang around for me to be at peak strength, and neither was I. Besides, we were all still waiting on Echidna to get out of her deep freeze, and Tobe had been pretty vague about when she might be ready. He'd said the end of the day, or tomorrow morning, which was all kinds of comforting given these latest side effects. *Not.*

I checked the clock and saw that it wasn't even five yet, which gave me two hours to shower and grab something to eat from the dining hall. Well, if I made it down there before Levi forced the kitchen to close. Dragging my ass out of bed, I padded over to the bathroom and sank down beneath a hot stream of water, letting it soothe away the aches of the past few weeks.

Half an hour later, I was dressed and filled up on coffee from the dining hall. The sight of the breakfast food had made me feel sick, and I could barely stomach a slice of dry toast. After forcing down a couple of bites, I gave up and headed for Nomura's office. Hopefully, the Euphoria would help with the Suppressor's current fluctuations and give me the chance to actually eat something.

I didn't hold out much hope of Nomura already being in his office at this cruel hour of the morning, but I knocked anyway. Surprisingly, he answered a few seconds later, a gloomy expression on his face. The scent of incense wafted out into the hallway, bringing on another wave of nausea. *Geez, it's like I'm pregnant or something.* At least the Suppressor hadn't stolen away my ability to drink coffee. If it had, I might as well have given up there and then.

"I wasn't expecting you until seven," he said abruptly.

"I had to get down to breakfast, so I figured I'd come a bit earlier."

He shrugged. "Very well, then you should come inside." He left the door open and stalked back into his office. I felt every touch of sadness and anger jolting off him, hitting me like tiny prickles in the chest. What was up with him? We were all sad about Alton, but we were getting on with things. We definitely weren't sulking about it.

"Everything okay, Nomura?" I closed the door behind me and moved over to the cushions on the floor. He stood on the far side of the room, preparing tea for our session. It smelled acrid and sour, even from here, but that was probably my Suppressor talking. *Everything* smelled nasty, thanks to this thing.

He turned over his shoulder and gave me a soft smile. "It's nothing to worry about. I've been unwell of late, and with the additional stresses of the coven... well, it doesn't make for jolly behavior, I'm afraid."

"Tell me about it." I grinned back, hoping to perk up his spirits. It didn't suit him to be so down and agitated, not when he was usually the picture of Zen. I wondered what he meant by "unwell," but I decided not to pry. I'd learned enough from my foster kid days to know when to stop with the questions, and health was always a big no-no.

"Are you ready to begin?"

I nodded. "When you are."

He brought over a tray of tea and handed me a small black ceramic bowl. That sour-smelling stuff sloshed around inside, stinging my nostrils. In a way, it reminded me of the scent of the bag around my neck, only not quite so vomit-inducing.

"Drink it all," he said. I watched as he drank first, then downed the contents of the bowl in one go. My stomach heaved and my throat went dry as the herbal concoction fought its way down into my belly, but I kept it there.

"What's next?"

He smiled. "First, you must be calm. You must clear your mind of all external thought and focus on the deepest part within. It should come to you as a light of some sort, though it varies from person to person. It may emerge as a figure from your past, or a happy memory."

I closed my eyes and listened to his guidance, focusing hard on my thoughts. It was harder than I expected to try and shove them all away, what with so much going on. Deciding to work at it piece by piece, I went through my mind like I was on some kind of combine-harvester, clearing each part of my brain one section at a time. My friends faded away into darkness as I pushed them to the side, feeling the tea churn in my stomach. The Smiths were next, followed by thoughts of Tobe and Echidna. I let memories of my mom and dad drift into the ether, until I came up against two huge roadblocks—Katherine and Wade.

"There may be some resistance, but you must have your mind entirely blank for this to work." Nomura's voice echoed in the darkness.

I focused on Katherine first, trying to combat every memory of her with warm thoughts of Wade instead. My anger toward her was overwhelming, made worse by the Suppressor, but if I didn't manage to achieve Euphoria, then all of this would be for nothing. Her face leered at me, but I pictured Wade slamming a ball of Fire right into her stupid grin and watched that thought evaporate. I envisioned Odette, rocking on the windowsill, and thought of the way that Wade had carried her over to the bed, taking care of her.

I picked through each furious thought until none remained, all of them altered enough by the presence of Wade to make them disappear. And then it came to Wade himself. The kiss still weighed heavily on my mind, and the desperation with which we'd clung to each other last night.

"You must release all your memories—happy and sad," Nomura coached. "Let them all go and clear your mind entirely."

I envisioned myself walking through every memory of Wade and boxing each one up, tucking them away for a later date. By now, my body was shaking and sweating with the exertion, but I had to keep going. I sent him away into the darkness, letting go of every feeling I had for him, until there was nothing left. I had no sense of time passing, but it felt like I'd been inside my own skull for days. As I let go of the final memory of him—where he stared at me in the parking lot of the casino, that first time—an odd sensation filled me. It was sort of like the syrupy creep of the Suppressor leak, but much warmer than that. With it came a hollowness, similar to the way I'd felt after my soul had been taken.

It was as if I were balancing on a precipice, completely alone and shrouded in darkness. It wasn't scary, just... weird, and almost peaceful. Had it not been for the nightmare I'd just had, it might have felt less unsettling.

"Reach inside and find that central light." Nomura's voice sounded so far away now.

I did as he asked, homing in on what remained inside my mind. With every thought and every memory gone, I couldn't see what he wanted me to. It was all just shadow and blankness and a gathering sense of deep calm.

A light emerged in the back of my head, spilling out across the shadows and chasing them away. My heart leapt in a way it hadn't since the Suppressor crack, feeding complete joy into my body. It ricocheted through my veins. My limbs felt heavy and sluggish, but not in an unpleasant way. The light morphed into a landscape I didn't recognize, with green hills and huge trees draped in Spanish moss.

A little girl was playing on the banks of a stream, with a man beside her. She had a tiny fishing net and was scooping it into the water to catch the silvery minnows that darted beneath the water's surface. In the near distance, I saw a quaint house with a picket fence and white-washed walls, with wildflowers swaying in the garden. The air felt cool and clean against my cheeks, and a figure stood in the doorway with a smile fixed on her face. She was watching the man and the girl playing together, a pendant glinting at her neck. A pendant I recognized because I wore a replica of it around my own neck.

Isadora...

The man turned to flash a grin at her, and I knew him instantly. My father was smiling at his sister because they were at peace, enjoying a simple moment of happiness. The girl on the bank was me, wearing a yellow summer dress. She turned to grab her father's hand and tugged on it to get his attention. She pointed at a fish caught in the net and let out a laugh so pure and heartwarming that I felt my own heart break in the most beautiful way.

"Did you catch one, sweetheart?" Hiram chuckled.

"A big one!" the girl squealed.

"Shall we put him back so he can swim with the rest of his fishy friends?"

The girl nodded. "Yes… he swims."

As soon as she'd let the fish go, my father scooped her up into his arms and threw her high into the air. She giggled and squealed with delight, stretching out her arms and pleading with him to throw her higher.

"I fly! I a bird!"

"No, honey, you're an angel." Hiram smiled as he tossed her higher.

"Like Mom?" the girl asked.

"No, not like Mom. She's flying much higher right now so she can watch you properly."

The girl grinned. "Mommy! See me fly!"

I didn't remember any of this, but it was definitely my memory, or a re-creation of one, since I was viewing it outside my own body. I realized it must have been buried in the very back of my mind, pushed down through years of heartache and loss and wondering why I'd been abandoned. I was vaguely aware of wetness on my cheeks. But they weren't sad tears, necessarily—they were happy ones, for the joy that I'd felt all those years ago, standing on the riverbank with my dad and calling out for my mom.

That happiness radiated through me. The real world fell away, until this was the only place I wanted to be. I'd never known a rush like it, the whole sensation completely intoxicating, like I was flying as high as the little version of me.

"Now, bring your Chaos into the light. Drag it all into that space." Nomura's voice was barely a whisper now.

I reached inside myself and felt for the familiar energy that flowed within my veins. It wasn't easy, and beneath the euphoric rush of joy, I could feel my body trembling with the exertion. I grabbed hold of the tendrils of Chaos and heaved them up into my mind, the sparking energy filling the landscape, making it look weird and psychedelic. Everything pulled away from my body and poured into my head instead, until I couldn't feel anything at all. I no longer existed in the real world—it was just me and this one scene, playing over and over on a sweet loop, while my Chaos tinged every figure and every aspect with vivid color and bright light. The sky seemed impossibly blue, and the silver glancing off the fish shone like a spotlight in my eyes. I'd never seen anything like it, but it didn't frighten me—it wasn't nightmarish at all. Instead, it felt like… well, like home.

My body felt weightless, and I realized that I was rising over the image below me. I was in the sky itself, flying on invisible wings, the air rushing across my face. Nothing could get me here, and I never wanted to leave.

Without warning, I plummeted to the ground. A sharp pain tore through my abdomen, connecting me back to the real world. The image faded, and the Chaos unraveled, and when I blinked my eyes open, I was standing next to my body. It lay on the cushions beside

Nomura's low table, my eyes still closed despite me seeing clearly. Nomura stood over me, glancing around in an agitated manner.

This isn't Euphoria... it was, but it isn't now. Everything felt wrong. I mean, I was staring down at my freaking body, and there was no kind of happiness in this. The rush had gone, and everything with it. My body was limp, and my chest barely seemed to be rising and falling.

"What have you done?" I hissed. My voice echoed outward, startling Nomura. He turned and narrowed his eyes, but I realized he couldn't see me. He was likely only hearing my voice because he'd done something to link us. *The tea... the freaking tea!* There was a reason I preferred coffee, and this was it.

Tears fell down his cheeks. "I am so sorry, Harley. I am so terribly sorry for this. I had no choice."

"What do you mean?" Although I was out of my body, I could still feel emotion. And right now, I was angry as all hell.

"About a week ago, the talisman I gave Shinsuke warned me that he was in grave danger. My son had fallen off the grid, so to speak. Two days later, I tracked him and found him with members of the Cult of Eris. Katherine had recruited him, and now she's using him as leverage against me... and against those who would seek to destroy her. The only way I can get my son out of there alive is if Katherine relieves him of his duties, and this is the price I must pay for that."

Son of a... I wasn't exactly disappointed in him, because what would I have done in that situation? Still, it stung like nothing else, filling me with fury and sadness. To think that Katherine had managed to manipulate another father into obeying her for the life of his child. She was beyond all boundaries and remorse, and I hated her for it. No, I despised her beyond words for it.

If only you knew how well that had worked out for Alton! Astrid had her soul missing because of what Alton had done. Nobody came out of a deal with Katherine in one piece, least of all the children who'd been turned into bartering chips.

"Put me back, and we'll figure something else out," I snapped. I'd trusted him, almost more than anyone else in this coven. I'd put my faith in him to help me and keep me from dying, and he'd done this. He had no right to use me for his benefit—no right! Nor did he have the right to sign my death warrant.

"I can't do that, Harley. I'm sorry."

I lashed out at him with my invisible hand, but it merely breezed through him like I was a ghost. Was that what I was now? A ghost? Whatever I was, I was locked out of my body, and Nomura was keeping me like this. The ultimate and most heartbreaking betrayal, from a man I'd trusted with everything.

TWENTY-EIGHT

Harley

Minutes passed as I paced the room in my ghostly form, invisible to Nomura. He kept saying sorry every few seconds, and it was starting to get annoying.

"If you were really sorry, you'd let me go," I said.

"I can't do that, I can't do that," he muttered. "You have to stay in your astral form. I will finish the spell that binds you here. It takes a while for the chants to be uttered. It's the only way. I am deeply sorry and deeply ashamed, but I can't allow Katherine to have my son. Please understand."

"What deal did you make? What exactly are you trading?" I struggled to push away my anger.

He glanced in the direction of my voice. "Katherine will release Shinsuke to me, and I will release you to her, at a designated time and location."

My astral heart lurched. What was Katherine planning, once she got her hands on me? It couldn't be good, whatever it was. Then again, maybe my body would give out before she could get to me. It wasn't what I wanted, but I would have given anything to see the look on her face when they made the exchange and she found out I was as dead as a doornail. *That'd serve you right, you evil cow.*

"We can think of another way to get your son back," I replied. "You don't have to do this. You don't have to stoop to her level."

He shook his head. "It has to be this way. I won't put your life above my son's, I'm sorry. I simply can't do that. The risk is too great."

"Please!" I felt helpless, hovering about with no way of getting back into my locked body. I understood that he was worried about his son, but I would face something far worse if Katherine got her hands on me.

Panic shot through me in a sudden rush, my astral veins pulsating with terror as I envisioned what might lay ahead. I didn't want to go to Katherine. I didn't want to be exchanged like an inanimate object. I didn't want to die, not because of the Suppressor and definitely not at Katherine's hands. My real body flinched suddenly, a vibration rippling through my limbs, making my fingertips tap violently on the ground. It seemed I wasn't completely cut off. All around the room, objects began to rise, spurred on by my Telekinesis glitching.

Yes, come on, body! That's it!

"I have planned for this, too," he said with a sigh. From the top drawer of his desk, he took out a pair of Atomic Cuffs and quickly slapped them on my real body's wrists. *Dammit!* I thought I'd had it then—a way out of this mess.

"So, what, am I a spirit now?" I demanded, infuriated.

He shook his head. "You are in your astral form. It's the only safe place to keep you until Katherine contacts me with her instructions."

A thought crept into my mind. If this was my astral form, then did that mean I was in some sort of astral projection? That was the thing we'd talked about with Marie Laveau and Remington, one of the two ways to reach out to a Child of Chaos. Until I figured out a way to get back into my body or warn the others, there was no harm in making my astral state useful.

Like this, I had the power to reach out to a Child of Chaos.

There was just one problem—well, a couple actually. *How* did I get to a Child of Chaos? Which one was I supposed to summon? Who was most likely to be helpful? And how was I supposed to summon them like this? Astral projection was the easy part; the rest... not so much.

My mind went blank. I knew one summoning spell, but Erebus was a scary bastard, and I didn't fancy giving a life to gain his services. Even though Nomura had betrayed me, I didn't want him dead. Plus, with those Cuffs on me, it probably wouldn't have worked anyway. *Maybe Gaia would be easier to approach?* Elementals were all connected to her in some way. She was the one who fed our energy to use Fire, Water, Air, and Earth—abilities that every magical was capable of, though most people were only capable of one.

Hey, Gaia? You listening? It was just as hopeless to ask for her help. I didn't know how to summon in this state, regardless of who I wanted to see. Nomura had probably been thinking this whole thing through ever since he got the news of his son, ironing out every little detail, and now I was stuck with nowhere to go.

Before I could blink, Nomura's office whirled away, and reality warped around me, morphing into the most beautiful place I'd ever seen. I found myself standing in front of a tumbling waterfall with a crystal-clear pool at the bottom, where colorful fish darted beneath the surface. Verdant trees hung across the falling water, exotic birds roosting in the branches, while pink-tinged blossoms drifted into the water below. Everything was green and lush and vibrant, with creatures chattering happily and sweet flowers growing all the way up the silvery rockface that the water rushed over.

I'm definitely not in Kansas anymore... But where was I?

I staggered back as a figure strode out from beneath the waterfall, the liquid parting. The woman was clad in a long gown made of interwoven leaves and flowers. Small green snakes wrapped around her arms like jewelry. They were still alive, just content to be there. A butterfly rested at the base of her throat, its blue wings spread out, looking like the prettiest pendant. It fluttered every now and again, flexing its wings before nestling against her pale skin once more. Long, flowing copper locks trailed all the way down her back, two tendrils framing her face, and a crown of leaves adorned her head.

In a strange way, she reminded me of myself.

The woman smiled. "I thought of you when I designed this body, Harley. I figured that a sense of familiarity would be more likely to keep you calm in a place such as this, given that it is your first official encounter with a Child of Chaos."

Did she just read my mind?

"I can hear your every thought," she replied with a warm chuckle.

"Are you... Gaia?" I'd have to learn to keep my thoughts toned down around her.

"A pleasure to make your acquaintance." She held out a slender hand covered in rings made of vines and daisies. I took it tentatively, not quite knowing the proper etiquette. I got the urge to curtsey, but I quickly pushed it aside.

"Did you hear me call for you?" I asked. "I mean, I'm guessing you did, otherwise I wouldn't be here."

"I heard your call."

"Then you know what kind of trouble I'm in? I wanted to contact a Child of Chaos, yeah, but I didn't want it to happen like this. I'm not even supposed to be astrally projecting, if that's even a term. Nomura tricked me so he could palm me off to Katherine, and now I'm stuck like this. Seriously, my body is down there—well, wherever Earth is—and I'm locked out. I don't know how long I have until he makes the exchange."

"Patience, my child." Gaia smiled warmly. "Time flows differently in my otherworld. By the time you are returned to your reality, barely minutes will have passed." She shifted her features until she'd become identical to me, which was as flattering as it was unsettling. "However, there are several things we must discuss before I can release you from this world. I have been waiting to speak with you for a very long time, and I'm rather glad that you have found your way to me."

I didn't know what to say to that. A Child of Chaos had been waiting to speak to *me*? That was impossible to wrap my head around. Still, there were things I needed to speak to her about, too, and I wasn't sure just how long she'd give me here.

"Since you've got the inside scoop, being a Child of Chaos and all, can you tell me anything about the five rituals to become one?" I asked. It was blunt, but I didn't care.

Gaia shook her head. "I cannot intervene in a challenge that has already begun, my child. Chaos forbids me from speaking of it, given the nature of my being. However, I am rather fond of you, given the nature of *your* being. It is rare to discover a Full Elemental, one who is in harmony with all of my gifts. You are one of the few who are truly connected to me." She paused. "But I can tell you that Katherine is getting closer to performing the second ritual. I can also warn you that it will involve a large gathering of magicals."

I frowned. "Her recruits?"

"I cannot say more, my child of the Elements." She looked sad about it, which was some comfort. "There is one other thing."

"What is it?" My eyes widened in hopeful anticipation.

"You must be careful when you contend with Echidna. She is ancient, almost as old as the Children of which I am one. She will not surrender the blood you seek with any great ease, and you will not find it as simple as you did with Giverny Le Fay."

So these Children could see and hear everything that was going down in the mortal realm? I wanted to be mad that they hadn't stepped in yet, but I understood the predicament they were in. Just like Marie and Papa Legba, they were bound by the rules and laws of Chaos, and those rules couldn't be bent, not even to save themselves. I guessed they were omniscient but not omnipotent, which had to suck.

"Do you know who the Challenged Child is—the one that Katherine is going to choose to face?" I'd been thinking about it a lot since Katherine's completion of the first ritual.

"I do not."

"Why don't you just stop her? Like, when you first found out what she was up to, why didn't you step in and stop her from doing the first ritual? I don't get it. Is it still about Chaos rules?"

She sighed sadly. "You are correct in your assumptions. It is the Chaos rule that we are forbidden from preventing such an action. Any magical may challenge a Child of Chaos, provided they have the right knowledge of the Chaos rituals. I confess, they were thought to be lost, remaining solely in the minds of the Librarians, who have passed it from generation to generation. We did not expect anyone to discover the secret of their last resting place, but Katherine is far more resourceful than we anticipated. She got to the current Librarian, it seems, and has learned all she needs to know. We could not have stopped her."

"So you're not quite gods?"

She laughed. "Not quite. However, I believe there's a chance you may stop her on our behalf, for the good of your own kind as well as ours. You are the hope of a generation, and far beyond that. Even if you cannot prevent her from performing the next ritual, or even the one after that, I believe you will find yourself with enough strength to fight her before the end."

"I hope so."

Compassion flickered across her eyes; her irises were entirely black. "You must not underestimate the magical spirit, Harley. There is a reason why we Children feed our Chaos into you. Power has very little to do with the ability to learn and perform the five rituals, just as studying hard cannot improve the overall intelligence of an individual. You are all gifted in your own ways, and you all have a strength that will only be revealed in the darkest of times. It is your greatest attribute —magicals and ordinary mortals alike."

"Anyone would think you're fond of us." I flashed her a smile.

"You are all exceptional beings, even those who fall into shadow. We have watched over all of you for more years than I care to count, and when we first made you, we knew there would be greatness and darkness in equal measure. We opened a Pandora's Box the day we made the first magicals, but we always hoped that those of good and pure hearts would triumph over those who sought evil. And, for the most part, we were right. A magical such as Katherine is rare in the world, and, as such, she will always be outnumbered. Now, a leader of equal strength is required to guide her downfall."

I gawked at her. "Please don't say you mean me. I'm happy to fight, but I'm no leader."

"Only time will tell, Harley." She chuckled. "You are born of two good souls, one of whom was especially dear to me. Your father was a Full Elemental, just as you are, and that bound us together in a manner beyond the ordinary. It bound us in the same way that I am bound to you. I always hold a soft spot in my heart for those who are closer to my central being."

"I was having the greatest memory of him just before Nomura left me locked out of my body." I smiled at the thought of me on the riverbank, catching fish and flying in his arms. I wished I could have had a memory like that with my mom, but that was impossible. She'd died shortly after my birth, and I doubted my memory went back that far. Still, I'd take what I could get.

"Euphoria?" Gaia said.

I nodded.

"It is not the average magical who can perform such a task on their first try, especially not under your current circumstances. That is most impressive," she said. "Then again, I am already aware of your more unusual specialties, which are beyond my Elemental gifts. I must implore you not to attempt to summon Erebus again, for he is the most volatile and dangerous amongst us Children. My own Children, the Elements themselves, fear him above all things."

"What about Lux and Nyx?"

"Nyx is somewhat distant in nature and cares very little for the world of mortals. Lux is more benevolent, I suppose, and shares my affinity for those within her jurisdiction of power. However, she can be somewhat wily, and often enjoys playing tricks to amuse herself. Even they fear Erebus."

Note to self: no more summoning. Gaia laughed at my thought.

"Can you tell me more about Katherine?" I asked. "Like, where she's hiding, or where the Cult of Eris is hiding? Think of it as a handy loophole in stopping her from getting these rituals done. You wouldn't technically be helping us stop the rituals, you'd just be helping us catch the Cult of Eris."

A mischievous grin spread across her face. "I would if I could, Harley. You should not underestimate me. I am a Child of Chaos, not a fool. I understand the rules of Chaos in a way you cannot." She tilted her head. "However, I can tell you more about Echidna. Enough to give you a chance of surviving your encounter with her—if luck is on your side."

TWENTY-NINE

Wade

I t'd been hours since I'd seen Harley. I'd woken up thinking about her. *Go figure.* Lunch had come and gone, and I was still thinking about her. After what I'd said to my mom, I knew I needed to do something about Harley. About my feelings for her. We weren't in an actual relationship, but we couldn't keep away from each other. And yeah, we'd agreed to focus on the Suppressor first, but what happened if she died? What if we couldn't fix it and she died without me telling her how I felt? Properly, this time. What if I didn't get to experience something real with her? I wanted to. I got the feeling she did, too. Not just because of last night, but because of everything else.

I checked my phone to see if she'd texted back. I'd tried to be subtle in my last three texts, but there'd been no reply to any of them. The Rag Team had been doing their own thing with regards to our mission, so I hadn't seen much of them, either. But it was weird that I hadn't seen any sign of Harley all day. Then again, she was exhausted. She was probably asleep somewhere, resting on the job. I was supposed to be on research duty, but I couldn't focus.

Giving up, I headed for the Bestiary. The rest of the Rag Team had planned to be there, and I hoped they'd have some info for me. Santana usually dropped in on Harley in the mornings, so she'd have some idea of Harley's whereabouts.

Up ahead, I noticed Nomura in the hallway. I was about to call out, to check whether Harley had been to see him, but he went into Levi's office before I could. Annoyed, I got my phone out and dialed Harley's number for the tenth time. It rang with no answer, just as it had before. Where the hell was she?

Feeling unsettled, I raced toward the Bestiary and pushed open the double doors. Making my usual excuses to the security team, I headed through to the back hall. Echidna was being defrosted here, under Tobe's guidance. The whole team was there, and they turned to look at me as I rushed in. Louella and Jacob were absent. So was Garrett, but that wasn't anything new. Harley's absence, however, felt wrong.

"Anyone seen any sign of Merlin today?" I asked. "Santana?"

"Today? No." She frowned. "Why, what's up?"

"I keep calling, but it just rings out. I haven't seen her all day, and she isn't replying to my texts."

Dylan smirked. "Did the two of you have a spat last night?"

"No, which is why it's weird." My throat constricted as I remembered last night. I just hoped my face didn't give me away. "Santana, you're sure you didn't check on her this morning?"

Santana shook her head. "I knocked, but there was no answer. I figured she could use the rest, so I just let her sleep."

"But you didn't actually check her room?"

"No." A flicker of fear crossed Santana's face.

I looked at Astrid. "Astrid, can you check Harley's GPS? This isn't like her at all. She wouldn't just drop off the face of the earth without saying something to someone. She wouldn't just miss a meeting because she was tired—she'd keep going until she dropped."

"I didn't even think…" Santana looked horrified. "I just thought she was sleeping."

"It's not your fault, and maybe she is sleeping, but we need to know for sure. She's in a vulnerable state with her Suppressor, and something doesn't feel right."

Astrid nodded. "Give me a minute. I'll find our girl." She whipped out Smartie, and her hands moved so fast they were almost a blur on the screen. I paced the floor anxiously and waited for the result. The others were on edge, too, although that might have had something to do with the great big box on the plinth ahead of us. It still looked like it was thawing out. And, since Tobe didn't look too stressed, I figured Echidna was some ways off from emerging.

"Anything?" I folded my arms across my chest.

"Two more seconds," Astrid replied. A beep sounded from Smartie. "Yep, got her. She's in the coven, but it's not exactly an accurate science. It doesn't give her precise location, just a vague search area."

"Which is?" My tone came out sharper than I'd intended.

"The west wing. Near the preceptors' training room."

"Great, thanks. Can you send the location to my phone?"

Astrid swiped her fingertip across the screen. "Already done. Are you going to go looking for her?"

"Yeah, I have to be sure she's okay. I'm sure she is, but... well, I need to know."

Santana nodded effusively. "I'll come with you." She clearly felt guilty about not properly checking on Harley this morning. "The rest of you should stay and keep an eye on Echidna. We're not far off, right?" She looked toward Tobe.

"We're rather close to her being fully functional again," Tobe replied. "I must confess, the deep freeze is melting far quicker than I anticipated. She is likely looking forward to stretching my entrails out like a rope—that's why she is thawing out faster." It dispelled my previous thought that he wasn't stressed. He was extremely bothered; he was just good at hiding it.

"Come on, then." I walked away without another word. My only focus was Harley. If Santana wanted to come along, that was fine, but we needed to move fast. A creeping doubt lurked in my mind. Harley had no reason to ignore us. If something had happened to her, I wanted to know. And with her Suppressor acting up, I feared the worst.

A thousand scenarios exploded into my head. She might have gone to do some private training and collapsed midway through. She might have gone for a walk and had a Chaos attack. She might have left her room to do some research and been gripped by the Suppressor while she was at it. We didn't have a timescale for her leak. In truth, none of us actually knew how long she had before it killed her. We'd been working on the idea that we had a lot of time left, but now I wasn't sure. What if it had run out already?

"You think she's okay?" Santana asked.

"I really don't know."

"Do you think she might be… uh…"

I shook my head. "I can't even think about that right now. She's so sick, and I…" I was about to spill my guts about Harley when a movement caught my eye. Up ahead, Nomura exited Levi's office. He didn't look very happy.

"I will report to you in the morning," Nomura said through the open door.

"I trust that you will." Levi's voice echoed from inside. A second later, Nomura closed the door and turned to leave. *Not so fast.*

"Nomura, wait up!" I sprinted toward him, with Santana at my side.

He whirled around, his eyes widening for a moment. "Ah, Wade, Santana, good to see you. Is something the matter?" The words came out a little too fast. He seemed tired and jumpy. Like we'd caught him red-handed.

"Have you seen Harley today?" I replied. No point beating around the bush.

"I saw her this morning, yes."

Santana and I exchanged a hopeful look.

"Did she seem okay? Do you know where she is?" Santana chimed in.

"We had our first round of Euphoria lessons, but then I sent her on her way. She said she wanted to grab some coffee, and she seemed rather tired. I presumed she was heading back to her room to sleep off the training." He made a point of looking us in the eye. "Should I be worried? Do I need to raise an alarm?"

The cogs whirred in my head. "No, I'm sure it's nothing. She's been pretty beat lately, so she probably grabbed her daily gallon of coffee and headed to bed. We were just going back to the living quarters, as it happens. I'm sure she's fine." Santana smacked me in the shoulder, but I ignored it. "I just thought I'd ask you so we could save ourselves the trek."

"Very well. Good day to you both." Nomura didn't even crack a smile. Instead, he breezed past us and walked away.

I waited until he'd disappeared around the corner. "Did you see that?" I hissed.

"What?" Santana looked baffled.

"Our dear preceptor here could barely hold it together." I tried to connect the pieces in my head. "Did you see the way his eyes widened when he saw us? It was like he didn't want to see us for some reason."

"What are you saying?"

"I'm still figuring it out, but the strain on his face and the lack of any kind of emotion—doesn't that seem odd to you?"

She frowned. "I guess."

"That's the go-to method for people desperate to keep a secret," I explained. "I've seen it before, in special training sessions they made us do back in Houston. My father led the classes. He was a specialist in interrogation before he joined the Texas Mage Council, and he taught us how to spot the subtle changes in speech and body language when someone is trying to hide something. There's a reason so many members of the Houston Coven end up in the intelligence services, and my father *is* that reason."

Santana scoffed. "It's probably got more to do with Nomura's oh-so-noble character. He's upset about Alton—he's been out of it ever since the news came about Levi. The man couldn't lie to save his life. There's probably some secret Japanese rule against it."

"This is Harley we're talking about. Do you really want to risk it?" I leveled my gaze at her. "He wouldn't be the first person acting weird in this place. Given our track record, I say we investigate."

She paused. It wasn't easy for any of us to be suspicious of the preceptors, but things had gotten strange lately. And there was no denying how odd it was that Harley had just vanished. All bets were off.

"If I get sent to Alaska for this, you're buying me every kind of thermal gear. Do you know what happens to Mexicans in Alaska?" Her voice carried a note of deep concern. But she was on board, and that was all that mattered.

"No, what happens to Mexicans in Alaska?"

"The same thing that happens to everyone else. They freeze their asses off."

I smiled. "So you're game?"

"You bet your hot pockets I am."

We took off down the hallway and followed Nomura. He was walking fast, and it was proving hard to keep our distance without losing him. He turned left and right without warning. For a moment, he disappeared completely. I pulled Santana to a halt with me. A second after, I heard his footsteps echo in the corridor off to the right and led the way down it. My stomach sank. I didn't want it to be true. However, he was heading straight into the west wing. I had a feeling I knew exactly where he was going, too.

Sure enough, five minutes later we ended up outside his office. He'd entered a minute earlier, and we were waiting for everything to fall silent. I pressed my ear to the door and listened closely. I heard shuffling inside and the subtle sound of a screen door closing. I had never been in Nomura's office before, but I'd heard rumors of a meditation studio. Was he going to meditate? I very much doubted it. Still, it meant he was out of his office for at least a short while.

"Are we sneaking in?" Santana whispered.

I nodded. "We need to find out where Harley is. I'm guessing he knows more than he's letting on. He's acting major-league shifty. Plus, the location Astrid sent me for Harley's phone is right around here."

"Come on then, before someone sets the dogs on us. Let's see what Nomura's really hiding in his place of Zen." She flashed me a grin and turned the handle. I let her go in ahead of me, slipping in after.

On first impression, nothing seemed out of place. Nomura's books and knick-knacks were all neatly organized. The pillows around his low table were perfectly arranged. The candles and incense were all set out at equidistant intervals. *There has to be something amiss.* My eyes fixed on a tea tray. It sat on a small table on the far side of the room, with two cups laid out. I approached and lifted one of them to my nostrils. A sharp scent stung them, a tiny drop of liquid still lying in the bottom of the cup.

Why two cups? I supposed he could have had a visitor after Harley.

Nomura's voice drifted through from behind the screen door. "... really am terribly sorry. You can speak to me, you know? I'm sorry for the trouble I have caused you. I didn't want it to be this way."

Santana shot me a worried look and pointed to the adjoining room. I nodded and crept toward it. Ducking down, I peered through a thin gap between the screen doors. Nomura paced the floor beyond. He was even more agitated than before and seemed to be looking at something on the ground. I squinted to get a closer look. My heart dropped like a stone. Harley lay slumped on the floor by Nomura's feet, and she wasn't moving.

I jumped up and tore the screen door aside. "I knew you'd done something to her!" I stormed into the meditation room, joined by Santana.

"*Dios mio!* Harley!" she yelped, catching sight of Harley's body.

"NO!" Nomura howled. He whirled around to face us with his hands up. Fire formed beneath his palms. If it was a fight he wanted, then he was going to get one.

I ducked, and the fireball struck the wall behind me. Gathering my energy, I formed a fireball of my own and hurled it at Nomura. He staggered out of the way and lashed another sparking orb at Santana. She sidestepped it with ease, given the smallness of the room. There was barely enough space for all three of us. Forgetting magical abilities, I sprinted straight for Nomura. I hit him with the full force of my weight and dragged him to the ground. He fought back with surprising strength, his fists aiming for my face. It was like trying to wrangle an eel. Just when I thought I had him, he'd writhe in a way that made me lose my grip.

Santana raced up beside me and pressed her knee into his chest.

"Get the Cuffs!" she shouted. "I'll handle this." Her Orishas whirled around her head and dove beneath Nomura's skin. His eyes widened in surprise.

I grabbed the keys from his waistband and ran for Harley. Unlocking the Cuffs, I unclipped them and carried them quickly back over to Nomura. A moment later, they were lashed to his wrists. He continued to struggle, but at least he couldn't use his magic on us.

"Can you hold him down?" I asked.

Santana nodded. "I've got this. See to Harley."

I nodded and ran back to her. Sinking down to my knees, I took her by the shoulders and lifted her into my lap. Her eyes were closed, but she was still breathing. "Harley? Harley, can you hear me?" I shook her gently. "Harley?" I smoothed back her hair and shook her harder. Desperation took hold of me as I kissed her forehead and rocked her in my arms. "Come back to me. Come on, I know you can pull through this."

Beside me, Nomura broke down in tears. "It is no good. I had no choice."

"You'd better start talking, you bastard." Santana dug her knee deeper into his chest, her face red. I'd never seen her so angry in all my life. "What the hell did you do to her? Speak quickly, before I start cutting things off!"

He shook his head. "I had no choice."

"I don't care. I want to know what you've done to her!" Santana screamed in his face. "My Orishas are raging right now. They like Harley, and you've hurt her. Right now, I'm the only thing standing between you and having your insides turned into your outsides."

He cowered beneath Santana's tirade. "I locked her in astral projection. It was the only way to restrain her without harming her, given the Suppressor crack. I had to be careful. I had to render her harmless before I could sneak her out of the coven. The location hasn't been sent to me yet. I had to keep her here until I had the details."

"Sneak her where?" I snarled at him. My arms were wrapped around Harley, but there was nothing I could do to wake her. I just wanted her to blink open her eyes and see me. I just wanted her to be okay.

"Away," he wept. "The associates are due to text me with the location and time of the exchange." It didn't take a genius to work out *whose* associates he was talking about. But why?

I stared at him. "Take this spell off her, now!"

"I can't do that. I have no choice. I can't free her, not with my son in danger. The only way to free him is to make this exchange. Even if it costs me everything, I will not forsake him."

"Take the spell off her!" Santana roared.

"You won't harm me, Santana." He looked up at her with weepy eyes. "If you do, you will have no means of freeing Harley. The spell is deadlocked. I won't fix it. It is the only way I can have my son back."

Nomura wouldn't budge. Even with Santana's threats, he wouldn't give in. Despair had clearly taken hold of his mind. There was no use in reasoning with him, not like this.

Nevertheless, I had to find a way to get through to him. I held my whole world in my arms, and I wasn't going to lose her. Not now. Not ever.

THIRTY

Harley

"To win Echidna over, you must appeal to her motherhood," Gaia explained. "Her children, as ghastly and terrible as they are, are her most precious possessions. If you are able to appeal to her maternal instinct in the proper way and use that to your advantage, then she may at least hear what you have to say. Otherwise, she will simply tear you to shreds before anyone can stop her."

I sighed heavily. "That's a risk I'll have to take. Everything is on the line here. Everything."

Gaia nodded slowly. "I thought you might say that. It is why I wished to help you as much as possible, even with all my restrictions."

"I'd love to stay and talk some more, but I need to get back." I glanced up at the azure sky and wondered what it'd be like to live in a place like this. "Can you help get me out of this astral projection? Nomura locked me out, but I'm guessing you've got some kind of magical goodies up your sleeve? Something that isn't covered in a bunch of Chaos red tape?"

She chuckled. "It is way past time that you were returned to your body. Spending too much time in astral projection wears upon one's spirit and makes the return much more difficult each time." She flashed me a smile. "Besides, your lover is waiting for you, and he is desperate to feel you breathe in his arms again."

"My who-said-what-now?" I spluttered, but I didn't get the chance to hear Gaia's reply as the otherworld warped around me. I landed back into my body with a brutal kick, my eyes flying wide as I sat up with a sharp wheeze.

"What the—" Wade almost dropped me out of fear as I dragged air into my lungs and stretched out my limbs. Everything seemed to be back in working order, but I had no idea why Wade and Santana were in the meditation room with me. I glanced down and saw Nomura on the floor, with Santana's knee on his chest and her Orishas whizzing about his head.

I clambered to my feet and marched over to Nomura, brushing past a startled Santana. "How did you break the spell?" he asked, his eyes wide in shock.

I slapped him hard in the face, his head snapping to one side. "Gaia helped, you asshole!"

"Hell yeah! You don't mess with *mi hermana!*" Santana laughed, despite her obvious awe. I was glad to have them here; it was way better than waking up alone and trying to figure out how to get out of Nomura's office without him realizing.

Strong arms grabbed me from behind and whirled me around. I barely had time to look into Wade's eyes before his lips were on mine, pressing against me with a desperate passion. I looped my arms around his neck and kissed him back, feeling an overwhelming sense of happiness to be back in action and not locked out of my own freaking body. After all, I couldn't have done this if I was lying on the ground, unconscious.

"I thought I'd lost you," he whispered as he pulled away. He held my face in his hands, his eyes glinting with un-spilled tears. I leaned in and kissed him again, reveling in the touch of his lips against mine. *I could get used to this.*

"You'll never lose me," I murmured back, holding him tight.

The sound of Nomura choking on a sob distracted us from our moment. "I am sorry, Harley. I am so very sorry for all of this. I had no choice. I really had no choice."

Wade glared at him, one hand sliding around my waist. "Your apology isn't worth a damn thing, Nomura. You weren't even willing to help get Harley out of her astral projection. You were happy to keep her locked in there, so don't even try and pretend that you're sorry."

"I couldn't think straight from sheer despair, Wade," he replied. "You must understand, I did not want any of this. I did not ask for it, but I had to do what I thought was best. I will forever be shamed by this action. You must believe me, I could not see any other—"

"Save it." I cut him off sharply. I was furious with him, but I couldn't hate him. "Katherine has his son, Wade. She recruited him to join the Cult of Eris, and now he's stuck with them. The only way Nomura could get him out was to make a deal—his son for me. Sound familiar? Man, she sure knows how to manipulate a father's emotions, right?"

The impact was no less terrible for knowing the truth, though. Katherine had managed to get to a preceptor, and a very important one at that. Even though she was in hiding, out there in the big bad world, she seemed to have this majorly annoying knack of weaseling her way into anywhere she wanted. Particularly the SDC.

Nomura lifted his cuffed hands and covered his face. "My son is lost now. I will never see him again." His body was wracked with sobs.

I took a minute to calm down, knowing the Suppressor was heightening my feelings of anger. Even without the leak, I'd have been furious, but I had to try and see it from his perspective. I'd forgiven Alton in my own way, and Nomura deserved the same kind of even judgment. His son was in danger, and Shinsuke was all that Nomura had left in the world. He'd already lost his wife in tragic circumstances, so it stood to reason that he'd want to do whatever he could to save his boy, even if that meant kidnapping me.

I turned to Nomura, breathing heavily. "I'll do whatever I can to rescue your son, Nomura. But you should've come to me first. You should've told me what she was up to, so we could've worked out something else. I understand impulse and panic, but you've been a total idiot." I dragged in another breath. "If Katherine is destroyed, the Cult of Eris will crumble. Cause and effect, Nomura. Your son would have come back to you without any of this. But it's too late for that now."

"What are you going to do?" Nomura mumbled.

"The only thing we can do," I replied. I felt bad for him, I really did, but we couldn't lie for every single person who made dodgy deals with Katherine Shipton. Someone had to be made an example of. I was just sorry it had to be Nomura. "Santana, give O'Halloran a call. He needs to deal with this."

Santana nodded. "I'm on it." She took out her phone and dialed, lifting it to her ear. "Hi, O'Halloran? Yeah, we need you in Nomura's office. There's been a… problem, and we need you to deal with it. Sure, five minutes? Okay, great."

"No, you can't. My son…" Nomura looked panicked. His entire reputation was on the line, that was true, but he didn't seem to understand that we were doing this for his benefit. If Katherine discovered that Nomura had been apprehended, she was more likely to keep hold of Shinsuke for her own purposes. This way, he was more likely to survive until we could find a way to rescue him. I wanted to tell him all of that, but he'd started to cry again, rocking violently on the spot. I couldn't have gotten through to him, even if I'd shouted at the top of my lungs.

Five minutes later, O'Halloran burst through the screen door. He skidded to a halt and scanned the scene in front of him, putting the pieces together. Wade took him to one side, hurriedly relaying everything to him. O'Halloran kept glancing back at Nomura, his eyebrows lifting higher and higher with every revelation.

"Nomura? Really?" O'Halloran gave a low whistle. "I can't believe it. Hiro Nomura. My own boss. Geez... I thought you were going to say something exploded. My money was on Merlin. I can't believe it." He ran a hand over his buzzed hair.

"You need to take him down to the cells until we can figure out what to do with him," Wade replied.

O'Halloran nodded. "Yeah, of course. Right away. Hiro Nomura... This is going to take some time to sink in." He walked over to where Nomura lay on the ground and hoisted him up into his arms like he was a child. Nomura didn't even bother to fight; he just lay there limply as O'Halloran took him away. We watched him go, wondering what would become of the great Nomura. I hated that he'd been brought so low, but it was just another thing to add to my list of reasons to despise Katherine. I was sick of her tearing families apart.

A shrill tune pierced the air. It was coming from Wade's pocket. Frowning, he took out his phone, swiping the answer button and lifting it to his ear. His expression darkened as the caller spoke, though he didn't say much in response. A few minutes later, he hung up and slid his phone back into his pocket.

"What is it?" I moved toward him.

"That was the Paris Coven," he said, his voice thick with emotion. "Dr. Fenélon found your card, but she said it rang out when she dialed your number. She tried the next number, which happened to be mine. It's Odette. She was killed this morning. They're still investigating who might have been responsible, but all of their tapes have been wiped. She just wanted to let us know."

I sank to my knees, overcome with grief. He knelt beside me and wrapped me up in his arms, but it did nothing to ease the pain. Odette was dead, and it was all Katherine's fault. Who else would be responsible? Odette had come to the end of her usefulness, so Katherine had had her killed. That was the only explanation for all of this.

"We promised we'd protect her," I murmured into Wade's neck. "*I* promised her. I said I'd never let Katherine hurt her again."

"I know." He held tighter to me. "My charms must have been over-ridden. I didn't sense anything at all. Whoever did this, they were prepared. They were stealthy, and they came without warning. I'm so sorry, Harley."

Santana watched us from where she stood, shifting awkwardly. She hadn't known Odette personally, but the loss of the Librarian was a huge blow to all of us. She was the only one who knew about the other rituals, and now she was gone. Even without the emotional kick in the gut, that was bad news.

"Should I call Alton?" Santana asked. "I don't know how far gone she is, but he could help. It might not be too late."

I peered up at her. "Yes... yes! Call Alton. He might be able to fix this." I could've kissed her.

She dialed his number. "Alton? We've just had some bad news from the Paris Coven. Odette, otherwise known as the Librarian, was murdered this morning. We were wondering if you could help." A small smile crept onto her lips as she hung up and turned back to us. "He says he'll go. He's on his way to Paris now to try and revive her with Necromancy."

"Thank G—" My throat seized up and my chest tightened. The cold syrup of the Suppressor leak flooded my veins as my lungs strained to grasp at a breath.

"Harley?" Wade sounded panicked. "Harley, what's wrong?"

I couldn't answer him. My muscles were going haywire, spasming all over the place, my eyes rolling back into my head. The Suppressor was finally coming apart, and I couldn't do anything to stop it.

It's too late... I'm too late.

Death had made her way up the steps to my door, and she was

knocking loudly. All around the room, cups and swords and candles flew, smashing into the walls, like a poltergeist with a vendetta. My abilities were no longer under my control. Fire sparked out of my hands. Wade and Santana covered their faces as things tore through the air with no sense of ally or enemy. The ground beneath me trembled, a crack splitting the wooden floor.

"It's happening!" Santana yelped, pressing herself against the wall.

"The Bestiary! We need to get her to Echidna!" Wade scooped me up into his arms and sprinted from the room. The hallways passed in a haze.

The Sanguine spell...

My time was almost out, and Isadora's charm bag had burned up at my throat.

THIRTY-ONE

Harley

Minutes later, we burst through the doors of the Bestiary and headed toward the back hall where Echidna was being defrosted. I drifted in and out of consciousness, aware of Wade's arms holding me tightly, but it was proving hard to keep a grip on reality. With every second that passed, the syrupy creep of the Suppressor leak spread deeper and deeper inside me, and I had no idea how much time I had left in this world.

"Hang in there, *mi hermosa*," Santana kept muttering. Her voice and Wade's grip were the only things keeping me in the land of the living. I had to make it through, because I wasn't about to lose everything I'd finally found, the things I'd been missing my entire life—love and friendship.

"What happened?" Isadora approached and touched her hand to my sweating brow.

"The Suppressor is taking over," Wade replied. His voice cracked, his words desperate.

"Set her down by Echidna's box. We need to get this Mother of Monsters out so she can speak to Harley." Isadora helped guide Wade toward the box, where he propped me up against the glass. From my vantage point, I saw that all the Rag Team was present, Garrett included. I hadn't expected to see him here.

He walked toward me and knelt down. "You keep at it, Merlin. This thing isn't taking you, you hear?"

I nodded and gripped my stomach as a jolt of pain shot through me.

"Astrid told me about this Echidna stuff. I figured I'd come over and help—wait for you to fix yourself up with that Sanguine spell, or whatever, so we can get back to work and kick Katherine's ass." He looked worried, which was oddly comforting.

Tobe sank down beside me and pulled me into his arms, wrapping me up in his furry embrace. "It will keep you warm, Harley," he explained as I buried my face in his fur. The others gathered around me, all of them wearing the same dire expression. *I must really look like crap.* Then again, I was on death's door, so what else could I expect? Even with Tobe's warm body feeding heat into me, I was shaking like crazy, every part of me hot and cold at the same time.

"How... much longer?" I rasped.

"Echidna is awakening," Tobe replied. Over his shoulder, I peered into the box behind me and saw a mass of black smoke encased in a thin layer of ice. Water dripped down onto the glass floor of the massive charmed box, filling it a fair way up. I hoped Echidna was ready to get her feet wet—if she even had feet. To be honest, I didn't know enough about her physical appearance to know what to expect from this Mother of Monsters.

"You've got this, Harley." Astrid made her way toward me. "You have to hold on. We're so close now."

I nodded and held tighter to Tobe to stop my body from disintegrating completely. I felt like I might implode at any moment, my heart racing, my lungs gasping for air, every muscle seized and spasming at once.

"She's almost awake, Harley," Tatyana added. "I can try and ease your pain, if it would make things better?"

I smiled up at her. "I don't think… it's going to cut it. But thanks."

"Get that fighting spirit going!" Dylan punched the air, but his eyes betrayed his fear. He was as scared as everyone else.

"I could see if the djinn can help," Raffe offered.

"One temperamental… monster is probably… enough for now," I wheezed.

Meanwhile, Jacob and Louella just stared at me. They didn't know what to say in a situation like this, but I could feel their despair drifting off them in sharp barbs that bit into my skin. It wasn't easy to keep positive when everyone around me was brimming with terror and hopelessness.

"I know you're tired, *mi preciosa*, but you've got to kick this in the *cajones*." Santana bent down and swept my damp hair out of my face. "You're stronger than anyone I know. The Suppressor isn't taking you yet—over my dead body!"

I grimaced. "No, I think it'll be over… mine."

"Just hold on, okay?" Wade added, his voice thick. "You have to hold on. I'm not losing you."

"I don't want to go." I looked up into his eyes and saw tears glistening. He tried to smile back, but he couldn't. Looking at me in this state wasn't fun for anyone, but he understood what he stood to lose if I didn't make it. He would lose all the possibilities we'd never explored, and all the words we'd never said to one another. To my mind, there was nothing worse than an unspoken love left to fester because time had run out. I wondered if my father had thought like this when he was faced with his dead wife and the weight of protecting his newborn child. I imagined all the things he might have said to her, if only he'd had the seconds left to pour out his heart.

"Keep your head in the game," he urged. "Try and focus, even though you're exhausted. You have to get that blood… you have to." He leaned over and kissed the edge of my shoulder, the only part of me left exposed by Tobe's embrace. The Beast Master himself seemed to be at a loss for words, his eyes cast down and his expression morose.

"Are you warm enough?" was all he could say.

"Better," I replied.

"It will not be much longer."

I glanced at him. "Echidna or me?"

"Echidna," he said hurriedly. "Of course, Echidna. You cannot die, Harley. I will not permit it."

I chuckled through the pain. "We may not have much choice."

Gaia had instructed me on how to appeal to Echidna's sensibilities, but there were no guarantees she'd listen after being trapped in a box for so long. I was as likely to die at her hand as I was from the Suppressor. Still, at least it'd be quicker. I didn't want to be defeatist, but things were looking pretty grim right now. Despite Wade's attempts at getting me to concentrate, trying to mentally prepare for this was a struggle of Everest proportions. I could barely think straight, let alone get myself in the right state to face Echidna.

With Odette's death, the Suppressor, the attack on Finch, Kenneth's sudden appearance, and Nomura's betrayal, mostly dictated by Katherine's grand plan, it was all weighing down on me way harder than before. Every time I tried to block out the bad thoughts, using the tips that Nomura had given me prior to locking me out of my own body, one of them jumped in without warning. I saw Odette on the windowsill and Finch curled up like a kid beneath the covers and Kenneth blinding Wade and Katherine staring me down in that pit I'd created.

"May I?" Wade glanced shyly at Tobe.

The Beast Master nodded. "It will not be long before she has to enter."

What, so everyone should say their goodbyes?

He frowned. "She's not going in there with that monster, Tobe."

"That box is the only thing strong enough to withstand the Chaos inside Harley. She is better off in there with Echidna than out here with us, where she may cause untold damage. I do not wish to be unfeeling, but I must consider what is best for the Bestiary, as well as for you." He looked torn, his expression downcast.

I smiled. "Hey, I'm supposed to go in there anyway. It's fine, Wade."

"How long does she have?" He looked at Tobe.

"A few minutes."

Wade moved into position where Tobe had been and wrapped me up in his arms. Although Tobe was much warmer, I preferred being in this embrace. Even if I didn't make it back out of the box, I'd have this memory to send me into... well, wherever people went when they died.

"Is it scary?" I asked, turning my gaze toward Tatyana.

A choked sob caught in her throat. "What do you mean, Harley?"

"Are the spirits scared when they die? Are they worried about where they'll end up?"

"You aren't going to die, Harley."

I smiled. "Humor me."

"They don't remember much of the actual dying. I believe it's like childbirth—they forget the pain as soon as it's over, and they're in the realm of the spirit world. As for what comes after, some are frightened, but most are eager to find out what awaits them." Tatyana wiped tears from her cheeks as Dylan put his arm around her.

Astrid turned her face away.

"Astrid?" I said softly.

"It is like coming home, Harley," she whispered. "It's peaceful and calm, and there's no pain anymore. It's like stepping into a hot bath after being out in the cold and sinking down beneath the warm water. It doesn't hurt. The coming back is the painful part."

Garrett stared at her. "It hurts?"

"Like you wouldn't believe," she replied. "But that won't happen to you, whatever the outcome."

With Alton in Paris, that definitely wasn't going to happen with me. I had no Necromantic backup to save me from the other side if I happened to die in the box with Echidna. There was a sense of calm in that, too—at least I wouldn't be ripped back to the land of the living, missing the one thing that made me who I was.

"Hey, but there's no point worrying about that," Santana cut in. "You're not dying, Harley. If you do, I swear I will hunt you down and kick your ass through every plane of existence."

I laughed. "Thanks, Santana. I'll look out for you if I don't make it out of the box."

Jacob sprinted toward me and threw his arms around Wade and me, burying his face in my shoulder. His tears seeped through my t-shirt and into my skin, his sobs stifled by my body. A moment later, everyone else gathered around for an impromptu huddle, their arms enveloping me and giving me strength. Even Garrett joined in, though he seemed awkward about it, while Tobe kept to the edges, brushing tears from his eyes with the edge of his wing.

"Go get that blood, Harley," Dylan said.

"Yeah, show that monster what you're made of." Raffe patted my back stiffly.

Santana grinned. "Show that Mother of Monsters what a mean mother—"

"Santana!" Tatyana interjected, sending a ripple of laughter around the group. That sound boosted my morale like nothing else, letting me know I was loved and that I could do this, for their sake as much as mine. The worse I felt, the more unstable what was left of my Suppressor became, and this was working wonders on heightening that sense of defiance in me. The one that had pushed me through a childhood of abandonment and bad homes, and the one that had helped me live on my own. The one that had given me the fight to face Katherine and live to tell the tale.

You're next, Katie. I'm going to get this blood, break this Suppressor, and then I'm coming for you.

"Echidna is emerging from her slumber," Tobe warned. "She must enter the box now."

"Come on, guys. It's time to get this show on the road." I broke away from them and allowed Wade to guide me toward the door of the glass box. I could barely stand on my own two feet but having him beside me gave me that extra push to carry on.

The door closed behind me, and I could just about make out the faces of Wade and my friends through the frosted panes. Ahead of me, Echidna rested, the ice melting off her. Any moment now, she'd wake up, and there'd be no going back.

THIRTY-TWO

Wade

I watched the glass. Closing that door behind her was one of the hardest things I'd ever done. Tobe stood beside me and restored the charms, but I couldn't settle down. I wouldn't until she was out again. Seeing her inside, slumped against the glass… it took everything I had not to storm back in and drag her out. What good would it do? She had to get the blood to survive. There was no alternative now.

Worst of all, I'd wanted to tell her I loved her before she went in. It had been on the tip of my tongue, but I hadn't been able to get the words out. I'd never said it before. Those words didn't come easily to me. I was kicking myself now. What if I never got the chance? If she got out of there, I vowed I'd tell her soon. When I could get my stupid tongue to cooperate.

The thought of losing her was impossible to comprehend. It kicked at my gut and squeezed at my heart. I paced the floor, but it didn't help. I wanted to punch the glass but knew I'd only get bruised knuckles. Man, I wanted to scream. I hated feeling helpless. Right now, I couldn't do a thing for her. Even so, I'd have done anything to save her. Anything. I'd have killed anyone who stood in the way of her survival. I couldn't lie and pretend I was okay; I was in deep. I loved Harley like I'd never loved anyone before. It felt wonderful and exciting and terrifying all at the same time.

I'd had girlfriends before, but they'd never lasted. Work was always the most important thing—work and career. Take this step, climb this ladder, reach this position. Do this, do that. I'd never stopped to smell the proverbial roses. I'd never stopped and looked at someone the way I looked at her. Then again, nobody had ever wrecking-balled into my life the way she had. Ignoring her had never been an option, and neither had stopping myself from falling for her.

"You sure know how to pick 'em, Crowley." Garrett's voice disturbed my anxious pacing. I'd almost forgotten there was anyone else in the room with me. The waiting was intolerable. This Echidna was taking her sweet time.

I glanced at him. "What?"

"You sure know how to pick 'em. You never did like a simple life, though, so I guess it makes sense." He wasn't trying to be funny. He was trying to pick my ass off the floor in his usual Garrett way. I knew he'd noticed the change between Harley and me. They'd all noticed. It was in their eyes as they stared at me. They all knew I loved her, and they were here for us both.

"She's not like any girl I've ever known. I think we can all agree on that," I replied quietly.

"She's a warrior, Wade." Raffe walked over and put his hand on my shoulder.

"I know." *But even warriors fall in battles they can't win.*

Just then, Harley tapped on the glass. All of us turned to look at her. She mouthed something, but we couldn't hear through the charmed box. I raised my eyebrows and tried to mime that we couldn't hear her. I probably looked like a prize idiot, but I didn't care. Did she want out? Did she not have anything left to give? Carrying her from Nomura's study, she'd been in a pretty bad state. It was only going to get worse.

She brought her fingertip to the last of the frost and scraped a word into it: *Odette?* The word was in reverse, but we could read it.

Astrid flashed her a thumbs-up and took out her phone. She punched in a number and lifted it to her ear. I guessed she was calling Alton, considering Harley's message. Even now, she was worrying about someone else. It annoyed me as much as it impressed me. She needed to be worrying about herself.

"I understand. I'll speak to you when you get back." Astrid swiped the end-call button. She seemed to want to be sad, but she couldn't manage it. Things had been weird with her ever since Alton brought her back. I didn't like to pry, but I knew something had gone wrong with her resurrection. We all did. The bright, bubbly Astrid we knew had been replaced with a cold, hollow version. It reminded me of Harley in New Orleans, after the soul thing.

I knew it hurt Garrett to see her like that. The revelation that being resurrected had hurt her had created an odd reaction in him. He couldn't stop staring at her.

Astrid approached the box and shook her head. Inside, Harley visibly deflated, her hopeful expression fading. And I didn't know if it was condensation running down the inside of the box or a tear falling from her eye. I'd have done anything to have been with her right then. But I couldn't even touch her.

"What's the news?" Santana prompted.

"Alton tried to revive Odette, but she died too many hours ago. His Necromancy barely lit up when he touched her body."

Tatyana frowned. "Could I be of any use?"

"I think it's too late for that," Astrid replied. "She's gone. There's nothing we can do about it." The words came out empty. Looking back at the box, Harley was trying to lip-read what Astrid was saying. I guessed she'd caught the gist. She was definitely crying now.

This isn't good for her. She needed to stay positive in order to combat the effects of the Suppressor. Too much of any emotion and she'd be spiraling out of control. I walked up to the glass to try and comfort her. The moment I reached out, the black smoke began to unravel. Echidna was waking up.

The last of the frost evaporated. Smoke spread through the box and obscured our view. Terrified of what might happen to Harley, I lunged for the door and tried to pull it open. Tobe was on me in seconds and yanked me away. He was too strong to fight physically. Still, I thrashed against him in an attempt to break free.

"You cannot help her." He bound me tight against him. "Echidna is not fond of males of any species, unless they have been birthed by her. You will destroy Harley if you attempt to get in, and Echidna will kill you, too. You must let Chaos take its course. Harley is the only one capable of doing this, and she will."

Isadora nodded, her voice trembling. "We must have faith in her now."

I stared at the box as a thickening haze filled it from pane to pane. In the center, a figure emerged.

THIRTY-THREE

Harley

A massive green-and-gold scaled tail lashed like a whip—a snake's tail, though much longer than any snake I'd ever seen, one that would put an anaconda to shame. An oddly human female upper body stretched out of the tail, like a messed-up mermaid. Wild black hair sprouted from her bone-pale skull, and six horns, pitch black, arched back from her forehead.

Her tail coiled around her, raising her up to give her more height over me. The scales vibrated, sending a shudder through the glass box and through my heart. Her face was drawn and skeletal, with two glowing red eyes peering at me through the black fog.

"Oh, it feels good to be free," Echidna hissed as she stretched out her bony arms. Her fingertips ended in long, sharp claws that glinted in the shadowy haze. "I am ready to kill something."

I backed up against the glass, but there was no escape. Terror splintered through me, a twist of pain searing my insides. My Suppressor didn't like this monster any more than I did. Either that, or it didn't want Echidna beating it to the punch and seeing me die first.

"You will do, girl." She lunged at me, but I ducked, and her head bounced off the door.

"No!" I cried, trying to get out of her way. The box was big, but not big enough to dodge her for long.

She lunged at me again, her fangs flashing. "I have been on ice for much too long. I must stretch my coils." I managed to roll out of her way, but I was too weak for this. If she kept lunging at me, I'd be a goner before I even mentioned a word about blood.

"Stop!" I screamed.

"A tasty morsel for starters, before I work my way out of this box and feed on the rest." She dove at me once more, and I barely escaped her attack, my limbs too slow and sluggish for this kind of assault. I caught a flash of her red eyes as her claws caught me in the ribs, my knees skidding along the wet floor and taking me out of her firing line.

Her scales rattled in excitement. "I do love the chase."

"Wait!" I urged breathlessly, still on my knees. "Listen to me, just for a minute. I've come to you, the Mother of Monsters, because I'm the daughter of a magical mother, and I need your help. Please." My lungs burned with the exertion of trying to escape her, and the horrible anticipation of her next attack sent a shiver of dread up my spine, like ants crawling all over me.

She sank back down into her coils. "What did you say?" Her voice carried a subtle hiss and rasped out of her throat when she spoke. I had her attention—holy crap, I had her attention! It was working... for now.

"I am the daughter of a magical mother, and I need the help of another mother to pull me through something that wants to kill me. Please, for her sake—for my mother's sake—you must listen to me." I knew that I was begging, but I didn't care. I thought of my mom and instantly felt strength in my chest, lifting me back to my feet in front of Echidna. She swayed from side to side like a cobra coming out of a basket, her red eyes fixed on me.

"The only thing standing between me and the rest of the world is this box. Why would I help you? Do you mean to let me out?" A creepy smile stretched her cracked, monstrous lips.

I held her demonic gaze. "You're better off in here than out there, believe me. There are other monsters out there now, ones who'd gobble you up for the sake of power. I already watched one die—a Purge beast who was very dear to me. I wouldn't want that to happen to you. Anyway, freedom isn't what it used to be."

"You are powerless to break me out, I presume?" she sneered, with a mocking tone. "Of course you are. You can't do anything. You can barely keep your Chaos under control." A bitter laugh rose from her throat as she swayed toward me.

"That's why I'm here, Mother." I bowed my head and prayed she wouldn't swipe it off my shoulders. In any situation, a show of respect and subservience was always a good way to go, and I'd already managed to capture her attention. I just needed to hold it until I could cut a deal with her—one that didn't involve her getting out into the world.

"I know I will return to ice, but my time will come… eventually. I am patient. Such is a mother's curse." She was so close I could smell her rancid breath and feel the cold mist drifting off her. She smelled of rotten earth, like decay and soil, mingled together with the salty tang of seawater.

"I'm here to ask for your help, from a daughter to a mother." I steeled myself and forced my legs to stop shaking. "And for my own mother, who can't save me herself because an evil, jealous woman took her life. A woman who killed my mother just after I was born. She stole my mother's chance to hold me in her arms and nurture me and see me grow into the woman I am today. On her behalf, I'm asking for your help, so that my life doesn't get taken, too."

Echidna reared back slowly, her eyes suddenly sad. "The bitter rage of mortals."

"I need some of your blood so that I can get my Chaos under control. I've got this thing inside me that's going to kill me, and I need your Dark blood in order to break it," I continued. I didn't know how much time I had to convince her, so I was rambling, quite literally, for my life.

Echidna looked stunned. "Why don't you quake before me? Why not beg for mercy?"

"What do I have to fear from a mother like you?" I urged my voice to stay calm. Truthfully, I had a *lot* to fear from this monster, but I wasn't going to show her that. I had to remember what Gaia had told me and keep a level head.

"So you do not quake, and you ask me for a favor?" She seemed completely boggled by me. "What are you?" She sniffed close to my skin, dragging her face up the side of my cheek and into my hair, leaving a thin film of rank slime. A grin split her features. "I smell it now. I did not before. Oh... I know you. Merlin and Shipton. Quite intoxicating. I know the scent all too well."

"At least we don't have to make any introductions, right?" I said, a little too brightly. "I know you, you know me, now we've gotten that out of the way."

She laughed. "You don't know me at all, do you?"

"I... uh, know enough."

"I was Purged by a Primus Anglicus. A predecessor of the Shipton bloodline." She brushed a claw against my cheek in a way that was both eerily tender and gut-wrenchingly terrifying. "You and I are related, in a way."

"Does that mean you'll help me?"

She didn't seem to be listening. "The power in you... I can taste it." She licked her lips, an oily bead dropping from her fangs to the floor. "Oh, the things we could do together."

Keep it together. I was getting through to her. I just needed to keep at it. But the longer I spent in here, the more time my Suppressor had to take its toll on my body and mind. I could already feel the pain creeping back in, slithering through my veins.

"The woman who killed my mother—Katherine Shipton—well, she wants to become a Child of Chaos, and I need to get my abilities under control so that I can stop her and take revenge for every mother she's killed and every child left without a parent because of her. If I don't manage to get my Chaos in order, and I fail in fighting her, then we're all screwed." I needed to make her see what we were up against.

Echidna smirked at me. "Why would I help you, since you can't help me?"

"Because if Katherine becomes a Child of Chaos, she'll destroy anyone she deems a threat, and that includes you, all-powerful Mother of Monsters." I realized I was lying through my teeth, but I had to convince Echidna that she was under threat, too. I was prepared to do whatever I had to do to survive, what with death lurking around the corner, waiting to pounce. I could feel it waiting for me.

"You think I don't know of Katherine Shipton? You have not been listening. I may have been frozen, but my Chaos connection runs deep. My ears have been hard at work." She darted toward me, stopping inches from my face. It took everything I had not to flinch. "There are five rituals for her to complete first. A simple magical cannot achieve such a mission. She will not succeed."

"And if she does?"

Echidna paused. "She will not. Those who tried before her failed before they even made it to Nyx's otherworld, the Asphodel Meadows."

"She's been there, done that, got the t-shirt." I lifted my gaze to hers. "Remember that Purge beast I told you about? Katherine killed him to gain the power of the first ritual. She killed him, right then and there, in the Asphodel Meadows, while we watched. We couldn't do anything to stop her then, but I can try and stop her from completing the second one, if you help me now."

Fear crept across Echidna's face. "She completed the first ritual?"

"She did."

Wait... did she just mention the five rituals? A sudden feeling of hope burst through me. Did Echidna know what the rituals were? It made perfect sense, considering how old she was. She was ancient. Of course she knew about them! But would she be willing to tell me more?

"Do you know what the rest of the rituals are? If you did, that would be really useful to us in stopping Katherine." I waited for her reply, pushing down the cold spread of the Suppressor leak.

Echidna cackled. "I am no Child of Chaos. I am not bound by secrecy."

"So you can tell me what they are?"

"I could." She was dangling a carrot in front of me.

"Would you be willing to spare some blood, too?"

Echidna swayed backward and tapped her long claws against her fangs. "I could do that, too. Although, maybe it would be kinder to kill you where you stand. End your suffering now. I'll make it quick and so very, very easy."

"I'm not ready to die yet, Mother. It might be quicker and easier for you to kill me now, I agree with that, but people in my family don't back down from a fight, even when we're at death's door. If you know us, then you know that," I replied firmly, terrified she might kill me anyway. "Katherine is already on her way toward success. She's already completed the first ritual. She killed Quetzi. She—"

"Quetzi?" Echidna barked sharply.

"He was the Purge beast I mentioned—the one I was fond of. Katherine killed him to complete the first ritual, like I said."

A sad glint flickered in Echidna's red eyes. "I was fond of him, too. An unruly child, but the young often are."

Young? Geez, just how old are you?

Echidna turned her back on me and swayed toward the back of the box. I wondered whether to jab something into her tail and get the blood that way, but I didn't have anything on me. Tobe had kept hold of my mini jar of Light blood for safekeeping, and I didn't have my knife or anything else to capture the blood. Before I could do anything stupid, Echidna swept back toward me.

"I will do it," she hissed. "I must."

"Why the change of heart?" I couldn't help asking.

"Because I am involved now." She sounded scared, genuinely scared. A weird thing, coming from a powerful monster like her.

I frowned. "What do you mean?"

"I am part of one of the rituals."

My mouth fell open. "What?"

"If Katherine has begun her mission, then she will come for me, too. You must stop her. I will give you what you need to prevent that witch from touching me." She smiled tightly. "Besides, I like the scent of you. The power within… it is delicious, to say the least."

I felt my chest swell with pride. My Suppressor and I were in the final stages of play, with the clock running out, and I was about to make a last dash for the touchdown. With Echidna's help, I might just make it before the buzzer went off.

"Thank you," I gasped.

"If anyone can stop Katherine from turning me into serpent sashimi, it must be you. This little fire-haired creature of Shipton blood. I have not seen Shipton fight Shipton in many a year. What a battle that shall be."

"I won't let you down."

Echidna laughed darkly. "Hold your horses, child. I am not done yet. I want something in return."

I rolled my eyes. "Nothing comes for free, right?"

Her grin was almost maniacal. "Wise girl."

THIRTY-FOUR

Wade

"What's going on in there?" I'd heard a couple of worrying thuds, but the black mist inside had shrouded everything, Harley included. It was like trying to see through a thick, dark blizzard.

"Your guess is as good as ours." Garrett shrugged. "As long as blood doesn't get sprayed on the glass, Harley should be okay in there."

Tobe swiped him across the back of the head with a clawed paw. "You are terribly insensitive, Garrett. You ought to work on your empathic side."

"Hey, I wasn't born with one." Garrett lifted a hand to the back of his head, where Tobe had swiped him. "You could've taken my head off!"

"I am in control of my strength, Garrett. I wouldn't have decapitated you unless I wished to. As you know, violence is not in my nature."

Garrett pouted. "Says the half-lion hybrid."

"Guys, can we focus on Harley for a—" The words died on my lips. On the far side of the room, the hall doors burst open and a horde of black-clad security guards poured in. The Rag Team whirled around.

Raffe's expression darkened. His father led the charge with narrowed eyes. O'Halloran and the preceptors flanked their new boss and looked equally grim-faced.

"Stop what you're doing this instant!" Levi bellowed.

Not now! Harley needed more time. I glanced frantically at the glass, but I still couldn't see a thing.

"Shouldn't you be downstairs dealing with Nomura?" Santana stepped forward and blocked their path.

"Not while this is happening right under my nose," Levi shot back. "Nomura will get what is coming to him, but this is far more concerning to me right now. How dare you go behind my back to attempt this!" His cheeks had turned scarlet.

"You aren't getting through." Tatyana walked up beside Santana, the two women ready to fight.

"Step aside this moment, or I will force you to move." Steam practically spurted from Levi's ears.

"Then force us," Santana replied.

Levi looked back at his security detail. "Get to the box. Seize anyone who stands in your way!"

The security personnel surged ahead. I sprinted forward and joined the rest of the Rag Team in forming a blockade between them and the glass box, all of us raising our hands to fight back. Magic sparked in the air as the two sides clashed. This was more than just a dispute. This was life and death—Harley's life, to be exact.

A security officer lunged at me and tried to land a punch against my jaw. I ducked it and swiped back, pushing the officer away. He staggered back, taking a small group with him. All along the line, the others were doing the same. Yet still the officers came at us. We pushed and shoved, a scuffle erupting. With fists and kicks and magic, we concentrated our forces against them. We were desperately outnumbered, but we'd never let that stop us before.

I grimaced as a kick landed just shy of my groin. A female officer bore down on me. Seizing her Kevlar vest in my hands, I pushed her back with every ounce of power I had. She careened backward like a bowling ball and fell to the ground, taking two more officers with her. But she was back up in an instant. Nobody was going to give up. The officers stood to face the wrath of Levi. We stood to lose one of our team members. Right now, all we needed to do was buy her more time. If Levi took her out of the box before she'd gathered the blood, it would be game over. There was no choice but to fight for her right to those vital minutes.

"Let the security team do their job!" Levi roared. "If you don't let them pass, it will be Avarice and Alaska for the lot of you!"

"Change the freaking record, Levi," Santana shot back. Levi looked like he'd been slapped. It took everything I had not to smirk.

"You will not undermine me!" Levi turned a brighter shade of beet and hurled a powerful lasso of Telekinesis toward Santana. It gripped her around the throat, and he pulled her to the ground. Her eyes bulged as she fought against the tightening lasso and tried to use her Orishas to get rid of Levi's vise-like hold.

A smoky shadow leapt through the line and made for Levi. Raffe darted around the officers who tried to stand in his way. His skin had turned scarlet, and his eyes flashed with red anger. The djinn was in control, and he was pissed. Smoke billowed from Raffe's body as he tore toward his father.

"Raffe, no!" Santana cried, but the lasso tightened before she could shout again.

The djinn leapt onto Levi and knocked him flat, forcing him to let go of Santana. Before Levi could even raise his fists, the djinn's hands tightened around Levi's throat and squeezed. Even from a distance, I could see Levi's eyes bulging as he fought to breathe. There was an irony to it, considering what he'd just done to Santana. Although, a few more minutes and he'd be a goner—and Raffe would be a murderer.

I wanted to stop him, but I had my own problems. The officers wouldn't back off. They just kept coming in waves, more determined than ever to break our line. I raised my palms and gathered an orb of sparking Fire between them. If I had to fight them to the bitter end, for Harley's sake, I would.

"ENOUGH!" Tobe's bestial roar cut through the hall. It echoed so loudly that the walls shook. Behind us, the glass box vibrated, and I worried it might crack. Everyone stopped and stared at Tobe in terror. He stood at his full height with his wings outspread. His fangs were bared, and his amber eyes shone with rage. "Look at yourselves! You are supposed to be a team, and yet you squabble like hapless mortals. Stop this at once!" His voice shook the ground, and his mighty chest heaved with angry breaths. None of us had seen him like this. We'd certainly never heard him raise his voice.

Even Levi looked about ready to crap his pants. He lay on the floor, pale and speechless and panting for everything he was worth. To my surprise, the djinn had obeyed too. He recoiled from Levi and stood, dusting off the front of Raffe's jeans. Slowly, the scarlet of his skin began to fade. Raffe had the reins again.

"Echidna is all that stands between Harley's life and her imminent death," Tobe said, his voice still booming. "You cannot stop her, and I will not permit it. She must be allowed to bargain for the ingredient she requires to save herself. If you so much as touch that box, I shall tear your hand from your wrist, and I shall not be sorry for it. If nothing else, you stand to release Echidna by accident, and I cannot allow that."

Levi sat up with his hands shaking. "Bargain for an ingredient? This is the first I'm hearing about it. What ingredient?"

"She needs Dark blood from Echidna in order to balance her affinities, which she will do with the use of a Sanguine spell," Tobe replied.

"A Sanguine spell?" Levi looked ready to blow. "And where the devil did she get her hands on one of those, huh?"

"I do not know, Director Levi. I only know what she requires."
Tobe's voice began to quieten.

Levi glowered at the Rag Team. "If she comes out of there and
releases all of that Chaos the Suppressor has been holding back, it shall
be on your heads!" He wheezed in a breath. "She could produce some
terrible monster, far worse than Echidna, or release a Purge plague into
the world. We will be done for! You have no understanding of the
forces you're playing with here!"

Tobe narrowed his eyes. "You realize to whom you're talking, do
you not? I know more about this matter than anyone else in existence,
and I will not be lectured by the very man who would have permitted
Harley to waste away from the poison in her veins. Do not pretend you
did not know that the Suppressor break would kill her, for we all know
that you did. And this entire mess might have been averted, had you
thought to listen to her. You forced her into this because you did not
try to help her, even without knowledge of the Sanguine spell, and all
because you are terrified of what she may become."

I stared at Tobe in shock. He'd hit the nail right on the head, but I
hadn't expected him to speak so boldly to Levi. The Bestiary was Tobe's
domain, but that didn't mean Levi couldn't find a way to get him fired.
He was taking a huge risk for us. I admired him more in that moment
than ever before.

"You're all done for, do you hear me? All of you!" Levi snarled. Even
the preceptors were looking at him with doubtful eyes now. It seemed
they were in the dark about Levi's efforts against Harley's survival.
They were horrified. I could see it on their faces.

"Nobody is done for." A voice cut in from the doorway. Alton stood
there with a sad smile on his face. "What will the Mage Council think if
they find that you, the great Leonidas Levi, are incapable of keeping a
bunch of younglings under control, hm? And what will they think of
your refusal to help Harley—a woman they value highly for her
potential?"

Levi dragged himself to his feet, though nobody stooped to help him. "You cannot come in here and—"

"Look at this mess. One of the coven's most prominent magicals is stuck inside a glass box with the Mother of Monsters because you wouldn't listen to her. The Librarian is dead. One of your preceptors nearly betrayed the coven to rescue his son from Katherine's grip. And all in... how many days has it been, Levi?"

"You are the one who caused—"

Alton shook his head. "How on earth will you even begin to explain all of this at the Washington Magical Assembly? How can you possibly hope to secure their vote of confidence, with all of *this* hanging over you?"

Levi shook violently, but he did not say a word. From Alton's lips, all of this sounded like a total PR nightmare for the new director. It was clear that he didn't know what to say in response to such obvious facts. There really was no way of explaining all of this without Levi immediately losing his position.

Raffe smirked. "Alton's right, Father. You can't excuse your way out of this one, not with so many witnesses." Both he and the djinn were taking satisfaction from this, I could tell.

"All is not completely lost, however." Alton walked toward Levi, and everyone watched him. "We may collaborate on this matter and seek to fix it together. I will help you maintain your reputation if you allow things here to take their natural course. I imagine the Washington Assembly will applaud you if they discover you have a fully powered Merlin in your ranks, no longer restrained by her Suppressor. It's what they've been hoping for, after all. I'm sure that would smooth over any cracks in your standing."

"She is a menace to this coven and the rest of the magical world," Levi spat.

So there it is. The admission we've been waiting for. The venom in his words rankled me. I wanted to smack him senseless for being so cold.

Harley was a living, breathing human being. She didn't deserve this kind of hatred. She hadn't chosen to be born with so many abilities. And if he was scared of what she might be, well, that was his tough luck.

"Whether you like it or not, Levi, you must admit that Harley is extremely valuable. She's of more use to this coven if she's on our side, rather than locked away or, worse, forced onto Katherine's side. Your obvious distaste for her does you no favors, and Washington would not want to hear of it." Alton folded his arms across his chest. He was right, and Levi knew it.

Alton turned to us. "Do we know how she is?"

I shook my head. "We can't see or hear anything." *And we're all worried sick.*

"Stand down from this, Levi," Alton warned.

"I will not take any action until Harley comes out of that box," he replied after a lengthy pause. "If her condition is deemed unsatisfactory, she will be taken into immediate custody. Those are my terms. I will not stand down if she threatens the safety of this coven and those within it."

Alton sighed. "Very well, if that's the best we can settle for right now." He glanced uncomfortably at the glass box, and the rest of us followed suit.

Now, it was just a waiting game. How would she come out of this? None of us could possibly know. But at least nobody was trying to barge into Echidna's private domain to take Harley by force. That would only have ended in disaster. And blood, most likely. If Tobe was frightened by Echidna, then we had to be absolutely terrified of what she was capable of. Monsters were wily by nature, and this one had to be restless and desperate after being locked up for way too long.

I walked up to the box and pressed my hands to the glass. The mist still shrouded what was going on inside. I imagined it was there like a wall, purely to block our view—although, Harley had to be able to see what stood in front of her. Still, I wanted to be as close to her as possible. All I could do now was pray to Chaos that Harley got through this okay. *Come on, keep her safe. She's one of yours.* After all, she deserved a shot at a full, magical life. Not even Levi could take that chance from her.

THIRTY-FIVE

Harley

"So what do you want in return?" I jumped straight to the point, knowing she could change her mind at any moment. That was the trouble with creatures like her: you could never tell what they were thinking.

Echidna swayed rhythmically. "All in good time, child."

It might have slipped your notice, but I don't have a lot of that, Mother of Monsters.

"Do want a gift of some kind?"

"I wonder why Katherine hasn't killed you yet." Oh, so we were digressing while my life was on the line? I couldn't exactly rush her, not with her fangs and claws at the ready to swipe my head from my shoulders.

I shrugged. "Maybe she's working up to it."

"Could be."

"What can I give you in return for your blood?" I pressed, feeling the creep of the Suppressor with every second that ticked by.

"Perhaps she might need you later." She tapped her claw against her lip, ignoring me. "It's the only viable reason she'd allow someone like you to live."

"Someone like me?"

She smirked. "That power, remember?"

How could I forget, when it was all anyone could talk about? Levi, Alton, the Mage Council, even the Rag Team were guilty of it at times —they saw my strength before anything else, with that apparently being my primary feature.

"You think that's why?" I figured I might as well get as much information out of her as possible before I made my escape out of this frigging box. The walls felt like they were closing in on me, the panic in my veins heightened by the Suppressor's influence. Two more steps, and I'd have this thing out of me for good. The Dark blood and then the Sanguine spell—those were the only tasks left for me to complete before I could break the Suppressor, and I had to keep my focus on that.

"It is the only reason a Challenger of a Child of Chaos would wait." She licked her lips. "Oh my stars and garters, that energy is delicious. So very delicious. I'd eat you up if I could." She seemed to be head over heels for the power inside me, to the point where I was actually worried she'd hold true to her word and literally devour me whole.

If that's the case and Katherine is waiting for something, then what is she waiting for? It got me thinking again. Katherine and I had faced each other, one-on-one, and she'd found plenty of ways to sneak her spies into the coven and manipulate good people like Nomura. So why had none of them come for me? I mean, Nomura had intended to exchange me, but Katherine hadn't asked him to kill me. He could have done it at any point, and it would have been way easier than locking me out of my body and making an exchange. She wanted me alive, but what for?

I vowed to find the answer once I got out of here in one piece. Escaping Echidna alive was my main concern, given the current circumstances... and that ravenous look in her red eyes.

"So what can I offer you in return?" I repeated for what felt like the millionth time. My body tingled with loose Chaos, my limbs feeling as heavy as lead and my heart slowing to a sluggish pound in my chest. If she didn't broker the deal soon, I wouldn't be alive enough to give her anything. My Chaos seemed to be trying to push through my skin, the energy practically seeping out of me. I shuddered, wondering what would happen if I didn't get out of here in time. With me dead on the ground, Echidna would probably eat me for the sake of not wanting my body to go to waste.

"I will give you my blood..." She trailed off in thought.

"In return for?" I prompted, after a good few minutes of silence. This was getting silly now.

"After—or rather, if—you defeat Katherine, you must bring your firstborn child to me within a week of its birth and allow me to name the infant."

I frowned at her. "You want to name my firstborn child?" That didn't seem like such a big deal, but she wouldn't have been asking if it didn't hold some weight. I just didn't know what kind of weight it could possibly have.

"Oh yes," she hissed with a smirk.

"Who says I'm having kids? Bit presumptuous, don't you think?"

She chuckled. "Then what do you have to fear?"

I don't know... What do I have to fear?

"And that's a long way off. Wouldn't you rather have something more immediate?" I replied.

"I am a patient mother. I can wait." She smiled at me. "You would be surprised how strong the maternal instinct can be. It pulls at the heart unlike anything else in this world. I am confident in my choice."

I shuddered. *What do you know that I don't?* I had horrible visions of one of her monster offspring creeping into my room in the dead of night and somehow injecting a Purge beast into me.

"Do you mean an actual child, or do you mean my first Purge

beast?" I wanted to be sure. Echidna was the Mother of Monsters, after all, so it could well have been either. Human or beastie, she saw them both in the same way, with the same level of importance.

"I mean a human child. Born of your womb."

There are no babies getting in this womb anytime soon, pal.

As if reading my mind, she barked a laugh. "As I say, I am patient."

"What if I shirk my promise and don't show up?" I asked bluntly. "Or I name it something else? *If* I ever have a kid, that is."

"Folks like you—the lost souls—feel the pull of motherhood more intently than most. It will surprise you, I am sure." She leered at me. "As for you shirking your promise, I have already thought of that, child. A curse will be on your shoulders the moment you walk from this box. I would not risk you breaking your promise, now, would I?"

I struggled not to roll my eyes. "No, of course you wouldn't."

"More to the point, you are currently the only thing standing between myself and the ritual that may take my life." A flicker of real fear moved across her red eyes.

"So if I stop Katherine before she gets to your ritual, will you rethink this whole firstborn thing?"

She chuckled coldly. "I will contemplate it. But if you can't stop her, and you break your word, you will be doomed. The curse will be slow —it will destroy you little by little."

"I'm sort of getting used to that," I muttered.

"Pardon?" She surged toward me until we were nose-to-nose, and I was staring straight into those deadly red eyes. The sour, fishy stench was so overwhelming I had to fight to control the vomit rising in my throat.

"A Suppressor joke. I meant no offense by it," I replied hastily, my body slicked in a cold sweat.

"Ah yes, very humorous." She reeled back, giving me a moment's respite from that foul smell.

"I'll do it. I'll agree to your terms." I exhaled sharply, swallowing my nausea. "I'll let you name my firstborn if I survive Katherine." *Good luck with that.* Me and babies seemed impossible. I'd never been a broody type of person who cooed over babies, and I didn't see that changing anytime soon.

Echidna laughed raucously. "And if you do not survive her—well, it's all the same to me. I will be doomed anyway, since Katherine requires me for one of those rituals. A cruel trick by those from whose energy I am forged."

"The Children of Chaos?"

"The Bastards of Chaos, as I like to call them." She grinned icily, sending beetles of fear crawling under my skin. "They could have picked anyone, but they chose me. Bastards, through and through."

"I'm sorry about that, but I'll do whatever I can to stop her before it gets to your ritual." I didn't know why I'd said that, since it wouldn't do me any favors whatsoever. Even if I did manage to stop Katherine before she reached Echidna's ritual, I had a sneaking suspicion that I'd still have to let her name my kid or risk a terrible curse. A very small part of me hoped she might change her mind in return for doing something that benefited her, but I could tell she wasn't the kind of monster who could be easily persuaded toward a good deed. This deal was proof of that.

She snickered. "I know what you're thinking. I won't promise it will change the terms, even if you do. There is much to be achieved first."

I ignored her, wishing I hadn't thought anything at all. "So does that mean we have a deal?"

"I suppose it does." She held out her wrist to me. "Take your blood, child."

I cast her a sheepish glance. "I don't have anything to cut you with, and I don't have anything to collect the blood, either."

"You are poorly organized for one in such dire need." Now the mom in her was really coming out. I could almost imagine Mrs. Smith saying the exact same thing to me the morning before an important exam.

"I know." I wanted to beat my head against the glass for being so idiotic. Tobe still had the jar full of Light blood, but he was all the way out there in the Bestiary hall, with no way for me to reach him.

"Allow me." Lifting her wrist to her mouth, she raked her sharp fang along the line of her human-like skin and tore open a gash. Black, oily blood leaked out, pooling in fat globules that turned my stomach into knots. From seemingly thin air, she produced a small green bottle into which she poured the promised blood. I guessed with all the magic at her disposal, creating something from nothing was child's play. Although, it showed just how strong these Bestiary boxes were, that they could keep so much power contained without inducing a single crack.

Once the bottle was halfway full, she passed it to me, and I took it gratefully, tightening my fingers around the glass in case it suddenly vanished.

"Is that it? Are we done?" I could hardly believe it.

She rushed toward me until we were nose-to-nose once more. "Not quite. I am in need of amusement. How about we make this more interesting?"

"What do you—" Before I could finish my sentence, she pressed her clammy hand to my forehead. A green flash lit up the glass box, and a hot stream of something fierce and overwhelming shot right into the center of my skull. It thundered down my spine, filling every vein with a searing sensation. My limbs shook, my teeth chattering as if I'd been dunked in an ice-cold lake. It felt as if I were sitting in an electric chair and someone had just flipped the switch. Worst of all, there was nothing I could do to stop whatever Echidna had done to me. *What the hell is this?!*

Then it hit my Suppressor, and I understood. Energy poured in all directions, taking control of my very being. A blinding pain tore through every cell in my body. I crashed to my knees. The Suppressor finally snapped in two, and all of my Chaos broke loose.

THIRTY-SIX

Harley

Struggling against the storm of raw Chaos twisting through my body, I crawled to the door of the glass box and slammed my fists against the pane over and over again, one hand still gripped around the vial. Every movement sent more Chaos into overdrive, the walls around me vibrating from the fierce pulsations of my free energy. *Please don't crack, please don't crack...*

Tobe appeared at the door, barely visible through Echidna's black fog. He caught sight of my face and reached into his wings, pulling out the jar of Light blood, a stick of chalk, and a small pipette—all the items I'd asked him to hold onto for when it came time for the Sanguine spell, to stop me accidentally breaking something in my current state. I had the spell itself tucked in the back of my head for safekeeping, but I needed the rest to get this done in time.

In the pane of glass, he opened a small square that was ordinarily used for food and threw the items in before snapping it shut behind him. He looked as panicked as I felt, which wasn't much comfort. Evidently, a forcefield stopped the energy leaking out into the real world through the food flap, but it wouldn't be long before nothing could hold this back. It was amazing enough that this box was keeping this mess contained for the time being.

"Hurry!" Echidna warned. "If the box cracks, I will escape and tear this coven apart."

"What about our deal?" I rasped.

She grinned. "It doesn't matter if you don't survive, does it?"

With black spots dancing in my field of vision and my head feeling like it might explode at any moment, I sat up against the glass and set out my tools. My hands shook as I gripped the chalk and drew a mandala on the floor before me. The Sanguine spell that I'd been given in the garden of Marie Laveau had sunk into my subconscious in the same way that the spells of my parents' Grimoire did, and I prayed this onslaught of Chaos wouldn't steal it from me as I fought to focus. Every couple of seconds, a new and terrible pain ricocheted through my nerve endings, playing a searing game of pinball that threatened to knock me unconscious.

Come on, Merlin! Hang in there! I pictured my friends telling me the same thing and concentrated on the idea of Wade's deep green eyes urging me onward. I had everything I needed—I just had to do this without falling apart, which was easier said than done given my current state.

With the mandala drawn, I settled into the center of the markings and laid out the green bottle, the jar, and the pipette. My limbs jolted as I tried to undo the lid of the jar, my hands sweating profusely as they slipped on the opening.

Twenty-six lines of a spell; that's all you've got to get through. Twenty-six.

I grasped for the pipette and dunked it into the jar, filling it all the way to the bulbous tip. Shuddering, I rested the edge of the pipette against the center of the mandala just in front of me and began to recite, the words coming back to me automatically, rising out of my brain and through my lips. I was constantly aware of Echidna leering over me.

"*De sanguine natu sumus, et non revertetur sanguis.*" I dropped the first bead inside the mandala, and the chalk-drawn shape lit up white with a steady, pulsing glow. "*Inter partes adversas pacem.*" The second droplet fell, brightening the glow of the mandala. "*Tenebris lux pugnae, sit aequilibrio.*" Another bead of Light blood fell. My hand trembled on the pipette, my heart gripped in terror, in case I accidentally dropped too much. It had to be thirteen of each exactly; there was no room for error.

"*Et non erit lux sine tenebris. Non sunt tenebrae et non lux: et erit lux. Currat et sanguine venas dubio compensetur. Educ de custodia animam meam et cor meum a pace animo corporeque caret. Educ de custodia animam in claritate ante omnia. Et magicae lenire dolorem viam inveniam de contritum est. Oblivione praeteritorum discordias et Chaos et risus sit. Scissa est in corde meo, et satisfacturos esse factum. Confregit in animam, unum sint. De sanguine natu sumus, et non revertetur sanguis.*"

I dropped a bead of Light blood into the mandala with every line of the spell I spoke, until the thirteenth line repeated the first: "We are born from blood, and to blood we return."

Hastily, I put the remaining Light blood back into the jar and reached for the green bottle of Dark blood. Feeling desperately sick, I put the empty pipette into the glass and let it suck up the thick blood within. Resting it against the center of the mandala once again, I recited the same thirteen lines, dropping a single bead at the end of each one. The white light of the mandala turned a startling crimson as the Dark blood mingled with the Light.

"I suppose it would do no harm to tell you of the five rituals," Echidna said as I struggled to concentrate on what I was doing. *Seriously, Echidna?* This wasn't exactly the best time.

"If I'm to have the name of your firstborn, I may as well give you better odds against Katherine," Echidna continued, clearly enjoying herself and my frustrated discomfort. "Number one, kill a god in the land of night. Number two, kill a Father of Magicals in the land of

Gaia. Number three, consume the spirit of thine greatest enemy in the land of Erebus on All Hallows' Eve."

How was I supposed to do everything at once? I was barely holding on to consciousness, and she was harping on about important freaking rituals. Couldn't she have told me this earlier, when I wasn't trying to concentrate on dropping one bead of blood at a time while whispering a spell in a language I barely understood? Oh, and she was loving every single moment. *Sadist.*

"Number four, cut the head off the Mother of Monsters in the Land of Light. Number five, the Challenger must acquire twelve powers and bathe in the blood of her blood under the light of a full moon. The twelve powers will thus be locked and become the twelve keys required to open the door to the realm of the challenged Child. Only upon the orderly completion of all five rituals will the Child of Chaos become unable to reject the Challenger's claim to their power. Or Bastard of Chaos, if you prefer."

I grimaced as an unbearable pain tore at my insides, ripping me apart. The Chaos from my broken Suppressor was tearing me to pieces on a subatomic level, pulling every magically drenched cell away from the flesh and muscle and bone that made up my body. With my hand still gripping the pipette, I screamed in agony. It felt like two extremely powerful magnets had been placed on either side of me, each pulling me toward its side—Light and Darkness, locked in a battle to the death. My death, if I couldn't get them balanced quickly enough.

Before I could utter another word of the six lines I had left, the whole world evaporated in a vortex of spiraling Chaos, spinning around me in a whirlwind of bronzed sparks. For a moment, there was nothing and everything, all at once. *Is this it... is this what crossing over feels like?* I couldn't feel my physical body anymore, but it wasn't like astral projection; this was a different, more permanent sensation entirely. The only things I could think about were the missing lines of the Sanguine spell and what might lie ahead.

I glanced down and tried to cry out, but no sound emerged. My body was coming apart. It was the same thing I'd seen happen to Jacob when he slipped up in the training room and almost took down the Bestiary's entire global defenses. The particles that made me who I was were drifting away in thin, sparkling streams of pure energy, feeding back into the whorl of Chaos that existed throughout the world.

I'm disintegrating. Dread and terror clawed at me with bitter hands, but I couldn't do anything to stop this from happening. I felt blocked, unable to react.

I have to do something! I can't die! I'm not ready to leave this world...

Bright images flashed in front of my eyes, vivid and heartbreaking. I saw it all. My life in impossible Technicolor. A blurry vision of my mom holding me close and whispering "I love you" in my ear. My dad on the riverbank by the cottage, laughing as I chased the minnows with my net. Isadora standing in the doorway with a smile on her face. And later, them both watching me sleep, muttering in quiet voices and wearing worried frowns. The orphanage where my father left me, at three years old. The jade-green corridors and peeling wallpaper of the room where I'd spent those first months after arriving there. The weekly line-up in front of potential foster parents, and the folder with my frightened picture in the corner. Every detail of my life within those pages. All the shoddy foster homes where I'd grown up and the dogs I'd loved and left. The Carraghers, the Gilligans, the McEvoys, the Rogerses, the Phillipsons, and everything that had come before the Smiths. All the terraced houses and cottages and apartments where I'd tried to make a space for myself, and the temporary siblings who'd pinched and shoved and called me names. The schools and the classes and the teachers, and the kids who'd never accepted me. The failures and the successes, all marked in red ink at the top of endless essays.

And then the Smiths and beautiful Ryann. Their house, on that tree-lined street, where I'd spent those last two years before heading out on my own. My room, with the posters of Springsteen, the Stones, and the

Foo Fighters, and Jared Leto in a pair of leather pants. And the rock music blaring from the speakers. The European movies that I'd thought made me look cool, all lined up by the TV. The smell of meatloaf wafting up from the kitchen.

The scene shifted rapidly to the casino and Malcolm the security guard, who'd become like a third father to me. Hiram, Mr. Smith, and Malcolm—three great men who'd shaped the course of my future. I heard the clatter of quarters in the slot machines and the shouts of winners and losers. I pictured the fuzzy green of the card tables and the satisfying slide of hands being dealt. That all seemed like forever ago. And the gargoyle in the parking lot that had changed everything. The green ropes lashed across its back, shooting up from scattered gems... and Wade. Oh, Wade. He'd been so arrogant back then, but I'd still felt drawn to his stupid face. The touch of his kiss against my lips and the muscle of his bare chest beneath his expensive shirt. His chest heaving as he struggled to pull away from me, and the race of my heart as I'd clung on to him. So much unexplored, never to be discovered.

Marie Laveau's garden and the scent of those lilies. Papa Legba in his fury to kick us out of the townhouse. That legendary love that existed between them. The dark silence of the Asphodel Meadows and the witty repartee of Quetzi, and my first day at the coven, every thought jumbled together as they sprinted through my head at break-neck speed. The preceptors, the traitors, the spies, Alton, Astrid, Dylan, Tatyana, Raffe, Santana, Garrett, Louella, Jacob... they all whizzed by in the blink of an eye. Even Katherine showed up for my farewell party, her voice ringing in my ears.

But the images always returned to glimpses of Wade. The most powerful and clearest images were of him, in any and all of the situations that we'd experienced together. I desperately tried to cling to the visions that blurred past, but it was like trying to catch melting butter in my hands. I saw Wade's arms around me, pulling me close, and heard him whispering of a promised future. His kiss again, against the wall of the coven's hallways. My knees buckling as the Suppressor had stolen the moment from me. Only... it felt like that hopeful future with him would never be now, not with my body drifting away from me on a wind of particles.

Wade... He felt so close and yet so far. I reached out to the image of him and could almost touch him. *Wade... help me.* I knew he couldn't hear me, but I didn't know what else to do. Half of me was already gone, vanished into thin air. In the distance somewhere, exploding from the darkness within, I heard Echidna laughing at the mayhem she'd caused. And something else... a loud banging nearby, as if someone was knocking on the glass box.

Wade, is that you? I forced myself to focus on the sound as I recited the last six lines of the Sanguine spell and made what was left of my hand move around the pipette, squeezing out the last six drops and letting them fall. That was it. The spell was done. I could do no more to save myself.

A deafening moment of utter silence followed. I'd expected bells and whistles, or at least a fanfare, but there was nothing but quiet. An endless, black silence. If this was death, then Astrid had been right—it was peaceful, if slightly terrifying. I looked around for the promised light at the end of life's tunnel, but there was only darkness.

What if I've gone... elsewhere? I'd never been a believer in heaven and hell, but now I doubted my entire existence. I tried to pinpoint moments when I might have done something unforgivable, something that might have bought me a one-way ticket to eternal damnation. Perhaps my name was enough, and the blood that ran through my disintegrating veins. Perhaps I was supposed to pay for the crimes of my family, like everyone who had come before. The thought made me quiver with fear. If I could have cried, I would have.

Without warning, everything began to rewind, like an old video-tape. The flashing images sped backward, and the particles that had drifted away whirled back toward me, replacing the parts that had evaporated. I became whole again, and the images disappeared with a sudden snap and a flash of blinding light. I expected to find myself back in the glass box with Echidna, but I was somewhere else—somewhere unknown. Behind me, a wall of darkness rose up to an unseen sky. In front of me, a shimmering blockade of incredible light that I could barely look at. Darkness and Light, and here I was, stuck in the middle.

I took a breath, the gasp of it splintering the silence. And, with that, the two sides rammed into me with all the fury of their cosmic force.

THIRTY-SEVEN

Harley

I woke up, head pounding, on the glass floor of Echidna's box. Chaos flowed through me in a rush of adrenaline that made me feel as if I could flip a fourteen-wheeler with one hand. This wasn't exactly the kind of balance I'd been hoping for, and it felt as scary as it did strange. It was almost like someone had strapped me to an atomic bomb and left me to figure out the rest. Deep down, I worried that this bomb could go off at any moment, the time ticking unseen beneath the shell.

But, on a more positive note, at least Chaos wasn't pushing at my skin and threatening to ooze out like Echidna's black smoke. And I felt practically invincible, like I could take on the whole world and win single-handed. I'd never felt so good in all my life. My blood was positively singing, and every single instinct was alert and attuned, my vision clearer, my hearing sharper, my strength more potent, my brain whirring with a million new and thrilling thoughts. Was this how I was supposed to be feeling? Was it meant to be this exhilarating and terrifying, all at once? Had I never had the Suppressor fitted, was this what my life would have been like—turning me into a source of pulsing energy that made me feel so utterly invincible?

I slowly blinked my eyes open, my vision clearing as I glanced around the box and remembered where I was. I almost leapt out of my skin as I saw Echidna flat on the ground like a creepy toad, barely six inches from my face, her red eyes peering at me with interest. That foul stench infiltrated my nostrils, but it didn't make me want to instantly hurl. Evidently, the broken Suppressor meant that my senses weren't as heightened as they'd been before, at least not in the smell department. She didn't say a word; she just looked at me like she wanted to gulp me down her throat or jab a pin through me and keep me in her collection.

This is going to ease off, right? Surely, this feeling of total power and exhilaration was just the initial stage of breaking the Suppressor, and I'd start to feel ordinary again soon? Whatever ordinary was. I'd never been ordinary, so I had no precedent to measure it against. What if this *was* what I was always meant to be? What if I was always destined to be this powerful? What if strong and invincible *was* my normal? If that was the case, then none of this was what I'd anticipated, but that wasn't exactly a bad thing. Heck, I could get used to this.

Echidna smirked and scuttled closer. "Not what you expected?"

"No… not really." I shuffled back, freaked out by how close she was getting. "I feel better than I thought I would."

"Did they teach you nothing here?"

I frowned. "What do you mean?"

"This 'good feeling' won't last, child. It's a high from the break and all that juicy power inside you. Sanguine spells are not a fix-all remedy. They merely smooth over the bigger problem within." An icy chuckle bubbled up from her throat.

"What?" That wasn't what I wanted to hear. I wanted her to tell me that this would last and everything was sorted, now that I'd performed the Sanguine spell. I wanted her to tell me that I wouldn't have to worry about the battle of Light and Dark ever again.

"You will have to learn to control all of this yourself... eventually." She lashed her tongue against her fangs, clearing away a globule of thick, oily slime.

I shook my head. "No, that can't be right. I did the spell. I should be cured."

"All this little gimmick does is delay the inevitable," she replied with a flick of her wrist.

"Which is?" I got the feeling I wasn't going to like her answer.

"The day when you will either take that control or be eaten alive by your own Chaos." She grinned with malice. "I know which side I am in favor of. How delicious."

"You're messing with me, right?" *Way to burst my bubble, Echidna.*

Her eyes glowed with amusement. "Try it, if you do not believe me. Feel the change and the lack of control for yourself."

I paused. "What... here?"

"Of course. If you explode yourself, the glass will capture the splatter."

She has to be messing with me.

"Do you mean try one of my abilities?"

She rolled her eyes. "Did you lose part of your brain when you performed the spell? Yes, I mean try your abilities. I suggest Fire. It tends to be my favorite. And if you combust, my, that will be a sight." Her cackle sent splinters of terror through me. I didn't know how much she was joking at my expense, but what if I *did* combust? This was all new territory for me, and the buzz in my atoms certainly seemed explosive.

"Okay." I got up on shaky legs and lifted my palms. I barely had to think before the sparks were flying and the tendrils of Chaos began to twirl around my fingertips, burning far brighter than they ever had before. The sheer force of the orb that took shape in my palms nearly sent me flying back against the glass, my insides vibrating with raw energy. *Yep, feels different.* But not necessarily a good different. The fireball in my hands was enormous, with a deep red center that I'd never seen before, the whole thing pulsating as if it were alive. There was so much power loose inside me now that it almost felt like it had been trapped in a glass box, like this, and it was desperate to get out.

I severed the ties between myself and the fireball, the whole thing disappearing in a flurry of bronze particles that drifted down like snow. They lay on the ground and blinked with continued life before they sputtered out and turned to ash on the glass. "I guess I'll have to take it easy," I murmured. If I didn't want to kill anyone by accident, I'd have to be very careful, going forward.

Echidna howled with manic glee. "Oh, so very delicious!" She was enjoying this turmoil way too much for my liking, considering she was the one responsible. Then again, would anything be different if I'd broken the Suppressor myself? This power had been building inside me for sixteen or so years—this outcome had probably always been inevitable.

"You're loving this, aren't you?"

She rushed at me, but I held my ground. With this much power in my veins, I had less reason to fear her. "You may get your chance to test these powers soon enough," she hissed.

"What do you mean?"

She darted back into her coils and sucked in the black fog that had filled the box. As the smoke dissipated, it revealed a whole bunch of people waiting for me to emerge. Not just the Rag Team but also members of the security detail stationed in the SDC. They stared at the box with worried expressions, every single one of their Esprits shining. Their guards were up, no doubt fearing the worst from me. *Crap.*

I glanced down at my own Esprit, more to make sure it was still there than anything else. I gasped at the change that had taken place without me even realizing. The metal had turned black, and every single stone had transformed into six pure white diamonds, the pearls included.

"What the—" I turned the Esprit under the soft lighting of the glass box. The Elemental stones contained a faint streak of the color that had once represented them, but the subtle flush could only be seen at a certain angle.

Everything is different. I'm different. I didn't know how long I'd actually been in the box, but my entire world had changed in one encounter with the Mother of Monsters. The way I felt, the way I moved, the way my Esprit looked, everything. This was going to take forever to get used to, if I ever did. And one thing was for sure: I needed to learn to control these changes before they grew beyond my reach, and my life hung in the balance again.

"Why the sad eyes?" Echidna taunted.

"It's nothing," I replied.

She smiled and scraped her claw across my cheek. "The Sanguine spell may not have saved you now, child. But it did prolong your life."

"Yeah, or my death," I retorted.

"Gratitude, child." She narrowed her eyes to reptilian slits. "You have a fighting chance now. Besides, you should have known not to expect a spell to fix everything. Have they taught you nothing?"

I flashed a grim smile. "Maybe I keep forgetting the lesson."

"I could teach you a thing or two." Her fangs flashed.

"No, thank you. You've already been way too generous." I couldn't swallow the bitter note in my voice.

"Then leave, before I change my mind and gobble you up. That scent is even more tantalizing now." Her scales vibrated, her eyes closing in a worrying display of ecstasy. "I don't know how long I can hold myself back."

I didn't need to be told twice. I walked the short distance to the charmed door, where Tobe was waiting. With every step, I felt Echidna's threatening presence behind me.

Tobe turned the key in the lock and let me out, his large paw cradling most of my shoulder with a warm pat. I expected him to slam the door shut behind me, to stop Echidna from escaping. However, to my surprise, he stepped into the glass box willingly and closed the door behind him. From my view through the glass, he seemed to be having a conversation with Echidna, but I couldn't hear a word of it.

That beast has balls of titanium. Nothing would have made me go back into that box voluntarily, absolutely nothing. I paused on the edge of the plinth before stepping down to where the crowd stood, taking a second to collect myself. My body didn't really feel like it belonged to me anymore; a constant tingling spiked at my limbs and danced across my chest. It was yet another thing that I'd have to get used to, but I could worry about it later. For now, I had to focus on Levi, O'Halloran, and the throng of security personnel that appeared to have joined the party.

I sought out the Rag Team amongst the crowd, wanting to see friendly faces. They stood as still as statues, their expressions panicked. Evidently, they knew something I didn't about this set-up, and none of them were saying a word. *Are they waiting for me to say something?* I didn't exactly have a grand speech prepared, after everything I'd just been through.

I dusted the chalk from my jeans in a bid to buy some time. Finally, I cleared my throat. "Well, that was fun. I'll be picking slime out of my hair for a week. Man, I doubt there's enough hot water in the entire coven to wash this smell off me."

I had hoped for laughter, but all I received were stony faces and a few wry smirks from the Rag Team. At the end of the day, they were all that mattered, and I prayed my little joke had let them know that I was okay. I was still me... sort of.

Levi sneered at me. "Security, take her away!"

I backed up. "Sorry, what?"

"You must undergo another Reading before I permit you to wander in public again. You may act the clown, Ms. Merlin, but we have no idea what has occurred within that… box. I will not put my coven in danger, not until I can be sure of the changes that have taken place."

Alton stepped forward. "She's perfectly fine. You can see it for yourself."

"She'd have blasted out of that box if she couldn't control her powers," Santana added. "She needs rest, not a freaking Reading."

"You made a promise, Levi." Wade glowered at the new director, his passion making my heart jolt. *Wade… you've got no idea what I owe you.* I'd never have made it out of that life-flashback if it hadn't been for him spurring me on to finish the spell. The memory of him and the promise of time with him in the future had seen me through.

"She's no danger to anyone," Isadora interjected. "Has anything exploded? No. Has she threatened anyone? No. This is nonsense. Absolute nonsense."

It was a comfort to hear them speaking out for me, even if they didn't know the full extent of what had happened. If they had, Isadora might not have been so quick to say everything she'd just said. And Levi would probably have had me locked up quicker than I could say "Get your hands off me, you asshole." The only person who wasn't focused on Levi was Raffe. His eyes flashed red, and they were fixed entirely on me, with an amused smirk twisting up the corners of his mouth. He knew something, for sure—more than anyone else. The djinn was sensitive to this kind of thing, and I guessed my new condition had made him temporarily rear his ugly head, even if he was keeping his presence quiet for once.

The security team crowded in to restrain me, their quick movements catching me off guard. As panic rose up in my throat, my Telekinesis erupted from within me, swatting them away like flies. One hit the far wall and slumped to the ground, but he still seemed to be breathing. It wouldn't look too good if I accidentally killed someone within my first few minutes of being the new and improved me.

"Whoa," I breathed, amazed by the strength of my ability. It didn't feel like a lasso anymore, but something much bigger and more powerful. In fact, it felt like I was connected to everything, tied to the very particles of Chaos. Every atom was within my reach—I only had to grasp for it, and the rest would do my bidding.

"Take her away!" Levi roared.

The remaining security hesitated, and I smiled, holding the gaze of Levi and the Rag Team. "I think it's time we had a talk, don't you?"

THIRTY-EIGHT

Wade

I couldn't stop staring at her. I'd have liked nothing more than to run to her and hold her close, even though I sensed it might be like hugging a tornado. Still, I was relieved she was alive. And worried, at the same time. Harley had changed. She was different than the girl who'd gone into the box. It was clear in the way she stood without fear, as if she could take on the world single-handed and win. Not to mention the way she'd hurled that guy against the wall as if he weighed nothing. I looked around to see if anyone else had noticed the difference, too, but they were all too focused on Levi. The little rat was trying to get his own way again.

"Security, seize her this instant or see yourselves without a job!" His voice wavered slightly and revealed his true fear. His staff was scared of Harley, and so was he. They didn't want to face her any more than Levi did, job or no job.

Harley descended the steps of Echidna's plinth. Man, she even moved differently. She had a swagger almost, but it wasn't cocky. It was the stride of someone powerful. "I assure you, Levi, I'm completely fine," she said. "I just don't like being manhandled, that's all. I'll happily have another Reading done soon, but right now we have more pressing matters to discuss. And I suggest you dismiss your security team first, unless you want them to hear everything I have to say?"

"I don't see what can be more pressing than your Reading, Harley," Levi shot back.

"I'll count to three before I start spilling my guts." A twinkle of mischief lit up her eyes. "Send the security teams away, or they hear everything Echidna told me. And before you try and tell me that everyone should hear, just remember what happened with Nomura."

Levi looked torn. He glanced at the black-clad security and back at Harley.

"One," she said. It hung heavy in the air.

He pulled a sour face. "You—"

"Two."

"Security, you are dismissed until I call for you." He shot a bitter look at Harley. "And I will certainly be calling upon you sooner rather than later." With a thunder of boots, the security personnel obediently left the hall. That left only Levi, Alton, O'Halloran, me, and the Rag Team in the hall. Even the preceptors had been sent away. They hadn't argued.

Harley smiled strangely. "Now that there are fewer of us, why don't you try this on for size, Levi? Number one, kill a god in the land of night. Sadly, that one's been done. Number two, kill a Father of Magicals in the land of Gaia. Number three, consume the spirit of thine greatest enemy in the land of Erebus on All Hallows' Eve. Don't think I've ever said 'thine' in my entire life. Anyway, number four, cut the head off the Mother of Monsters in the Land of Light. Number five, the Challenger must acquire twelve powers and bathe in the blood of her blood, in the light of a full moon. The twelve powers will become the twelve keys required to open the door to the realm of the challenged Child of Chaos. Only upon the orderly completion of all five rituals will the Child become unable to reject the Challenger's claim to their power."

The remaining people in the room gaped at her. Myself included. She'd just rattled off the entire list of rituals as if they were groceries. Echidna must have revealed them to her inside the box. After all, she wasn't bound by Chaos in the same way as the Children.

"But the rituals are prone to wider interpretation, so what you see on the tin might not be what's in it, if you catch my drift," she added. "Our focus has to be on the second ritual. Gaia told me that Katherine is about to perform it, but she hasn't completed it, which means there's still time to get in her way."

"Kill a Father of Magicals in the land of Gaia?" I replied. We'd already heard that one from the Librarian.

Harley smiled at me. "Precisely."

"And just who is this Father of Magicals?" Levi snorted.

"That's what we have to figure out, and fast." Harley came closer and ignored our shocked faces.

"We thought it might be a descendant of one of the Primus Anglicus," Dylan chimed in.

Tatyana nodded. "Or the spirit of one of them? The first one, presumably."

"Is there a Father of Monsters?" Raffe said.

"Wouldn't it have said 'Father of Monsters' if that was the clue? It states the Mother of Monsters in one of the later rituals, so I don't think that would make sense," Santana replied. She put her arm around Raffe's shoulders. The djinn had been a little unruly of late, and he was still visibly on edge.

Levi shook his head. "Well, this is stupid. Why would these rituals be so vague? Why not spell it out more clearly?"

"I imagine it's meant to be difficult. Otherwise, everyone would be trying it." Isadora cast him a dry smile.

O'Halloran lifted his hand abruptly. "What if it means a leader of magicals? Leaders can sometimes be seen as paternal figures, right? The founding fathers of our great nation, for example, and that sort of thing?"

Movement swirled in Echidna's box, distracting us. Inside, the monster had turned back into smoke that billowed out and hit the glass in powdery waves. A second later, frost crept up the inside pane and encased her in a bubble of ice. The charms had been restored. Echidna was asleep again. *Thank goodness for that.* Tobe exited shortly afterward and locked the box. He dusted off his paws and slipped the keys into his wings.

"What are we talking about?" He looked at us expectantly.

"The second ritual," I said. "We need to figure out what 'Father of Magicals' means."

O'Halloran nodded. "I thought it might have something to do with a leader of some kind. A metaphorical father figure."

Tobe tilted his head. "What about a coven director? They are often looked up to as paternal figures, especially by those who have no parents of their own. Take Alton for example; he is surely a father figure to the magicals of the San Diego Coven."

Levi turned up his nose. "Alton is no longer the coven director here, so it cannot be him."

"That was only a suggestion, Levi," Alton said. "I don't think it's me, either, for what it's worth. Directors are very localized, so it would be impossible to figure out which one might be considered a Father of Magicals. It could be someone with far greater reach." Alton glanced down at Levi. Tobe's remark had clearly irked him, given his new position here. It was still a pissing contest between the two of them.

Levi's eyes widened suddenly. "I've got it!"

"What have you got?" Harley leveled her gaze at him.

"The president of the United Covens of America, Steven Price. He would most certainly be considered a Father of Magicals; he's the leader of an entire nation." He tapped the side of his chin. "Not to mention the fact that Katherine knows him very well indeed. The two of them came up together in the New York Coven and tended to move in the same elite circles. Naturally, he has renounced any affiliation with her, but they were close acquaintances, once upon a time."

Isadora gasped. "That's got Katherine written all over it. That would be one hell of a statement, wouldn't it? 'Here I am, Katherine Shipton, and I've just murdered the president of the UCA.' It's exactly what she'd do, if given the opportunity. She won't be able to resist it!"

Harley nodded. "I was told that the next ritual would happen in a place with lots of people. If our assumptions are right, then that points to one place in particular."

"The Washington Assembly," I said. The pieces fit perfectly. Katherine wanted a grand stage to prove her power, and Washington was it. A ripple of shock bubbled around the gathered group. The implications were all too clear.

"We've got to move fast on this," Harley urged. "The Assembly is only a day away, which means we've got a super brief window to stop Katherine. Levi, what do you say to letting us plan our form of attack? The fewer people who know what we know, the better. After that stunt with Nomura this morning, we're just about the only people you can trust in this joint, whether you like it or not."

All of us looked at Levi. I didn't know which way the dice would fall on this one.

Levi grimaced. "I suppose I have very little choice." He glanced at Harley. "However, you must remain under constant supervision, from either your team, your aunt, or… frankly, whoever is willing to take on the job. All I care about is that you are being watched around the clock. I'm simply not comfortable with you like this, having free run of the coven."

"Well, I'm not comfortable with you as our coven director, but hey, we can't all get what we want in life, right?" Harley snarked. A grin tugged at my lips.

"You may not like it, but I am still your director," Levi retorted. "And I won't forget your actions today. You disobeyed direct orders. Rest assured that I will be thinking of appropriate penalties for all of you and will execute them once we have completed our mission in Washington. Now, I suggest you all get some rest and stand by. We will reconvene in the morning."

Garrett pushed through the group. "Actually, Director, I was wondering if I might have a quick word with you in your office? I wanted to discuss my latest task with the LA Coven."

I cast him a withering look. The rest of the Rag Team joined me. From where we were standing, it looked like Garrett had just weaseled back out of our group and sided with the boss in order to gain favors. *It's a slippery climb to the top, pal.* Then again, "slippery" should have been Garrett's middle name. He'd always been good at getting out of trouble and in with the right people. Nothing had changed in all the years I'd known him.

Not that I really cared what Garrett was up to. With all the talk of Washington out of the way for tonight, my focus returned to Harley. I couldn't take my eyes off her. The others were walking toward the door, but I lingered a moment. I took her hand. She glanced at me in surprise. I didn't want to bombard her with questions, but I needed to know what had changed. She looked the same. She felt the same. She sounded the same. But something was off.

She said she was okay, Wade. I repeated the words over and over in my head. I wanted to take solace in them, I really did. The only trouble was, I didn't know whether to believe her.

THIRTY-NINE

Harley

The following morning, with the sun barely risen, we gathered in Wade's office. I'd hoped for a decent sleep, but in the aftermath of my Suppressor breaking my mind had had other ideas. I'd been buzzing away all night, waking every couple of hours with a start and a sudden realization that the Suppressor was actually gone. At least there were no more nightmares, but I could've done with one whole night without being woken up by something out of my control. The others seemed equally tired, standing around like zombies with gigantic flasks of coffee, all pilfered from Santana's secret stash.

"So what happened in that box?" Dylan was the first to speak. I hadn't really said much about it, with the whole Levi debacle after the fact, and they'd been nice enough not to bombard me with questions right away. To be honest, I was still making sense of it in my own head.

"A lot," I replied with a sleepy smile. "After making a deal with Echidna, she put her hand on my head and broke the Suppressor with her own powers. I think she wanted to watch me squirm a bit more. I had to rush to get the Sanguine spell completed, otherwise... well, I don't think I'd be standing here right now."

Wade moved closer to me. "What do you mean?"

"When the Suppressor broke, I couldn't control any of the energy coming out of it. I... uh, sort of disappeared for a while. 'Disintegrated' is probably a better way of describing it. All that power was tearing me apart, quite literally. There was so much going on, and I was trying to get the freaking words of that spell out." I took a deep sip of coffee. "My life flashed in front of my eyes, and I was pretty sure that was it. Game over. Done. Dead. Pushing up daisies. And then... well, I thought of you, the people I care about most in the world, and I managed to get the last few lines of the spell out. Light and Dark collided, and I guess they figured out a balance. More or less."

I expected at least one of them to crack a joke at my cheesiness. Instead, sad eyes stared at me from around Wade's tiny office. Their emotions, a mix of fear, relief, sorrow, and anxiety, drifted off them in steady waves. I understood why they felt that way. They'd been stuck outside the box, unable to help me and not knowing what the outcome might be.

"I know how that feels," Jacob murmured.

I nodded. "If I hadn't been able to think of you guys, I honestly don't know where I'd be right now. It was everything Astrid had described to me about dying, and I... man, I thought I was a goner." I stole a glance at Wade and leaned closer to him, wanting him to somehow know that *he* was the true source of my survival. Thoughts of him had pulled me through.

"How do you feel now?" Tatyana asked.

"Weird."

"How so?" Raffe asked.

I shrugged. "I don't feel like it's over yet. The Sanguine spell was more of a Band-Aid than a cure-all for the broken Suppressor. I mean, the Suppressor is definitely gone, but all of that power is still there, and the Light and Dark sides aren't exactly as balanced as I'd hoped they might be. Something still feels strange, if that makes sense?"

"Maybe it just needs time," Louella suggested, though she didn't seem convinced. She was smarter than that, and I could feel the nerves brimming through her. I'd become truly dangerous overnight, and they all knew it.

Isadora put her arm around my shoulders, giving me a hug. "We're all just glad you came out of that box in one piece, Harley," she said softly. "But I have to ask, what was Echidna's price for giving you her blood? She must've wanted something in return."

Santana snorted. "I think it's a freaking miracle that Echidna didn't eat her whole the moment she stepped into the box. Monsters love power, and Harley must have walked in like a frigging all-you-can-eat buffet." She glanced at me. "I can say that now that you're out of there, right?"

"I had the same thought a couple of times," I replied with a laugh. "She threatened to eat me more than once, too. I must have had about three showers when I got back to my room, and I can still smell her."

"We didn't want to say anything." Raffe nudged me in the arm, a mischievous glint in his eyes.

About the smell, or about what your djinn knows? I cast him a meaningful glance, which made him dip his head in understanding. It seemed like he could sense the intense power in me, and my fight to control it, even now.

I turned back to the others. "So if I'm wandering around in a cloud of perfume for a while, that's why." I gave a nervous laugh. "She really was scary as hell. Imagine your worst nightmare and multiply it by about a thousand, and then add fangs and scales."

"Harley?" Isadora prompted, no levity in her voice. "What did she ask for?"

I sighed, knowing I couldn't put it off. "She gave me the blood in return for… being given the right to name my firstborn child. Only if I survive Katherine, of course. She put a curse on me to make sure I come back and do as she's asked."

"She asked you to do *what?*" Santana sounded outraged, her shock mirrored on the rest of the Rag Team's faces. Wade looked particularly troubled, though he didn't say anything. I guessed the thought of me and babies was as terrifying to him as it was to me. His emotions were certainly nervous and shocked, all at once.

"Name my firstborn." It was a weird prospect, but it felt improbably far away. There was a lot to get done before I even had to worry about it, and there was no telling if it would ever matter. "I don't even know if I want kids, so I probably got the better end of the deal."

"You understand the significance of names, though, right?" Santana asked.

Raffe nodded. "Names have untold power. You should never give that gift to someone else."

I forced down a sudden bubble of panic. "Hey, it's not like she asked me to fight Leviathan or something! I really don't think we need to worry about this, not anytime soon. In ten years, maybe, but even then... I don't know. I might never want one." I was flustered, the words tumbling out. Having Wade nearby made it even worse, because I could see him looking at me in confusion and fear.

Wade stared down at me. "Harley's right. We can't worry about this too much now. We've got Washington to think about." He was trying to bring the team back into the moment while covering his own discomfort around the subject, and for that I was grateful. Still, the flood of anxiety and concern coming off him was hard to ignore. I was still getting used to controlling my new, supercharged Empathy, and blocking out emotions wasn't as easy as it had been before.

"At least my father can't keep us out of this one," Raffe muttered. "He's got no choice but to trust us and let us lead the charge."

"You really think he'll do that?" Garrett retorted. Both he and Astrid had been silent since entering Wade's office, making me wonder if they'd had some sort of talk about her current state.

"Yeah, unless you know something we don't?" Raffe shot back. "You seemed pretty cozy with him yesterday, when you walked off to have a little 'chat' about some bullcrap or other."

Garrett narrowed his eyes. "I was trying to do something to give us the upper hand. He's got his concerns about all of you, which means you need someone who's in his good books to get the inside scoop."

"Did he say anything about keeping us out of it?" Astrid asked.

"Like Raffe said, he doesn't feel like he has much choice but to let us in on this mission." Garrett's expression softened, though a glimpse of sadness moved across his eyes. Yeah, they'd definitely had some kind of talk, but there wasn't time to delve too deeply into it, not with the event in Washington on our heels.

"Even if he does try something funny, you've got me to portal us all there," Jacob piped up.

Isadora nodded. "That will be especially important if he decides to use me for the same purpose."

"Wouldn't he just use the mirrors?" Santana replied.

"With the Katherine situation, he might wish to be a little more secretive about his arrival. Plus, if he wants to keep us from getting involved, he'll take me just to be sure that you have no way of reaching Washington in time," she explained. *Sneaky bastard.*

"No matter what Levi has to say about it, we're reaching Katherine before she can get to the president." I looked at the gathered group. "It's pretty clear that there are a lot of people withholding vital information from the magical public, especially about Katherine. The president included. Nobody wants to be associated with her, for good reason. But that doesn't change the fact that the president knew her well a long time ago, which makes him vulnerable to her attack. She'll know things about him that we don't, and Levi seems to know more than he's letting on, too."

Garrett nodded. "It seemed like it to me, too."

"Care to elaborate?" Raffe replied.

"Levi didn't say too much last night when I spoke with him, but I got the feeling he had something in mind—like, he was coming up with a plan of his own to try and intercept Katherine."

I shook my head. "Right, so we need to get to the president before Levi *and* Katherine if we want to stand any chance of succeeding."

A knock at the door startled us. "Come in," Wade said, a note of reluctance in his voice.

O'Halloran peered around the door with a grim look on his face. "I was hoping I'd find you all here."

"O'Halloran? What's up?" Wade replied.

"Levi sent me to give you all a message," he announced, evidently none too pleased with what he was about to say. "None of you are permitted to get involved in the mission in Washington. He's mobilizing the National Council—the members he can trust, anyway—and a group of experienced magicals to increase the overall security at the gathering." He looked at me specifically. "He doesn't want you or the Rag Team involved in any way. I tried to convince him otherwise, but he's resolute about it. I believe 'ticking time bomb' was thrown about a few times. For what it's worth, I don't agree."

Anger spiked through me, though I wasn't sure what else I'd expected from Levi. He hated me even more now than he had before.

"Are you serious?" Santana grumbled.

O'Halloran pulled a sour face. "Unfortunately, yes."

"This is ridiculous!" Raffe snapped. "There's no freaking reasoning with him!"

"Easy there, *mi amor*." Santana put her hand on his shoulder.

"I had a feeling he might do something like this," Garrett murmured. "I thought I'd managed to get through to the guy."

Tatyana glowered. "The man is an idiot. An absolute idiot."

"Can't argue you with you there," O'Halloran replied.

"Doesn't he understand how far Katherine's reach is?" Dylan added grimly.

Jacob nodded. "Yeah, what if she's already manipulated the National Council?"

"It wouldn't be so outlandish," Isadora said bitterly. "I don't think any of us could have imagined her bending Nomura's loyalty to benefit her. And yet he's downstairs in one of the cells, and she's running around, free as a bird." We were all pissed off by this decision. It flowed around the room in dark, angry waves.

"I should've tried to read Levi's mind when I had the chance; then we could have gone to Washington without him even knowing," Louella muttered. "Not that I've made much progress with my Telepathy."

O'Halloran gave an awkward little bow. "I'm needed elsewhere in the coven in a couple of minutes. Hopefully, I'll end up someplace where I can't hear about how you plan to sneak out of the coven and get to Washington." He gave a conspiratorial wink and headed for the door. "Just a heads up—you have ten minutes before I send a team of security magicals to keep you on site. They'll watch and listen to your every word, so be cautious. Isadora, you'll have to come with me. I'm sorry, but I have to follow my orders."

Isadora nodded. "No need to be sorry, O'Halloran. I was expecting it." She joined him at the door, and the two of them left the room together, leaving us to contemplate our next move. It was clear what we had to do now, though time was running out.

Even if it got us shipped off to Alaska or Avarice, we had to get to Washington and stop Katherine ourselves. And we needed to move quickly. The Assembly was tonight.

FORTY

Wade

———————

The security magicals kept us together in one room. A big mistake, but they didn't know it. We behaved until late afternoon. We stayed quiet and gathered our things together without much fuss. I had a stash of weapons in my office. Even before the security team had come for us, we were able to slip knives and tasers about our persons. They'd pushed us into one of the reading rooms and barred the door. Every half hour or so, one of them came in to check on us. That gave Jacob plenty of time to do his thing before the next check-in.

The only two people who'd been taken away were Louella and Garrett. Apparently, Levi wanted another word with Garrett before he went back to the LA Coven. Louella, on the other hand, had lessons to attend. I was starting to doubt Garrett's integrity. Yeah, he'd said he was speaking with Levi for us, but he didn't often put others first. He had a lot to lose if Levi discovered he was truly on our side. So maybe he wasn't. Not that it mattered. He wasn't coming with us anyway. We had to go, and he wasn't here.

"Now?" Raffe kept his voice to a whisper.

I nodded. "Jacob, you ready?"

"I've got this." He raised his palms and began to feed energy between his fingertips. A moment later, a hole tore in time and space and opened to let us in. It sparked at the edges. I didn't think I'd ever get used to portal travel. We moved quickly through it, and I made sure to stay close to Harley.

I didn't understand the full extent of what had happened to her, but I still felt as if I needed to be at her side. She was dealing with a lot. I knew she'd changed, just not the exact details. She was definitely way more powerful now, and that worried me. My mom's words came back to my mind. She'd warned me that Harley might be dangerous, but I hadn't given it much thought until now. Dangerous or not, I'd stay close until she told me otherwise.

We burst out into a huge ballroom, which had been decorated for the occasion. Circular tables were spread across the space, with fine tableware and white silk cloths. Pale flowers filled the room, and serving staff rushed in and out. The ballroom stood inside the walls of the Washington Coven; I hadn't been here too many times before, but I recognized the décor.

We'd barely taken a step forward when an icy grip took hold of me. Pain shot through my legs and seized my chest. I fought against it, but it held me fast. I had lost complete control of my limbs, the pain growing inside me. It splintered through every vein and prompted my muscles to spasm wildly. Beside me, the others were suffering the same fate. Raffe buckled completely and sank to the ground, while the rest of my friends tried to keep moving forward. Nobody could take a single step.

"What's happening?" Dylan hissed. A vein at his temple throbbed with the exertion of pushing against the hex. As a Herculean, meeting a powerful force he couldn't break was probably tough on him.

"Levi," I spat back. He'd clearly warned the Washington Coven that we might appear and had ensured that the coven warded itself against us. Beside me, Harley's brow furrowed, and her eyes looked dead ahead. I'd never seen her so determined.

"Screw this." She closed her eyes, and her body vibrated. Bronze particles flowed over her skin and lit her up from the inside. If I could've protected my eyes from the glow, I would've. Sweat dripped from her forehead as she powered against the hex. I didn't know what she was doing, but a tremor of fear shot through me.

Her hands balled into fists as the bronze light grew brighter. I opened my mouth to tell her to stop, but a blast burst outward and enveloped us all. I fell to the ground, and the pain subsided. When the explosion faded, Harley emerged from the epicenter, her skin glowing completely white. More to the point, we could move again.

"Harley?" I jumped to my feet and ran to her. She crumpled in my arms the moment they folded around her. I propped her up with ease, but her eyes rolled back into her head for a moment, as if she were about to pass out. "Harley, are you okay?"

She nodded weakly. "I think so."

I glanced at Jacob. "You should go back to the SDC. Jacob can take you."

She shook her head. "I'm fine. I need a sec to catch my breath, that's all. Anyway, we've got work to do. If Levi has laid any more of these hexes, you'll need me around."

"I'm not sure about this." I held her tighter, but she straightened up and brushed me off.

"I'll be back to normal in a minute."

I wanted to take her back myself, right then and there. But she was right. We had work to do, and we couldn't do it without Harley's strength. That didn't stop me from being worried sick about her, though. These newly altered abilities of hers were terrifying. More so because I had no idea just what she was capable of anymore. What if she defended herself against a security officer and ended up doing something more harmful than she'd intended? One thing was clear: she still had very little control.

"Everyone okay?" Tatyana dusted herself off as she got to her feet. Fortunately, the serving staff had been out of the room during Harley's hex-breaking. Now, we were just more guests to avoid.

A ripple of assent moved around the group.

"We should join the party." I nodded toward the ballroom door. Loud chatter could be heard from the hallway beyond. I unzipped my coat and revealed the suit beneath. I always wore at least a vest, but I'd changed into something a little more formal. In the ten minutes before security took us, I'd grabbed every spare suit I had stashed in my office and handed them out. We'd dressed in the reading room and put our jackets over the evidence. My tailor always did a great job with my suits, adding charms that ensured they adjusted to fit anyone who wore them, but the navy-blue one looked especially good on Harley.

Leaving our jackets in one of the storage cupboards, we made our way out into the hallway. We blended in well enough. Everyone was smartly dressed and snatching flutes of champagne from passing trays. I politely declined when a server came near; we all needed to keep a clear head this evening. At least they'd mistaken me for a guest.

We infiltrated the crowd and kept an eye on one another. Naturally, I stuck by Harley's side, while the others spread out a bit more. Not too much, but enough not to draw attention. I hadn't seen Levi anywhere, which was a good sign. He'd have outed us the moment he saw us.

"Ladies and gentlemen, if you would care to join us in the main ballroom, we may begin the first meeting of the Assembly!" a firm voice called from within the crowd. Immediately, the masses began to move toward the door we'd just come out of. I took Harley's hand and led her in the same direction. However, before we could step through the doors, a figure intercepted us. It took me a second to realize it was Garrett, all gussied up in a black tuxedo.

He grabbed my lapel and yanked me away from the main entrance, and the others followed. Anger pulsed through me. *Whose side are you on, pal?* If he tried to stop us from doing this, he would have the entire wrath of the Rag Team to contend with.

"What are you playing at?" I held his gaze.

Garrett rolled his eyes. "You people need to understand that I do keep my word. We can slip in through the side door, where nobody will see us." He pointed to the door beside him, which he opened. Beyond, I could see the ballroom. "Levi took me into his office and told me he wanted me here. I've been looking for you guys, since I figured you'd sneak in. I saw some security magicals laying hexes earlier. Did you manage to avoid them?"

I looked at Harley. "Not exactly."

"Well, you're here now, so let's keep a low profile." Garrett led the way through the side door. A heavy curtain stood between us and the rest of the ballroom. In this instance, I figured that was better, since it meant nobody could see us. Garrett was truly on our side.

We hung back as the crowd took their seats at the circular tables. Waiters brought cocktails, and a relaxed chatter filled the air. It reminded me of all the galas and parties that my parents had dragged me to when I was younger. I'd hated them then, and I hated them now. They were just an excuse to show wealth and power, and this Assembly wasn't much different. Thinking of my mom and dad, I scoured the tables to see if they were there. As director of the Houston Coven and a member of the Texas Mage Council, they would have definitely been invited to this. Fortunately, there was no sign of them. That was one less thing for me to worry about.

"Katherine's associates have already made it in." Astrid pointed to a man who sat nearby.

I frowned. "A cultist?"

"Yeah, he's on the Most Wanted list." She brought up Smartie and showed us the man's face on the screen. It was a grainy mugshot, but it was definitely him. "I'm scanning the database of her potential associates now, and the list of missing magicals who've been presumed dead or missing from other covens."

I could've hugged her. Without being able to see the tattoos on their chests, we had no idea whether they were part of the Cult of Eris or not. But Smartie seemed to have the right idea, and Astrid was forever thinking outside the box. She ran a few more faces through the facial recognition technology she had installed. Windows kept opening, showing the faces of potential cultists—a young woman with jet-black hair shaved on the sides, a grizzled older man with a long beard, a stocky guy with tattoos on his face, and a whole bevy of others, who looked a bit more ordinary. All of whom were somewhere in the ball-room at this very minute.

"How are you spotting them so fast?" Garrett sounded mystified.

"I hacked into the cameras before we arrived. I've got a good view of the entire ballroom, and Smartie is cross-referencing the faces with the database." She smiled up at him. "The only ones I can't pick out are the Shapeshifters, if Katherine has any in this particular cell of her associates."

"Right, so we need to keep an eye on these creeps," Harley said. "Everyone is a suspect."

I nodded. "Once the speeches get underway, we can move into the ballroom. Let's follow them as closely as we can without alerting their suspicions. Then, when the time is right, we engage them. We can't stir up any trouble before the president comes on stage, or all of this will go up in smoke and Katherine will find another way to complete this ritual."

"We have to wait until we see her." Harley looked as if she was holding her breath. Her eyes were fixed on the far stage, like she expected Katherine to appear at any moment. We knew she was going to show up. It was all a matter of when. And when that moment *did* come, Harley would have her shot to take Katherine on.

Astrid sucked air through her teeth. "Crap."

"What is it?" Santana peered over Astrid's shoulder.

"I've had a program running in the background, to try and hack into Levi's emails. Smartie just broke in."

"Isn't that good news?" Harley asked, her tone anxious.

Astrid shook her head and showed us the screen. It had opened onto one email in particular. "Levi's mobilized the security magicals and the National Council—we already know that—but, judging by this, he's asked that the president be kept in the dark about why. If that's the case, then Steven Price doesn't know Katherine's coming for him." She swiped down to the end of the email. "Yeah, see, right here—Levi was worried the president might cancel his appearance and cause him to miss out on nabbing Katherine. So nobody's informed President Price about what the heck is going on."

"We need to get out there." Harley gestured toward the front stage. "Right now, we're all that's standing between the president and Katherine. Those security magicals won't be able to stop her. They might think they're prepared, but they've got no idea what's coming."

I nodded. "Let's move out and draw as little attention to ourselves as possible."

We slid out from behind the curtain and began to mingle. The speeches hadn't started yet, so people were still up and about. About half sat at their tables and looked over the night's running order, but the rest were standing and chatting. I looked to Harley and dipped my head toward the stage. We'd chosen the right side of the room. On the opposite side, I could see Jacob walking casually toward the front of the room, too. The president was in the wings somewhere, and he was totally unaware of the danger he was in. We needed to remedy that.

"How the hell did Levi end up on the Mage Council when he thinks *this* is a good idea?" I frowned up at the stage. Hopefully, we weren't too late.

Raffe gave a wry chuckle from close behind me. "He rubbed elbows with the right people. How else do people like him get in power?"

"Ladies and gentlemen, proceedings will shortly get underway." The event's MC, a middle-aged woman with half-moon glasses and way too much energy, bounded up on stage to make the announcement. "Please stand for the president of the United Covens of America."

With a rustle of expensive fabric, the assembled guests stood, the cultists included. Even the guy with the tattooed face didn't look out of place. They'd all been dressed and prepped to fit in. Katherine was very good at her job, I had to give her that.

My gaze turned toward the stage. The president hadn't appeared yet, even though he'd been announced. *Weird.* Peering closer, I saw a figure in the wings. He was flanked by one too many security magicals. Their black uniforms stood out like sore thumbs. I realized that I had to take the chance before it was too late to do anything. The president *had* to know what was going on. At least then he'd be more prepared if Katherine showed her face.

"Hurry," I whispered to the others on my side of the room. Raffe, Tatyana, Harley, and Garrett followed me as I walked up the steps of the stage and into the wings. I hoped we looked like additional plain-clothes security. Otherwise, we'd just blown our cover.

"Mr. President, might I have a word before you go out there?" I flashed my Crowley credentials at him. I always carried a name card or two, in case I needed my surname to get me out of a fix. It had worked in Paris, and I prayed it worked for me now.

Steven Price stood at six feet, with the broad figure to match. He looked like a linebacker in a sharp suit. However, his forty-something face was open and welcoming. The face of a politician. If he was worried about our sudden presence, he didn't show it. I supposed my name helped, but still, we were interrupting him on a very important night.

"Can it wait until after the opening speech, Mr. Crowley?" He spoke with a rich, deep baritone that reminded me of my dad. I'd actually met the president a few times before, but I didn't know if he'd remember me personally.

"I'm afraid it can't, sir."

"What do you need to speak to me about?"

I caught sight of another figure waiting in the opposite wing. Even drenched in shadow, I knew him instantly. Levi watched us, with fire and brimstone burning in his eyes.

FORTY-ONE

Harley

The president wasn't what I'd expected at all. I always pictured national leaders as stuffy old men. Instead, Steven Price was lean and well put together, with salt-and-pepper hair and steady brown eyes. Even his voice was weirdly soothing, making me wonder if he was using some magical charm to give off a calm and reliable air.

"Well, it's about—" Wade started to speak, but I cut him off. I had no idea why; I just felt a sudden urge to make myself known to this man.

"We've come from the SDC." I was aware that I was staring at him in a fairly creepy way as he turned to look at me. I stuck out my hand. "It's a pleasure to meet you, sir. It's Harley… uh, Harley Merlin, sir."

"Hang on a moment," the president said, his eyes fixed on me. "*The* Harley Merlin? I suppose there can't be too many of you. Your reputation precedes you." He chuckled and took my hand, giving it a firm shake. "I must say, I've been watching your situation closely, and with great curiosity, ever since your identity came to light. It's not too often that we discover a magical of your caliber simply wandering the streets. It's a delight to have you safely within our midst. It would not do to have a young lady of such skill out there alone in the world."

I melted into a puddle right about then. He was generating some serious Robert Downey, Jr. and Bruce Springsteen vibes, and I'd always been a sucker for that type of star power. He had a nobility about him that was hard to ignore, and a charismatic, soft way of speaking that made you want to lean in and listen more closely. *This has got to be some sort of sorcery.*

"You know about me?" I gushed.

"Of course I do, Ms. Merlin. I've heard a great deal about you, and I'm impressed by what I've been hearing. We multi-skilled magicals have got to stick together." He flashed me a bright smile that made me feel a little gooey inside.

"You can do more than one thing, too?" I realized I sounded like an idiot, but I was at a total loss for words. I'd almost forgotten the real reason we were up here in the first place, speaking to him one-on-one.

He nodded. "Water, Magneton, and Telekinesis. Although, I don't get to use them all too often these days."

"Magneton?" I practically choked. "I don't know that one."

"I can manipulate metal," he replied with a grin. "As a kid, I was always getting in trouble for ruining my mother's silverware. Needless to say, there are many people who find my talent far less impressive than you do, although it has been known to come in handy from time to time."

"Incoming," Wade hissed in my ear.

I turned to see what he was talking about, just in time to watch Levi attempt to cross the stage without being seen by the gathered guests. He stepped forward and backward as if he were in some kind of comic sketch, before disappearing into the shadows. I realized he was going to try and find another way to reach us, by taking the long way around, which meant we didn't have long to get the president up to speed.

"Mr. President, I know you're very busy and you've got a heck of a schedule ahead of you, but we have to tell you something," I rambled, keeping my eye on the stage door behind him.

Wade nodded. "There's an imminent attack on your life, though the National Council has seen fit to keep it from you. They know about it, but they've kept you in the dark," he explained at breakneck speed. "Katherine Shipton is coming here tonight because you are part of one of the rituals. You know about her wanting to become a Child of Chaos, right?"

"I have been made aware, yes," the president replied. *Good, otherwise we'd be screwed.*

"Well, like I said, you're part of the second ritual she needs to complete in order to become a Child of Chaos, and she's coming here to take you out."

He frowned. "I've known of Katherine's desire to become a Child of Chaos for a long time. She used to float the theory when we were younger and studied together in New York. At first, it was a wild idea—we even used to joke about it. Then, after your mother and father got married, Ms. Merlin, it became more of a definite goal."

"You knew her well, then?" I asked, even though I already knew the answer.

He nodded sadly. "We were good friends, once upon a time. We both had the same sort of potential. I tried to persuade her to get into magical politics, but she had already started to unravel. In the end, I had my career to think of, and I couldn't coddle her any more. I had to let her go. I realize now that I should've done so much more. When you're young, you so often fail to see where things might lead."

I shook my head. Katherine certainly had all the right attributes to get into politics. She'd already amassed a huge following, even though she was obviously unhinged. Cult leaders and politicians often had a lot in common, and Katherine was no exception.

The stage door burst open, and Levi came running over with a face like thunder. He clearly wanted to send us to Alaska right then but had to keep up appearances. The president held up his hand before Levi could speak.

"If Katherine wants to come after me, then she's welcome to try," he said firmly. "You ought to have told me of this, but I can understand your reasoning. I imagine you thought I would cancel this whole affair and ruin the plan to apprehend Katherine, correct?"

Levi nodded sheepishly. "We were fully prepared to protect—"

"Fortunately, I know that I can count on Mr. Crowley and Ms. Merlin here to stop Katherine if she attempts anything." His firm tone cut like a knife. "I have also been busy, Director Levi. In fact, I had my security team draw up files on the so-called Rag Team so that I could become better acquainted with their specific traits and skillsets, since their name kept coming up so often."

Levi's mouth hung open in shock. "You... did what, Mr. President?"

I was equally surprised, although it made sense. Of course, someone as powerful as the president would be keeping tabs on everything related to Katherine, the biggest national security threat of the decade.

"I wouldn't expect you to know, Levi." The president chuckled. "Even Alton didn't know, and he was director far longer than you. I am firmly up to speed on all matters regarding Katherine, though I should like to hear more about these rituals. Those, I'm not so well versed in."

"The second ritual is something about killing a Father of Magicals in the land of Gaia," I explained. "You're the Father of Magicals in this instance, and the land of Gaia... well, that's one of the otherworlds belonging to the Children of Chaos. She's going to take you there, whenever she decides to strike."

He tapped his chin. "An otherworld, you say?"

"Yes, sir."

"But she's without a Portal Opener, from my understanding? I know she was in possession of one for a time, but I'd heard that your aunt had been rescued from her, Ms. Merlin?"

I nodded. "She has, sir."

My mind completely blanked. That was a very good point. How *was* Katherine going to take the president to the land of Gaia if she didn't have a Portal Opener anymore? She was hella resourceful when she needed to be, but I figured even that was beyond her current powers.

"How will she take me to the land of Gaia without one?" The president asked the same question I'd been thinking. He seemed surprisingly calm for someone who'd just been told his life was at risk, and that Katherine Shipton was coming for him. Maybe he wasn't worried. Maybe he thought he could reason with her, for old time's sake. Or maybe he was confident enough in her lack of Portal Opener to not be overly concerned.

"I... I don't know," I admitted.

"Well then, until she shows her face, we must go on with the show." The president fixed his bow tie and smoothed down the lapels of his tux. "If you'll wait here and remain vigilant, I have a speech to give. We can't let Katherine know there's something the matter now, can we? If this is our chance to capture her, then we must take it. Be bold, be brave, but don't do anything overly heroic."

He strode out onto the stage to the roar of rapturous applause. Levi had definitely underestimated him—there's no way he would have canceled. It was clear now that he would never have cowered before Katherine or tried to save his own life in favor of catching her.

He'd lifted his hand to the microphone, to check that it was working, and smiled at the crowd. "Ladies and Gentlemen, it is my pleasure to address you this evening, on the day of our Annual Assembly. I know we are in the midst of a time of turmoil, but I wish to alleviate your fears. My people and I are doing all we can to solve the problem that faces us and to defeat the enemy that looms over us. I don't like to start on a negative note, and I hope you'll not take negativity from my words. We are hopeful, and I would urge you to be, too. Together, we are united. Together, we will overcome."

I glanced around the curtain and took a look at the congregation. "Over there!" I hissed, as I spotted one of our Most Wanted turning to whisper to his accomplice. It was the guy with the covered tattoos, speaking with the girl who'd shrouded her buzzcut in a blond wig.

Wade nodded. "I've got my eye on them." He glanced at Garrett, who stood on the opposite side of the room, and signaled to him with a set of subtle hand gestures. Garrett turned his head to look at the whispering pair before giving a slight dip of his head in Wade's direction. If they moved to strike at the president, we'd be ready. It looked as though Katherine wasn't going to appear after all. The headliner of this gig had canceled.

Still, I kept my eyes fixed on every possible entrance and exit, keeping watch over the stage door and every shadow that the evil witch could slink out of. If she tried anything and thought she could pop up and catch us unawares, we'd be on her like flies on crap. As I watched the crowd, I sent out my Empath ability to try and weed out anyone I couldn't sense, thus picking out the Shapeshifters in the audience.

I was halfway through scanning the room when I caught sight of a uniformed figure slipping in through one of the side doors in the left-hand wall. They wore a long black coat and a peaked cap that covered their face. It was hard to make out their figure in a get-up like that, but the person moved with a feminine fluidity that seemed eerily familiar, even though they wore the face of a man. I'd had my suspicions about Katherine being a Shapeshifter for a long while, after having her emotions blocked from me in our previous meetings. If she was here, there was every chance I'd have to identify her by a process of Shapeshifter elimination.

I launched my Empath senses toward the uniformed figure and felt nothing come back. I grabbed Wade's arm. "I think that's her. Look."

His eyes widened. "Do you think so? It could be one of the president's guard."

"Then why aren't they with the president?" The rest of his personal guard surrounded him in a semicircle, standing with their heads bowed and their arms behind their backs. This creeping uniformed figure had no emotions coming from them and was acting shifty. It had Katherine written all over.

"I'll apprehend them. Wait here and cover me if you have to." Wade turned to leave through the stage door, but a discreet movement made me reach out and pull him back. One of the president's personal guard, dressed in the telltale uniform of his officers, lifted his head in a sharp movement and darted forward before anyone could move. I realized a split second too late that they didn't have any brimming emotions, either.

"It's her! It's Katherine!" I yelled, hoping my voice would be enough to alert the president. But in one swift movement, she grabbed him around the throat with one arm and shoved him forward, the two of them vanishing instantly into what looked like a portal that had suddenly appeared in front of them both. It snapped shut a second later, leaving the whole room in a state of shock and panic.

The president had been taken.

Screams and shouts of alarm rose from the gathered crowd. Many of them ducked for cover under their tables, as if they expected Katherine to come back and kill them all, while others simply stared in wide-eyed horror at the empty space where they'd disappeared. A few sprinted for the doors, panicking as they found their way barred by security officers, who were in an instant state of lockdown. They didn't know what had happened, but they knew it wasn't good. We all did.

"Was that her?" one voice howled. "She'll kill us all!"

"She took the president!" another screamed, the sound blood-curdling.

"She'll kill him. Oh my God, she's going to kill him!" a third shrieked, filling the air with the sound of terror and grief.

"How the hell did she make that portal?" Wade bit out, his eyes steely.

I shook my head. "This is Katherine we're talking about."

My body was gripped in a numb sort of fear, but I had to force myself to focus. The rest of the Rag Team was looking around in complete shock, their faces drained of color, all of them looking to Wade and Levi for some kind of explanation. The truth was, none of us had an answer, but we did have a shot at getting him back. But only if we moved quickly. My mind jumped into action, and I ran toward Jacob, who stood by the opposite stairs, which led up to the stage. He was trembling, his eyes wide in panic.

"Jacob, you need to take us to Gaia's otherworld. You need to do it now!" I grasped his shoulders, trying to get him to focus on me.

He shook his head frantically. "I can't. I'm not familiar with this kind of portal trail, and if I get it wrong, we could end up stuck between the otherworld and some other place, like my dad. I'm not risking losing us all in some interdimensional gap where we'll never be heard from again."

"Look, I need you to calm down." I gripped his shoulders tighter. "It might not be the same, but can you smell a portal trail?"

He frowned. "Sort of."

"Then follow that. Use all that adrenaline and fear about us getting stuck and take us to Katherine!" The others had arrived behind me, and all of us were staring down at Jacob. Right now, he was our only hope. I knew it was a lot to put on his young shoulders, but we had no other option, not if we wanted to stop Katherine now.

"I... I'll do my best." His voice shook as he spoke. Slowly, he lifted his hands and closed his eyes and let the Chaos inside him wrap around his fingertips. The bronze light pulsed beneath his skin as he surged the energy outward, tearing a hole in the fabric of reality. The guests screamed as a savage gust of dusty wind blew across the tables, their panicked cries rising to a crescendo. They hurried for any available exit, knocking over glasses and overturning chairs in their rush to get out. This portal was definitely different. The edges swirled and snapped like wild whips, violent and unsettled, while a distant, deep rumble could be heard from within the portal's dark mouth, unlike anything we'd ever witnessed before.

We won't get stuck, we won't get stuck...

I didn't wait for the others as I turned on my heel and sprinted through the portal, praying that Jacob had managed to send us to the right place. I knew they would follow, but I needed to show Jacob that I believed in him by being the first one through. He'd done it before with Nyx's otherworld, and he could do it again.

I stumbled through to the other side and gasped in surprise, almost losing my balance. The world opening up before me was incredible...

FORTY-TWO

Harley

I'd expected to end up in the same waterfall realm that I'd gone to when Gaia had called me to her, but this was something else entirely. Sunlight shone down from a clear, azure sky, glowing from two small twin suns. A jeweled rainforest surrounded us on all sides, with multicolored birds and strange monkey-like beasts with blue-and-purple fur traveling from tree to tree. Vines, interwoven with huge scarlet flowers, hung down from the branches like Spanish moss.

To my right, a wide stream trickled through the verdant landscape, the babbling sound soothing to my ears. Koi fish darted beneath the surface. This place was beautiful, and green, and bursting with shimmering life—the kind of place that shouldn't be touched by evil of any kind. But Katherine was here, somewhere. The exodus of flapping birds told me she'd already made her presence known.

"This way!" I shouted to the others as they tumbled through the portal after me. I followed the sound of frightened animals and charged through the dense undergrowth, careful to avoid the glittering snakes that slithered beneath.

I skidded to a halt as a clearing appeared in the rainforest. It looked like the ruins of an ancient civilization, though nature had long since reclaimed the towers and spires that had once been here. A few emboldened monkeys, with that same startling fur, lingered on the crumbling walls, their eyes turned to the sight below. An open altar stood in the wreckage of the ancient temple, or whatever it had once been, and Katherine stood in front of it.

The president lay on the moss-covered surface of the altar, strapped down with golden ropes.

Déjà vu much? This time, I wasn't afraid of what might happen. This time, I was confident I had the power to help. Thanks to the Suppressor break, I was on more equal footing with Katherine here. The only trouble was, she wasn't alone. Naima and her band of cloaked cultists stood on the perimeter, ready to fight anyone who might try and stop the ritual. *Well, it's your lucky day.*

With the others at my back, I sprinted forward with a gigantic ball of fire between my palms. Only, it didn't quite feel like the usual fire. There was something almost alive about it as it struggled to break free of my grip. The first wave of cultists headed toward me, and I let loose. My fireball bounded between the cultists, slamming into them with a powerful force that sent them flying backward. And it didn't stop there. I realized I was partially controlling where it went and whom it hurt.

Trying to wield it with my mind, I sent it careening toward the next wave of cultists, where it exploded with one enormous blast that disintegrated three of the cloaked figures. Their bodies drifted away on a breeze of bronzed particles, leaving nothing but three limp cloaks on the ground.

You need to be more careful. All of this is new. If that weird bomb somehow turned on one of my people, I didn't know if I'd be able to stop it from doing something terrible. My friends were already staring at me as if I'd grown two heads, and even the cultists seemed scared. However, it had opened a path between us and the altar.

"Wade, I'll cover you," I shouted back to him. He was dealing with a cultist of his own, but he quickly dispatched her with his Fire and headed for the altar. Meanwhile, the rest of the Rag Team spread out in a circle, taking one cultist each. Elements roared and rumbled all around.

"Eat this!" Santana cried as she shoved an Orisha down the throat of a burly man.

"Oh, you have no idea how long I have waited for this." Raffe's eyes flashed red, his skin already crimson and smoking, as he lunged for a young man with bright green hair. The djinn was hungry and wasn't about to stop now that he had carte blanche to do what he liked.

Dylan grinned as he tackled another guy to the ground, pounding on him with his Herculean fists. Meanwhile, Tatyana had just slammed a woman into a nearby tree with a lasso of powerful Telekinesis. Garrett had a different woman in a headlock, the two of them brawling on the ground.

"Did you just bite me?" Garrett snarled, driving his elbow down into the woman's shoulder.

"You thought we were playing nice?" the woman shot back.

The only one who was standing back from the fight was Jacob, who'd ducked out of the way behind a berry bush. Astrid hadn't come through the portal at all, which I figured was a good thing, after what had happened last time she came to an otherworld. I didn't want that happening again.

Building another ball of temperamental energy in my hands, I lashed it toward Katherine, using a blend of Telekinesis and Fire. I sensed there was something else in the mix, too, something that made it crackle and spark in a worrying way, but I couldn't think too much about that now. I was barely able to keep hold of it, let alone control all the elements inside it. I essentially had an atomic bomb in my grasp and no idea how to properly use it.

"Hey!" I yelled across the clearing. "I'm going to give you a choice, Katherine. Stop what you're doing, or I unleash this on you!"

Katherine barely glanced up as the ball hurtled toward her. She stood inside a forcefield once again and was evidently too confident in the forcefield's ability to protect her. But I had a feeling it wouldn't matter this time.

The moment my energy ball connected with the forcefield, the whole thing blew to smithereens. Bits of stone and moss flew everywhere. Golden smoke billowed away from the center of the blast, shrouding everything in a thick cloud. I tried to peer through, to see if I'd managed to maim Katherine, but the smoke obscured my view.

As the dust settled, I noticed Katherine slumped against the back wall of the ruins, a trickle of blood sliding down the side of her face. *So you do bleed?*

Unfortunately, the blast had also knocked Wade down, but the president seemed unharmed. A second later, Wade jumped up and sprinted for the altar, his fingers working away at the golden ropes around the president's body.

"Mr. President, are you okay? Mr. President?" Wade shook him, but he was out cold. He worked faster at the ropes, until he'd managed to break the president free. He'd just looped the man's arm around his neck when Naima suddenly appeared out of nowhere.

"This time, I will finish the job and snap your neck like a twig," she growled at Wade.

I surged toward them, but Katherine drew my eye again. This might be the only chance we had to capture her while she was out cold. I couldn't risk missing an opportunity like this, even though Wade was in danger. Naima was already advancing on him, and he tried to stagger back with the president's weight leaning against him. Wade was tough—he had the strength to overcome someone like Naima. *Fight with everything you have, Wade.*

I darted around the side of the altar and reached out for the unconscious Katherine. As soon as my hand touched her arm, her eyes snapped open, a cruel smirk on her face. She grasped my wrist and yanked me against the wall, driving me headfirst into the hard stone. I shot out a cushion of air to lessen the impact, but it was too wild and too strong, sending me bouncing backward with a nasty case of whiplash. Still, at least I hadn't been brained against the ruins.

"It looks like someone's not quite out of their training pants," Katherine jeered. "A little too much for you, is it? Come here and let me relieve you of some of that power. I'd be more than happy to."

I stepped back. "I'm sure you would."

Before I could even move, she sent a twist of Telekinesis toward me. It snaked around my throat and pulled tight. I scrambled to get a defense up in time, but I didn't have the dexterity to handle someone like Katherine. It didn't take a genius to realize that she'd become far more powerful than I'd anticipated. She'd barely flicked a finger, and the Telekinesis had done her bidding. Feeling the pulse of my energy deep beneath my skin, I forced it upward to try and break apart the grip of the Telekinesis around my throat. She was strong... incredibly strong.

Powering my Chaos harder and harder into the stream of Telekinesis, I already knew I was using too much energy on breaking this. I didn't have the time or knowledge to carefully pick it apart—I had to use brute force instead. The Telekinesis solidified around my neck into a glass-like collar and shattered into a million pieces. A rush of light-headedness overwhelmed me as I fought to stay on my feet. I wasn't going to crumble in front of her, no matter how much that had taken out of me.

"Oh dear, have things not worked out the way you expected them to?" She smiled at me. "Disappointing when that happens, isn't it? It's all about preparation, Harley. You've got to make sure your ass is covered from every angle; otherwise, you'll end up mooning someone. A sticky metaphor, maybe, but I like the visual." She hammered a barrage of fireballs at me without moving a muscle. The sparking orbs just appeared in the air in front of her before hurtling toward me. I managed to dodge most of them, but one seared past my shoulder with a hiss of smoking flesh and fabric.

"How can you be here?" I gasped, catching my breath. Maybe I was the one who'd been too confident. I knew the first ritual must have given Katherine power, but this was freaking excessive—she was more like a god than a woman right now.

"Always underestimating me, huh? Honestly, Harley, what lengths must I go to, to get you to see that I'm more powerful than you think? Shall I... kill the president? Would that do it? I mean, I'm already going to do that, but two birds, one stone. It's kind of insulting, really, that you keep doubting me." She chuckled as she shot another barrage of fire my way. This time, I was ready, building a rapid blockade of water from the nearby stream.

"Nice try!" I panted.

"Hey, I always said I could be a good teacher to you, but you kept saying, 'No, I don't want to join sides with you. I'm going to stay at the SDC where it's all safe and proper.' How's that been working out for you? Nomura and Alton giving you some good lessons?" She sighed. "Men are so easy to manipulate. Honestly, they're like origami."

I scowled at her. "What?"

"They fold under pressure."

"You didn't answer my question!" I shot back. "How can you be here? You went through a portal, but you don't have anyone to open them for you anymore. Did you steal from Isadora? I bet you've got a bunch of Ephemera lined up, right?"

She sighed. "Contrary to popular belief, I'm not much of a thief. Hah, that rhymed. In this case, there was no theft necessary. I earned the right to interdimensional travel when I performed the first ritual. Not for the faint-hearted. I suppose it's lucky I've got the heart of a bull."

With every sentence she spoke, another attack came. It was impossible to gauge her next move when she didn't even have to move a muscle to get her Chaos to do what she wanted. I managed to hold off an attack of Earth, with vines slithering toward my legs and trying to trip me up, but her attacks were coming too quickly for me to think clearly.

"You can just travel however and wherever you want to now?" I flung a tornado of water away into the rainforest, the swirling pillar exploding as it hit the trees, soaking Tatyana and Dylan, who were fighting nearby. Fortunately, it soaked the two cultists they were battling, too, giving my people a moment's distraction to take them down.

"Handy, isn't it?" she replied. "It's a load off my mind, not having to worry about where my next Portal Opener is going to come from. You'd think Chaos would have made more, but I guess it's like small-batch gin—you only make a few of the best. Actually, you've got me thinking. If I don't need a Portal Opener anymore, why don't I just kill Isadora and Jacob now? Your aunt won't be too hard to find, and it's nice of you to have brought Jacob with you. Saves me the trouble of sniffing him out."

"You won't touch either of them!" I squared up to her, using my newfound power to build a wall of shimmering air between us.

She nodded slowly. "No, I really think I will kill them, right after I kill you." For the first time, Katherine actually raised her hand to send out her abilities. A steady stream of molten fire poured out of her palms and struck the barrier of air, making it disintegrate in a puff of smoke. I hurried to get my defenses up, but a vine tugged at my leg without warning and yanked me to the ground in one jarring movement. Katherine appeared above me, her palms raised.

"I thought you had plans for me, alive." I strained to speak as the vines crisscrossed over me, squeezing like pythons.

"Oh, Harley, I wanted it to be you. I really did. All the family, back together again." Bronzed tendrils wrapped around her fingertips, and I could see the power building in the center of her palms. "But you keep causing too much trouble, so I'll have to find someone else to fill your shoes. A shame, yes, but that's on you. And with all that power unleashed in you—what a pity."

I let fire stream out of my hands and singe the vines, prompting them to let me go. "It's not ending like this," I spat as I struggled free. "You don't get to win this time."

"Why won't you just STAY DOWN!" she snapped suddenly, pressing her foot down hard on my chest. Her grin turned cold on her lips. "Why do you refuse to learn? You've got so much of your mother in you. Too much, if you ask me." Her voice echoed across the clearing, drawing the surprised glances of her followers. Watching her, I could see it was taking every ounce of strength she had to calm down again.

"I'd rather be like her than like you. Heck, I'd rather be like freaking Echidna than like you!" I grabbed at her ankle, but my hands jolted away. Chaos drifted across her skin in a thin layer, giving me an electric shock if I tried to touch her. *Sneaky.*

An amused smile turned up her lips. "That could be arranged. I've been trying out this new splicing spell, and I'd love to see the outcome on a human test subject. I was going to say 'human guinea pig,' but then you might've been confused. What do you say—you and a lizard, or you and a scorpion, or you and a hobgoblin? I'd like to see that. I could do with a laugh."

A movement beside the ruins distracted my attention away from Katherine's ramblings. Naima had Wade pinned up against the wall, her fangs headed straight for his jugular. This time, there was no Marie Laveau to save him. One slice, and he'd be done for. I opened my mouth to beg for his life, but no sound came out. Instead, a rush of white light exploded out of me, knocking Katherine back and freeing my chest from her foot. I scrabbled against the ground to get to my feet, but the blast had only done so much to keep Katherine away. She regained her footing and pounced on me, slamming my back into the dirt.

"I said STAY DOWN!" she roared. "I guess I need to *put* you down, huh?" She squeezed my throat, her hands pulsating with bronze light. Her tendrils of Chaos poured through my skin and into my throat, filling it up like water, until I couldn't drag in a single breath. I panicked and thrashed against her, but she just knelt harder on my chest and stared down at me with calm, dead eyes.

This is it... I was going to die here in Gaia's otherworld. Katherine was going to kill me.

"Take me, Katherine. Spare her. Take me and be done with it." The president's voice boomed across the clearing as he rose from the ground where he'd fallen. He'd somehow broken free of the last few ropes and stood proud, facing her.

Naima had Wade pinned, but his hand was reaching for something in his pocket. A second later, he threw a bright red dust into her face before whispering something I couldn't quite hear. It sounded Latin, and I knew what that meant. She fell backward, crashing into the ground with an almighty crack that split the earth. Whatever curse he'd used, it sounded like it had broken or dislocated some joints, too.

Wade smiled. "I've upped my game since last time."

Naima snarled at him. "I will see you strangled with your own entrails, Crowley!"

The president stepped toward Katherine. "I know about the ritual. I know what you need." He held out his hand. "Please, Katherine—take my life in exchange for Harley's."

"How about I kill you both? Buy one get one free?" she shot back. "Then nobody needs to feel left out."

"You have to hurry, Katherine. If you waste time on killing Harley, you may not have the chance to kill me. These Children of Chaos don't like people lingering in their otherworlds."

She snorted. "What would you know about it?"

"I know you'll find yourself kicked out if you wait too long."

"How do you know that?"

He smiled at her. "You always did underestimate me, Katherine."

"If I let Harley live, she'll just keep on meddling. She can't help it. It's in her blood." An amused glint flashed across her eyes.

The president took a swift step back and snatched something from his waistband—a sharp, golden knife that he must have taken from the altar when Wade freed him. "Then I'll kill myself. You won't have the satisfaction of killing me, and you'll have to find another Father of Magicals. But, more than that, your failure to kill me will reverberate across the magical world, and you won't be able to outrun the ripples."

FORTY-THREE

Harley

Katherine stepped off me and left me on the ground. Before I could catch my breath, she swiped her hand and sent me flying into the trees on a wave of Telekinesis. The moment I landed, I jumped back up and ran to the perimeter of the clearing. I had probably bruised a rib or two, but right now, panic overwhelmed any pain I might've felt.

Katherine approached the president. He wasn't moving, he wasn't shaking, he wasn't doing anything. He was just looking right at her, totally unafraid of what might happen next.

The sight of him standing there, all noble and stoic, was confusing and eerie and awful. Was he really going to do this? I supposed, if he wanted to stop Katherine from performing the second ritual, his death was the fastest way to go about it, but I didn't dare think about it for too long. There had to be something else going on here.

Near to where the president stood, Wade shuffled through the grass to get to Naima. He didn't have a Mason jar handy to capture her with, but at least she was temporarily trapped.

Katherine stalked toward President Price like he was the sick wildebeest in the herd, but he didn't flinch. Surely, he had something else in mind. He had to be thinking up a plan that he was going to surprise us all with in a couple of seconds.

"You really want to aggravate me like that?" Katherine asked. "You think I'm not making ripples of my own, Steve?"

He held her gaze. "I know you are, but I also know you can't continue in your pursuit of power without me. You might find another Father of Magicals, but how long is that going to take you? Can you really afford that kind of delay?"

I stared at him. What was he playing at? It was making less and less sense with every second that passed. Either he was going to kill himself to stop Katherine achieving what she wanted, or he was going to hand himself over to her, which would ensure she succeeded. I couldn't understand it. Instead, all I could do was watch as it unfolded.

"I'm a patient woman. If I have to wait, I will. It'll just annoy me and make me more inclined to indulge in some random killings. Is that a price *you* are willing to pay?" Katherine folded her arms across her chest. "You might be dead, but what about all those other poor souls who wind up dead because of what you decided to do today? Your choice, old friend."

"Then, I choose—" A blinding light interrupted the president as a portal tore open in the space behind him. Jacob tumbled out and grabbed the president around the waist, dragging him away from Katherine's reach. Even with the draw of the portal, Jacob struggled against the president's height and strength, the older man unwilling to follow.

Oh, Jacob. He was playing a dangerous game here, and it wasn't what we'd agreed on, but I couldn't help feeling grateful toward his actions this time. Thanks to Jacob, the president was going to live. Yes, it made me think back to our last visit to an otherworld, where he'd done this same thing and given up Quetzi's life in favor of Isadora's. But this time I wanted him to do it, for all of our sakes. I wanted the president to survive, and I knew Jacob was doing everything he could to make amends for his previous mistake. Only, the president wasn't budging.

He pushed Jacob back toward the portal. "Don't intervene, not unless you want to get yourself or your friends killed."

"But we can all—" Jacob began.

The president shook his head. "This ends now, with Katherine and me. I don't need saving, though I thank you for your courage."

Even when confronted with his own impending death, the president still managed to be benevolent. I was in awe of him, although I didn't completely understand why he was doing this. There had to be another way. If Katherine killed the president, *that* would leave ripples through the nation.

Jacob looked confused and conflicted, but he fell back into the portal, alone. I pushed through the undergrowth and staggered out into the clearing, drawing the attention of everyone inside it. The cultists had stopped fighting, and so had the rest of the Rag Team. All eyes darted between me and the president, no doubt wondering what I was going to do next. The truth was, I couldn't just stand here and let him take his own life, or let Katherine take it from him, either. And yet, my mind couldn't picture a way out of this without the president dying. His death was imminent and destined, and that shook me to my very core.

"You can't." A fierce sob heaved at my chest. "You can't give her what she wants. If you kill yourself, she'll keep going. We need to fight her. We need to stop her."

Katherine smiled. "My niece is very right."

As I took another few steps, I felt something shift inside me. It felt similar to what had happened back in the ballroom, when we'd first arrived and we'd hit those hexes. My desperation to get free had caused the balance inside me to change for a moment, unleashing a whole barrage of raw energy from the side I'd suddenly leaned toward. Teetering on the brink of grief and desperation now, it happened again. My body glowed bronze, and then white, as every single cell in my body vibrated. The energy felt unstable, like I was about to disintegrate and flicker away on the breeze.

"Harley, focus on my voice," the president said calmly. "I'm doing this for you, so that you have that chance in the future—that chance to stop her. Katherine will always find a way to complete the rituals. She was always going to. From the moment she performed the first one, and even before then, I knew this was it—that her life would only end with her challenging a Child of Chaos. The only thing I can do for you now is to give you a fighting chance."

I shook my head. "We can fight her now!"

"She's too strong, Harley. You need time to find a weakness." His gaze held mine and brought my vibrating cells back under control. "Go now, and plan for the future. Let me do my duty to Chaos and to magicals so that you may do yours."

"No! She's not having you!" I leapt toward them, but Raffe cut me off, darting out of the shadows and knocking me to the side. His eyes flashed a red warning, and his scarlet arms gripped me.

"He's right, Merlin," the djinn hissed in his savage snarl. "He has to do this. We can't fight her here—not if we want to win. And if we're all dead, then what? You think she'll stop and have a change of heart?"

I glowered at him. "No, but I—"

"But nothing. He gets it, he understands what's at stake, so listen to him." He cast a glance into the trees. "Because we've got to go."

"What? I'm not leaving." I struggled against him, but he was too strong in his djinn form. Glancing around, I saw the entire Rag Team running toward us, with Wade following close behind. *What's going on? Why was everyone making a run for it?*

The djinn smirked. "I'd be more than happy to let Katherine roast you until the tender meat just dropped off the bone, but things can't always go my way. This isn't where you go out with a bang, kiddo."

"Let me go, you asshole!"

"Normally, I like 'em lively, but you need to stop thrashing and be a good girl for Papa Kadar. This is all for the best. You'll see." I could feel the searing heat of his skin as he grasped me even tighter, sandwiching my arms down by my sides.

The djinn knew that I couldn't unleash my newfound abilities without hurting Raffe, too. The bastard was using my friend to his advantage, and for what? Why was he so invested in stopping me from getting to the president and letting Katherine have her wicked way with him? With the djinn, it was impossible to tell which way his loyalties lay. He had ties to Erebus, I knew that, which didn't exactly fill me with confidence.

"Raffe! Tell him to let go of me!" I wriggled to try and break free of his grasp, but he didn't move.

The djinn chuckled. "Raffe isn't here right now; would you like to leave a message?"

A gust of wind barreled toward us, throwing dirt and debris into my eyes. Peering over the djinn's shoulder, I gasped as a portal appeared close by, with Jacob leaping out. Raffe forcibly dragged me over to the spot, while the others went on ahead. Wade looked back at me with an apologetic glance, but he wasn't on my side, either. I wanted to stay, I wanted to help the president, and we were all just abandoning him to Queen Nutjob and her courtiers!

"WE HAVE TO SAVE HIM!" I screamed as Raffe brought me closer to the edge of the portal. I had a front row seat to the sight of Katherine taking the knife from the president's hand as she began to chant her ritual spells. I supposed the poor Librarian had been forced to give her all the details, not just the headlines. The president didn't put up a fight at all—he just let her take the knife, even though he knew it spelled his own demise.

"NO!" I howled, trying to headbutt Raffe's shoulder in a last-ditch attempt to break free. Why was everyone just leaving him here? Why wasn't anyone doing anything? Why were we all just giving up, when Katherine was right there? I didn't understand, and I didn't want to.

"Sorry, kiddo," the djinn replied. He carried me into the portal.

The president turned to look at me as I was pulled away, a small smile on his face. He didn't look at Katherine, only me. With tears streaming down my face, I wanted to reach out to him. His smile widened ever so slightly.

No, no, no, no, no...

He kept his eyes fixed on me, showing no fear at all, until the moment Katherine plunged the blade deep into his chest. Then, his features flickered, as if he understood what this truly meant. It meant oblivion and uncertainty. It was the selfish moment before the bitter end, the moment of "I don't want to go," and I felt it so keenly that I wanted to scream at the top of my lungs.

The portal snapped shut behind us and the image evaporated, but I'd never forget the look on his face for as long as I lived.

I turned sharply as something tore through the portal tunnel behind us. Before I could even shout a warning, reality warped.

FORTY-FOUR

Wade

W e thundered back into the Washington ballroom to the sound
of screams. It looked like no time had passed at all since we'd
gone through the portal and come back again. Floods of people were
hurrying for the door, squashing and crushing one another in their
desperation to escape. Everyone was sobbing—men, women, everyone.
Those who weren't running away stood around in hollow disbelief.
They kept staring at the stage. They were terrified that their president
had been kidnapped by a crazy woman in a Security Services uniform.
And they'd been there to witness it. When the news of his assassination
came out, it would hit them all the harder.

Levi hurried down the steps. "Is he with you...?"

Hot tears stung my eyes. I couldn't even speak. I just shook my head
slowly. Now they would know; Levi would pass on the message. The
president didn't make it. The president was dead.

This would be a huge blow to the magical community. We were
talking irreparable damage. The ripples that Katherine and the president had spoken about were already in motion. This would spark

nationwide panic, when the news filtered out. It would, soon enough. People already had their phones out, typing frantically on the screens.

Meanwhile, with blurry eyes, I looked around for Harley. I'd watched Raffe pull her into the portal behind me. But... she wasn't here. The portal had closed, and she wasn't here! I ran to Jacob, who looked a bit woozy.

"Jacob, did you close the portal too early? Jacob?" I shook him firmly.

He frowned. "I felt something weird come through behind us."

"Jacob, did you close the portal too early?! Harley isn't here!" My voice cracked as I stared into Jacob's eyes. He looked startled and afraid, but I couldn't stop until I knew where she was.

"I don't think so." Jacob trembled in my grasp. "I... I don't know. I really don't think so. All I know is... there was a weird rush following us."

"A weird rush? That's all you can give me?" I knew it wasn't his fault, but I was on the edge of a nervous breakdown. Where the heck was she? If she'd somehow gotten stuck in the portal tunnel, then that was it... I'd just lost her, too.

My heart pounded in my chest and a cold sweat crept across my skin. My mind raced a mile a minute. I punched the nearby wall and let the pain jolt through me. *I can't have lost her... not her, not now.* I punched the wall again. I needed the pain to help my head focus. Otherwise, I was tumbling into a pit of despair from which there was no return. If Harley was gone, then I didn't want to be here anymore.

What if Katherine held her back?

FORTY-FIVE

Harley

I hit the deck with a thud that echoed through my ribcage and jarred my teeth together. Slowly, I blinked my eyes open to find daylight streaming down. It took a minute or two for me to realize that I was still in Gaia's otherworld, but I wasn't in the rainforest or the ruins anymore. Instead, I was back by the waterfall where I'd first met her, lying on the slick rocks and staring up at the birds that flew across the tumbling water.

I sat up just as Gaia emerged from the parting water. She'd mirrored my image once again, her red hair long and loose, wearing the same elegant gown of interwoven flowers and leaves from last time. She edged along the rocky path toward me, looking so sad it broke my heart.

"I am sorry for what you have had to endure." She spoke first, then offered a hand to help me up. I took it gratefully and dragged myself to my feet. Tears stained my cheeks, though they'd dried somewhere between being zapped out of the tunnel and landing here.

"I need to get back to my friends. They'll be worried sick if they get to Washington and find I'm not there," I replied, feeling a nervous tension gather in my stomach. I needed to be there when they told everyone about the president. I needed to be there so I could ask them why the hell they hadn't stepped in to try and save him. That had been our moment, and we'd wasted it out of fear.

Gaia smiled. "Time flows differently here, remember?"

I covered my face, overtaken by a sudden, painful urge to cry again. So much had happened, and it was all rattling around in my head like loose strings, with me unable to make sense of any of it. Katherine had found her sacrificial lamb all right, and now the magical world was going to be in turmoil. She would be the nation's most wanted for the murder of Steven Price, but what made matters worse was people would still freaking follow her. The president had been right about her; she was charismatic and charming and could bend just about anyone to her will.

"You are alight, dear Harley," Gaia said softly. I glanced down and found that the white light had returned to my skin, pulsing underneath with the thrum of every vibrating cell. The more I cried, the brighter the light became. The more desperate and hopeless I felt, the more it glowed.

"I can't help it," I murmured, wiping my nose on the back of my sleeve.

"Let us see if we can remedy that." Gaia touched my cheek, brushing away my tears with her fingertip. I froze at her strange touch—I couldn't feel the pressure of her skin at all. It was almost like being touched by a ghost, not that I knew what that felt like. Somehow, her touch made the glow fade and tilted the shifted balance inside me back to a centered position.

I blinked up at her. "Did you fix me?"

"I encouraged the balance between Light and Dark into a steadier equilibrium," she replied. "But you are by no means fixed, dear child. You are still in the woods."

"What's happening to me, Gaia?" I choked out, feeling vulnerable in her presence. "Is this glowy stuff happening because Echidna snapped the Suppressor? Is this her idea of a joke?"

Gaia shook her head. "It would seem the Sanguine spell you performed was not strong enough for all of that Chaos inside you. After all, such levels of raw energy are more or less unheard of, even with previous sufferers of the Dempsey Suppressor. You are unique, and, as such, the more generic spell was unable to contend with the release of two almighty forces rushing forward with such violence at once." She tapped her chin. "A useful human metaphor might be 'closing the stable door after the horse has bolted,' especially as you were unable to use Euphoria to mediate the release."

"So this is Echidna's fault? Partially, at least?"

"By breaking the Suppressor so instantaneously, I would say that she is responsible for some of these side effects, yes. Your body had no time to prepare, and it is still attempting to figure out how it is supposed to fix itself. Meanwhile, the Light and Dark within you continue to battle for prevalence."

I shook my head, feeling like an utter failure. "Great."

"You are making more progress than you know, Harley, and you must continue to fight. I know it seems like a relentless road of obstacles, but you will endure, and you will triumph if you keep your will strong and your heart fierce." She paused. "You must stop Katherine before she can complete the next ritual, for you will be stronger then. You will know what to do the next time you meet. But if you cannot beat her before she succeeds in the rituals, then you must prepare yourself for a further step. The last chance you will have to win."

I glanced at her in sudden dread. "What do you mean?"

"If you cannot prevent Katherine from succeeding in the rituals, then you must prepare yourself to defeat her in her final form, when she has become a Child of Chaos."

My jaw dropped. "What are you talking about?" How the hell was I supposed to do that? I'd been preparing to fight Katherine and stop her *before* she became a Child of Chaos, not after.

"If you cannot stop her before she changes, then you must change in your own way and defeat her before she can unleash her final form upon the world."

"And how am I supposed to do that?" The words tumbled out.

Gaia sighed. "I cannot say."

"Let me guess, Chaos rules?"

"Precisely." She smiled. "I can say one thing, however. You were rushed in this fight today. That is why you did not succeed in stopping her. It takes more than brute force and blind luck to defeat someone like Katherine, and you had not been given the time to prepare properly."

Against Katherine, it didn't seem like any amount of preparation would've helped us, but I let Gaia continue.

"Your Suppressor has only just broken. You cannot be too hard on yourself. You need more time to figure out the new differences in your abilities before you can fully use them to your advantage. You have greater potential within you, but it requires your strength of will and character to coax it out."

"You think I'll do better next time?" I didn't feel too hopeful. We'd just lost the president of the UCA because I couldn't get my crap together and take her down. It had all been pinned on my newfound strength, and I'd totally screwed it up. Then again, the security personnel wouldn't have fared much better if they'd been utilized against her. Right now, there'd be a lot more dead people, if Levi's squad had gone after her instead of us. *Small mercies, right?*

"You know the rituals now, don't you?" Gaia asked.

I nodded.

"Then you may plan ahead. A day is not long enough to organize a mission against Katherine. When you meet her again, you will have had more time to think and prepare, and you will not falter."

"Can you see that in your crystal ball, or whatever it is you Children have?"

She chuckled. "I cannot. It is merely a feeling that I have about you. I pray that I am right."

"Yeah, so do I."

"Goodbye, Harley. I wish you the best of luck." Gaia gave me one last brilliant smile as the waterfall world warped away from me. My body twisted through darkness, and cold air rushed around me. Gaia faded into the distance, and I became aware of nothing but falling.

I had a lot to think about as I fell, but my mind kept drifting back to that sad final image of President Price, with the hilt of a knife sticking out of his chest. He'd realized the true extent of his sacrifice in that moment, and I didn't think I'd ever get over the frightened, boyish look on his face. In the space of a second, he'd regressed to a child, terrified that the world was going to end. And his did.

I winced as I landed hard on my knees, on the floor of the Washington ballroom. My body had taken a battering already, and I could still feel the heavy bruise where Katherine's foot had stomped into my chest. *I'm going to kill you, one of these days.* I made the promise with the memory of the president still fresh in my head.

"Harley?" Wade sprinted over to me and helped me to my feet. He gripped my shoulders so tight that his fingernails started to bite into my skin, his eyes wide with panic. "Are you okay? What happened to you? I was just about losing my mind over here!"

Raffe nodded. "He really was."

Jacob edged forward, his body trembling. "I don't know what happened, Harley. I really don't. If it was something I did to the portal, I'm so sorry."

I squeezed his arm. "It wasn't you, Jacob."

"It wasn't?" He instantly relaxed.

"No, it was Gaia." I looked toward the far side of the room, where a group of cultists had been corralled into the corner by Santana,

Tatyana, Garrett, Dylan, Astrid, and what remained of the president's Secret Service team. The only cultist that was on our list that we hadn't seen was Nomura's son, Shinsuke. He hadn't been at the ruins, and he wasn't here at the Washington Coven. All throughout Astrid's facial recognition scans, he hadn't shown up once. Katherine clearly knew his value and was keeping him out of our reach in case we tried to use him to turn the tables on her.

She's going to be so freaking cocky after today. As if her ego wasn't inflated enough.

"You've been busy." I nodded to the group of cultists.

Wade nodded, refusing to release me. "Yeah, they got caught in the rush to get out, and we've been rounding up as many as we can. They're headed straight to Purgatory. Those gold tattoos on their chests are enough to show their guilt." He tilted my chin up. "I thought I'd lost you, Harley. When I turned around and you weren't there…"

"I'm here now," I replied. "What have I told you, Crowley? You're never getting rid of me."

I held his gaze and lifted my palms to his chest, pressing gently on his heart. I didn't know how much time had passed here since I'd been in Gaia's world, but it seemed to be a lot longer than she'd promised. The sadness and fear in his eyes broke my heart. Even the relief washing over him was overwhelming as it hit me in a sudden, intense rush.

A small smile crept onto his lips. "It's good to have you back in one piece, Merlin. I like you in one piece."

I love you too, Wade. All I could do was nod.

Levi strode toward us, with the rest of the Rag Team crossing the room to join us. "Ah, Ms. Merlin, I see you've decided to join the party. Would you care to tell us where you've been, exactly? It's not every day that young ladies just drop out of the skies like that. And, since your young Portal Opener is here, I'm certain you didn't use him to return."

Jacob pulled an apologetic face. "He knows."

"It didn't take a rocket scientist to put the pieces together, not when I saw you tear a hole in the air!" Levi retorted. "Now, Harley, explain yourself."

I shook my head. "I've got a question first." I looked at the rest of my team. "Why did you all just leave him there? He needed our help, and you all ran instead of backing me to save him."

"She was too strong for us, Harley," Dylan replied. "If we'd stayed, she would have killed all of us."

Santana nodded. "We didn't want to leave him any more than you did, but this way we have a chance to stop her before she gets to ritual three. It was hopeless. He wouldn't have come with us, and if we'd managed to get him out of there, do you really think Katherine would have stopped?"

"She would have gone after him until she got what she wanted," Tatyana added. "She evaded all this security. It would only be a matter of time before she finally got her hands on him and dragged him right back to that otherworld and that altar."

I sighed. "I hadn't thought of it like that." Seeing it from their perspective, they had a valid point. As long as the president had remained alive, he would have continued to be Katherine's target. She would have hounded him to the ends of the Earth until she got him, and with us like this, there was no way we could have prevented it.

Levi sucked in a sharp breath. "When you're quite done wallowing in self-pity, would you mind giving me an explanation?"

We've all had a long day, pal. Get to the back of the line. Still, I knew he'd get off my case quicker if I just responded.

"Gaia sucked me out of the portal somehow, and I woke up in another part of her world. It's a part I've been to before."

Levi looked flabbergasted. I'd guessed it was pretty unusual for a Child of Chaos to pull a mortal into their realm.

Ignoring Levi, I soldiered on. "She told me that, now we know the rituals, we'll have more time to plan our next move instead of rushing at it all guns blazing." I peered at everyone. "But she said if that isn't possible, I'll have to prepare myself to fight her when she becomes a Child of Chaos. She couldn't tell me how or when or why—Chaos rules and all that jazz—but that might become a possibility."

"It'll never get that far," Santana said, though a note of astonishment lingered in her voice.

Tatyana nodded. "She's likely preparing you for a worst-case scenario, but we have plenty of time to intercept Katherine before then."

"Like you said, now that we know what the rituals are, we'll have a lot more time to make the proper preparations," Astrid added. She flashed a smile, which felt all the more comforting coming from her.

To my surprise, Levi unleashed a deep, exhausted sigh that seemed to shake him to the core. "I imagine you all are correct. Gaia is likely making everything seem worse than it is so you will do your best to avoid that possibility. Katherine will be apprehended long before then." A sad glint flashed in his eyes. "Now, thanks to the tragic events of this evening, I have an incredible mess to clean up. You should all return to the SDC this minute and leave me to deal with the fallout of this. I don't even know where I'll begin."

His pain and anguish drifted off him in tired waves, his vulnerability exposed for just a moment. He had wanted the president to survive, too, but he evidently agreed with our verdict: we couldn't have saved him tonight, no matter what we'd done. Judging by his emotions, he felt partially responsible for the mission's failure and the shockwave it would send through the nation.

You're not so different, after all, are you? It was a strange realization. As I glanced at Levi's pale face, I understood that he was just a man trying to do the right thing for the safety of others, in his own mind. He might have flawed ideas at times, but didn't we all?

"I would be only too happy to help with the cleanup, Director Levi," a voice echoed from behind us. We turned to find Alton standing there, though I had no idea where he'd appeared from. He'd picked up an unusual habit of loitering furtively in doorways recently. "Apologies for my lateness. I seem to have missed everything, though the stream of panicked guests led me here. Is it true about the president?"

"Unfortunately, yes." Levi huffed out an unsteady breath. "I will get you up to speed on the rest while we make reparations here."

"There is a great deal to do and not a lot of time to do it, I gather," Alton said.

"I fear the news tomorrow, Alton," Levi murmured. "This will destroy our nation's hope. The last thing I want for the president's memory is a thousand grainy videos of his capture at the hands of Katherine. That kind of image will only be used for further propaganda, to spur on her cause and highlight her power. And it is not becoming of a man as great and noble as President Price."

Alton gave a small, sad smile. "I can help with that, too. An EM pulse within a five-mile radius should prevent any images being released before we can speak with the magical news channels. We will make sure his legacy is honored in the proper way."

"Then we must get started right away." Levi hurried away toward the far exit, with Alton following close behind. Weirdly, it looked like some kind of peace had been reached between the two men, at least temporarily. *Well, that's one half-decent thing to come out of this nightmare.*

After all, Katherine had likely completed the second ritual by now, which meant she would be even more powerful and even deadlier than she had ever been before. We had three more to stop, or else we'd be faced with a new and extremely vindictive, not to mention psychopathic, Child of Chaos...

FORTY-SIX

Wade

A few days had passed since the tragic events in Washington, and the entire nation was in mourning. I couldn't bear to look at another magical newspaper or TV headline on the magical-only networks. I wasn't burying my head in the sand. It was just too sad. Steven Price had been a hero amongst men. He'd been well loved, not only for his politics, but for the kind of man he was. Noble, intelligent, kind, and humorous; he was going to be sorely missed.

Not only that, but the Rag Team had turned notorious overnight. And Harley had become infamous. The president had likely hoped that, by martyring himself, the country would rally together toward a mutual goal: defeating Katherine. Sadly, it had had the opposite effect. The magical world feared Katherine Shipton more than ever before. Plus, the crazies were coming out of the woodwork. There were riots in the streets already, all interwoven with the heavy loss the country had endured. Vigils were being held in the president's honor, but it was like a huge split had torn the nation in two. On one news channel, there'd be a video of candles being lit and kind words being spoken about President Price. On the next, windows being smashed and hooligans running amok in the name of Eris.

She sure made her damn statement. Still, thanks to the president's sacrifice, we now had more time to plan our next move. That was the idea, anyway. The only trouble was, since Washington, we'd found ourselves under review. Alton was doing a stellar job of keeping Levi restrained and playing the PR nightmare angle to stop him from actually punishing us. But we still felt watched. Our every movement was under scrutiny. We couldn't go to the bathroom without some security officer popping up out of nowhere. This morning, I could've sworn one came into the stall next to me and waited until I was done.

We were the nation's most feared, just below Katherine, and that didn't feel like a nice place to be. My parents had already given me enough grief about it—the usual "I told you so" and "we warned you" stuff. Not that I listened. Even when they discovered the true story, they were still worried about their reputations. I'd been thrown in with the same bad press, and they hated it. Then again, the Crowley name was due a couple of scuffs. We'd hardly had any bad press since my ancestor Aleister; it could take a hit or two without too much trouble.

Harley wasn't dealing with it too well, though. She hadn't left her room since we got back from Washington. Santana had been feeding her from her secret stash, leaving trays outside her door, but Harley didn't make any contact. The only way we knew she was alive was by the empty trays that returned. In fact, she refused to speak to anyone. I'd given her all the space she needed, but four days without seeing her was enough. I couldn't take it anymore. I needed to talk to her. She'd been through so much, and it pained me to have to stay silent. She'd always been alone, but I wanted to show her that she didn't have to be. Not now. Not with me.

So, that's how I found myself at her door on the fourth morning after the tragic events. I paused outside and lifted my hand to knock. My knuckles hadn't even made contact when I heard a loud noise coming from inside. I knocked but got no answer. The loud noises persisted. I knocked again, but still no answer. Fearing the worst, I pressed my hand to the lock and charged up my Fire power. It melted the lock completely, and I gave the door a firm kick and busted it wide open.

Sweating and panicked, I scoured the room for any sign of foul play. Instead, I found Harley in the middle of her bed. She seemed to be using her Telekinesis to slip tiny glass beads onto a thread of fine silk. All without using her hands. None of it dropped as she turned and raised an eyebrow at me.

"Did you have to break the door down again?" she asked. The silk thread still hovered steadily in the air.

"You weren't answering." I glanced back at the melted lock. "I'll get it fixed for you."

"Much appreciated."

"What are you doing?" I took a step forward.

"Practicing."

I smiled. "That's...very impressive."

"I've been at it since I got back from Washington. I'm getting much better." She flashed me an excited grin. "Look at this, Wade! I can do things with so much more detail. Finesse, as I like to call it."

I paused as I took a closer look at her. At first, I'd thought the sunlight was coming in through the blinds and was casting its glow on her. However, the blinds were half shut, and the day outside was a gloomy one. The light was coming from within her—that same glowing white light that had swept through her when she'd broken the defense hexes. *That's not normal.* Even in Kolduny like Tatyana, it stayed focused in the eyes. Even a spirit glow wasn't as bright as this.

"Your skin—it's glowing, Harley." I couldn't keep the concern from my voice. What if this was a dangerous side effect of the Suppressor break?

Harley took a few deep breaths. "I need to keep the glow under control. It's like a computer overheating. That's how I feel right now. I have to remind myself to take it easy. One step at a time. Strong will and fierce heart, like Gaia said, but all at a steady pace."

"Okay, well, cool it for a moment." I crossed the gap between us and sat down beside her. Slowly, she brought the thin thread down onto the bed. It lay flat, all of it done without a single touch. She looked elated, which was always a nice thing to see.

She dipped her head. "Everyone's worried about me, huh?"

"You've kind of been a hermit for four days, so yeah, we're worried. At least you've been eating, though."

"I've been eating like a horse. Santana must be out of food by now."

I chuckled. "I doubt it. She's robbed the kitchens blind."

"Nobody's caught her yet?"

"She's a stealthy one. Either that or she's bribed one of the chefs." I leaned over and put my arm around her shoulders. She didn't flinch. Instead, she nuzzled into my side. "How are you doing, Harley? Really, I mean?"

She shrugged. "I'm getting there."

"You seem more determined than ever."

"I am. I have to be. My Light and Dark are never going to behave if I don't learn to control them," she explained. "And I'm tired of my abilities dictating what I do. Echidna told me that the Sanguine spell wasn't a fix-all, and Gaia said it might not have been strong enough for me. So I've got to make myself strong enough. Even if I can't fully fix my balance problems, I need to be strong enough to face Katherine again. We walked into a huge mess the other day, and I didn't have the means to fight her properly. I won't put myself, or any of us, in that position again."

"I guess asking you to chill out is out of the question?" I smiled down at her and drank in the strawberry scent of her hair.

"Absolutely."

"Whatever you need, I'll help. I don't want you to feel like it's all on you. You've got enough to deal with without that kind of pressure."

She chuckled. "You scared you might lose me again?"

I lifted her chin up. "Always. That's what happens when you have something precious."

"Do we have something precious?" The question rested anxiously on her lips.

"I'd like us to, if you're ready for that." I took a nervous breath. "If you're not, I'll wait. I know we said we'd talk about this when your Suppressor broke, but there's no rush. This is all on your time."

She sat up taller and looped her arms around my neck. In one movement, I picked her up and pulled her into my lap. She grinned as I leaned down and pressed my forehead to hers. She was warm from the Telekinesis, though the glow had faded. Her loose hairs tickled my cheeks as I cupped her face in my hands, keeping my forehead against hers. My heart beat faster, and I swallowed hard. I wanted to kiss her, but I also wanted her to be the one to close the gap. That way, I'd know we were on the same page. I'd almost lost her too many times to risk that again. I held my world in my lap, and I wanted it to stay that way.

"See, I told you it wasn't the Suppressor," I murmured.

She pressed a tender kiss to the tip of my nose. "I believe you now."

"You do?"

She nodded and leaned closer. Her lips grazed mine. It was all the permission I needed to kiss her the way I really wanted to. My mouth caught hers and moved with slow intensity. She kissed back with equal desperation, and her tongue danced softly with mine. She wriggled in my lap and wrapped her legs around my waist, while her arms pulled me tighter and our kiss deepened.

I trailed sweet kisses away from her mouth and left gentle touches along the curve of her neck, moving down to the exposed line of her clavicle. My hands slid down and smoothed over the contours of her waist, before moving up beneath her t-shirt to touch her bare skin. It felt soft and warm, as if she'd just woken up from a nap. I smiled against her neck as a quiet gasp bubbled from her throat. I liked having this effect on her, especially now. For the first time, we could be sure it was real.

I pulled away slightly and gazed into her eyes. "Does this mean you want us to be together?" I figured I might as well get straight to the point.

"I do if you do," she replied.

"You know I do."

She grinned. "Then kiss me again."

I did as she asked. Scooping her into my arms, I pressed her gently down onto the bed and kissed her hard on the lips. She pulled me close and kissed me harder, the two of us entwined on the covers. The beads and thread went skittering off the edge, but neither of us stopped to pick them up. From now on, I didn't want to waste another second.

With her in my arms, things didn't seem so grim. We knew what the remaining rituals were, more or less, and Harley was getting stronger. We could look toward the future with hope and determination because we had each other. Nothing was insurmountable if we had that.

Harley's phone rang. I tried to push it under the pillow, but she twisted away from me and picked it up.

"I need to get this," she said with a note of apology in her voice. She swiped the answer button and lifted it to her ear. I went back to kissing the bare skin at the top of her t-shirt as she spoke to the person on the other end. I couldn't hear much, but I figured she'd tell me what was going on soon enough. A few moments later, she put the phone down and lay back on the bed. She stared up at the ceiling.

"What's the matter?" I propped myself up on my elbows.

"That was the prison. Finch is awake, and he wants to talk to me."

FORTY-SEVEN

Harley

Half an hour later, after speaking with Alton about smuggling us through the mirrors, Wade and I were being led through the familiar hallways of Purgatory toward the infirmary. Mallenberg had been the one to make the call, and he'd met us at the mirrors the moment we came through. I was glad to see that he looked better, after our last encounter. The guilt still remained as a faint hum in the background of his emotions, but the job seemed to be distracting him enough.

"Did you ever find any sign of Kenneth Willow?" I asked as we walked along.

Mallenberg shook his head. "The devil managed to escape, but we have heightened security everywhere, and all of the entrances and exits have been double-checked for any potential weaknesses. It won't be happening again. Not on my watch."

"And Giverny? How's she?" Wade chimed in.

"She's been locked away in a new cell and doesn't seem to be causing any trouble. We have a four-guard team stationed outside her doors at all times, and nobody is allowed in or out without a full body scan and magical detection scan. Kenneth Willow had some strange hex bags on him, it seems, and we have to make sure that doesn't happen again."

I recalled the blinding spell he'd used on Wade and shuddered at the memory. Kenneth was a dangerous man, and it terrified me to think he was still out there somewhere. Katherine had a keen eye for the worst, and most powerful, of people. How she'd managed to rope Nomura's son into her cult, we still didn't know. But that had caused so much heartache and damage, and I knew Katherine would only continue to create pain and suffering until either we stopped her, or she got what she wanted.

We walked through an empty ICU and headed toward the only occupied bed. There were guards stationed absolutely everywhere, intent on keeping Finch safe from any further attacks. Still, he'd managed to survive whatever Kenneth had done to him and was sitting up in his bed as we approached. He turned to face us, a bitter glint in his eyes. The platinum in his hair had all but faded now, revealing a dark auburn that looked like a perfect blend of my hair and my father's. Or, rather, Katherine's and my father's.

"Did you finally run out of dye?" I spoke first, wanting to break the ice.

He smiled. "What can I say, I figured it was time for a change."

"It suits you. Well, it will, once the frosted tips are gone. That's a little too '90s for you."

"I'm surprised you came," he said as we sat down on either side of his bed. Wade sat opposite, his eyes fixed on me. I drew comfort from them, though I was sort of annoyed at Finch's timing. I missed Wade's lips on mine already. Still, at least we'd made a decision about our future, and it was one I was more than happy with.

I shrugged. "I wanted to hear what happened with Kenneth."

Finch scoffed. "He attacked me on my mom's orders, which means she wanted me dead. Probably didn't have the courage to do it herself."

"Why do you think she tried to kill you?" I pressed. We'd speculated about the reasons, but I still didn't know for sure.

"Because she thought Adley made me weak."

"Because you loved her?"

A pained expression crossed Finch's face, and I almost felt bad for asking the question. "Yeah. Yeah, I did. Garrett told me what happened. About how Katherine had Adley killed. She thought I wouldn't find out. That cold-blooded bitch," he muttered.

You've finally realized that Katherine doesn't give a damn about you, huh, Finch?

"I'm sorry about Adley." I smiled sadly at him. Although I couldn't read his emotions, regret was written all over him. "So Katherine found out that you'd heard about her orders to kill Adley, and she worried that—what, exactly? That you'd turn on her?"

Finch smirked. "Something like that. When Garrett came to visit, I told him I'd consider telling the guards everything I knew about my mom. I was done bowing and scraping. But there was a mole in the prison somewhere. The same person who let Kenneth in and out, no doubt. Anyway, once she discovered that, she wanted me out of the picture. I was no use to her anymore, and I'd become a huge risk to her empire."

"Does this mean you're ready to cooperate with us?" Wade asked.

Finch ignored Wade and looked at me. I was startled by just how similar his sky-blue eyes were to my own. "I'm guessing you know more than you did last time we talked, so you've found out that the rituals can be pretty vague, right?"

"You can say that again," I said.

"And you know the gist of the third ritual?"

Wade leaned forward in his chair. "Consume the spirit of thine greatest enemy, in the land of Erebus, on All Hallows' Eve."

"Confusing, isn't it?" Finch raised an eyebrow.

"But you know more?" I replied.

"I do." He took a shaky breath. "The spirit that the ritual is talking about, in Katherine's case, is Hester Merlin's spirit. Katherine is looking to consume her."

I gasped. "What?"

"Hester was Katherine's greatest enemy. So she's the spirit in question."

Wade shook his head. "Hester has been dead for a long time. There's no way her spirit is still floating around, not unless she lingered in the spirit world for Harley's sake." He gave me a sympathetic look, and I knew he wanted to reach right over Finch to take my hand.

"You'd think that, but she trapped Hester's spirit the moment she killed her. And I know where she's keeping it," Finch went on. "I can help you find it, but I need to get out of Purgatory. My mom won't hesitate to keep trying to kill me until the job is done."

I stared at him in disbelief. "Tell me you're not asking what I think you're asking."

Finch grinned. "You'll need me at your side if you want to infiltrate the Cult of Eris and get to Hester's spirit. I can't do that from here."

I sat back in my chair and let his words sink in. He wanted us to get him out of here so we could sneak into Katherine's cult together. Wade looked like he'd just been smacked in the face with a wet fish. I didn't know whether to laugh or cry—this whole thing was absurd, and yet weirdness had somehow become my reality.

"You realize you're asking something impossible here, right?" I said.

He shrugged. "Either you do the impossible, or Katherine gets ritual three done, and you have a whole mess of power to deal with. If she's two rituals down, then she's already on the verge of being godlike. What I'm asking is pretty small in comparison to having an almighty Katherine on the loose, if you ask me."

I cast a hopeless look at Wade, who seemed equally resigned. Our list of improbable tasks was getting longer by the day. But if what

Finch said was true, then he knew more about the third ritual than any of us. And that made him our only hope in this future mission.

A man was dead because I hadn't been prepared to stop Katherine, and I'd already vowed never to let that happen again. The path forward seemed clear to me now, though it was littered with a million potential landmines. If we didn't have Finch, then we had nothing. With the Librarian dead and Echidna tight-lipped inside her frozen box, he was our only remaining source of intel.

Nothing comes for free, remember?

I turned to Finch. "Well then, I guess it's time we got the family back together."

Ready for the next part of Harley's journey?

Dear Reader,

Thank you for reading *Harley Merlin and the Broken Spell.* I hope it lived up to your expectations!

Book 6 - *Harley Merlin and the Cult of Eris* - releases **February 23rd, 2019**.

Not too long to wait!

I'm incredibly excited for what comes next—and to explore the head of a most interesting character...

Visit: www.bellaforrest.net for details.

See you soon!

Love,

Bella x

P.S. Sign up to my VIP email list and you'll be the first to know when my next book releases: **www.morebellaforrest.com**

(Your email will be kept 100% private and you can unsubscribe at any time.)

P.P.S. I'd also love to hear from you. Come say hi on Facebook: Facebook.com/BellaForrestAuthor. Or Twitter: @ashadeofvampire. Or Instagram: @ashadeofvampire.

Read more by Bella Forrest

HARLEY MERLIN

Harley Merlin and the Secret Coven (Book 1)

Harley Merlin and the Mystery Twins (Book 2)

Harley Merlin and the Stolen Magicals (Book 3)

Harley Merlin and the First Ritual (Book 4)

Harley Merlin and the Broken Spell (Book 5)

Harley Merlin and the Cult of Eris (Book 6)

THE GENDER GAME

(Action-adventure/romance. Completed series.)

The Gender Game (Book 1)

The Gender Secret (Book 2)

The Gender Lie (Book 3)

The Gender War (Book 4)

The Gender Fall (Book 5)

The Gender Plan (Book 6)

The Gender End (Book 7)

THE GIRL WHO DARED TO THINK

(Action-adventure/romance. Completed series.)

The Girl Who Dared to Think (Book 1)

The Girl Who Dared to Stand (Book 2)

The Girl Who Dared to Descend (Book 3)

The Girl Who Dared to Rise (Book 4)

A Castle of Sand (Book 3)

A Shadow of Light (Book 4)

A Blaze of Sun (Book 5)

A Gate of Night (Book 6)

A Break of Day (Book 7)

Series 2: Rose & Caleb's story

A Shade of Novak (Book 8)

A Bond of Blood (Book 9)

A Spell of Time (Book 10)

A Chase of Prey (Book 11)

A Shade of Doubt (Book 12)

A Turn of Tides (Book 13)

A Dawn of Strength (Book 14)

A Fall of Secrets (Book 15)

An End of Night (Book 16)

Series 3: The Shade continues with a new hero...

A Wind of Change (Book 17)

A Trail of Echoes (Book 18)

A Soldier of Shadows (Book 19)

A Hero of Realms (Book 20)

A Vial of Life (Book 21)

A Fork of Paths (Book 22)

A Flight of Souls (Book 23)

A Bridge of Stars (Book 24)

Series 4: A Clan of Novaks

A Clan of Novaks (Book 25)

A World of New (Book 26)

A Web of Lies (Book 27)

A Hunt of Fiends (Book 53)

A Den of Tricks (Book 54)

A City of Lies (Book 55)

A League of Exiles (Book 56)

A Charge of Allies (Book 57)

A Snare of Vengeance (Book 58)

A Battle of Souls (Book 59)

Series 8: A Voyage of Founders

A Voyage of Founders (Book 60)

A Land of Perfects (Book 61)

A Citadel of Captives (Book 62)

A Jungle of Rogues (Book 63)

A Camp of Savages (Book 64)

A Plague of Deceit (Book 65)

An Edge of Malice (Book 66)

A Dome of Blood (Book 67)

A Purge of Nature (Book 68)

Season 9: A Birth of Fire

A Birth of Fire (Book 69)

A Breed of Elements (Book 70)

A Sacrifice of Flames (Book 71)

A SHADE OF DRAGON TRILOGY

A Shade of Dragon 1

A Shade of Dragon 2

A Shade of Dragon 3

A SHADE OF KIEV TRILOGY

A Shade of Kiev 1

A Shade of Kiev 2

A Shade of Kiev 3

THE SECRET OF SPELLSHADOW MANOR

(Supernatural/Magic YA. Completed series)

The Secret of Spellshadow Manor (Book 1)

The Breaker (Book 2)

The Chain (Book 3)

The Keep (Book 4)

The Test (Book 5)

The Spell (Book 6)

BEAUTIFUL MONSTER DUOLOGY

(Supernatural romance)

Beautiful Monster 1

Beautiful Monster 2

DETECTIVE ERIN BOND

(Adult thriller/mystery)

Lights, Camera, GONE

Write, Edit, KILL

For an updated list of Bella's books, please visit her website:
www.bellaforrest.net

Join Bella's VIP email list and she'll send you an email reminder as soon as her next book is out. Visit: www.morebellaforrest.com

Made in the USA
San Bernardino, CA
09 July 2019